"You like me, Dana. Admit it."

She had no intention of admitting anything, but she couldn't look away from him. He leaned closer, bending toward her mouth. "Admit it," he repeated, his voice husky and low.

Without waiting for an answer, he cupped her face with his large hand, cradling it in his palm and stroking her lower lip with the pad of his thumb. A languorous weakness flowed through her body like the lulling sound of the surf rushing softly across the sand.

He seemed to sense that the fight had gone out of her. Gently, he drew her head back as he lowered her to the towel. His lips brushed the rim of her ear as he spoke, sending a rush of warm air with each word. "I'm the one. The only one."

He could make a woman—even the sanest woman—do anything, she thought, slow heat unfurling in her belly. She waited, anxious to see what he'd do next.

PROMISE ME ANYTHING

"A VERY INTERESTING AND ENJOYABLE NOVEL."—*The Talisman*

"WONDERFUL ROMANCE combined with a smartly plotted mystery and intrigue makes the well-written novel one you do not want to put down."
—*Affaire de Coeur*

NEVER KISS A STRANGER

"EXCITING . . . Writing with perception and power, she takes her rightful place as one of today's most exciting authors of women's fiction."
—*Romantic Times*

"A splendidly intricate tale full of rich characterizations and sweeping passion . . . Bravo Ms. Sawyer."
—*Rave Reviews*

Dell Books by Meryl Sawyer

A KISS IN THE DARK
LAST NIGHT

LAST
NIGHT

Meryl
Sawyer

A DELL BOOK

Published by
Dell Publishing
a division of
Bantam Doubleday Dell Publishing Group, Inc.
1540 Broadway
New York, New York 10036

The trademark Dell® is registered in the U.S. Patent and Trademark Office.

ISBN: 0-440-22050-5

Printed in the United States of America

Published simultaneously in Canada

January 1996

10 9 8 7 6 5 4 3 2

RAD

For Jeffrey

The best way to love anything
is as if it might be lost.

G. K. CHESTERTON

1

"It looked like a chicken—you know, feathers 'n all —but it was a jockstrap."

A titter rippled across the courtroom and the witness stopped, a flush rising up her cheeks to her gray hair. Judge Dana Hamilton tapped her gavel, silencing the courtroom crowded with snowbirds who had retired to Hawaii and found themselves bored. She could count on having them pack her court whenever the weather was hot or a sensational case was being tried. Today the temperature hit triple digits, and the "Fowl Flasher" was on trial.

"You may continue," Dana told the witness. Behind the concealing judge's bench she hiked up her robes and skirt to the tops of her thighs. Lordy, would they ever fix the air conditioner? It wheezed audibly, puffing moist air like a vaporizer.

"The man was standing on the beach wearing a trench coat," the witness said. "He motioned to me and I walked over. That's when he threw open his

1

coat and I saw this . . . this . . . chicken thing. Then he tore it off and threw it into the water."

A volley of laughter erupted and Dana whacked the gavel on the wood, adding one more dent to the countless nicks left by fifty-plus years of judges in department seven, Municipal Court of Honolulu. The resounding bang was an effective substitute for her own pent-up laughter. The image of the flasher tossing the jockstrap in the surf tickled her. It shouldn't have—judges were supposed to be above such a human failing—but it did.

She had a bit of a temper and an irreverent sense of humor that made her a little sarcastic at times. Hide your emotions, she told herself. The tough grind through law school and the years in the district attorney's office were finally paying off. She had a place on the municipal court; in time she hoped to move to a higher court. She'd better learn more self-control.

As she silenced the crowd with another thump of the gavel, she accidentally glanced at Rob Tagett. She had noticed him that morning when she'd ascended the two steps to the bench, but she'd never once permitted her gaze to stray to the first row where the members of the fourth estate had reserved seats. She had absolutely no use for reporters. And Rob Tagett, star reporter for the *Honolulu Sun*, ranked right at the top of her list of creeps.

Sometimes, late at night, when she was in bed alone, she thought about his rich, smoky laugh and the twilight blue of his eyes. During the day she had no trouble recalling how he'd gone for her jugular with one of his typically damning articles. Were the ugly rumors she'd heard about him true? Charges had never been filed against him. Still, the gossip about Rob was too consistent to discount entirely.

Rob was smiling, evidently finding the Fowl Flasher as humorous as she did. He winked at her, but she pretended not to notice.

"Please go on," she told the witness, warning the crowd with a frown.

Finally the testimony concluded and Dana gave the jury its instructions, then quickly left the courtroom through the judge's door directly behind her without glancing at Rob Tagett. She yanked off her robe, telling her secretary, "Call maintenance again about the air. Scream this time."

"Right away," Anita said, reaching for the telephone.

Dana hung her robe on the padded hanger she kept on the back of her door and glanced around the room. She'd inherited the shelves of leather-bound books and the oak desk from the previous judge. She'd added her own personality to the small office with a Wyland sea-life print. She'd splurged on it, giving herself a present for being appointed a judge after so few years in the district attorney's office.

Of course, she'd received dozens of small presents and enough flowers for a gangster's funeral, but no one knew her well enough to realize how much she loved this painting. It showed the sea with the dolphins playing on the surface chasing a whale. What fascinated her more was the activity beneath the sea: the fishes, the coral, the deep-blue current sweeping the sand along the bottom.

A hidden world. Just like people, she thought. What you couldn't see was often more interesting than what was on the surface.

Anita buzzed her on the intercom. "Judge Sihida's on the line."

Dana glanced at the school clock on the wall between the American flag and the Hawaiian state flag. Two o'clock. Gwen should be back in court by now.

"Why are you taking such a late lunch recess?" Gwen Sihida asked. "I'm keeping my entire court waiting just to talk to you."

Dana knew this had to be important. Gwen never kept anyone waiting. Petite, fortyish, with jet black hair and eyes to match, Gwen was Dana's closest friend on the court. "I wanted this flasher case to go to the jury. With any luck they'll have a verdict today."

"How did my brother do with your wisdom teeth?"

Dana almost said that she'd rather preside over a serial killer's case than go to Gwen's brother again. "It hurts a little."

"That's to be expected. Frank said you had the most impacted wisdom teeth he'd ever seen." Gwen laughed as Dana touched her sore gum with the tip of her tongue, hoping she had another pain pill. Otherwise she would be miserable all afternoon.

4

"Are you sitting down?" Gwen asked. Dana dropped into her chair, then swiveled nervously from one side to the other. "Judge Parker announced his retirement this morning. Guess who's being considered for his seat on the superior court?"

"You," Dana responded, thinking how great this would be for her friend. After years on the municipal bench Gwen had run for superior court and lost. "It's about time. They need a woman."

"They're considering you, Dana."

"Me?" Shocked, Dana stopped swinging from side to side. "I'm too young."

"Bullshit," Gwen said with characteristic frankness. "Thirty-four isn't too young. The last appointee was thirty-six."

"And a man." Dana took a deep breath, shocked yet thrilled at the unexpected news. "I'm sorry they're not considering you, Gwen. They'll never appoint me. They're just paying lip service to women. That post will go to a man. You watch."

"Don't bet on it."

Dana understood the bitterness she heard in Gwen's voice. She had five brothers. One was a dentist, the others were well-placed politicians. The family, especially Gwen's father—Boss Sihida—expected more from her than just a seat on the municipal court, handling traffic violations and family squabbles.

Boss had goaded Gwen into running for superior court and had been furious when she'd lost. Well, what did he expect? This might be paradise, but women weren't accepted the way they were on the mainland. The route to higher court was to be appointed—a sign that you were accepted by the establishment—then run as an incumbent. And pray you'd be elected.

"You have the best record," Gwen said. "How many of your decisions have been overturned on appeal?"

"A few." Very few actually, and she was proud of it. Cases criminal attorneys didn't win, they appealed, creating a legal log jam. "But the Tenaka case will be a black mark against me."

"That was three years ago, your first month on the bench."

"And I received letters about it for a year." She cradled the phone against her shoulder and began arranging the files on her desk. "Just this morning I received a black rose with a note that said: *I know what you did.*"

"Kooks," Gwen said, and Dana imagined the dismissive wave of her gavel hand. "Judges are threatened all the time. Nothing usually comes of it."

Dana wasn't sure she agreed; she found the dark side of the criminal mind frightening and unpredictable. The black rose and its note disturbed her, but she didn't voice her concerns, changing the subject instead.

"Rob Tagett was in court today," Dana said. "When he gets wind of the vacancy he'll make dead certain the world remembers the Tenaka case."

"Really? He was in your court?"

Dana attributed Gwen's caustic tone to Rob. Gwen had gone out with him once, but then had the good sense not to see him anymore. She knew Rob Tagett would hurt her career. Dana admired Gwen's willpower. Women were drawn to Rob despite their better judgment.

"Look, I've got to run," Gwen told her. "See you later."

Dana hung up and glanced at the desk covered with probation reports, motions, and briefs. She should work through lunch if she hoped to clear her desk for her vacation, but she felt light-headed. Considering the pain medication she was taking for the wisdom teeth she'd had extracted yesterday, she decided she should eat something.

Despite her throbbing tooth, she felt like waltzing on the ceiling. Superior court. Dare she hope? She might have a shot at it, if . . .

If she hadn't been assigned the Tenaka case another judge might have tried it. Not hotshot Dana Hamilton. She'd looked at the DA's botched evidence and did what the letter of the law required her to do: She granted the defense's motion to dismiss charges against the child molester.

The press, led by Rob Tagett, attacked her like starving pit bulls. Her achievements—a stellar record for someone so young—were forgotten in a barrage of negative press. That's why she hadn't called the police when she'd found the black rose and the note this morning. She'd had enough of the press to last a lifetime. Hopefully Gwen was right and this was just some kook who'd gotten his kicks.

There were few people in the cafeteria when Dana walked in; most of the other courts were back in session. She slid her plastic tray along the guide rail and looked at the mound of spaghetti in a pool of grease. Airline food was haute cuisine compared to anything the court cafeteria served. She selected a cup of coffee and a prepackaged sandwich that claimed to be tuna fish.

She found a table that was almost clean and sat with her back to the room. When she'd come in she'd spotted Rob Tagett with a group in the corner. She didn't even want to look at him.

"Your Honor." The tone was light, mocking.

She glanced up and saw Rob Tagett swinging a chair around backward. He sat opposite her, straddling the seat with his long legs, his arms resting casually across the back of the chair as he grinned at her.

Tall and well-built, Rob had blue eyes that flickered with amusement—as if he got a kick out of life in general. Of course, his hair needed to be cut. What else was new? Thick and jet black, it dusted his collar and swept low across his brow, making him look younger than thirty-eight.

There was something subtly sexy about Rob. Maybe it was his arresting smile. Or his limber athletic stride. Whatever it was, the female population —despite his questionable reputation—adored him.

Even now one of the cute ADAs was scouring him with admiring glances.

Dana knew better. Rob Tagett was trouble, and any woman who allowed herself to become involved with him deserved what she got.

"Thrilled to see me, huh?" he asked with his familiar mix of Texas drawl and gall. "And here I walked all the way across the room to ask if you wanted to see my chicken."

"Rob, don't unzip your pants. Your brains will fall out."

"Thanks," he said with a grin that could have convinced the toughest jury that he'd just received a supreme compliment.

"Look, I can't talk to you." She shoved the sandwich aside, her appetite gone. "You're covering my trial and the jury is out."

"S'okay. I'm not covering the Fowl Flasher. I kinda' like the guy, though. Not your ordinary wienie-wagger, but a flasher with flair."

"Then why are you sitting in my court?"

"Parker's bailing out. The booze finally got to him. You're up for his spot on the superior court."

"Really?" She tried to sound surprised, but obviously missed the mark, because he winked at her. The only way she could lie was to rehearse over and over and over. She'd done it; she could rise to the occasion. This time she'd been caught off-guard. "How'd you find out?"

He shrugged, his powerful shoulders stretching

the cotton fabric of his polo shirt. "Jungle drums. You know how it is. I heard about it two days ago."

She silently fumed; Gwen had found out only this morning, while Rob had known for days. No doubt he'd hopped in the sack with one of the secretaries. They always knew everything first.

"I'm here to get a statement from you."

"No comment." Did he really think she'd talk to him? Rob had a weekly column called "Exposed." It was devoted to controversial issues. He loved to blow the whistle on government waste and foul-ups. Just having your name appear in his column was the kiss of death.

"You stand a good chance of getting appointed, you know." He leaned forward, balancing his weight on the back two chair legs. "I'd hate to lose you. Most of the other judges around here are so ugly they could haunt a house and charge by the room."

She didn't acknowledge the backhanded compliment. She knew she was passable, but not pretty. Her sister, Vanessa, now there was pretty—beautiful, actually. It was a leap of faith to think they were even from the same gene pool.

Ever mindful of the testosterone brigade who ran the judicial system, Dana strived for a professional appearance. Glasses instead of contacts made her look older, more like a judge, and kept her green eyes from appearing so large. Cutting her warm brown hair into a wedge that brushed her chin gave her a no-nonsense look. She dressed carefully, conservatively, in keeping with her position—except for her underwear. She adored lacy, feminine undies, the frillier the better.

Now Rob's grin was positively wicked. "None of the other judges pulls their robes up to the tops of their thighs during a trial."

"It was broiling—" She snapped her mouth shut, realizing he couldn't possibly have seen anything. The judge's bench was totally enclosed. But Rob was smart, too smart for his own darn good. "You're a real jerk, you know."

"Let me get back to you on that." He winked at her again, then straightened, bringing his chair to rest on all four legs again. "I have tickets for the Eagles' concert—front row."

Dana stifled a gasp. He wasn't asking her out, was he? Well, it didn't matter. Rob might be sexy and devastatingly masculine, the kind of man who made you dream about him at night, but she couldn't go out with him. The last thing her career needed right now—when she was up for that coveted spot on the bench—was to become involved with a cut-throat reporter.

Oh, go on, Dana, admit it. It's more than the appointment that's keeping you from going out with Rob. Something about him frightened her. Maybe it was that he was unpredictable; maybe it was something more.

She'd first met Rob at the cocktail party the DA threw to celebrate her appointment to the court three years earlier. She'd heard the ugly rumors about him, of course, but she didn't pay much attention to gossip. Still, she wondered why he'd left the police force so suddenly, then become a reporter. She'd been attracted to Rob and thought he'd liked her too. A week later he wrote the article that triggered a cry of public outrage that still echoed in her ears.

"You interested in seeing the Eagles?" Rob repeated, his tone now serious.

She picked up her purse and scooted her chair back from the table. "Thanks, but I'm busy."

"I haven't even said which night yet."

Oh, boy, he was going to press it. If she refused, was he going to crucify her in print? Again?

"Still sore about that article I wrote?"

"Of course not," she said a little too quickly. He wasn't fooled.

"You hate me, don't you?"

"Hate you? No. I like you. I've always gone for creeps."

That evening when Dana drove behind Diamond Head to her home on Maunalua Bay, she was still cursing her sharp tongue. Really, what had gotten into her? She had walked away as soon as the words were out of her mouth, but not before she'd seen the look in Rob's eyes. He wouldn't forget the insult.

What was wrong with her? She really must need this vacation. Lately she'd lost her temper much too easily. It's the pressure, she silently cried. No, it was more than that. It was the isolation.

When she'd been in the DA's office she'd had lots of friends. Well, not friends exactly, just people to go out to lunch or dinner with. Now she couldn't see those lawyers and have them try cases in her court. Of course, some judges did, but it wasn't proper. Dana always did things by the book. She always had.

She was too busy to be lonely, too ambitious to be lonely—or so she told herself. Once in a while something would trigger a wellspring of emptiness buried inside her like the secret life beneath the surface in the Wyland painting. Somehow, just seeing Rob made her lonely.

He was nothing like the men she admired. The ideal man was intellectual. Sensitive. Safe. Everything Rob Tagett wasn't. Like a lone wolf, Rob had an elusiveness about him, a hint of risk and adventure. And danger.

She slowed her car as she rounded the corner overlooking Maunalua Bay, catching her breath as she always did at its beauty. The sun had slipped behind Diamond Head, leaving the bay in a purple twilight and firing the clouds with amber and gold. On the point, cloaked in early evening shadows, was Koko Head. A smaller version of Diamond Head, the ancient volcano stood like a lonely sentinel guarding Maunalua Bay. To Dana, Koko Head was as majestic as Diamond Head, yet friendlier, the symbol of the back bay.

Buying a home here had been a stretch. Right out of law school she'd gone into the DA's office. She'd always been a public-service employee. It had taken her years to pay off her student loans.

When she was finally out of debt she began saving for a house. The other judges had come from lucrative private practices and lived in luxurious high rises or at the foot of Diamond Head in the ritzy Kahala area. She didn't envy them. Maunalua Bay might not be as prestigious, but she preferred the serenity of the back bay.

As she stopped in her driveway and stepped out of her car to get the mail, her friend came running over. Lillian Hurley was a widow in her mid-eighties who'd lived here since Pearl Harbor. She was a trifle forgetful at times, so Dana helped her, making it possible for Lillian to live at home.

Tears pooled in Lillian's eyes. "My daughter's coming to visit."

"Wonderful." Dana gave her a quick hug and hoped the tears were tears of happiness. She'd long since decided the daughter was strange. What kind of a person forgot Mother's Day? In the three years Dana had lived here the daughter had never visited. "Don't forget to mark the date on your calendar."

"I did already—just the way you told me." Tears spilled out of Lillian's pale blue eyes. "I don't want to go into a nursing home."

"I'm sure when you explain to your daughter that I'm working with your doctor, she'll understand that you're fine here." Dana hugged her again.

It was true—for now—but Dana knew the day would come when Lillian would need more help than she could give. That's what happens to the elderly, she thought. They're warehoused, lonely and forgotten, until they die. An American tragedy. She wasn't letting that happen to Lillian.

"Will you talk to Fran for me?"

"Of course." Dana smiled reassuringly, silently pledging to take time out of her busy schedule to talk to the daughter. "Don't worry. I'll take care of it."

"I knew you'd help me. That's why I came over." She looked around suspiciously as if she expected someone to jump out of the dense oleander bushes. "I'm so frightened."

"Of what?" A frisson of alarm shot through Dana. This was just Lillian's nerves, wasn't it? Dana moved here because this was a safe neighborhood. They weren't having trouble, were they? During the past year the Panama Jack's rapist had attacked several women. Dana had always been careful. Now she kept pepper spray in her purse.

"I'm so-o-o frightened," Lillian repeated. "Last night I heard the night marchers. I'm going to die."

Oh, boy, Dana said to herself. How could Lillian believe that island lore? According to superstition the restless spirits of Hawaii's ancient warriors marched at night. If you heard them someone was going to die.

"You're not going to die, Lillian. Remember what the doctor said? You're perfectly healthy. Just remember to take your blood pressure medication."

15

Lillian perked up. "Oh, I almost forgot. I brought in your package."

"Thanks." Dana wasn't expecting anything, but she did buy most of her clothes mail order because she despised shopping.

"I put the box in the refrigerator," Lillian said with pride. "A bottle must have broken. It's leaking. I didn't want the food to spoil."

"Food? I never order food. It must be a gift. I'd better come get it now." She tossed the mail on the front seat of the temperamental Toyota she'd driven for years and followed Lillian up the walk.

Inside Lillian's modest home the white linoleum floor had surrendered to time and was now a depressing amber, but it was clean. The dishes were drying in a wire rack on the counter. Lillian was doing just fine on her own in the home she loved, Dana thought as her friend opened a boxy Frigidaire that had been new in the fifties.

"Here it is." She handed Dana the package.

With a growing sense of apprehension Dana accepted it, recalling the black rose and the ominous note that she had received at the office. There was no return address on the plain brown wrapping paper. She touched the bottom of the package, then quickly pulled back her hand and stared at it.

"Sweetie, is anything the matter?"

"No." Dana beelined for the door, realizing just how poor Lillian's vision had become. Whatever was inside was leaking blood.

16

2

Dana raced to her house, holding the dripping package away from her suit. She dumped it in the kitchen sink, half-tempted to call the police. Perhaps she was overreacting, she thought, as she peeled back the soggy brown paper. There might be a perfectly innocent explanation for this.

Inside a Ziploc plastic bag was a rabbit-skinning knife slathered with blood. The blade had punctured the plastic, causing the leak. She tested the blade. It wiggled, not quite anchored securely in the handle.

"Oh my God!" she cried, her voice echoing through the small kitchen. "It can't be!"

She inspected the bloody knife more closely. It looked *exactly* like the one she remembered so well —even though it had been over twenty years since they'd thrown it into the swamp.

Bile rose up in her throat and the memory she'd blocked for years intruded with sickening clarity. There was a bloodstained note the size of a business card with the package.

I know what you did. Pack your bags, bitch.

The words echoed in her mind. A similar message had come with the black rose she had received that morning. Twenty years without a word. Nothing. Until today.

Why, after all these years, when her career was really taking off, did the past have to come back to curse her? She'd grown complacent, believing that after all this time she was safe. You were never safe from something like this. Somehow—someone—knew what had happened that night so long ago.

She picked up the telephone to call her sister. Then she remembered Vanessa wasn't in Maui. She was here in Honolulu for the evening. Thank God. The Coltrane family compound where Vanessa lived with her husband and young son was her father-in-law's home. Thornton "Big Daddy" Coltrane had his nose in everyone's business.

She checked her watch. If she hurried she could make the cocktail hour at the Royal Corinthian Yacht Club where the Coltranes were staying. It was always crowded and noisy. No one would overhear her talking to Vanessa.

Dana arrived at the Royal Corinthian Yacht Club, the pinnacle of society in the islands. While the elite on the mainland congregated at country clubs, Hawaii's wealthy socialized at yacht clubs. The security guard opened the gate and Dana hurried in. Normally she would have smiled at the ridiculousness of having a statue of King Kamehameha overlooking the club's courtyard. Generations ago the wise king had united the warring islands, but now—thanks to the Coltranes and the other white settlers—the king's descendants were in the kitchen or waiting on tables, she thought with disgust.

Inside, burgees of the great yacht clubs of the world hung from the ceiling. The small, triangular flags all had one thing in common: the red star. A yacht club wasn't a "serious" club until some member earned a star in a death-wish yacht race.

Naturally, the Royal Corinthian had a star. And the R.C. had what Dana thought of as "yacht snot" —an attitude. The real reason the club existed was to exclude "undesirables." She didn't belong. The welcoming smiles were for a judge, for Vanessa Coltrane's sister. Not for a girl from the backwoods of Georgia.

Dana spotted Vanessa in two seconds. As usual, her sister was standing in a cluster of men, flirting. Vanessa had a presence about her that would have shouted, "Look at me!" had she been in Levi's instead of tonight's designer gown with a diamond necklace that circled her throat as regally as a crown graced the head of a reigning monarch.

Dana waved, suddenly a young girl again, fondly waving to her older sister. After the death of their parents Vanessa had raised Dana, but since her marriage to Eric Coltrane they had grown apart. What had happened to the bond of trust that they had shared for so many years? The Coltranes. And

Dana's career. She wasn't seeing her sister often enough and she missed her terribly.

"Dana, darling." Vanessa threw her arms around her and hugged tight.

For just a second Dana clung to her. She loved Vanessa so much—and owed her so much—that she couldn't quite bring herself to destroy Vanessa's happiness by telling her about the knife. Her sister had every right to enjoy her life, even if it wasn't a life Dana would have chosen.

Vanessa's blue eyes became serious. "I wasn't expecting to see you until Monday. You're still vacationing with me, aren't you?"

"I'm flying over to Maui first thing Monday, just as we planned." Dana steered Vanessa toward the terrace that overlooked the yacht harbor where the members' boats were docked. "But I have to talk to you tonight."

In the semidarkness of the terrace Dana explained what had happened. Vanessa quickly cast an apprehensive glance at the interior of the club to her husband, Eric. As usual he was standing with his brother, Travis, and their father, Big Daddy Coltrane.

"It's just a joke," Vanessa whispered.

"Someone must know *something*. A rabbit-skinning knife with a loose blade. That's not a wild guess. I haven't mentioned what happened that night to anyone—ever."

It was true. She had tried to block out that fatal night and everything that had happened. She thought she'd done it with amazing success—until this evening. But there was always some hidden corner of the mind set to betray with terrifying memories of the past.

"I never told anyone, not even Eric." Vanessa glared at her husband, who was standing inside, his back to them. "We never talk."

Normally Dana would have been sad for her sister, who'd married for money, not love, but tonight she was too upset. "There must be an explanation—"

"Help me," Vanessa pleaded suddenly, and Dana was stunned by the turn their relationship had taken. Once she would have expected Vanessa to help her, to mother her as she had when they'd been teenagers alone in the world. Time had bolstered Dana's confidence, while it had eroded Vanessa's. "This has to be a Coltrane plot. They're going to take Jason away from me."

The panicked look in her sister's eyes alarmed Dana as much as Vanessa's convoluted logic. This was totally out of left field. "How could they take your son away from you?"

Vanessa stared out at the harbor, where the lights atop the forest of masts swayed rhythmically with the surge of the ocean. "You don't know Big Daddy. He has his ways."

"The notes were sent to me, not you. I don't think this has anything to do with the Coltranes," Dana said. "It must be a blackmail scheme. Someone must think I have money. Obviously they haven't checked to see how little municipal court judges make."

"I can't get any money to pay off a blackmailer." Vanessa's voice was trembling now. "Big Daddy sees all my bills."

"We have to find out who's behind this and . . ." And what? What would she do when she found the blackmailer?

"You've got to do something," Vanessa cried, clutching Dana's arm. "Don't let them take Jason away from me. He's all I have."

"Don't panic," Dana said with more confidence than she felt. "I have a friend who can help us. I'm going to see him right now."

Vanessa followed her outside, whispering, "Don't call me at home. Wait until you see me on Monday to tell me what's happening. I don't trust the Coltranes."

Convinced Vanessa was paranoid, Dana walked out to her car. Vanessa had never had a childhood; their parents' death had robbed her of any semblance of a normal youth. Men flocked to her, yet she had never found love.

Dana had prayed that having a child would help Vanessa, and it had. Vanessa loved Jason, so much so that she was overly protective. Borderline obsessive.

Was Vanessa's paranoia about Big Daddy justified? Even if he had discovered their secret, why would he send notes to Dana, not Vanessa? The whole thing was strange, confusing. Right now she needed an objective, analytical mind to help her, someone clear-headed and intelligent.

Garth Bradford. The criminal attorney was the best legal mind in the islands—probably in the country—and he was the man she'd choose to defend her. If it came to that.

She called him on her car phone. There was a momentary pause at the other end of the line after she identified herself. She knew what he was thinking. They'd been friendly for years, but not so close that she ever had called him at home on a Friday evening.

"What's on your mind?" As usual, there was a smile in Garth's voice.

"I need to discuss something with you in private." Suddenly she thought he might be with a woman. "Are you busy?"

"No," he responded. "Have you eaten? I'm fixing dinner. Come over and we'll talk."

"I'm starving," she fibbed, already mentally calculating just how much to tell him.

She drove along the shore into the exclusive Kahala section of the city, where the homes were nestled at the foot of Diamond Head, fronting a private beach. Just hearing Garth's voice had calmed her, and she recalled the first time she'd met him. The DA had assigned her to a murder case where Garth had been defending the man. She had seen him sitting at the counsel table, but didn't consider him much of a threat.

He'd looked like a sandy-haired jock who'd be

more at home on the football field, if he hadn't been confined to a wheelchair. But it wasn't his handicap that had totally disarmed her. It was his easygoing smile. How serious could he be?

Well, she found out. He annihilated her case, only half-trying. She could laugh now, but she'd been humiliated then. It had taught her an important lesson: Never underestimate Garth Bradford.

He was the most honest, ethical man she'd ever met. He accepted his handicap with complete dignity. She'd never once heard him complain. Come to think of it, Garth never even mentioned it. All she knew about the accident that had left him without the use of his legs, she'd heard from others.

Just thinking about how Garth must have suffered, then rebuilt his life, gave her courage. Vanessa had a child and Dana had a career. Their only option was to stay—and fight.

Garth Bradford stared at the telephone receiver still in his hand. "I'll be damned. Dana Hamilton just invited herself over."

"Sue the bastards! Sue the bastards!" shrieked his parrot, Puni, cocking his crimson head to one side and ruffling his bright blue feathers. "Sue their asses!"

"Give me a break. Be quiet for *one* minute." Garth wheeled himself into the kitchen, thankful he had enough veal for two people. He liked to cook on the weekends and fancied himself to be an amateur chef.

Tonight was suddenly special. He rarely entertained. Too often people felt sorry for him, tried too hard to help him. It was simply easier to eat alone. Dana was different. She never made him feel awkward; she always treated him the way she did the rest of the guys—with cool disdain.

Some called her a ball buster. Others claimed she was a frigid bitch. Garth figured she was a little shy, secure only when she was in court. She was most comfortable when doing something like ruling on points of law. When it came to personal relationships, that confidence evaporated.

He knew the feeling. He never dwelled on his handicap. It had made him stronger, wiser, and twice the man he would have been. Except physically.

He wanted to be friends with Dana, sensing a kindred spirit. She had always kept her distance though. That made her unexpected call even more surprising.

"Sue the bastards! Sue the bastards!" Puni chanted rap-style. "Sue their asses!"

Garth didn't have the heart to cover the cage. Maybe Puni would provide comic relief. It was as hard to get Dana to laugh as it was to appeal her decisions. She was one tough judge.

He loved the challenge. That's what he lived for.

He answered the doorbell and had to concentrate to keep from gasping. Dana? Right, but she wasn't wearing those hideous glasses. Makeup made her look younger, more feminine. The dress—well, there ought to be a law against wearing anything that sexy.

She wasn't his type—not that he could afford to be picky. Still, something in him yearned for a leggy blonde. His last relationship had ended months ago, but he was too weary to try again. He had his career. That had to be enough.

"Thanks for letting me come over," Dana said as she followed him, putting him at ease because she ignored his wheelchair.

"Sit, sit." He poured wine and she wearily dropped into the chair.

"Your call surprised me," Garth admitted after they'd chatted for a few minutes. He placed a salad before her, then wheeled to his place. He reached for his fork, saying, "Are you concerned about the superior court appointment?"

"Not at all. They're going to select a man."

"You're the best candidate. If there's any justice you'll—"

"Sue the bastards! Sue the bastards!" screeched Puni.

Dana laughed. "What a great parrot."

"Appeal, appeal." Puni moonwalked along his perch. Obviously he'd been watching too much MTV while Garth had been at work. "Sue the bastards! Sue the bastards! Sue their asses!"

"What's your parrot's name?"

"Puni." He caught the quizzical look in her eyes. "Short for Punitive Damages."

She laughed again. "I should have known."

Dana dutifully consumed two forkfuls of the salad, never commenting on the raspberry vinaigrette that he'd made himself. Something was on her mind and it wasn't the pending court appointment. He didn't press. Patience was his long suit. Not always, of course, but the accident had changed everything.

Dana wasn't an easy woman to get to know. Oh, she was friendly enough—up to a point. One of the advantages of his handicap—he'd managed to find several—was that people thought he was harmless. True, it was a subconscious thing, but people tended to trust him, to open up to him more than they would have otherwise.

Except Dana. There was an invisible shield between Dana and everyone around her. Why?

"This is fabulous," Dana said with a sigh after he served the veal Normandy.

"You've been eating at the courthouse cafeteria too much. The only place with worse food is the county jail." He grinned, but asked himself why he always discounted his talents. For some reason he was uncomfortable with compliments.

"Garth," Dana began, then stopped. She gazed into her wineglass for a moment. "Over twenty years ago something happened to me. I thought it was done, forgotten—until today."

He did a quick mental calculation. How old could Dana have been twenty years ago? Fourteen? Fifteen? He saw acute pain and the kind of fear he often noticed in his clients' eyes. Uh-oh.

"I'm afraid I'm being blackmailed."

That simple statement sent a shock wave through Garth. Blackmail implied the person had something on Dana. What? She was straighter than Cochise's arrow. More ethical than St. Peter. Still, something had happened to her twenty years ago. Now it was back to haunt her.

"I may need you to represent me . . . in court. I want to retain you."

Garth splayed his hands across his knees, touching the legs that felt nothing, experiencing a squeezing sensation in his chest. How could she be worried about being tried for something that happened twenty years ago? The statute of limitations had run its course, unless . . . His anxiety kicked up another notch; his chest felt so tight now that it was hard to breathe. Dana had to be involved in something that had an extended statute.

Murder. It could only be murder.

It took a second for his breathing to become normal and for his usual self-control to return. He struggled to keep his tone level, shaken by what she'd told him. "I'll represent you, Dana, but do you really think this will go to trial?"

Dana didn't respond, and Garth wasn't surprised that she'd stopped without telling him everything. She had retained him, professionally assuring his silence, yet she couldn't quite bring herself to trust him.

"I need to find out who is blackmailing me," she

said quietly. "Then I'll know what to do. But I haven't any idea who to call."

"Well, the two PI's in the islands who do most of the investigations aren't worth a damn. When I'm stuck on a case—and I have been several times—I use Rob Tagett."

"Really? Why?"

"Rob used to be a homicide detective, remember?"

"I was away at law school then."

"He was a damn good detective until . . ." Garth lifted his shoulders. "Rape charges were never filed against him. It was all some sort of . . . mix-up."

"Then why did he leave the police force?"

Garth didn't have an answer to the question so many people asked about Rob Tagett. His unexpected departure in the wake of the scandal still fueled the rumor mill even though years had passed. "I'm positive that Rob had a good reason for leaving the force."

"I can't call him. He crucified me for dismissing the Tenaka case. I couldn't possibly work with him."

"The presiding judge, Binkley, is the one you should blame. That case should have been heard in superior court, but they kicked it down to the muni bench because it was a political hot potato. Binkley would be damned before he'd put any of his buddies on the court on the spot, so he dumped it on you, hoping to ruin your career."

"True, but what choice did I have? I had to dismiss."

"What do you think Gwen Sihida would have done?"

"Gwen would have tried the case so that it would have been appealed and let the appeals court get the blame. Her father's pressing her hard to move up the judicial ladder. She wouldn't risk angering the public."

"Exactly. Justice is influenced by politics. Do you suppose the Fowl Flasher would have been tried in New York? No way. But Hawaii isn't going to become another Miami—an urban basket case. Mess with a tourist and you're in court. It's politics."

"True," she agreed with a weary sigh.

"You're not perfect. No judge is. Expect criticism." Garth took a deep breath. "Forget what Rob said in his column. Remember, he gets paid to assassinate people in print. Call Rob. I'd trust him with my life."

3

Rob Tagett sat on his sofa, his long legs propped up on the glass coffee table, the receiver cradled against his shoulder as he listened to his son. He could almost see the defiant thrust of Zach's chin. How similar he'd been at fifteen. Rebellious as hell. You were either hungry or horny. Usually both.

"Listen to me." He gestured with both hands as if Zach were in the room with him instead of a thousand miles away.

"Yeah?"

How could you discuss something like this over the telephone? "Your mother says she found you and your girlfriend naked in the hot tub." Two beats of dead silence. "If you're having sex with a girl you need protection."

"Puh-leeze."

How in hell was he supposed to supervise a son who lived in L.A.? For the millionth time he cursed Ellen. If she'd believed in him, in their marriage . . . but she hadn't. He didn't miss Ellen so much anymore, but he missed Zach terribly. He hated having these intimate father-son discussions via Ma Bell, but Ellen made it impossible for Zach to visit him very often.

Yet Ellen expected him to be the one to administer discipline, to control a teenager whose hormones had staged a coup. It was really just a way of getting back at Rob, torturing him for what Ellen saw as his betrayal. Didn't she care that he was the one who'd suffered? He'd been the one accused, his name, his career ruined—not Ellen's.

"Da-ad," Zach said, his tone insolent as usual, "I can't just pull out a life jacket. The babe will think I planned to screw her. That would be, like, totally nerd city."

Life jacket? Jesus, was that what kids were calling condoms these days? Fitting, but depressing as hell. "Here's how you handle it. Explain that you really care for her and want to protect her."

Silence, then, "Awesome. Totally awesome. That's it, Dad . . . thanks. Gotta go."

"Put your mother on, Zach. I'll call you next week." Rob waited while Ellen came on the line. "I expect Zach this summer. I don't want any bullshit about parties, ball camps—anything. I want to see my son."

Ellen reluctantly agreed and he hung up but stayed on the sofa, too upset to trek into the kitchen to see if there were any egg burritos in the freezer. The only light in the room came from the aquarium, where dozens of tropical fish as colorful as a Hawaiian sunrise swam in slow circles. His life was like his aquarium, he realized, moving in endless circles but going nowhere.

"Oh, crap. What's the matter with you?" He vaulted to his feet and strode out onto the deck overlooking Sunset Beach. "You don't have a damn thing to complain about."

It was true; his private security company earned a bundle without him spending much time at it. His weekly column, "Exposed," made him a local celebrity. He was doing all right for a kid from Galveston's back bay who'd come to Hawaii almost twenty years ago.

He gazed out at the sea, heeding the call of the ocean as the surf broke on the shore. A hunter's moon rode across a cloudless sky, spilling blue-white light on the waves. The *menehune* claimed their spirits became the wind on the north shore, their presence creating the pipeline waves that marched in from the sea like an invading army.

Not that he believed in the legendary dwarfs the way the natives did. Even on a night like tonight, when the wind was nothing more than a fickle breeze, the waves formed perfect tubes. Still, the ocean had an almost hypnotic effect on him, as if something magical *was* at work. At dawn the surfers would be back—not as many here as farther down the beach at the Banzai Pipeline—and the quiet beauty of the night would be lost. For now, though, he let the sea mesmerize him, his thoughts drifting along with the waves.

He remembered his run-in with Dana Hamilton at lunch. Aw, hell, what had he expected? She avoided him all the time. Why did he think she'd want to go out with him? Why did he ask her out anyway? There were plenty of women around.

What a crock. He was lying to himself. Since he'd been accused of rape he didn't quite trust any woman. He doubted that he ever would again. He was always aware of the damage to a career—to a marriage—that even an unfounded accusation could do.

Women could be such treacherous liars.

To protect himself he dated women with no more morals than an alley cat in heat, or the opposite, saints who'd never lie. Trouble was, the saints, like Gwen Sihida, tended to be boring. He suspected Dana was different, but he'd never have the chance to find out.

Of course, the article he'd written hadn't helped win him any points with her. Not that he regretted it. Too often justice was a four-letter word. A pervert walked because the DA blew the case. Too bad Dana had to catch the flak.

"Let it go, Rob," he said out loud. "Forget her."

He knew his pent-up anger, which he tried to disguise with offbeat jokes, was making him bitter. He'd thought that as time passed and that fateful night became a distant memory that his old personality would return. It hadn't. If anything he was getting worse and he hadn't a clue why.

The telephone rang and he rushed to answer it,

hoping it was Zach, yet knowing better. "Garth? Hey, this is a surprise."

The image of Garth wheeling himself into the courtroom made Rob ashamed for moping around. Garth never felt sorry for himself, nor had he allowed himself to become bitter.

What in hell is wrong with you?

"I have a client who needs help—tonight," Garth said. "What are you doing?"

"Nothing. Send him over."

"Great. Hold on a second." He heard Garth give his client the address, then cover the phone with his hand.

Rob checked his watch. Almost eleven. What couldn't wait until the morning? There were a few seconds of silence and Rob imagined the guy leaving Garth's spectacular home.

He'd been there once for a trial lawyers' cocktail reception. Not his favorite group. If he found himself with more than two lawyers at once, he reached critical mass and wanted to run. But he liked Garth, even if he did have some crazy parrot that kept spitting birdseed and threatening to "sue your ass."

"Rob, this case is important to me. I don't think my client can afford you. I'm willing to pay whatever it takes to straighten this out. Keep that between the two of us."

"Okay. What am I supposed to straighten out?"

"Blackmail." There was a long pause. "Maybe something more. I'm not sure. That's what I want you to find out."

"You got it." Rob hung up, then stood there a moment, realizing Garth had forgotten to tell him the client's name. He almost called Garth back, but decided it didn't matter. He would find out soon enough.

He should shower before the guy arrived. On his way to the bathroom he stopped by the refrigerator, his rumbling stomach getting the better of him. Nothing. Not even a frozen egg burrito.

He rarely ate at home. What fun was eating unless you had someone to eat with you? The best he could do was take a handful of crack seed from the jar on the counter. The sweet-and-sour taste of the bits of dried plum, assorted nuts, and lemon peel did little to fill his stomach.

He was supposed to meet one of his sources later at Coconut Willie's. He could get something there if he was still hungry.

He showered and toweled his hair dry. He was overdue for a haircut, he decided, checking his reflection in the mirror. S'okay. Tomorrow he'd hit the grocery store and the Clip Joint. Should he shave? Nah. Why bother?

He pulled on cutoffs that weren't too raunchy and found a clean T-shirt in the dryer, along with a load of underwear he'd forgotten. The shirt had more wrinkles than crepe paper and it was a little tight. He'd probably used water that was too hot again.

The doorbell rang and he flicked on the porch light as he opened the door. For a moment he stood there like a cigar-store Indian. "Well, I'll be damned."

"Hello." Dana's voice was low, uncertain.

"Garth sent you?" he asked, half-hoping she'd come on her own and she wasn't Garth's client.

She nodded and he took one step back to let her in, wishing he'd shaved. Look at her! The black robes that made her look like Mother Superior were gone. She was wearing a slinky blue number that fit her cute ass like shrink wrap. Those God-awful glasses were history. Her eyes shone a luminous green. And serious as hell.

Okay, Garth said she was in trouble, but come on. This was Dana Hamilton. Blackmail? Over what? Making personal calls on the court's phone? Better yet, she'd fudged on her taxes and the IRS would be on her cute tail if the informant turned her in to get the government reward.

"Garth explained?" she asked.

Not nearly enough. "A little."

"I have some reservations about our being able to work together."

That got him. He stabbed at the air between them with his finger. "Don't be such a tight ass, Dana." Honest to God, why couldn't he control his temper? More and more he lashed out and was disgusted with himself later. "Go ahead, say what you mean. You must be desperate to be knocking on my door."

She glared at him, her eyes telegraphing what she couldn't bring herself to say. Finally, she looked at the toes of her pumps. "Garth said you were the best, or I wouldn't be here. I'd like to hire you."

"I don't know if I want to work for you." He leaned one shoulder against the doorjamb. "I don't like being treated like shit."

There was a moment of total silence, punctuated by the sound of the surf breaking on the beach and the wind rustling through the palms. The night was balmy, slightly warmer than usual, and filled with the scent of the tropical flowers that grew along his terrace, separating his home from his neighbors.

"I'm . . . sorry. I was rude to you today at lunch."

All right. He'd gotten to her. She'd apologized, but only because he'd forced her. And she was pissed—big time—about it. That meant she'd had no choice. She really did need him. His stomach chose that moment to rumble like distant thunder.

He grabbed her arm and steered her back outside. "I'm starving. Let's run down to Coconut Willie's and talk. I'm supposed to meet someone there in an hour anyway."

Dana held on, her hands gripping the Porsche's seat as Rob drove down the highway. Really, this was more terrifying than bungee jumping. If she didn't need help so desperately she'd tell the creep to drop dead. But she needed Rob Tagett.

Hard as that was to believe. He looked nothing like a detective in his grubby cutoffs and a T-shirt that was two sizes too small. She would have to work with him. That's what happened when you made a bargain with the devil the way she had two decades ago.

Now she had to rely on a man who'd already proven how much damage he could do to her career. Was she crazy? Probably, but Garth had convinced her. She had the queasy feeling that she was going to regret this.

They drove along the blacktop road into the outskirts of the old sugar mill village of Kahuku. Wooden homes with rusted tin roofs, roadside vegetable stands with hand-painted signs, boarded-up company stores. Somehow the twentieth century had bypassed Kahuku, leaving a vestige of the island's plantation days.

They pulled into a roadside tavern. Tourists never stopped at grass shacks like Coconut Willie's, Dana thought. It was on the water, but the battered vehicles in the parking lot and the toilet seats haphazardly nailed to the exterior discouraged tourists who happened to venture beyond their territory to this stretch of the north shore.

The landscaping consisted of old tires sprouting weeds and a lone palm, a dusky silhouette against the night sky. A scuttling noise announced a rat in the dried fronds that hung like a hula skirt from the tree. They followed the well-worn path around the tires and passed by a rusted-out engine partially covered with tropical vines.

Inside, the lights were nothing more than candles planted in bottles of island beer, Primo, leaving petticoats of wax. The scent of mildew and beer was almost eclipsed by the cigarette smoke. Willie's had been there since the war, and it had been that long since anyone swept the floor or sponged off a wooden table. Its saving grace was its location on a tranquil cove where waves tumbled across silver-white sand.

Dana followed Rob into the bar, whose back wall was a roll of woven bamboo that had been pulled aside so the patrons could stroll out onto the beach or sit at one of the tables outside. The neon PRIMO sign over the bar flickered spasmodically, threatening to die any second. The behemoth bartender, definitely a descendant of King Kamehameha, greeted Rob as if he were his brother.

"Two S.O.B.s," Rob said, "and four orders of *saimin*."

"No *saimin* for me," she spoke up, thinking of Garth's delicious veal. *Saimin* was such an island staple that even McDonald's served the noodles, but she'd never cared for them.

"They're all for me." He patted a tummy as flat as Kansas. "I'm a growing boy." He pointed to a vacant table on the sand. "We'll be outside, Willie."

Dana let Rob take her arm, not missing the crowded room full of *mokes*, island toughs. There wasn't a designated driver present. Not that anyone in Willie's cared. She'd probably prosecuted half these *mokes* on DUIs when she'd been a deputy DA. Being in court with them was one thing; being here, another. Women who strayed into dives like this

40

were inviting trouble. Not that she was straying. She was with Rob on his home turf.

"What's in an S.O.B.?" she asked as they sat at a table a few feet from the breaking waves. The candle in the Primo bottle was dying an agonizing death, its wick casting nothing more than a dim glow and leaving a smoky mist that drifted into the night air.

"S.O.B.—sex on the beach." He had the audacity to wink and roll his eyes toward the water. *"Okolehao."*

"Moonshine," Dana snapped, just to show him she knew the score. "They're brewing ti roots in a tub nearby. Drink it and you'll be declared a vegetable by the court on Monday."

Rob smiled, that narcotic smile backlit by the impish twinkle in his blue eyes. "That's it, Dana. Let your temper show."

The waitress, a *tita*, a tough girl who'd be more at home wrestling gorillas, slammed the drinks on the table with a "sex on the beach"—or anywhere— smile for Rob.

"Okole maluna," Rob said. Bottoms up. He tossed back his drink.

Dana picked up her glass, but didn't drink for fear her brain would be pickled in an instant. The stuff smelled vile. How could anyone drink it? "Let's talk about my problem."

"Sure." Rob leaned back, stretching the T-shirt even tighter, revealing a powerful torso. Obviously he took his workouts seriously. "Fill me in."

"Does this mean we can work together?" she asked, all her doubts returning full force.

He studied her for a moment, his hands clasped across his broad chest. "If the price is right."

She hesitated, knowing how strained her finances were and that Vanessa was rich on paper but a pauper in reality. "What's your fee?"

"Forget the article I wrote about you."

"What article?"

"Cut the bullshit. You know what article."

"All right," she conceded. "I haven't read a thing you've written."

"Forget whatever you've heard about me."

"What makes you think I've heard anything?"

"You won't go out with me because you think I raped that woman. And you're still pissed—big time —about the article."

She kept her face expressionless—or tried to—but Rob was right on target. She had heard the rumors and they made her leery of him. Would she ever live long enough to forgive him for his vicious column? "Ever think I won't go out with you because I don't like you?"

"Nope." Incredibly, he grinned as if he knew his smile was a lethal weapon. "You like me."

Why bother denying it? Obviously the man had a bulletproof ego. "You're okay, I guess."

"We can build on that."

"Rob, we're not building anything," she shot back, justifiably proud of her stern tone. "I need a good detective. Sex isn't included in the job description."

"Could have fooled me."

She was more than a little overwhelmed by his nearness and the way he was behaving. She didn't like aggressive men. "Don't you ever think about anything but sex?"

"Mmmmm." He pondered the question. "Sometimes I think about food."

He was something, wasn't he? Obviously he didn't believe she was in serious trouble, or he wouldn't be joking like this. "Are you helping me or not?"

"I'm helping Garth."

Oh, God, she was in over her head with this man. Why now, when everything she'd worked for was at risk? "Where should I start?"

"At the beginning."

She stared over his shoulder at the surf tumbling lazily onto the shore. She'd thought about what to tell him. And what to omit. Driving from Garth's she'd rehearsed. There was only so much she was going to tell anyone about that fateful night.

"I suppose it started when my parents were killed in an auto accident. My sister and I had no relatives, so we were sent to a foster home. It was so bad that Vanessa and I ran away." She looked into his eyes and was relieved to see he was dead serious now. "You may have heard of my sister. She's married to Eric Coltrane."

"One of the big-five families," he said with disgust.

The history of the five families was common knowledge. They had achieved so much power that they entered the realm of the mythical Hawaiian gods. The Factors, the Alexanders, the Baldwins, the Cookes—and, of course, the Coltranes—had once had a stranglehold on Hawaiian business and owned most of the valuable land. Their influence had diminished with time, but here, in the islands, they were still powerful. Dana wanted Rob to know what they were up against—should Big Daddy prove to be the blackmailer.

"It was a little over twenty years ago when Vanessa hot-wired a car and we headed west toward California."

Rob listened to Dana's story with interest, convinced she wasn't making it up. She wasn't much of an actress. Her eyes were too expressive. They had a future; she just didn't realize it yet.

He concentrated on what she was saying, trying to imagine two girls, aged fourteen and sixteen, driving across the country with nothing more than a beat-up Ford and a pocketful of change. Apparently they stopped in several towns, never daring to tell the authorities they were runaways. A damn shame someone hadn't helped them.

"We ran out of money and had to stop in a town so small it wasn't even a wide spot in the road." The downshift in her tone forewarned Rob. This was the heart of the story. "Vanessa took a job in a bar"— Dana looked around—"not unlike this one. We lived in a trailer behind the joint."

He didn't like the picture he was getting. He'd been a hell raiser, yet he'd always had his parents to help him. Pop had died long before Rob set out for Hawaii, but his mother had always been there. She still was. He'd brought her to Kauai years ago, setting her up in a new home that she loved.

"There was this horrible man who worked at the bar. Hank Rawlins was always after Vanessa, saying how much he liked girls who were . . ."

"Were what?" Rob prompted, tensing at the raw emotion in her voice.

Dana looked away, her eyes seeking the moonlit water. "Virgins."

There were sons of bitches like that everywhere. Too often women didn't have anyone to protect them.

"One night Vanessa didn't come home. I found her in the storage shed behind the bar where they kept beer and stuff. Hank was on top of her." Dana's voice trailed off, but he didn't have to hear the details to know what was going on. He thought of himself as a callous bastard who'd seen it all, heard it all, but the pain in Dana's voice and the anger flaring in her eyes made him want to kill the son of a bitch.

"He was attacking her. I . . . I had to stop him. There was a knife used to skin rabbits hanging on a hook. I grabbed it. He lunged toward me . . ."

Rob waited for Dana to continue, but she didn't. He studied her and saw that her gaze was directed at the undulating surge of the sea where it broke on the rocks. "Go on."

"He shoved me up against the wall. His pants were down around his knees. I could see his hairy belly and . . . everything. I should have been able to get away from him. He was dead drunk, stumbling around, but he was too strong. He got the knife away from me."

Rob could just picture two young girls fending off a burly man. He heard the terror in her voice. And the desperation. Jesus. The waiter interrupted them to plunk down the *saimin* in the traditional wooden bowls. He shoved them aside. Who could listen to this and still want to eat?

"He pulled up my dress, saying he was going to . . ." she said, her voice dropping with every word. "Vanessa jumped on him from behind. I kicked him between the legs as hard as I could."

"Atta girl."

"It wasn't hard enough. He didn't drop the knife. He stabbed at me, but I moved at the last second. That's when Vanessa went for his eyes. He spun around, swearing he'd kill her. Then he tripped on a carton."

She paused to let a couple pass their table, then said very quietly, "Hank fell facedown on the dirt floor. I kicked him and Vanessa clobbered him with a bottle of bourbon. When he didn't move, we rolled him over and saw the knife in his chest." She closed her eyes for a moment. "He was dead."

Two panic-stricken girls. One dead bastard who'd

gotten what he deserved. Rob shook his head, suspecting what was coming. They hadn't called the police.

"Vanessa and I would have called the police, but we were terrified no one would believe it was an accident when they saw the cuts on his head from the bottle and bruises where I'd kicked him. We decided to drag him into the parking lot. Then we ran away. We didn't stop to pack."

"I see," Rob said, even though he had his doubts. He didn't give a damn about the dead man, but it was real tricky to fall on a knife you were holding. Yet not impossible.

He didn't challenge Dana's version of that night's events. She seemed totally sincere and obviously still shaken by what had happened. It *could* have been an accident. He didn't blame the girls, yet his years as a detective had honed his sixth sense. He was certain that one of them had deliberately plunged the knife into the bastard's heart.

4

Dana studied Rob, but it was impossible to tell what he was thinking. His steady gaze remained fixed on the weathered rocks that formed a barrier between the placid cove and the savage waves of the north shore. Had he believed her story? She'd tried not to stray too far from the truth, but perhaps her delivery had been off-key.

The uncomfortable silence was punctuated by the lulling sound of the surf and the raucous noise coming from inside Coconut Willie's. Dana couldn't resist asking, "Do you think you can help me?"

Rob turned slowly, the flickering light from the candle on the table playing across his face. He suddenly looked younger, less cynical. Dead serious.

She grabbed her drink and sipped it quickly. The S.O.B. hit her stomach in a second and flared back up her throat like a blast of napalm. She coughed and blinked rapidly to quell the tears the deadly concoction brought to her eyes. She knew better than to drink it, but this situation had her completely off-balance.

Rob's inquisitive stare didn't make her feel any better. "I can probably help you. How many people know about this?"

"Just you." She quickly added, "My sister and I have never told anyone. I didn't even tell Garth. I wouldn't have told you now except I had no choice. I received a blackmail note and a knife just like the one Hank had."

Rob leaned forward, both elbows on the table, his turbulent blue eyes never leaving her face. "Someone talked, or the blackmailer wouldn't have the goods on you."

"Neither of us told," Dana insisted, "but I have a theory. While we were in that horrible town Vanessa met Slade Carter. It was one of those first love things. That night, after we'd dragged Hank's body into the parking lot, we met Slade. Vanessa said I was sick and we were going to the all-night pharmacy in the next town. She promised to call him in the morning. Of course, she never did."

"Has Carter shown up in Hawaii?"

"No, but two months ago *Town and Country* did a feature article on the Coltranes. There were several close-ups of Vanessa. She hasn't changed much since she was sixteen. She even wears her hair long and straight the way she did then."

"Okay, so you think this guy subscribes to a hoity-toity magazine that's geared to East Coast WASPS?"

"I admit it's far-fetched, but I don't know how else to explain it. I never told a soul . . . until tonight." The impact of what she'd done overwhelmed her. She'd put her future—as well as Vanessa's and Jason's—on the line with a man she barely knew.

"Then your sister told," he said flatly. "Someone here in the islands is behind this, not some boyfriend from twenty years ago."

"I'm positive Vanessa hasn't told anyone."

"Aw, come on. Not even her husband?"

"They don't have that kind of relationship. She married him for his money and he knows it. They barely speak."

Rob kicked back the rest of his S.O.B.—apparently his throat was lined with asbestos—but he didn't look one bit convinced.

"Vanessa believes the Coltranes are behind this. She thinks they want to take her son, Jason, away from her."

"That makes more sense than the old boyfriend." Rob stood and thrust his hand into the pocket of his tight-fitting cutoffs and yanked out some bills. She rose as he tossed a few on the table. "Let's head over to your place and take a look at that blackmail note and knife."

"Weren't you going to meet someone?"

"I'll phone him from the car and reschedule. This is more important."

She didn't move away when Rob put his hand on the small of her back to guide her through the grass

51

shack, which was so packed that people were forced to stand. Up on the small stage three men were playing ukuleles and chanting Hawaiian rap while a dozen men stood near them in nothing but their underwear.

"Free Willie! Free Willie!" yelled the *titas*.

"It's the Saturday night Wet Willie contest." Rob nodded toward the group of tough-looking women, who were now whistling at the men. "The *titas* love it."

The men began dousing their flies with pitchers of beer. Dana was grateful for Rob's strong arm as he prized his way through the crowd to the door. Clearly women couldn't be too careful where they went. She didn't belong in a place like this; it reminded her too much of the Road Kill Bar, where all the trouble had begun. Places like this, wild people like this, frightened her.

Yet Rob Tagett was right at home with these people. As he helped her into his sports car, she reminded herself that she wasn't looking for a soulmate. This was a professional relationship. Rob could frequent every sleazy bar in the islands for all she cared. What mattered to her was that he could help her when no one else could.

They rode back to his home in silence. She didn't ask herself what he was really thinking. Thank heavens he hadn't challenged her account of what happened that fateful night. She'd said as little as possible, afraid he'd detect that she wasn't telling him the whole truth.

"I'll follow you home," Rob said as he pulled his silver Porsche up behind her Toyota. "Where do you live?"

"Go—" She hesitated, almost saying east, but quickly changed it to, "Diamond Head."

Islanders didn't rely on geographical terms like east/west. They used points on the island like Diamond Head or *mauka*, meaning toward the mountains that dominated the center of the island. Even after living in the islands for almost twenty years, she still had to stop herself from giving proper directions. Vanessa always said Dana was too formal to be a real islander.

"I live on Lanai Road. Number four eleven."

"Don't worry, you won't lose me."

So true, Dana thought ten minutes later as she again glanced at her rearview mirror and found Rob's Porsche hugging her bumper. No doubt her pace irked him, but she'd never gotten a speeding ticket and she wasn't going to get one tonight. Finally they pulled into her drive, and Dana was relieved to see that Mrs. Hurley's lights were out. The fewer people who knew that she was associated with Rob Tagett the better.

Inside her kitchen she poured water into the Brewmatic while Rob stood beside her at the counter, reading the note and inspecting the rabbit-skinning knife. She threw open the windows and switched on the ceiling fan, conscious of how warm the room seemed after being shut all day.

"I'll run a fingerprint check on the knife," he said.

"I don't want the police involved. That's why I hired you."

He stared at her, his incisive blue eyes saying he wasn't accustomed to being questioned. "I never said I was using the police lab."

She motioned for Rob to sit at the dinette, then took mugs out of the cabinet. "I forgot. You have your own security company."

"True, but it's not a private investigation firm. Rent-a-cops. I specialize in hotel security. This is paradise, remember? We don't want tourists' rooms robbed or hookers soliciting in the bars. Private security, dressed like tourists, handle potential problems. That kind of operation doesn't need a lab."

"Garth said—"

"Occasionally I do some investigating—when the case is interesting and the price is right. I'm taking the evidence to the lab at the University of Hawaii. They have a first-rate criminology department with equipment that's better than what the HPD has."

Suddenly she felt foolish for questioning him. Garth was right; Rob knew what to do. She poured the coffee into blue-striped mugs and sat down opposite him.

"I don't expect to get any prints though. The perp's probably been careful." He inspected the knife. "This handle looks really old and the blade is slightly loose." He stared directly into her eyes, expecting an answer.

"It's exactly like the one I grabbed off the wall that night," she heard herself whisper. "The blade was loose, the handle worn from years of skinning rabbits."

His gaze never wavered. "That's an amazing detail for anyone but you or your sister to know."

"Exactly. That's what has me worried. This isn't some wild guess."

Her voice must have had more of an emotional edge than she realized, because he leaned forward and covered her hand with his. She couldn't help noticing how wide and strong his hand looked. Everything about Rob Tagett projected strength, from his long runner's legs to his powerful torso to his personality.

He withdrew his hand and took a swig of coffee, his eyes never leaving her face. "At work next week, keep to your normal routine. Don't—"

"I'm on vacation next week. I'm going over to the Coltrane ranch on Maui to spend time with Vanessa and my nephew, Jason."

"Perfect. I'm coming with you."

"What for?" she gasped, stunned that he'd even suggest such a thing.

He leaned forward until he was halfway across the small table, face to face with her. "I want to check out the Coltranes. I agree with your sister. They're the most likely suspects, unless you have an enemy you haven't mentioned."

"I've racked my brain. I can't think of anyone who'd blackmail me." She stared into her cup, aware that she'd been nervous and had poured more cream into the coffee than she liked. "You know the municipal court only hears misdemeanors. I don't get the psychos the superior court does. I don't think anyone I sentenced is after me."

"What about Davis Binkley? He tried to kill your career the first week you were on the bench by assigning you the Tenaka case."

You didn't do me any favors either, she almost said. Now was not the time to give in to her temper. Rob's article had been as devastating as the presiding judge's maneuvers. "True, but how would Judge Binkley know about the knife?"

"Good question. It must be someone close to you —or your sister. Probably the Coltranes. That's why I'm coming with you."

"I don't need you. I can check on the Coltranes myself."

"You're too emotionally involved to be worth a damn, and you aren't trained as an investigator. I pick up on things most people miss."

Rob leaned forward again, so close this time that she could see her reflection in his eyes. He took both her hands in his, a subtle gesture that wouldn't mean anything—if it had been anyone but Rob Tagett. Her pulse skyrocketed, surprising her, making her furious.

"I'm a damn good detective," he said. "I'll bet no one but your sister knows your hair is really blonde."

Dana couldn't stifle a gasp. She'd been dying her hair since high school, when she'd decided that being a blonde attracted the wrong kind of attention from men. That was okay for Vanessa; men were her stock-in-trade, but even back then Dana had other plans for herself.

"What makes you think I'm a blonde?" she asked with as much sincerity as she could muster. She touched up her roots each week without fail. He couldn't know. He was just guessing, trying to trap her the way he'd guessed that she'd hiked up her skirts in her hot courtroom that morning.

In one fluid motion he dropped her hands and stood up. He walked around the table, the movement of his thigh muscles clearly visible beneath the worn fabric of his cutoffs. She started to get up, but he steadied her by putting both his hands on her shoulders as he stood behind her.

"Face forward," he said, his voice low.

The air stalled in her lungs. For some reason she did as she was told. With his thumbs he traced a feather-light path across the base of her neck. Oh, Lord, what was he doing? Why couldn't she breathe?

Her hair hung halfway down her neck. He parted it with his thumbs. "When you bend over," he said, stroking her neck, exerting a gentle yet extremely sensual pressure, "your hair falls forward and anyone can see the short wisps along the back of your neck. They're a natural blonde."

Stunned that he'd discovered her secret, she let her chin drop to her chest, but then a surge of anger came to her rescue. Why was she allowing him to touch her in a way that felt more like a caress? She jerked her head away from his talented hands and spun around to face him.

"All right. I confess. I dye my hair. So what? I look more professional with darker hair."

He chuckled and muttered, "My, such a temper." He sat on the kitchen table, one leg hitched up on the edge, grinning. "How do you explain the sexy underwear?"

This time she didn't gasp, but she must have looked shocked because Rob hooted and slapped his knee. "You know, anyone can see those lacy bras when you bend forward."

"Only if you're looking down the front of my blouse."

Rob didn't bother to deny it; he just smirked. "You wear the sheerest nylons possible"—his eyes took a leisurely tour of her body, making her even more aware of the provocative dress she should have returned—"and sexy garter belts."

She banked a groan, unable to believe he'd detected the sexy lingerie she loved to wear. It made her feel feminine even though she was wearing a power suit under her judge's robe. "So what?"

His finger roamed up the rise of her cheek. "You don't want people to know what you're really like, do you?"

"I'm just trying to make it in a man's world," she insisted, reluctant to admit he was right. She was a very private person. The only one who really knew her was Vanessa, and over the last few years they had grown apart.

"Uh-huh," he replied, his voice leaving no doubt he didn't really believe her. "Noticing your hair proves my point. I'm good at what I do. I'm coming with you to the Coltranes."

She wanted to argue with him, but she stopped herself. Too much was at stake. Rob was uniquely observant, and he had resources she didn't have. As much as she wanted to distance herself from him, she believed he had a talent for investigating.

Rob stood and placed the knife and note in a paper bag. "Don't tell anyone, even your sister, that we aren't lovers—"

"Lovers?" She jumped to her feet. "Now just a minute! I agree that you should come with me to check out the Coltranes, but why can't I say you're my friend?"

"Okay, whatever. Use the word *friend* if you like, but the impression they should get is that we're lovers."

"Why on earth would I want to do that?"

He rolled his shoulders back as if stretching a tight muscle, pulling the snug-fitting T-shirt even tighter across the well-defined contours of his chest. "I'm not the type of man who's 'just friends' with a woman. No one's going to buy that. Might as well pretend we're lovers, then they won't be suspicious about why I'm really there. The last thing we want is for the Coltranes to think I'm investigating them."

As much as she hated to admit it, he was right. No woman could be "just friends" with a man like Rob

59

Tagett. And the last thing she needed was to make Big Daddy Coltrane suspicious.

His slow grin told her he sensed victory and was savoring every second of it. "I'm coming to Maui because I'm hot for you, right?"

It took her a few seconds to get the word out. "Right."

Bag in hand, he moved toward the door, grinning at her response.

"I have to tell Vanessa the truth. I never keep anything from her."

Rob stopped just short of opening the back door; his eyes assessed her from head to toe. "Bullshit. You don't tell your sister everything. Convince her that you've flipped for me. Then she'll treat me like a potential brother-in-law. Otherwise she may blow my cover. We don't want that, do we?"

"No," she conceded, irritated that Rob had a way of seeing through people, pinpointing weaknesses. She supposed she should be thankful. No doubt such a talent would be helpful with the case. But she wasn't happy; she was frustrated. Was she really so transparent?

Rob dropped the paper bag with the evidence on the counter. The thud echoed through the tiny kitchen like a warning shot.

What was he up to?

Nothing, apparently. He was just standing so close that she had to battle the cowardly urge to back up. She didn't look into his eyes, not wanting to acknowledge the raw sensuality she knew would be there. As she stood waiting for him to speak, she was overwhelmed by his size. Until now she hadn't realized he was quite so tall—well over six feet—or that he was quite so powerfully built.

The pulse in her throat jumped, alerting her. His hand slipped under her chin, cupping it and slowly forcing her to look directly into his eyes. She met the challenge with a clenched jaw.

Close up his eyes were a marine blue shot with minute stitches of silver that danced like summer lightning. At a loss for words, furious with herself for noticing how attractive he was, she angrily pursed her lips, ready to do something infantile like kick him in the shins.

She opened her mouth to tell him off, but before she could utter a sound he bent his head and angled his lips over hers. He slid his strong hand into the hair at the base of her neck, anchoring her in place while his other hand clutched the small of her back, bringing her flush against him.

She braced herself to endure his kiss. Didn't all men think they were world-class lovers? Instead of boredom, an unanticipated surge of pleasure almost buckled her knees as her lips willingly parted and his tongue aggressively mated with hers. The heat of his body engulfed her, molding her smaller frame against his with shocking intimacy.

For a moment she reveled in the unique sensations, allowing herself to respond even though she knew better. Suddenly the insistent bulge of his arousal chilled her like an arctic wind across Waikiki.

She pulled back her head, her lips still inches from his. "You creep!"

"Temper. Temper," he chided with an infuriatingly sensual grin that said he didn't take her one bit seriously. He kept his arms locked around her, pinning them together from chest to thigh. He bent forward as if to whisper something. His lips grazed her ear and she bit back a moan. Then he nipped gently at her earlobe and took its softness into his mouth.

Suddenly her body felt heavy and weak, yet alive with sensations that she'd never felt before this moment. He moved away unexpectedly and she rocked back on her heels. His eyes were almost black now, the irises dilated. And there was no mistaking the jutting ridge in his jeans.

"Let's get something straight." Oh, Lordy, why did she sound so breathless? "This is a professional relationship. Nothing more."

He picked up the bag on the counter and said with a drawl that evoked the image of a hot cowboy on a Saturday night, "Coulda fooled me."

5

The jet swept low across Maui, tipping its silver wings and giving the tourists aboard a better view of the crystalline beaches. The incandescent blue of the sky echoed the deeper blue of the sea. Even at this distance the water was so clear that Dana could see the reefs, dark shadows against the ocean floor.

She looked away from the dazzling white sand that was almost blinding in the morning sun, barely glancing at the rows of hotels nestled in groves of palms along the shore. She gazed inland at the green, rolling fields of sugar cane and pineapples that climbed up the hills to Maui's crowning glory, the dormant volcano Haleakala. As usual, the "house of the sun" was floating in a sea of its own, an ocean of clouds that nourished the rain forest along its slopes. It was early for the showers that came daily, but by afternoon the warm tropical rain would begin to fall in the hills.

Below Haleakala was the lush "up-country" area of Maui, with its myriad waterfalls, enormous tree ferns, and stretches of grassy pastureland where herds of cattle grazed. The Coltrane ranch was located there in a picture-postcard setting.

How would the Coltrane family take the news that Rob would be joining her for vacation? Dana wondered. He had decided to have Dana come alone while he ran tests on the knife and note. It was Dana's job to prepare Vanessa and the Coltranes for the arrival tomorrow of her "boyfriend."

Dana knew it wouldn't be an imposition. Kau Ranch, the Coltrane family compound, was huge, with a large main house and several guest cottages. She'd never been the only guest.

Big Daddy had always encouraged her to bring a friend. Last night she'd called to say someone would be with her. Big Daddy had taken the call and said he'd be delighted to have another guest. Not that he was imbued with typical Hawaiian hospitality. Dana had decided that he liked to have a court of people around him so he could play king.

An unexpected guest wouldn't be a problem, but her choice of Rob as a boyfriend would surprise everyone, particularly Vanessa. She knew how upset Dana had been over the negative article. Not only had she told Vanessa she despised the man, but Rob was nothing like the men she usually dated.

Convincing anyone she cared about Rob would require some top-notch acting, something she wasn't very good at. Too often her temper flared and she let her true feelings show. Could she pull it off?

Yes, she assured herself, remembering all that was at stake. Her career. Vanessa and Jason's future.

Dana stopped inside the terminal and looked around for Vanessa, but she wasn't there. Strange. Vanessa was rarely late. Even after Dana had claimed her bags Vanessa hadn't appeared. Dana was waiting in the long line for rental cars when Vanessa dashed up.

"Sorry," Vanessa said, struggling to catch her breath. "I-I—"

"It's okay. I just arrived." Dana hugged her sister and kissed her cheek.

As usual, Vanessa was stylishly dressed, in a floral-print skirt and a blouse piped in a matching print. Her thick blonde hair brushed her shoulders, and she wore sunglasses that covered half her face.

They walked outside into the moist tropical heat fanned by the ever-present breeze from the trade winds. At the curb was a Range Rover with the Kau Ranch sign painted on the door and the Coltrane logo, a black Angus cow wearing an orchid lei.

Dana decided to immediately tell Vanessa about Rob. Waiting wouldn't make it any easier. "Vanessa"—she drew in a calming breath—"I've met someone."

"Really?" To her surprise Vanessa sounded only mildly interested.

"I hope you don't mind, but I've invited him to come here and spend my vacation with me." The words were coming out in a breathless rush now. "I've been seeing Rob Tagett."

"Great," Vanessa replied as she tossed the suitcase she'd been carrying into the back seat and waited for Dana to put hers in.

Great? Dana silently climbed into the passenger seat. Was that all she had to say about a man that Dana had once insisted she hated? Vanessa pulled away from the curb without asking a single question. Though relieved, Dana had mixed feelings. Didn't Vanessa care?

Without making another comment Vanessa took the Haleakala highway toward Maui's up-country. Dana glanced at her, but Vanessa didn't look her way. If she didn't care about Dana's love life, didn't Vanessa at least wonder about the blackmailer? If the truth came out she might lose her son. Something had to be troubling Vanessa, distracting her. "Vanessa"—Dana put her hand on her sister's arm—"what's wrong?"

Vanessa's lower lip quivered. "It's Jason."

She realized Vanessa was crying, silent tears dripping from beneath her oversize sunglasses. The car veered toward the lane of oncoming traffic. "Pull over." Dana pointed to the parking lot of the Bad Dog Gym. Vanessa drove in and slammed on the breaks, bringing the Rover to a jarring halt. "What happened? Is Jason ill?"

Vanessa whipped off her sunglasses. Beneath the sheen of tears, anger burned like a white-hot flame in her blue eyes. "Jason's fine. At least he was when he left with Big Daddy and the boys to go pig sticking."

"No! Jason's barely five. He's much too young to go on a pig hunt."

"Big Daddy doesn't think so."

"What about Jason's father? Didn't Eric put his foot down?"

"Are you kidding?" Vanessa's tears had stopped. She swiped at her wet cheeks with the back of her hand, where a doorknob-size diamond gleamed on her ring finger like a beacon. "Have you ever known Eric to cross his father?"

So true. Dana shook her head. The Coltrane brothers might look like men—rough, macho men's men—but Vanessa's husband Eric and his brother, Travis, were dominated by Big Daddy.

"Maybe they won't find the pig," Dana said.

"They'll find him. They took Rambo and the other tracker dogs."

Dana stared out the window at the clouds skirting Haleakala like billowing petticoats, reminding herself that wild pigs were a nuisance. Descended from the boars brought by settlers in the eighteenth century, the pigs had "gone wild." Even environmentalists agreed that they were a severe threat to Hawaii's fragile ecosystem. They devoured native plants that took generations to grow and they stripped the bark from trees, killing them.

"I know the pigs are a problem," Dana said, "but I can't condone hunting them down on horseback with vicious tracker dogs like Rambo when they could use Havahart traps or stun guns."

"Big Daddy will see that Jason is safe, but watching the pig sticking is bound to give him nightmares. I know. I went on a hunt once because Big Daddy insisted," Vanessa said, her voice full of bitterness. "The tracker dogs cornered the pig. Then grabber dogs nipped at the pig's hind legs to distract it, so it couldn't gore anyone with its tusks. While the dogs tormented the pig, the hunters stabbed it with long knives."

"Only a mental case would drag a child to see something so bloody and inhumane," Dana said, disgusted.

"Try telling that to Big Daddy. He claims pig sticking is like fox hunting."

Dana hated both sports—if you could call them that. "Where's the sport in hunting an animal with a pack of dogs? I don't care if it's a fox or pig. They're totally outnumbered, the odds so against them that it sickens me to even think about it."

"Me too." Vanessa's voice was barely above a whisper. "How will Jason react?"

Dana didn't have an answer. Like most little boys, Jason was so inquisitive that he got himself into a lot of scrapes. Yet there was a sensitive side to him that reminded Dana of herself. He loved unusual animals like the geckos. The small lizards, a symbol of good luck in Hawaii, were everywhere on the ranch. Jason had made pets of several, giving them special names.

"It's not going to get any better." Vanessa interrupted Dana's thoughts. "Big Daddy won't be happy until he molds Jason the way he did his boys. I can't allow that to happen."

"You're right." During her visits to the ranch Dana had noticed that Big Daddy was almost as obsessed with Jason as Vanessa was.

"Big Daddy has this unshakable image of the perfect Coltrane male, a Hawaiian cowboy, hard-riding, hard-drinking, hard-hearted. Just plain hard."

Dana was tempted to remind Vanessa that she'd warned her about Eric's father. All anyone had to do was look at the way Big Daddy dominated his sons to realize that his grandson would be treated the same way. But Vanessa hadn't seen it, or hadn't wanted to.

Vanessa started the car and pulled onto the highway. "I'm getting a divorce. I can't let them ruin Jason's life. I can't." Vanessa wearily lifted her shoulders. "It's hard to admit I made a mistake. You tried to tell me . . ."

Dana told herself not to be angry, but on some level she was. How long had Vanessa been miserable? She'd told her sister everything about her own private life—what little there was to tell—and yet her sister hadn't confided in her.

"Will you let us live with you until I can make other arrangements?"

"Of course. Stay as long as you like." Inwardly Dana sighed, the uphill battle facing Vanessa starkly apparent to her. "What did Big Daddy say about the divorce?"

It took a few seconds for Vanessa to admit, "I haven't told him. I haven't even mentioned it to Eric. But this morning when they hauled Jason away I knew I had no choice."

"Big Daddy will fight, you know. He'll do anything to keep his only grandson. And the Coltranes will have the big five behind them. I don't have to tell you how much power the founding families still have."

"You're right," Vanessa conceded. "It's going to be a battle royal to keep Jason. That's why I'm glad you're here. I need you."

A tight band formed across Dana's chest as she recalled her childhood, every memory colored by Vanessa's presence. She'd been more of a mother than a sister. And she'd always been there to help her younger, shyer sister. Now Vanessa—and Jason —needed her. "We're in this together, like always."

"Like always."

Vanessa turned off the highway and headed for Makawao—which meant "where the forest begins" —driving into the lush up-country ranch lands at the base of Haleakala. Tall eucalyptus and jacaranda trees shaded banks of ferns. Endless meadows of wild ginger danced in the breeze, their white blossoms sending a fragrant scent into the warm air.

Kentucky must look something like this, Dana thought as she always did when nearing Makawao. White wood fences enclosed pastures of shimmering blue-green grass where horses and cattle grazed. The tall trees and rolling hills blocked the view of the ocean. Only a hint of the sea on the wind reminded Dana that this was Maui.

The up-country was so different from the tourist beach area that it was difficult to imagine they were within half an hour's drive of the ocean. From experience Dana knew people here were socially as well as geographically isolated from the hotels full of tourists who rarely ventured beyond Maui's shoreline. Many up-country families went back generations, most living in homes they'd inherited.

Besides ranchers, a number of artists resided in the area, their studios hidden along country lanes that were hardly wide enough for a car. Dropouts from the seventies still lived in enclaves concealed behind banks of tree ferns. New age types had discovered the up-country, too. From gates hung hand painted advertisements for Tarot card readings and psychics. A few signs heralded the up-country's own volcanic crystals, a sure cure for whatever ailed you.

"Vanessa, when do you intend to leave?" She carefully broached the subject, the blackmail threat uppermost in her mind. Had Big Daddy anticipated this divorce? Was the bloody knife a warning meant to keep Dana from helping her sister?

"I'm going back to Honolulu with you."

"Remember that knife and note I told you about?"

"Sure. You found out it was some kind of joke, right?"

"No. I think it's a blackmail attempt. Your intuition may have picked up on something when you said it was the Coltranes."

"Impossible. No one knows anything about that night except us. I was just being paranoid when I said it was the Coltranes."

Dana expelled a deep breath. Lordy, Vanessa could be unbelievably stubborn sometimes. "The knife was exactly like the rabbit-skinning knife that hung in the shed. Someone knows."

"Well, I didn't tell anyone."

Vanessa wheeled the Range Rover onto the private side road with an electric gate and a large orange sign that read: KAPU. The literal translation of the word based on ancient Hawaiian meant *forbidden*, but throughout the islands today the sign meant *keep out*.

Dana thought the older meaning better fit the Coltrane ranch. There was something forbidding about the place. Oh, it was beautiful, more stunning than most island resorts. But Dana was never quite comfortable there. With each visit her wariness increased.

Vanessa pressed the remote control and the gate swung open. Just beyond it was a huge painted sign: KAU RANCH. Below the letters was a painting of a steer wearing an orchid lei. The cow looked so happy you'd never think all the Coltrane cattle were destined for the slaughterhouse.

When Dana had first met Big Daddy she'd asked him what *kau* meant, and he'd claimed it meant *king.* The ranch had originally been called Coltrane Ranch, until Big Daddy had renamed it Kau Ranch. King. It fit, all right.

Coltrane considered himself a king. He was obsessed with old Hawaii, when the white settlers ruled the islands like feudal kings. It wasn't until much later that Dana's friend on the court, Gwen Sihida, told her that *kau* meant *king shark.* In Hawaiian lore shark gods played a predominant role, and Kau, king of the sharks, was by far the most troublesome. And dangerous.

"Vanessa, I hired an attorney to represent us . . . just in case. We have to be prepared to take on the Coltranes. Assuming they don't know about the knife, the blackmailer may tell them if your divorce gets nasty."

"You know best." Vanessa sounded so trusting. It was hard to believe that only a few years ago their roles had been reversed.

"Is there anything I should know about the Coltranes?" Is there anything you haven't told me, Dana silently added. All this was so unexpected.

"No. But sometimes . . . well, sometimes Big Daddy finds out things long before you think he will. I don't talk much on the telephone—I think he listens on one of the extensions."

Ahead of them the ranch house was a modern creation set on a rise and flanked by several smaller houses and clusters of guest cottages. All the buildings faced the sea, which beckoned on the distant horizon, a mirrorlike glimmer in the midday sun.

Hidden by a grove of trees were the stables and paddocks. Near the mammoth barn was a bunkhouse where the *paniolos* lived. The cowboys' quarters were constructed Hawaiian style, like the other buildings, with bleached wood to reflect the sun and huge louvered windows to admit the cooling trade winds.

The main house was shaded by lacy jacaranda trees and ferns so tall they brushed the roof. Drifts of rare orchids with deep throats of scarlet or lavender grew in the shade. An arched bridge brought guests across a lagoon of koi fish to the double-wide doors of polished teak.

Eustace, the housekeeper who'd taken over when Big Daddy's wife died leaving him with two sons, greeted them. Stern-faced and as wide as she was tall, Eustace wore the Kau Ranch uniform, a violet muumuu with splashes of white orchids. She was flanked by several servants, who took Dana's suitcases.

The interior of the house was a series of huge rooms with vaulted ceilings and soaring glass that rose two stories above the marble floors, creating an illusion of cool tranquillity, of being part of the spectacular landscape. When the weather was nice, as it was most days, the glass slid into wall pockets to allow the gentle breeze to blow up the green valleys into the house. Display cases in the whitewashed wood walls contained priceless Hawaiian art and artifacts that had been collected by Big Daddy's great-grandfather.

Spotlighted on a wall was one of Big Daddy's own contributions to the collection, Duke Kahanumoku's longboard. Surfing, a sport of ancient Hawaiians, was almost a lost art in the twenties when Duke built his longboard and took to the beach off Waikiki. Fascinated tourists made surfing—and Duke—world famous. Surrounding the wooden board, which was much longer than contemporary surfboards, were three stuffed sharks, looking every bit as vicious as they'd been when Big Daddy had speared them off the Molokini Crater. Each time Dana visited, he told her how he'd single-handedly killed three sharks in one day.

At first Dana thought he'd forgotten he'd already told her the story. She later decided there was nothing wrong with Big Daddy's memory. He simply loved basking in his own glory.

"You're in Makai House," Eustace informed Dana.

Dana arranged to meet Vanessa by the pool later and followed the men with her suitcases along the crushed-lava rock path to a small cottage. As soon as she entered she saw why it was called Makai House. *Makai—toward the ocean.* The cottage faced the sea, with an awesome view of the water and the blown-out cone of the Molokini Crater rising from the waves like the crown of an ancient Hawaiian king.

The cottage was too small, she realized with a jolt of alarm. It had a sitting area with a love seat and a chair that was adjacent to a king-size bed. There was an alcove with a minibar and beyond it a marble bathroom with a sunken tub.

She couldn't possibly share these quarters with Rob. She'd always had one of the two-bedroom bungalows, and she hadn't expected this visit to be any different. She marched back to the main house, but had no luck in persuading Eustace to give her a bigger cottage. Lots of guests would be arriving to celebrate Big Daddy's birthday on Saturday night. There wasn't any other cottage available.

Dana returned to Makai House and surveyed the situation. She could sleep on the love seat and let Rob have the bed. Six nights. It sounded like a life sentence with a man that she didn't quite trust. Today she'd purged Rob from her thoughts. Well, most of the time anyway. The emotional aftershock of that kiss was undeniable. How could she have kissed him like that?

She'd never lost her composure when other men had kissed her. Temporary insanity, she decided, reluctant to admit that she was actually attracted to him. Rob Tagett frightened her. Massive shoulders. Intimidating height. But it was much more than the threatening power of his body that disturbed her.

And it was much more than the ugly rumors she'd heard about him.

He'd been studying her. How else had he detected her dyed hair and her penchant for sexy undies? Add his talent for keen observation to his skill for assassinating people in print and she might as well be swimming with one of Big Daddy's deadly sharks.

What choice did she have?

She stretched out across the bed, listening to the birds singing in the jacaranda trees and the lulling sound of the ferns brushing against each other as the wind softly swept through the glade of ferns and wild orchids where the cottage was located. Her head on the pillow, she listened to the "oh-oh" call of the islands' most elusive bird, the 'o'o.

She must have fallen asleep, she thought, jerking upright with a neck-wrenching jolt, not realizing at first what had awakened her.

Another keening wail pierced the bosky stillness. A child's cry.

6

Dana sprinted up the path to the main house, drawn by the sobs. It had to be Jason; he was the only child at the ranch. As she crossed the terrace Dana could see into the house. Eustace was kneeling beside Jason while Big Daddy towered over Vanessa's young son.

Nearby were Eric and Travis Coltrane, but neither of the brothers appeared particularly concerned about the sobbing five-year-old. Dana saw their blood-splattered clothes and knew they'd killed the pig. She could just see them "sticking" the cornered animal with the knives that were now in scabbards at their sides.

And Jason had been forced to watch.

"Shut him up before his mother hears him," Big Daddy told Eustace.

A white-hot flare of anger rocketed through Dana. Swear to God, if she'd had a gun she would have shot the three of them. She charged into the room. "What have you done to him?"

Big Daddy raked his hand through his arctic-white hair, which swept back from his face in thick waves and emphasized jet black eyes and matching eyebrows that shot upward like a Russian dictator's. "The boy's pussy-whipped. Started bawling the minute the dogs cornered the pig."

"W-Wilbur," Jason got out between sobs, reaching his little arms out for Dana.

She took him from Eustace and cradled him against her bosom with an overwhelming surge of affection. As young as he was, Jason sensed he could trust her even though he didn't see her as frequently as he did the others in the room. She kissed Jason's blonde head, silently praying that all he'd inherited was the Coltranes' square jaw and distinctive cleft chin. She didn't want him to be anything like these men. "Honey, who's Wilbur?"

He lifted his head from the crook of her neck. "Y-You know, Charlotte's friend Wilbur."

It took a second for it to register that he'd thought the pig was the one from *Charlotte's Web*. Dana had given him the book at Christmas, and she'd been the first one to read the story to him. To Jason, the sticking had been like watching a beloved pet die.

"The dogs jump on Wilbur and bite him bad." His blue eyes—so like his mother's—were swimming with tears. He sniffed and swiped at his runny nose with his fist. "R-Rambo tore Wilbur's ear off."

Imagining the dogs attacking the trapped pig, Dana gazed into Jason's eyes and saw the anguish of innocence destroyed. The charming world of *Char-*

lotte's Web, where pigs talked to spiders, had been cruelly wiped away in a bloody pig sticking.

She knew only too well how one traumatic incident could emotionally cripple someone for life. She never dwelled on the past, but she was intelligent enough to know her psychological scars came from that horrible night. She didn't want Jason to suffer for years because he'd been forced to watch this.

"Den they cut Wilbur." Jason pointed an accusing finger at his father and grandfather. "He cry and cry, but they don't stop cutting him."

She longed to scream at the Coltranes, but she didn't. There would be time for that later. It wouldn't do Jason any good to see adults fighting. "Honey, it wasn't Wilbur. It was a *bad* pig."

"Hell. I tried to tell him that," Big Daddy interrupted, "but he wouldn't listen. Started crying like some pantywaist."

"You're barbaric," Dana said, certain Jason didn't know what the word meant.

Vanessa burst into the room, her wet hair dripping on her shoulders. Obviously she'd just gotten out of the shower and heard the crying. Her beautiful face was contorted with an emotion too intense to be mere anger. The only other time Dana had seen her this upset had been that night so long ago.

"You bastard!" she yelled at Big Daddy. "You won't be satisfied until you ruin my son!"

"You coddle him too much," Big Daddy said, his tone placating. He reached out to put his hand on her arm, but she jerked away.

Vanessa wheeled around to face her husband. Eric was standing behind his father, his hands crammed into the pockets of his blood-splattered jeans.

"I want a divorce," Vanessa said, her voice now deadly calm.

Eric glared at his wife with black eyes that were exactly like his father's; he shrugged, clearly conveying his indifference to his wife. Dana battled the urge to slap him.

Travis, standing nearby, spoke up. "Hey, Vanessa, babe, you're overreacting. So the kid freaked. He'll get over it." Travis pointed at Dana, who was rocking from side to side, comforting Jason. "See? He's already better."

Vanessa ignored Travis. "I mean it." She glared at Eric. "I want a divorce."

"Okay by me," Eric responded, then looked at his father.

"You'll change your mind," Big Daddy said with such characteristic confidence that Dana gritted her teeth instead of responding in anger.

Dana grabbed Vanessa's arm with her free hand. "Let's put Jason down for a nap." At the door she paused and looked over her shoulder. "I wouldn't bet on Vanessa changing her mind, Big Daddy."

Side by side they walked out of the house and across a lawn that would put most golf courses to shame. On the far side of the swimming pool that looked like a mountain lake and a row of cabanas was the house Vanessa and Eric shared. Already Jason was half-asleep, exhausted from crying for so long.

Vanessa opened the door to her home, which was a smaller version of the main house, with floor-to-ceiling windows that accentuated the panoramic view and vaulted ceilings. They went into Jason's bedroom and put him to bed.

"Mommie," he said, his voice groggy with sleep, "don't leave me."

Dana watched as Vanessa kissed her son's forehead and said, "I won't. Aunt Dana and I will be sitting right outside your door." She pointed to the French doors that opened onto a redwood deck outside Jason's bedroom.

Vanessa and Dana slipped outside and sat in bent-willow chairs surrounded by an armada of toys. Dana could still feel Jason's little arms around her neck. She never thought that she wanted children. Oh, she liked them, but she never considered having her own. Now she had a glimpse of what she'd been missing. She wanted a home and a family; her life wasn't going to be complete without a child.

"I've been thinking," Vanessa said, her voice so low that Dana had to lean toward her to hear. "I'm going to act as if Big Daddy's right and I've decided to stay here. I don't want him to suspect that I'm really leaving. He has enough men here to stop us from taking Jason. On the night of his birthday luau we'll go. It'll be hours before anyone misses us."

"What about the knife I received in the mail? That might be Big Daddy's weird way of warning me about helping you. If he knows what happened, there isn't a judge in the country who wouldn't give Eric full custody of Jason."

"It doesn't sound like something Big Daddy would do. He would have picked up the telephone and threatened you himself. Besides, this is the first time I've ever mentioned divorce. He wouldn't have any reason to warn you."

"Maybe," Dana halfheartedly agreed.

"Whatever you do, don't discuss this when anyone can overhear you," Vanessa warned. "I swear. The walls have ears. Eustace and her helpers must tell Big Daddy everything."

Hours later Dana was just putting on her lipstick, already dreading going to the main house for a tension-filled dinner, when she heard a knock on her door. She swung it open and found Big Daddy standing there with two glasses in his hand.

"Champagne," he said as he offered her a glass. "I thought we should have a drink before dinner."

Dana reluctantly took the glass as he swept past her through the small cottage to the open doors that led out to the deck. She wanted to throttle him, to scream what a heartless bastard he was, but she and Vanessa had a plan. Besides his two burly sons, Big Daddy had a phalanx of servants and a bunkhouse full of *paniolos*. No doubt about it; they could physically prevent Vanessa from taking Jason.

As much as Dana hated indulging this pompous jerk, she had no other choice, so she followed him outside and stood on the deck, sipping expensive champagne and looking at the sunset. The sun's crescent was barely visible, firing the rim of the Molokini Crater with golden light. The submerged volcano had blown its top eons ago and was now a popular dive site. Dana had been promising herself for years that she'd dive there and see what it was like to swim with the sharks. As she waited for Big Daddy to speak, she realized this might be her last trip to Maui.

Who knew what the future held?

"I've decided to set Vanessa up in a business of her own. What do you think about a boutique in Makawao?"

Big Daddy rarely asked anyone's opinion on anything. Just asking the question showed he was concerned that Vanessa might actually divorce his son.

"Vanessa has never mentioned to me that she was interested in having a boutique."

"Well, she shops enough. A boutique would be right up her alley." He drained his glass. "Vanessa's too focused on Jason. He's growing up. She needs to learn to let him go."

Dana had to grip her glass firmly to keep from tossing her champagne in his arrogant face.

"Vanessa listens to you. Since she's not going to be able to have any more children, she needs an outside interest."

Dana took a quick gulp of champagne. Why couldn't Vanessa have any more children? She'd never mentioned not being able to have another baby. What was going on here? Vanessa wasn't telling her everything.

"I have no intention of letting Vanessa take Jason away." There was more than a note of menace in his voice, and Dana held her breath, waiting for him to mention the knife and the note.

When he didn't, Dana asked, "What does Eric say? After all, he's Jason's father."

"Nothing. My sons are as worthless as tits on a bull. Do you seriously think they can lead Coltrane Consolidated into the twenty-first century? I need Jason."

She nodded, surprised that he understood what mental lightweights he'd fathered. True, both Eric and Travis were outrageously good-looking, with full heads of hair that would turn a lush white like their father's and square jaws with cleft chins that belied their weak personalities, but they weren't intellectually capable of—or interested in—running a multifaceted company.

The original Coltranes had made their fortune in macadamia nuts. Local society matrons liked to dip the nuts in warm chocolate and eat them. Soon the Coltranes began exporting not only nuts, but boxes of chocolate-covered macadamia nuts. Big Daddy's great-grandfather had also purchased the rich pastureland at the base of Haleakala and began raising cattle.

The family fortune had been made and the Coltranes became one of the wealthiest families in the islands, but that was then and this was now. Today the vast groves necessary to cultivate the nuts were costly to maintain, and environmentalists were constantly pressuring them about using pesticides on the crop. The ranch itself carried an unbelievable tax burden. No doubt about it, Coltrane Consolidated, which also included numerous buildings in Honolulu and several exclusive hotels in Maui and Kauai, needed top-flight management. But Jason was a good twenty years from being able to help.

"I'm not as old as I look," Big Daddy answered her unspoken question. "I'm fifty-two. I'll be in my seventies when Jason's ready to take over. I can hang on until then."

Not for the first time, Dana wondered who really ran Coltrane Consolidated. Big Daddy seemed content to laze around the ranch and ride out each day with the *paniolos* to check on the herd. She doubted he had much more ambition than his sons. Why would he expect so much of Jason?

"I married young, too young," Big Daddy said, an unusual wistfulness to his voice. "When my boys were growing up I was still sowing my wild oats. I didn't give them proper guidance. I'm not going to make that mistake with Jason."

Rob spotted Dana among the swarms of tourists in Maui's air terminal. She was dressed in white shorts and a T-shirt with splashes of pink and aqua on it. She looked incredibly young, incredibly sexy.

He gave her the slow grin that could coax most women out of their panties in two shakes. Naturally it didn't work on Dana. She parted her lips, revealing an even set of white teeth, which was about as close to a smile as he was likely to get.

She didn't like him, didn't like being forced to work with him, and for an instant he wondered why he was trying so hard to change her mind. Because he felt challenged, truly challenged, not just by the case, which was proving to be a doozy, but by the woman herself.

"What did you find out?" she asked the minute he was within hearing range.

He put his hand on her shoulder. "Hey, is that any way to greet someone you're crazy about?" He gave her a quick peck on the cheek, knowing it would piss her off. "You can at least notice I cut my hair. And I have new clothes."

She gave the navy blue polo shirt and his khaki shorts a quick once over. "You look nice."

"That's better," he said with another encouraging smile that had about as much impact as the first one.

They started walking toward the baggage claim area and Dana asked, "Did you test the knife? What did it show?"

"The knife is brand-new. Someone hammered it and rubbed it with dirt to make it look old. There were scratch marks where someone deliberately loosened the screw so the blade would wiggle."

She stopped dead in her tracks and put her hand on his arm. Her green eyes echoed the disbelief in her voice. "Someone knows. How?"

Rob was betting on Vanessa Coltrane, but he didn't verbalize his thoughts. Dana was unbelievably touchy about her sister. He could hardly wait to meet Vanessa and confirm his suspicions.

"Someone told." Rob started walking again and Dana followed. She seemed to be taking care not to stand too close to him, he decided, as they stopped at the baggage carousel. "You know, Dana, we're not going to fool the Coltranes for one second if you act like I'm dog shit."

"What do you mean?"

"For starters try smiling at me. Pretend you're glad to see me." She responded with a halfhearted smile. "And whenever you're near me, stand in my space."

"Your what?"

"About three feet around everyone is their 'space.' We're uncomfortable if strangers stand too close to us. Lovers always stand close. They want that intimacy, and people pick up on that closeness. If you just stand closer to me it'll send a silent message about your feelings."

She moved closer, her body not quite touching his, and tried a smile that made her look adorable.

"That's better," he said. "If you make certain to stand close it'll make it easier to whisper anything I don't want the Coltranes to hear."

"Good idea," she said so earnestly that he almost kissed her. "My sister says Big Daddy has the servants eavesdrop and report back to him."

"Wanna hear about the blood on the knife?" he

asked, leaning close to her, his voice low. "It was snake blood."

"There aren't any snakes in the islands." Her eyes widened as she spoke, and he decided being this close to her was damn nice. He caught a whiff of her perfume, a light floral with a trace of spice, and he could see the double tiers of her lashes. They were long and unusually thick for a blonde.

"It was harder than hell to identify the blood. My friend at UH did the tests. Cost me nothing except a round of drinks at Panama Jack's." He couldn't resist bragging just a little. He didn't want her to think of him as some sleazeball reporter. He wanted her to know that there was more to him. Much more. "This tells us a lot about the perp. Snake blood can be bought in Chinatown, if you know where to go."

She was looking at him now with genuine admiration in her eyes, and he experienced a charge of excitement that he hadn't felt in years. "Really?"

"They sell so much snake blood in Chinatown—it's an aphrodisiac, you know—that I couldn't ID the person." He reached into his back pocket and pulled out an envelope. "This came for you in yesterday's mail."

She took it and quickly opened it. They'd agreed that he'd open any of her mail if it appeared to be a blackmail letter. This plain white envelope with no return address and a Honolulu postmark had been a dead giveaway.

The note read: *Get out of Hawaii or I'll go to the police and tell them what you did.*

7

For a second Dana looked so shocked, Rob thought she was going to fall into his arms. "Hey, at least we know what they want."

"It's the Coltranes," Dana informed him. "They're blackmailing me."

"What makes you think so?" Rob pulled his bag off the luggage carousel. He guided Dana over to the car rental desk while she told him about the pig hunt. He rented a red Mustang convertible and escorted her to it, listening to Dana's explanation that Vanessa planned to leave the ranch during Big Daddy's birthday luau and divorce Eric Coltrane.

"Somehow Big Daddy knows about Hank Rawlins," Dana said as he tossed his bag in the trunk. "If he can get rid of me, then Vanessa will think twice before divorcing Eric. She has no money of her own. Without me she won't be able to fight the Coltranes. They're too rich, too powerful."

"The way things work in these islands, anyone's crazy to tackle one of the big-five families."

"The Coltranes know we were orphaned as children. Vanessa doesn't have anyone but me. She has no education beyond high school. Without me it'll be impossible for her to fight them—though she might try." Dana turned to him as he helped her into the convertible. "Believe me, Big Daddy's worried. Last night he tried to convince me that Vanessa should open a boutique here on the island."

"That's interesting." Rob climbed into the car and started the engine. "From what I've heard that's not Coltrane's style."

"It isn't. I don't think he wants a confrontation with Vanessa. That's why he's trying to frighten us. That's why he's trying to placate her with a boutique. For some reason Big Daddy's acting out of character."

Rob stepped on the accelerator and passed a slow-moving truck filled with sugar cane. "Maybe you're right, but I've been thinking. This threat seems more directed at you than Vanessa. I'm betting Davis Binkley is pissed—big time—that his name wasn't on the list for superior court. Hell, he's been presiding judge for years. You come in and do an end run around him. When I get back I'm checking the guy out."

"I'm telling you, there's something wrong at Kau Ranch. I can *feel* it. Big Daddy is the prime suspect."

Rob wasn't certain that he agreed with her analysis of the situation. He figured he'd have a much better idea of what was happening when he met Vanessa and the Coltranes and could judge for himself.

They lapsed into silence as he drove down the Haleakala highway, the wind ruffling his hair and bringing with it the scent of pineapples. He couldn't help smiling. As much as he loved the excitement of Honolulu, there was nothing quite like Maui, where fields of pineapples and sugar cane covered much of the island. Between fields, thickets of ferns and dense bamboo encouraged the birds to take sanctuary. Their songs, as bright as the sunshine, brought him an astonishing sense of peace.

He glanced over at Dana. The wind had whipped her hair aside, leaving the gentle curve of her face exposed to the sun. He wondered if she knew how attractive she was. Probably not; she'd grown up in the shadow of a beautiful sister. She deliberately minimized her looks, concentrating on her intelligence.

He had the feeling it wasn't as simple as that. Dana Hamilton was a complex person. She hid so much about herself that he couldn't help wondering what she was really like.

"Where are you going?" Dana asked when he turned off the highway.

"I'm taking you to lunch at Mama's." He didn't add that he planned to spend as much time alone with her as possible and still thoroughly investigate the Coltranes.

"You know your way around Maui."

"Yeah. I've been here a lot." He could have said

93

this was Ellen's favorite island. When they'd been married they'd come over as often as they could. This was the first time he'd come back since the divorce.

Dana had always liked Mama's. The restaurant sat on a bluff overlooking a cove buffeted by the trades. The perpetual wind and the high waves brought dozens of windsurfers to the cove. From Mama's, people could watch the windsurfers with their colorful sails jet around the cove and fly off waves with awesome agility.

Rob sat beside her, making it hard for Dana to keep her mind on the surfers. She'd managed to get herself under control, but since Rob had walked off that plane, looking incredibly attractive with his fresh haircut and new clothes, she'd been off-balance.

As he'd walked toward her, a welcoming smile making him even more handsome, she'd been stunned to realize how much she'd wanted him to come despite all the negative feelings she had about him. He could look at the situation with an outsider's detachment, she'd told herself. It horrified her to think she actually needed him. She'd been on her own for so long and had been able to control most situations. Not this time. Now she needed Rob.

If he'd been what she'd thought, a crude reporter with a shady past but a talent for investigating, she could have easily dealt with that man. Instead, he was someone else entirely—and he wanted her to know it. Intelligent and streetwise, Rob was also a keen observer of people.

Of her.

He'd picked up on things no one else had discovered. Worse, he seemed to know *exactly* how to get to her. That unexpected kiss in her kitchen had been one thing. What had gone on today was another entirely. *His space.*

Didn't he know what he was asking?

Of course he did. And he was clever enough to veil his intentions by insisting the Coltranes would notice if they didn't appear to be lovers. He was right, but she had to be a total idiot to go along with it. Still, here she was smiling at him, leaning across the table at Mama's into *his space.*

They ordered the fresh fish that was Mama's specialty. Dana braced herself, knowing if she didn't explain their sleeping arrangements before they arrived at the ranch that Rob would see the room and misunderstand.

"They've given us a really small cottage," she began. "I tried to get it changed, but because of all the guests coming for the party, I couldn't. There's only one king-size bed. You can have it. I'll sleep on the love seat."

He greeted the news with a wolfish grin.

"I don't have any intention of sleeping with you," she insisted. "This is a business arrangement."

"Suit yourself, but you don't know what you're missing."

"Rein in your ego and concentrate on this case."

"Ooookay." He pulled the cover off his camera and leaned so close to her that she could see the stitches of silver that made his blue eyes so unique. "This isn't any ordinary Nikon. See this flash? It blinks twice, not to tell me the battery is low, but to indicate the presence of electronic listening devices."

"Surely you don't think the Coltranes—"

"Did I ever mention that I was trained by the FBI at their facility in Quantico, Virginia?"

"You know you didn't."

"The United States is divided into crime districts, and the FBI trains someone from a local police department to work each territory as a perp pro."

She knew perp pros were specially trained to create psychological profiles of criminals, but she was surprised to learn Rob had been chosen to go to FBI headquarters to receive the advanced training. Obviously he'd been an exceptional detective. Why would he leave the force?

"Perp pros have been damn successful with repeat offenders like serial killers, who are often outgoing, seemingly trustworthy," Rob said. She knew all this, but didn't interrupt him, noting the boyish enthusiasm in his voice. Clearly he was in his element. "They usually keep something to remember the crime—pictures, tapes of the killing, something belonging to the victim."

Dana shuddered. "Gruesome, just gruesome."

"The HPD still calls me in to consult—unofficially, of course. Remember that woman who was murdered on Kauai last year?"

"The one who'd been strangled with a silk scarf?"

"That's right. It was a ritual killing, and I suspected the killer had done this before, even though there hadn't been any similar crimes in Hawaii. Ritual murderers get a thrill from the ritual, and they tend to repeat their crimes with astonishing accuracy. I put the details in the FBI's master computer and found murders in other tourist meccas."

"So that's how they found that travel agent who'd strangled all those women," she said as the waiter served their lunch. She couldn't help being impressed. Despite his sexual overtures, Rob was extremely competent. "What have you decided about the person blackmailing me?"

"Well, I think the blackmailer is nonconfrontational." He put his hand on her arm, his strong fingers exerting just the slightest pressure as he gazed directly into her eyes. "Someone you'd never suspect."

"If Vanessa hadn't mentioned it I'd never suspect Big Daddy."

Picking up his fork Rob said, "I did a little checking on Thornton Coltrane. Big Daddy's a real hardcase." He chewed a bite of *opakapaka*, obviously savoring the pink snapper before continuing. "This isn't his style, but it's possible he might deliberately do something out of character so he wouldn't be suspected."

"That's what I think. As I told you earlier, he really doesn't want a fight with Vanessa."

By the time they'd finished it was midafternoon and the wind had died down. Voluminous clouds promised the typical late-afternoon showers, not here in the arid beach area, but in the verdant hills and valleys of the up-country. They stood on the bluff watching the surfers pack up their boards. Rob turned to her, his expression earnest, and put his hands on her shoulders.

"That's better," he said when she didn't back up. "By the end of the week I'll need a baseball bat to fend you off."

"Dream on," she said. Really, his bark was worse than his bite. Not that she was going to let him bite her again. Too often she remembered the way he'd nipped her earlobe the night he kissed her.

They drove to the ranch the back way through a labyrinth of country lanes. Too soon they turned onto the private road that lead to Kau Ranch. The gate had been left open for the guests arriving for the party. The orange KAPU sign caught Dana's eyes like a beacon on a moonless night. She told herself she was being silly. She reminded herself yet again that the modern meaning of *kapu* was *keep out*.

So, why did *kapu—forbidden—*seem so right?

"Wow! This is some place," Rob said with a Texas drawl as Kau Ranch came into view. "Back in Texas we'd call this a spread—and a half. How many people live here?"

"They have about one hundred *paniolos*, I think. Besides the cowboys, Big Daddy probably has twenty-five servants to keep up the house and grounds. One man's job is to maintain the koi ponds."

Rob whistled. "It's no sin to be poor, but it sure is inconvenient."

Dana couldn't help laughing as she pointed to a narrow drive half-concealed by tree ferns. "Take the back road down to the cottage."

Rob skillfully maneuvered the convertible past the main house and several guest cottages until they came to Makai House. He switched off the ignition and put his arm around her shoulder, leaning close. This wasn't a come-on; his expression was totally serious as he whispered into her ear, "When we go in, you chatter about the place and tell me to take pictures."

"You've been watching too much television," she said, opening the door. Nevertheless, as they entered the cottage she said, "Look, Rob, isn't this a spectacular view of the Molokini Crater? You'll have to get a picture of it."

"Right, babe," Rob responded, and she decided they almost sounded natural. "I like the bed better. Why don't you plant your cute tush on it, and I'll take a picture."

Dana did as she was told, demurely sitting on the bed, legs crossed, watching Rob silently laugh at her as he pulled his camera out of the case. He wasn't laughing two seconds later; the red monitor light on his flash was blinking, indicating the presence of a listening device. Rob motioned for her to keep talking as he climbed across the bed to inspect the large Hawaiian quilt mounted on the wall above the bed.

Big Daddy collected native art. This spectacular quilt was white with yellow geometric designs and pineapples, the symbol of hospitality and friendship. The missionaries had taught the island women to quilt, believing this would keep them too occupied to do "the devil's business"—hula dancing. It didn't, but the islanders loved quilting, producing magnificent quilts with a unique Hawaiian flair.

"Wait till you see the bathroom," Dana rushed on, suddenly chilled by the knowledge that someone was listening to every word. "It has a sunken tub and a magnificent view of the ocean."

Rob pointed to a tiny protrusion of metal a bit smaller than a thumbtack. It jutted out from the wall a fraction of an inch, well concealed by the hem of the quilt. If you didn't know what you were looking for, you'd never have noticed it.

He jumped off the bed. "Let's get a shot of that sunken tub."

The bathroom was almost as large as the bedroom, with a marble dais that featured a sunken tub angled to face the windowed walls. The panoramic view took in the up-country's rolling green meadows, dotted with clusters of black Angus cattle, and in the distance the enticing glimmer of the sea. Rising from the azure waters, a black horseshoe of volcanic rock, was the Molokini Crater.

"Hey," Rob said, "we'll have to christen this tub."

Dana almost came back with a cutting remark, remembering in time that Rob had made the comment for the benefit of the bug in the adjacent room. He was concentrating on his flash attachment. It wasn't blinking.

"Okay, sweet cheeks," he said, "out on the terrace. Let's get a shot of you with the Molokini Crater in the background."

Dana followed him outside, and he closed the sliding glass door behind them. Feeling like an idiot, she struck a pose with the crater visible over her shoulder. Rob clicked off several shots, positioning her on the bent-willow chaise lounge, against the cottage wall, and finally in the thicket of ferns and wild orchids with silky white petals and deep throats of lavender that lined the side of the house.

"Nothing," Rob said when he'd finished. "Just the one bug above the bed." He looked around, scanning the roofline, obviously wondering if he'd missed something.

Suddenly he grabbed her and swung her into his arms. His abrupt change of mood caught her offguard. Before she knew it he was kissing her, his strong arms locking her in place.

He broke the kiss, his forehead pressed against hers. "Stop fighting me," he whispered, his breath uneven. "There's a man with white hair on the balcony at the far side of the big house. Has to be Big

Daddy. He's watching us through some kind of telescope, so make this look good.''

"Big Daddy loves to watch the humpback whales migrate. He's probably sighted some off Lahaina.''

Rob didn't move; his lips were still a mere inch from hers. "Right. Whales winter here. What month is this?''

"July," she admitted as his fingers combed through her hair. "He couldn't be looking at whales.''

"Kiss me again, then let's move around to the side of the cottage where he can't possibly read our lips.''

He pulled her close; his chest meshed against hers, flattening the mounds of her breasts. For a moment he gazed into her eyes. A strange but exciting feeling feathered up through her chest. Lordy, what he could do to her only half-trying. No wonder he kept insisting she couldn't resist him.

His eyes rested on her lips for an uncomfortably long time, then he lowered his head. It was just a kiss—for Big Daddy's benefit—she assured herself. But the caress of his mouth on hers, his agile tongue parting her lips, his talented hand stroking the back of her neck fired a primal urge to kiss him back.

Rob pulled back, ending the wondrous, searching kiss that promised more to come between them. Much more.

"The worst thing we could possibly do," he said, "is tip our hand and let him know we've found the bug. We'll have to play along and act exactly like two lovers enjoying a freebie vacation."

Dana groaned out loud. Wasn't it bad enough that she had to stand in Rob's "space"? Now she was going to have to pull a real Sarah Bernhardt for the bug planted above their bed. "I'm still sleeping on the love seat."

"No, you're not. We're taking the toss pillows off it and using them to divide the bed in half, but we're getting into that bed at night and giving Big Daddy enough pillow talk to satisfy him."

"Won't he be suspicious if we don't . . ."

Rob grinned. "Dana, you're such a prude. Can't you say it?"

She wrinkled her nose, barely getting out the words. "Make love."

"That's better." Rob put his hand on both her shoulders, the heat penetrating the lightweight fabric of her blouse. For a second she thought he was going to try to kiss her. Instead, he said, "We'll say things to convince him that we're so kinky that we screw in the tub, or outside on the chaise, or in the grass—anywhere except the bed."

She honestly didn't know if she could trust him in the same bed with her, but what choice did she have?

"We're going to make love. Count on it." His hands skimmed down her arms and came to rest on the curve of her waist. He was the kind of man who could convince a woman to do anything, she realized, half-liking the sensation, half-afraid she wouldn't muster the willpower to defy him.

"When we make love, Dana, it won't be with some dirty old man listening." He lowered his head until his lips were almost touching hers. "I'm not sharing you with anyone."

8

Rob went back inside the cottage and yanked the telephone out of its jack. He motioned for Dana to keep talking while he unscrewed the receiver and checked for a bug. Sure enough, there it was. Small. Hardly state-of-the-art, but it would do the trick.

"Come on," he said to Dana as he plugged in the phone again. "I'm dying to meet your sister."

They left the cottage and walked along the crushed-lava rock path that wound through artistically placed beds of native Hawaiian flowers toward the pool area. Rob put his arm around Dana and pulled her close. For once she didn't resist.

She gazed up at him, her green eyes wide with concern. "You know, I've always felt there was something wrong here. *Kapu*—forbidden. Now I know I was right."

Rob stopped, but didn't move his arm. "We have to be very careful. It's more important than ever that no one suspect why I'm really here. We'll have to watch every word we say, especially inside our cottage."

"What about out here?" she whispered. "Are there bugs?"

"Nah. Too much humidity. They'd have to replace the bugs every few days. Judging from the one in our room this is an amateur operation, otherwise Big Daddy would be using one of the new supersensitive devices that can hear a pin drop five miles away." He started walking again. "Let's see what's in your sister's house."

Rob didn't know who he'd been expecting, certainly not the knockout blonde who answered the door. Tall. Dynamite figure. Sexy as hell.

But he wasn't a horny kid anymore. He'd long since stopped drooling over beautiful women. Ellen had been pretty. Girl-next-door looks, really. That's what turned him on. He pulled Dana a little bit closer and kicked up his killer smile another notch.

"Vanessa," Dana said, "this is Rob Tagett."

Rob extended his hand. "Howdy."

"Hello." Vanessa Coltrane responded with a lot more warmth in her voice than her cool blonde appearance indicated. "How do you like Kau Ranch so far?"

He was half-tempted to tell her. "Great."

Vanessa stood aside and motioned for them to come in, her eyes on Rob's arm draped casually over Dana's shoulder.

"You're an amateur photographer?" Vanessa asked, glancing at his camera.

"Yeah. It's my hobby," he answered in his best good-ole-boy tone. When he'd been working homicide he'd found the more harmless you appeared, the quicker perps let their guard down.

"Rob's a reporter," Dana put in as they sat on a wicker sofa with cushions so enormous he doubted if anyone really ever used it.

"That's right." Vanessa sat opposite them in a fanback chair that made her look like a queen on a throne, her eyes narrowing. "I read your column, 'Exposed,' all the time."

Rob wasn't surprised; the *Honolulu Sun* was the main paper in the islands. He stole a glance at Dana. She was seated next to him, as much "in his space" as those damn cushions would allow. She seemed totally at ease with him. But would Vanessa detect some small gesture he couldn't?

He studied the two sisters. Their eyes. Now there was the major physical difference between the two. Dana's expressive green eyes dominated her face, a sharp contrast to her brown hair. Vanessa had sensual blue eyes and Nordic blonde hair worn long in a style designed to maximize her sex appeal.

No one could deny they were sisters though. It was there in the graceful curve of their cheekbones. They had matching widow's peaks, one so blonde it was barely noticeable, the other more prominent because of the darker hair.

"Mommi-e-e," came a sleepy cry from down the hall.

Vanessa vaulted to her feet. "I'll be right back."

"Jason's up from his nap," Dana explained.

"Let's shoot a couple of pictures while Vanessa's with Jason." Rob stood and centered Dana in his viewfinder. She treated him to one of her irresistible smiles. Okay, it was a camera-ready, phony-as-hell smile. But he was getting to like this. A lot.

The detector flashed red as he took the picture. Was he surprised? Hell, no. Anyone who puts bugs in guest suites was bound to eavesdrop on his sons.

Dana was frowning now, having detected the signal. "Let's get a picture of Jason in his room. He has a great rocking horse that I had made in Kauai."

As he followed her out of the living room, Rob noticed that the flash monitor was winking again. Two bugs in one room? Why? There was another in the hall. It was probably hidden behind the picture frame. Still another device seemed to be in the potted palm in the alcove that separated the bedrooms. Interesting.

"I'm going to the head," he said to Dana, tilting his head toward the hallway, knowing she'd get the idea that he wanted to check out the other rooms. "Meet you in Jason's room."

Rob quickly swung into the first bedroom, which was set up as an office. Sure enough, it was bugged. The master bedroom, like a scene straight out of *Casablanca*, had a ceiling fan and a bed swathed in a tropical print with huge green palm leaves and woven bamboo covering the walls. And four bugs.

Jesus! What was going on here?

There was yet another bug in the master bath. It

seemed to be attached to the wall-mounted television.

He wandered back down the hall to Jason's room and paused at the door. Inside, Dana sat on the bed with Jason on her lap. She was struggling to pull on his second cowboy boot. It would hit the kid's knees when she succeeded, but it wasn't the comically tall boots that made him clutch his camera tighter. It was the expression on Dana's face.

Tender. Full of love. *Love.* The word registered, bringing a jolt of emotion he hadn't experienced in years. The air in his chest compressed, lodging at the base of his throat. A child had stripped away her emotional armor and revealed the sensitive, loving side of Dana Hamilton that he'd always suspected was there. Could a man get her to open her heart so easily?

Beneath the professional demeanor, beneath the unexpected flaring of her temper, beneath the psychological fortress Dana kept around herself was a wellspring of sadness. She was too intent on protecting herself to open up to a man. He wasn't certain how he knew all this. Okay, sometimes his sixth sense just kicked in. It rarely failed him. Even on the night when his career had been ruined, he'd sensed he was in trouble, but he couldn't do a damn thing about it.

Suddenly Dana glanced up, saw him, and her expression instantly changed. "Rob, this is my nephew, Jason."

From under blonde bangs that brushed his brows

the boy surveyed Rob with blue eyes that were exactly like Vanessa's. In another ten years all the fathers in a fifty-mile radius would be fitting their daughters with chastity belts.

Vanessa emerged from a closet that looked like a preemptive strike in a kids' clothing store. Clothes were tossed everywhere; a tiny space suit hung haphazardly from a hook along with an Indian chief's headdress; socks and shoes littered the floor, half-hidden by T-shirts.

"Stick 'em up." Jason pulled a toy six-shooter from the holster on his hip, and Rob dutifully raised his hands as he walked into the room.

"Isn't he cute?" Vanessa asked.

"Real cute," he answered, his eyes on Dana's provocative fanny as she rolled onto her side, tugging madly to get Jason's second boot on.

"There," Dana said to Jason, the second boot finally in place. "You're all set."

Jason jumped to his feet and grabbed his Stetson off the bedpost. He jammed the hat down so far that his little ears flared out like bat's wings.

Vanessa touched Rob's arm. "Take a picture for me."

He fired off two shots, picking up at least one bug in the room. "Why don't I take a picture of Jason on the rocking horse?" he asked Dana, conscious that Vanessa had moved closer to him and hoping to distract her if she noticed the winking red light.

"Yippe-e-e!" Jason launched himself onto the colorfully painted rocking horse and started bouncing on it, kicking the wooden beast for all he was worth.

"Jason, hold still," Dana said as Rob centered him in the viewfinder.

Rob didn't like the wall-mounted television that would ruin the picture. He reminded himself that he was merely looking for another bug on this side of the room, not an artistic shot. The second his finger pressed on the button, the red light blinked. He quickly depressed the button to fire the flash.

"Is something wrong with your camera?" Vanessa's voice was low. She was right at his elbow. If he moved, he'd bump into her.

"Just a low flash battery."

Jason hopped off the horse and sprinted from the room, his gun trained on imaginary bandits. Rob chuckled, reminded of his son at that same age. The age of innocence, he thought. How quickly it ended.

He turned and collided with Vanessa. "Sorry."

She didn't back away. Instead, she peered at him intently, her blue eyes as soft as a caress. "You're good with children."

Where the hell did she get that idea? He was—or more accurately he had been when Zach had lived with him. But Vanessa couldn't know anything about his parenting skills. She was just trying to be nice, he realized. He orchestrated a smile and reached for Dana.

"So what do you think?" Dana asked Rob.

"Big Daddy's a control freak . . . and maybe

worse. I won't know until I get a long look at the command center, which is probably in his suite."

They'd left Jason and Vanessa and were walking past the pool toward Makai House. Twilight came earlier in the hilly up-country than it did miles away at the beach. Mauve shadows deepened into purple, and the breeze, always cooler here than on the coast, was moist against Dana's face, bringing with it the fragrant scent of plumeria.

"Big Daddy can't listen to everyone at once. He must have a sophisticated tape system that he can play back later." Rob stopped at the turnout for the spa that was separated from the pool by a few feet.

"You're right. He's out riding with the *paniolos* most days. At night he holds a cocktail hour from six until dinner is served at eight." Even now she could hear the sounds of guests gathering on the terrace, appreciating the spectacular sunset. "He must listen later."

"He probably tunes in for the bedtime follies." There was no mistaking the sensual light in Rob's eyes. "We won't want to disappoint him."

Dana drew in her breath and crossed her arms as if to protect herself. "I think we should get a few things straight."

"Really?" All innocence. "Like what?"

"Like this is a serious situation. I've hired you and I can fire you."

"I love it when you talk dirty," he said with a pronounced Texas drawl. "You aren't going to fire me. You're up to your eyeballs in alligators and you know it. What's really bothering you?"

She gazed out across the swimming pool designed to look like a mountain lake. The rumors she'd heard about him echoed in her mind like distant thunder. He'd never actually been charged with rape, but when he'd brought it up that night at Coconut Willie's, he hadn't denied it. Why not?

"I guess what's bothering me is the size of the cottage," she fibbed. "I'm not used to living in close quarters with a man. I think we should establish some guidelines."

He chuckled, an undeniably masculine laugh. "Like who gets the bathroom first? You can have it, sweetcakes, as long as you don't stay in there all day."

"I don't take long," she informed him, her annoyance showing in her tone. She swallowed twice. "I was wondering what you planned to wear to bed."

His smirk made her want to whack him. "Hey, I sleep nude. Doesn't everybody?"

She wished she owned a more modest nightgown than the black lace one she'd brought with her, believing she'd have a room of her own. "Wear your shorts, or I'm sleeping on the love seat."

"And tip off Big Daddy?"

"I'm serious." She shot him the look that made attorneys who ventured into her courtroom cower. Rob had the audacity to wink at her.

"All right," he finally conceded with a wise-guy

smile, and she couldn't help wondering if he'd been deliberately baiting her. "Anything else?"

She was tempted to tell him to keep his shirt on too, but considering the warm temperatures that would be tantamount to admitting she found his body physically disturbing, which she didn't. She was merely more comfortable around fully clothed men. "No. That's all."

"Then it's okay to snore?"

She laughed, even though the cockiness in his voice told her that he hadn't taken her seriously. No telling what he might pull later.

9

They'd forgotten to leave the door open, so it was hot inside Makai House. Like most homes in the up-country, Kau Ranch wasn't air-conditioned. It relied on the steady trade winds and ceiling fans to cool the rooms. Dana watched as Rob slid open the door that led onto the terrace, uncertain of just what to say, considering someone was listening to every word.

"Darling," she almost choked on the word. Rob spun around, silently laughing. "First dibs on the shower."

"Sure." He stripped off his shirt, pulling it over his head and ruffling his dark hair.

She scanned his torso, noting the hard planes of his chest and the contours of his muscles. A skein of hair darker than his tanned body trailed down his chest to the waistband of his shorts. Of their own volition, her eyes dropped to his crotch and the masculine bulge barely concealed by the fabric.

Instantly she forced her eyes back to his face,

hoping he hadn't noticed. Of course, he had. He flashed her a sensual grin, his shirt dangling from his hand. He tossed it over a chair and reached for his belt buckle. It was off and hanging over the same chair before she could open her mouth.

"See something you like?" he asked.

"Drop dead," she mouthed, then quickly turned to gather her clothes. She grabbed the first dress she saw and fresh undies. It took all her willpower not to slam the bathroom door shut.

Inside, she leaned against the door, letting it support all her weight. She'd be lying to herself if she didn't admit she found Rob disturbingly attractive. "Don't be a fool," she muttered to herself. But even after she was in the shower the image of Rob standing there half-undressed stayed with her.

She stepped out of the shower and wound a towel turban-style around her freshly shampooed hair. She was reaching for another towel to dry herself when there was an insistent knock on the door. "What do you want?"

"Telephone."

Still wet, she shrugged into one of the terry robes that hung on the back of the door. She walked into the living area and picked up the phone. It was Lillian Hurley. Guilt swamped Dana. Hadn't she promised to call her elderly neighbor yesterday? Yes. And she'd forgotten.

"Lillian, is anything wrong?" Dana asked, turning her back on Rob. He was stretched out across the king-size bed, his tanned legs casually crossed at the ankles. His shorts were now unbuttoned at the waist, the zipper threatening to open.

"The night marchers," Lillian responded. "I heard them again last night. Someone is going to die."

"It's just the wind in the palms," Dana insisted, alarmed that Lillian's mind seemed to be slipping. "You know how those dry fronds rustle when they haven't been trimmed. That's what you're hearing."

It took Dana a full five minutes to calm her friend. By the time she returned to the bathroom her hair was half-dry and its natural curl had sprung to life. She tried to blow it straight, but it didn't do any good. Chalk it up to another bad hair day, she thought as she inspected her reflection in the mirror.

The spaghetti-strap sundress, a deep shade of lilac, made her eyes appear greener, and the pleated bodice made her breasts seem fuller. Not bad, she told herself, suddenly wondering what Vanessa would be wearing. It didn't matter; Vanessa was always the center of attention.

She always had been.

Dana emerged from the bathroom and saw that Rob had fallen asleep. She stood over him, taking the opportunity to study him without him knowing it. There wasn't a spare ounce of flesh on his tall frame. You could count his ribs below his well-honed pecs. You could see the jutting bones of his hips. You couldn't miss the fullness between his legs, the stark evidence of his maleness.

A secret thrill shot through the barrier of her self-control. She'd never been in a situation like this. She had to admit she found Rob exciting. Oh, she knew he was the wrong man for her. From his powerful torso to his strong biceps, Rob Tagett radiated masculine virility. And domination. Here was a man who'd take command of every situation.

No telling what he might try in bed.

Wake him, she told herself, before you forget why you're here and how much trouble you're in. Don't look for any more.

"Darling," she said for the benefit of the stupid bug that was just above Rob's head, "it's time to shower. We're going to be late for dinner."

He didn't open his eyes. At least she didn't think he did, but she couldn't be sure. Quicker than a snake, he grabbed her waist and pulled her down on the bed.

He stared directly into her eyes, their sharp breathing the only sound in the room except for the blood pounding in her temples. His lids widened, any trace of drowsiness gone, replaced by a more intimate look. A new awareness swept over her, bringing with it some hidden emotion that rose like a phoenix from the core of her being.

What was happening to her?

Without warning his mouth covered hers, hot and firm and unbelievably insistent. She twisted her head away, determined not to let him take advantage of her, yet aware she couldn't curse him the

118

way she wanted to. The intrusive bug was inches from them.

Moving her head only gave him access to the sensitive curve of her throat. He ran the tip of his tongue along the soft skin, gently nipping as he went. The sound that escaped from her lips wasn't a moan, was it?

He responded by kissing the base of her neck where it met her shoulder, an unbelievably erotic spot. She hadn't known it existed until this very second. Gooseflesh blossomed across her breasts and down her legs.

With the palm of his hand he turned her face toward his. Their lips almost touching, their breathing sharp and deep, she gazed into his eyes. His irises were nothing more than a narrow band of blue around dilated pupils; his heavy lids were spiked with thick black lashes.

She'd never been faced with such an uninhibited look of passion before. She should have been frightened—considering all she'd heard about him—but she wasn't. Just the opposite.

The warmth of his bare chest so intimately brushing hers and the heat of his powerful thighs snug against her legs demanded a corresponding reaction in her own body. She radiated the warmth of a woman willing—and ready—to make love.

Her logical brain insisted she damn him to hell. When she parted her lips he instantly took advantage, his mouth coaxing hers to open even more, his tongue invading the moist chamber. The motion was rhythmic and sensual, as if he wanted to remind her of how another, harder part of his body could perform.

Why was she responding? she asked herself. *Because you can't help it,* came the answer as her tongue sought his. The contact jolted her, erupting in a surge of heat between her thighs.

She twisted her body against his in a primitive rush of passion she'd never experienced before. She wanted to feel the entire hard, oh-so-masculine length of him against her. She wanted . . . she didn't dare think what she wanted, allowing herself to be swept away on a swift-rising tide of arousal.

Rob pulled his head back and surveyed her with an insolent grin as he sat up. "Time to shower."

No! He wasn't leaving her here like this. "You jerk—"

He was on his feet now, his finger to his lips, reminding her about the bug. "Temper, temper." He had the audacity to wink. "I'll take care of you later."

With two loose-limbed, athletic strides he was at the bathroom door. For a second he paused, and she had the feeling he wanted her to see just how aroused he was. An impressive erection jutted against the confining fabric of his shorts, a promise and a threat.

A half hour later they were on the terrace having cocktails. Dana hadn't said a word to Rob on the way over. That little stunt he'd pulled still had her so furious—and humiliated—that if she hadn't been trapped by circumstances she would have told him to drop dead.

But here she was, sipping Cristal champagne, holding Rob's arm like a possessive girlfriend, and chatting with the half dozen guests who'd already arrived for the extended birthday celebration that would culminate with a luau on Saturday night. The Coltrane brothers were on the far side of the terrace talking to Big Daddy and Minerva Mallory, the society widow whom Dana had met at dinner last night.

Where was Vanessa? she wondered. Just then her sister appeared out of the shadows at the far end of the terrace, wearing a white sheath that emphasized each luscious curve, provocative but still classy. The white set off her tan, a rich golden color that gave her a healthy glow.

Just right, Dana thought. Everything—physically —about her sister was just right. She instantly saw that all the men present, except Vanessa's husband Eric, agreed. Male eyes swung in Vanessa's direction; masculine voices halted midsentence.

Rob stared at Vanessa, an unreadable expression on his face, his glass halfway to his lips. Even Big Daddy, who saw Vanessa every day and should have been immune to her charms, was gazing at her. Dana left Rob to drool in his wineglass, half-wondering how her sister would have handled the little scene back in the cottage. She walked up to Vanessa and gave her a hug.

"I like your Rob," Vanessa said, her eyes on him.

Dana wanted to scream that he wasn't "her" anything. She reined in her temper, reminding herself that she needed Rob Tagett. "He's nice," she managed with a smile that had to be as flat as her voice.

"I hope he likes me," Vanessa said.

"Of course he does."

"What did he say?" Vanessa asked with girlish enthusiasm that somehow bothered Dana.

Actually, she couldn't recall Rob making any direct comment about Vanessa. He'd said over and over what a great kid Jason was, but he hadn't verbalized anything about her sister. Still, only a fool could have missed the look on his face when Vanessa had appeared tonight. He had practically stepped on his tongue.

"Rob thinks you're fantastic."

"I'm not so sure. He didn't seem very friendly." Vanessa gazed at Rob, who was now in the center of a cluster of people. "Be careful of him, Dana. He's the type of man that women can't resist. That kind of man is nothing but trouble."

She knew Vanessa was right. Even now several of the women, two of them married, were bombarding Rob with "I'm available" glances.

Dana tried to allay her sister's concerns. "We're not serious."

"Really?" Vanessa said, shocked. "The way he looks at you, I assumed he was nuts about you."

Dana shook her head. Rob must be a whole lot better actor than she'd thought. They drifted toward the main group and one of the men stopped Vanessa. Dana kept walking rather than link up with Rob again.

She went inside the house and stood alone in front of the wall where glass cases held *leimano*, ancient Hawaiian weapons made from sharks' teeth. The war clubs and spears were studded with teeth from two of the most dangerous sharks in Hawaii, the great white and the tiger shark.

"The native Hawaiians didn't have metal, you know." Big Daddy suddenly appeared at her side.

He was tall, with a muscular body kept trim by hours in the saddle and skin tanned a rich caramel color. His full head of white hair and dark brows added to his impressive bearing. As usual he wore an aloha shirt, but this wasn't one of the cheap versions sold in Waikiki boutiques. Like the original aloha shirts, which were made from the cast-off kimonos that the Japanese islanders wore, this shirt had a more oriental print and was made of silk.

"Sharks' teeth were the sharpest thing around," he informed her. "That's why Captain Cook was able to take advantage of the islanders so easily. For a handful of nails they traded barrels of fruit and casks of *'awa*."

This was another of his favorite stories. How many times had he told her that the *'awa*, made from kava roots, had a druglike effect that Cook's men craved? Waiting for an opportunity to get away, Dana reminded herself to be polite. She didn't want him to suspect Vanessa was really leaving.

"The ancient Hawaiians believed the shark was a symbol of fertility."

Undoubtedly, Big Daddy would now "talk story" in the typical Hawaiian fashion and launch into how he had speared three sharks in one day. Hawaiians liked to retell family stories as much as they did Hawaiian lore, thoroughly enjoying each retelling even though everyone already knew the tale. But Big Daddy didn't have the Hawaiian flair for details, nor did he have a sense of humor. He did nothing more than brag.

"Really? The shark was a fertility symbol?" she asked, playing along the way everyone did when someone was talking story, pretending she didn't know the legend.

"Yes." Big Daddy studied her, his dark eyes ominous beneath those wild black brows. Or was it her imagination?

Dana turned away from his piercing gaze and tried to imagine what kind of man put fertility symbols on his living room wall along with a surfboard. "Interesting."

"In old Hawaii," he continued, and she could tell he was on a roll now. When he got going there was nothing to do but wait him out. "The shark was believed to be all-powerful. The islanders thought he was Pele's brother."

Dana couldn't resist. "That's what I love about old Hawaii. They understood power."

"What do you mean?"

"Notice their chief deity wasn't a god, but a goddess. Pele was the goddess of fire and volcanoes. She gave birth to these islands. Pele was a woman, an all-powerful woman. Next in line was her brother . . . a man. A shark."

He chuckled, but she doubted he found her comment funny. Barefoot and pregnant was his vision of the ideal woman, not a fiery goddess superior to his beloved sharks. She couldn't help wondering what he thought about Rob. She'd introduced them and Rob had thanked Big Daddy for his hospitality, but the older man hadn't said much. Surely he knew about Rob's column in the *Honolulu Sun*. But if he read it he didn't mention it.

Odd, Dana thought, studying Coltrane. He'd always been strange, but now that she knew he eavesdropped on his guests and had forced Jason to watch a pig sticking, she positively despised the man. She strolled outside, hoping to get away from Big Daddy, but he followed her.

At the far end of the terrace Rob and Vanessa stood alone. Vanessa was talking and Rob had an odd expression on his face. He stepped away from Vanessa to take a drink from a passing waiter, and Dana stole a quick look at Big Daddy. Sure enough, he was watching. Her gaze swung back to the couple and a thought niggled at the back of Dana's mind. Vanessa had moved forward.

She was standing in Rob's space.

10

At dinner Dana was seated in the place of honor next to Big Daddy, with Travis Coltrane beside her. How lucky could she get? The floor-to-ceiling doors were open and another table had been set up on the terrace. Rob was seated there with Vanessa at his side, and judging from the laughter they were having fun.

She could hardly imagine the Coltrane brothers really enjoying themselves. They were too intimidated by their father to have fun while he was around. She cast a quick glance at Travis. Like his brother, Eric, who'd married Vanessa so quickly, Travis Coltrane was the image of his father. He had thick dark hair that would never creep backward like most men's, jet black shark's eyes, and the distinctive Coltrane cleft chin.

To give him credit, Travis had a better personality than his brother or father. He wasn't sullen like Eric or a domineering braggart like his father. Travis was always nice to her, and she had the impression he'd be a lot more fun if he ever got away from his father.

"I'm surprised you're here with Rob Tagett. *Ho'omano*," said Travis.

A fitting description, Dana thought with a sigh. *Ho'omano* meant that Rob behaved like a shark with women. On the mainland they would call him a wolf.

"Rob and I are just friends," she responded, though she could see she'd be more likely to sell him a bridge than convince him that she wasn't having an affair with Rob.

"Your timing stinks," Big Daddy added, obviously listening intently to their conversation. "You're up for a superior court appointment. Why would you get involved with a man with a reputation for—"

"It's my life," Dana cut him off, not surprised that he knew about the appointment. The Coltranes had numerous political connections. She couldn't help noticing Travis's smile of approval. No one put Big Daddy in his place, certainly not his sons. He pointedly turned his attention to Minerva Mallory, discussing his upcoming birthday luau with the red-haired widow.

"How are your girls?" Dana asked, curious about his divorce.

Travis shrugged. "I haven't seen them in over a year."

So Travis didn't see his children. Would Eric even want to see his son? Dana glanced down the table to where her brother-in-law was sitting. She'd never had the impression Eric cared one whit about Jason.

Big Daddy, though, doted on the boy. He would insist on seeing his grandson and force Eric to press for custody. Like it or not, Vanessa had no chance of getting rid of the Coltranes entirely. Any judge would grant Eric and Vanessa joint custody.

Travis leaned close and whispered, "Looks like your sister is about to steal your man."

Dana glanced up and saw Vanessa and Rob's heads close together. They were engaged in an animated conversation that didn't include anyone else at the table. "Vanessa's just being friendly," Dana said, determined not to allow Travis to incite a competitive situation with her sister.

"She's a flirt, and she doesn't know when to quit." Travis glanced meaningfully at Big Daddy, who was watching Vanessa gaze into Rob's eyes as if he were about to impart the location of the Holy Grail.

That kind of man is nothing but trouble. Her sister's prophetic words echoed in her ears.

Dana summoned a smile, aware that Travis was studying her, but she couldn't forestall a twinge of anger. She wanted to march over and tell Vanessa that she wasn't a child anymore. She didn't need her help.

She already knew Rob Tagett wasn't the man for her.

* * *

Garth Bradford looked at the clock as he hung up the telephone. 10:30. Was it too late to call Dana in Maui and give her the news? Probably not.

"Sue the bastards, sue the bastards," chanted Puni, moonwalking along his perch. "Sue their asses."

He picked up the telephone, wondering for the hundredth time if Dana could possibly be involved in a murder. He doubted it, but still, Rob had been incredibly cagey when he'd given Garth a preliminary report. All Rob would say was that he was "checking."

There wasn't any answer at the number Rob had given him, so Garth tried the main house. "May I speak with Dana Hamilton?" he asked and was told to hang on.

Garth waited, thinking it had been divine inspiration to throw Dana and Rob together. Not that he'd misled Dana. Rob Tagett was the best detective in the islands, but he was also a lonely, troubled man. And Dana Hamilton, despite her successful career, was a lonely, troubled woman.

He'd deliberately not told Rob who was coming to see him. He didn't really know how Rob felt about Dana, but he thought that if Rob saw her in person he'd have trouble refusing her request for help. And he'd been right.

"Hello?" The voice was as sultry as a tropical night. "This is Dana's sister, Vanessa." Garth conjured up an image of Dana, but with long, dark hair and makeup. "Dana left some time ago, but they must have stopped somewhere. Is there any message?"

The breathless quality of Vanessa's voice gave Garth a glimpse of how provocative Dana could be —if she wanted to. Should he tell her sister why he'd called? It might be better if Vanessa broke the news to Dana. "Please tell Dana that Garth Bradford called. The superior court appointment went to Craig Olsen."

"Oh, no!" The sultry voice was no longer so sexy. There was genuine disappointment in Vanessa's tone. "That's not fair."

"You're right. It's not fair. Dana deserved it."

"I know she's going to be disappointed." The voice was low again, provocative. "Her career means so much."

Garth didn't say anything, but he agreed. He suspected that, like himself, all Dana had was her career. That's why it meant so much to her.

"Do you know Rob Tagett very well?" Vanessa unexpectedly asked.

"About as well as anybody knows him."

"I'm worried about Dana. She doesn't have much experience with men. Someone like Rob is so out of character for her." Vanessa sighed, a soft rush of air across the receiver, but it raced down Garth's spine and stopped where all feeling ended at his waist. "I mean, well, Rob seems genuinely interested in Dana, but the stories I've heard—"

"Forget them. Rob's a good man. He's perfect for Dana." Garth decided the situation must indeed be

131

serious. They hadn't told Vanessa that Rob was working for Dana. Interesting.

"He's not good for her career."

"True," Garth conceded. Rob Tagett wasn't right for Dana. A husband with a sterling reputation and a job outside the legal community would be perfect. Still . . .

"I hear there's been more trouble." Vanessa interrupted his thoughts. "Gwen called here to ask Dana where she bought her pepper spray. She said the Panama Jack's rapist attacked another woman last night."

"That's right." Garth shook his head in disgust. Some nut in Honolulu had been following women home from bars and raping them. The press had dubbed the guy the Panama Jack's rapist because two of the victims had been stalked after leaving the popular nightclub.

"I hope the police catch him soon."

"I'm sure they will," Garth said, although he had his doubts. The creep was clever. So far they only had a generic description that fit half the men in Hawaii. Tall, broad-shouldered, dark hair.

"Thanks for calling," Vanessa said. "I'll break the news to Dana."

Garth would have liked to keep talking, but what could he say to someone he didn't know, someone who was nothing more than a sexy voice. Someone who was married to another man.

He hung up and wheeled himself out onto the terrace, where it was pitch dark. Beyond the barbecue area was the swimming pool he'd designed. It stretched out, appearing to be part of the ocean, one continuous shimmer of water. At night he liked to sit outside and listen to the symphony of the ocean and the wind in the stately palms. Usually he kept Puni on his shoulder for company. A foul-tempered parrot might not be everyone's idea of the ideal companion, but he was better than the overwhelming silence, broken only by the lonely call of the sea.

Dana followed Rob down the lava rock path toward Makai House after dinner. They went around to the terrace that faced the sea. She honestly didn't know what to say. If he kissed her again she was going to whack him. Obviously, he thought he was irresistible to every woman. Well, he was dead wrong.

"Did you find out anything?" Dana tried to keep sarcasm out of her voice, but heard a hint of it despite her best efforts.

Rob flopped down on one of the bent-willow chairs and propped his feet up on the deck rail. The only light came from a lover's moon, a soft glow as romantic as candlelight. It played across his dark hair and caught the enigmatic blue of his eyes as he pulled the other chair close to his and motioned for her to sit.

Dana yanked the chair back to where it had been and reluctantly lowered herself into the soft cushions.

"Big Daddy's banging Moneybags Minerva."

"Possibly," Dana admitted, recalling all the meltdown looks Minerva cast at Big Daddy during the interminable dinner. "What does that have to do with anything?" She knew she sounded bitchy; she couldn't help herself. Sometimes she had trouble hiding her temper.

"Coltrane doesn't allow anyone up in his suite except when Eustace cleans it. That means he has to go to Minerva's bungalow, right?"

"Right." She assumed Vanessa had told him all this. Perhaps their conversation had been more businesslike than it had appeared.

"Tomorrow night, when Big Daddy's with Minerva, I'm checking his suite. I'd like to know just what's up there."

"What if he catches you? No telling what he might do."

"He's not going to. I've got a pair of two-way radios. You're going to hide in the bushes outside Minerva's cottage and warn me."

"All right," she whispered, finding it hard to imagine herself doing such a thing. She'd always been extraordinarily careful not to break any laws. In the back of her mind she always knew she'd been wrong not to report Hank's death. Sometimes, when she stepped up to the bench, she asked herself, *What right do I have to be here?*

Under ordinary circumstances she'd never spy on anyone or be a party to a break-in. But these weren't normal circumstances. She honestly believed Big Daddy had sent the blackmail notes. He seemed to be the blunt, forthright type. The bugs planted everywhere proved he was an out-and-out sneak—the kind of man who *would* send blackmail notes.

Dana stared at the starry reflection of the moon as it danced across the waves in the distance, thinking that Rob was in his element. Apparently he had no qualms about breaking in or counterblackmail. While she admired the ruthlessness she saw in him, because she didn't have it herself, Rob frightened her.

"Aren't you going to ask me what else I learned?"

"There's more? You've been busier than I thought." She'd assumed that he'd done nothing more tonight than drool over her sister.

"Eric Coltrane spends every night in town with his mistress. He comes back just in time to shower and go to work on the ranch."

"Vanessa told you that?" She heard the anger in her voice. Vanessa had never told her Eric had a mistress.

"Nah. I got it out of one of the maids."

Rob's cocky smile should have forewarned her, but she asked anyway. "There's more?"

"Yeah. Travis has the hots for you."

"What makes you think that?"

"The way he kept pawing you at dinner. Every time you leaned forward, he checked out your bra."

A surge of heat rose to her cheeks. She was wearing a demi-bra, and it was possible that if you looked down the front of her dress you could see the

135

edge of her breasts. Rob must have looked or he
wouldn't know what someone else might see. He
was a totally incorrigible leech. He could probably
tell her exactly what Vanessa was wearing beneath
that white sheath—if anything.

"Travis just better watch it," Rob said. "If he
doesn't keep his hands off you I'm going to deck
him."

Something in his tone left no doubt in Dana's
mind that Rob meant what he said. Part of her felt
protected in a way that she'd never felt protected
before, but she couldn't help resenting his attitude.
What right did he have to be so possessive?

She hesitated, her thoughts turning to Vanessa.
She almost asked Rob what he thought about her
sister. Then she decided that she didn't really want
to hear him put it into words.

"Let's go inside." Rob rose from his chair and
offered her his hand. His strong fingers curled
around her palm as he pulled her to her feet. "Remember, we've been in the grotto making love."

Who but Rob would have thought of the grotto?
The mountain-lake pool was surrounded by artfully
placed boulders. Waterfalls flowed into it, creating
"slides" over the rocks just like the "slides" in the
rain forest, which had been Mother Nature's inspiration rather than a showcase for some jet-set landscape architect.

Between two slides was a grotto concealed by a
thicket of ferns. Jason and his friends played on the
rocks, jumping off them into the pool or sliding

down the mossy boulders as if they were on some amusement-park ride. When they tired of this, they played hide and seek, often hiding in the grotto.

"It's *so* dark in the grotto," was all Dana could think to say once they were back in the cottage.

Rob laughed, a rich, deep masculine laugh that was as wanton as sin on Sunday. "I don't need light. I go by feel. Admit it, you loved it."

"Well," Dana struggled to keep her voice light. "It was more fun than doing it in bed, but those ferns tickled. And I think I lost my bra somewhere."

"Nah, it's right here in my pocket." He stopped dead in his tracks and she nearly bumped into him.

He turned to face her, staring into her eyes and grinning. Oh, Lord, what was he up to now? Before she could stop him, he hooked one finger over the top of her sundress and pulled it back, exposing the sexy demi-bra. He silently whistled and winked.

She swatted his hand away, but not before his warm palm accidentally grazed one breast. The nipple sprang to life, and his mocking eyes didn't miss the raised fabric. He slowly ran his tongue over his lower lip.

Furious, she turned away. Rob was into sexual games; she wasn't a player. She never had been. He was a bum who would hustle her sister at dinner, then fondle her later. She grabbed her nightgown and robe from the closet and headed for the bathroom. "I won't be in here too long."

She shut the door and kicked off her shoes, wondering what Rob would pull when she came out.

Bug or no bug, she was sleeping on the love seat. Sure, it would be cramped, but anything would be better than getting in bed with that lout. She unzipped her dress, pausing when she heard a knock on the cottage door. Wondering who it could be, she moved closer to the door.

"Hello, Rob." It was Vanessa's voice.

"Dana's in the bathroom," he said. "Do you want to come in and wait?"

"No. I want to talk to you."

Dana kept her ear to the bathroom door. The next sound was the soft click of the cottage door shutting behind them. Dana whirled around and stared at her reflection in the mirror. What was her beloved sister doing? She'd never known Vanessa to be so brazen.

But then, Vanessa had never met Rob Tagett. He was the kind of man who'd be a challenge for a woman like Vanessa. Even so, didn't her sister care about her feelings? What if she really loved Rob?

Dana turned on the water in the tub and told herself it didn't matter. Vanessa was welcome to the leech. All she'd hired Rob to do was find the blackmailer, and she had to admit he had made more progress than she could have on her own.

She sprinkled lavender bath salts into the tub and slipped into the water. At least she didn't have to hurry. Surely he wouldn't be back for hours. When she finally emerged from the bathroom, her robe tied tight, she saw that Rob had returned. He'd turned the sheets down and placed the narrow cushions from the love seat down the middle of the bed, creating an effective barrier. You'd have to be dead to roll over those cushions without waking up.

He'd turned out the lights, but the full moon streamed through the open door, bringing with it a cool breeze and the aroma of wild ginger. Crickets called to their mates, and in the distance came the deep *ribbit-ribbit* of the bullfrogs, who lived in the lagoon with the koi. The ceiling fan was on, its wide blades circulating the air with a comforting *whoosh* that usually lulled her to sleep.

Rob was sprawled across his side of the bed, facedown, wearing nothing but Joe Boxer shorts. Dana knew Joe Boxers from advertisements in the *Honolulu Sun*. They were printed with outrageous sayings.

She edged nearer, recalling the last time she thought he was asleep. She leaned closer, so close that she could see the pulse throbbing at the base of his neck. He was asleep all right, breathing evenly, his tanned face and dusky eyelashes a stark contrast to the white pillowcase.

Her hand hovered just above his bare shoulders. Heat radiated from his skin, warming her palm and drawing her hand downward. She knew she should stay away from him, but she couldn't help herself. She honestly couldn't.

With a tremor in her fingers, she touched his shoulder. She inhaled sharply, half-expecting him to awaken and round on her as he had earlier. She waited a moment, her fingers resting lightly on him.

139

He didn't move, although the whisper-soft ceiling fan ruffled his dark hair.

His skin was smooth, but beneath her fingertips she detected the raw power she always associated with him. Knowing he was truly asleep, she couldn't resist letting her hand glide down the masculine plane of his back across the bare skin that was surprisingly soft. The muscles beneath were firm though, as solid as the beat of his heart.

Her hand drifted downward a scant inch at a time, stopping at the waistband of his Joe Boxers. She could tell that the underwear was brand-new. It was crisp and had deep creases from being in the package. Using the moonlight, she had to squint to read what was written on them.

Just Say Yo!

11

A bar of sunlight warmed Dana's cheek, and she raised her arm to cover her face, thinking this had to be the weekend—the alarm hadn't gone off—and she could sleep past six. As she lay there not quite awake, she remembered she wasn't home.

She was in bed with Rob Tagett.

She kept her eyes shut tight, questioning the wisdom of her decision last night. Rob had been sound asleep; the love seat was so small. She'd eased herself onto the bed and positioned herself with her back to him and the barricade of sofa cushions.

Her arm still sheltering her face, Dana peeked out and saw that she'd turned over during the night and was a mere inch from the cushions that divided the bed. She dropped her arm, set to sneak out of bed before Rob awoke, but he was already gazing at her, his cocked arm propping his head up.

In the mellow sunlight his eyes were twilight blue, shaded by double tiers of lashes the same dark color as the rasp of stubble shading his jaw. He smiled, a slow sensual smile, his eyes traveling across her face and down her neck. As his gaze drifted lower yet, Dana glanced down.

The lacy bodice of her black silk gown gaped open, exposing most of her breasts. Searing heat flared up to her cheeks as she recalled the way he'd looked down the front of her dress last night. The man had only one thing on his mind. She reached down to grab the sheet and saw that her gown had inched up, revealing her legs right up to the tops of her thighs. She straightened her gown and started to roll out of bed.

Rob's arm came down on her shoulder. "Morning, princess."

His eyes swung to the quilt with the intrusive bug, and she snapped her mouth shut before she said something ugly. "Good morning," she managed to respond.

"I need to talk to you." He sat up and propped his back against the headboard, completely comfortable with his near-nude state.

Dana didn't know where to look, certainly not at the bulge in his Joe Boxers. She knew what men were like first thing in the morning. Couldn't he at least pull up the sheet?

"Last night Garth called, and Vanessa spoke with him," Rob began, his tone gentle. "The superior court appointment went to Craig Olsen."

"Really?" was all Dana could say. That must have been why Vanessa had come out to Makai House. True, she was disappointed about not getting that appointment, but she was much more relieved that Vanessa hadn't been chasing Rob. "It doesn't matter."

He reached across the blockade of cushions and put his large hand over hers, lacing his strong fingers between her smaller ones. For a change there was nothing aggressive about the gesture. It was tender, reassuring. "Once your name is on the list of acceptable candidates, it stays. You'll get another shot at it."

She was so astounded by his concern that she didn't know what to say. It seemed so out of character for him. He kept looking at her until she pulled her hand from his. "It's your turn to get the bathroom first," she said, forcing a light tone.

He jumped up, his more familiar joking expression back in place. "Yeah, you really hogged the head last night. I fell asleep waiting."

While Rob was in the shower Dana dressed, putting on crisp white shorts and a navy shirt trimmed in white. She inspected her reflection in the full-length mirror. She wanted to look professional. Rob had a friend on the Maui police force. They were going to see him this morning, although Dana couldn't imagine what help he'd be.

Rob opened the bathroom door and steam billowed out, but she could see that all he was wearing was a towel carelessly tucked around his hips. One quick turn and the thing would fall off. "We're going to the beach this afternoon. Can you round up towels and an umbrella?"

"Sure," she said, thankful to have an excuse to get out of the cottage. "There's beach equipment in the cabana. I'll get what we need."

She was halfway down the lava rock path to the pool when she realized that going to the beach hadn't been part of the original plan. She gathered towels and an umbrella, wondering what Rob was up to now.

Back at the cottage, Rob was standing in the bathroom, shaving, not bothering to shut the door. Dana tossed the towels on the bed as he motioned for her to come inside. Wary, she edged in and he closed the door.

Before she could protest Rob said, "Don't mention the police. I don't want that bug to pick it up."

"Do I look stupid?"

"Now that you mention it—yes," he said, unfazed by her sudden burst of temper.

She quickly backed out, ignoring the water droplets on the wedge of hair feathering his chest and the cute puff of shaving cream on his earlobe.

"Don't you want to use the bathroom too?"

Did he honestly think that she'd be willing to share the bathroom? *Look at him!* The towel had worked its way down on his hips, dangerously close to coming undone. Yet he didn't seem to notice. Or care.

"I used the cabana," she said as she left.

Rob was much more comfortable with his body than she was with hers, Dana decided as she changed into a swimsuit, then put on her shorts again. Evidently he was accustomed to parading around in front of adoring women. But she wasn't used to wearing skimpy clothes. She was thankful she'd brought a conservative swimsuit. The more clothes she had on around Rob, the safer she felt.

Kahului was the main city on Maui, but few tourists visited it, Rob thought as he drove the convertible through the streets. The flip side of paradise. It wasn't a bad town, if you liked Buffalo in the fifties, Hawaiian style. It was populated mostly by hotel workers and other service personnel who couldn't afford to live in the exclusive beachfront condos.

Around the clock a volcano of steam erupted from the Clean-Rite linen service. Between hotel bedding and towels and uniforms, the commercial laundry ran continuous shifts. Rob drove past, thankful he didn't have to stand for hours over a vat of hot bleach, getting lipstick-stained napkins pristine white so tourists could soil them again.

He turned onto Hana Road, moving his head slightly to look at Dana. She hadn't said much since they'd left the ranch. He thought maybe she was brooding about losing that spot on the bench. Tough break. She'd have been damn good.

He eased up on the gas, checking the street signs for the police department and noticing that the car he'd spotted earlier in his rearview mirror was still there. The blue Toyota was lagging back almost a full block.

"Part of the problem is that too many people from

Pacific Rim countries live here," Rob said, making a quick turn down a narrow lane.

Dana's expression said she hadn't a clue what he was talking about. "What problem?"

"Why there aren't more women on the bench or in executive positions in Hawaii." Rob checked the rearview mirror again. Sure enough, there was the blue Toyota. "So many of the islanders come from the Philippines or Japan or China that they have an Eastern attitude toward women."

"I hadn't thought about it until now," Dana agreed, "but I'd say Hawaii's heart is in the United States—freedom-loving and fair—but its soul is in the East—full of traditional customs and superstitions handed down from generation to generation. Gwen found out the hard way that many islanders have a double standard for women."

"Right. She would have been smarter to wait until she was appointed to a higher court, then run as an incumbent. Like it or not, what's seen as assertive in men is considered pushy for women—in Hawaii anyway."

Dana's eyes followed his as he looked in the mirror again. "What's wrong?"

She started to look around, which would have been a dead giveaway in a convertible with the top down, but he put his hand on her shoulder. "Don't look back. We're being followed."

"Big Daddy's men?"

"Probably. They drove off one of the *kuleana* roads just beyond Kau Ranch." The *kuleanas* were independent farmers with their own system of roads, which were little more than dirt tracks through the sugar cane fields. The car must have been hiding behind a thicket of cane that was taller than full-grown corn, waiting for them to pass.

"Hang on." Rob gunned the engine and cut sharply to the right.

Dana gripped the armrest as the convertible shot down the street, swerved to the left, and entered a one-way street. Going the wrong way, Rob barreled up the short road, then veered off to the right into traffic.

They rode around until Rob was certain that they'd lost Big Daddy's men. They drove into the police station lot and parked by a fence that was sagging under the weight of a scarlet bougainvillea. Rob pulled so close to the bush that the thorns scraped the side of the car, but at least it couldn't be spotted easily should the blue Toyota pass by.

The station was little more than a heap of concrete blocks once painted beige but now a mottled gray and tan. Nothing about it inspired confidence or reminded Dana of the Honolulu police station. It made her wonder about Rob's friend. Bruce Kenae had once been on the Honolulu Police Department with Rob. What was he doing in this backwater?

Rob hopped out of the car. "Wait here."

"I'm coming with you."

"Forget it. Bruce won't talk—off the record—with someone around." He walked away, leaving her to silently fume.

147

Twenty minutes later he reappeared, striding across the cracked concrete lot that was sprouting weeds. "Any sign of our friends in the Toyota?"

She shook her head. "What did you find out?"

He slid behind the wheel. "No IRs on any of the Coltranes."

She knew those were incident reports. Every time a policeman stopped someone, it didn't result in an arrest or a ticket—especially in paradise where tourists were sacred. They wrote an incident report in their logbook instead.

Rob turned the key in the ignition and the motor grumbled, but finally caught. "Kenae did know a little about Eric's mistress though. Word is he wanted to marry her, but his father had a fit. She's *hapa haole.*"

"Half white. That would upset Big Daddy. He detests marriages with native Hawaiians. He's a total bigot."

"The only other thing Kenae mentioned was that Coltrane looks the other way when some of the islanders raise a little Maui Wowie on his land."

"Marijuana?"

"It's not the same old weed you smoked in the seventies." He looked at Dana, then obviously decided she hadn't smoked anything at anytime and shrugged. "It's kick-ass stuff and sells for big bucks on the mainland."

"The police don't care?"

"Now that they've closed down so many sugar mills and tourism has stalled, it's the only source of income some people have." Rob shrugged as if to say, That's the way it goes. Clearly, raising Maui Wowie didn't rate high on his list of serious crimes.

She sympathized with the islanders. Life in Hawaii was harsh—despite the tour guides' air-brushed version of paradise—and exceedingly expensive. Food and housing were three or maybe four times what they were on the mainland. Few homes had air conditioning; it simply cost too much.

"This doesn't give us much leverage against Big Daddy, does it?"

Rob pulled out of the lot, saying, "Image is everything to Big Daddy. He loves being thought of as a god. Kenae says he's a hero around here. He donated all the money to build the hospital and medical center."

"Then he's going to hate a lot of negative publicity about the divorce. I know what's going to happen." Dana frowned, shaking her head. "He'll make certain my sister gets blamed."

"Coltrane's on a power trip. That kind of person thinks he's untouchable. He'll hate to be crossed. That makes him dangerous—and don't forget it. We need to be careful. Real careful."

12

"Big Daddy's concern with his image is the key," Rob told Dana as they drove along the Hana highway, slowed by yet another truck laden with sugar cane, typical of harvest time. "What do you suppose would happen if people knew he eavesdropped on his guests?"

"He'd do *anything* to keep that from coming out. Anything." Now she was smiling, seeming to warm to Rob's idea.

"That's what I'm counting on."

"We'll need proof."

"I'm getting into Big Daddy's suite. The proof's there, trust me."

She was silent for a few minutes, then she asked, "Do you see them?"

"The third car back might be the same one I spotted earlier. I'm going to pull in at Pic-Nic's and get something for lunch. You watch the blue Toyota and see what it does."

Rob slowed the car as they drove into Paia, the

last town on the isolated thirty-mile stretch to Hana. Once a sugar plantation, today Paia catered to the tourists bound for the serpentine road that would take them past countless waterfalls and through tunnels of ferns to the remote village of Hana. A cluster of gas stations and a general store plus several specialty food shops was all there was left of the historic site.

He pulled into Pic-Nic's small lot and left Dana to watch for the blue car. He came out a few minutes later with a small rental cooler full of sodas and a picnic box with sandwiches and fresh fruit.

"They're in the gas station across the street," Dana said. "They didn't get any gas. They're just sitting in their car—"

"Waiting for us to pull out." Rob placed the food in the trunk on top of the towels, then got in. He leaned toward Dana. "Kiss me. We need to look like lovers out for the day."

Before she could protest he leaned down and touched his lips to hers, gently covering her mouth. It was more of a caress than a kiss. He'd wanted to catch her off-guard, and judging by her startled expression, he had. Evidently she'd been expecting another searing kiss.

Her seductive lashes lowered, but not before he saw the flash of regret in her eyes. *Okay, babe. You asked for it.* He tipped her head up and touched the soft underside of her chin with the pad of his thumb.

She rewarded him by parting her lips. This time his mouth captured hers in a fierce, hot kiss that

152

sent currents of arousal through his body. Reflexively, her arms circled his neck. His awareness focused, excluding everything except the erotic signals her body was sending.

His tongue flirted with hers, touching, moving away, then touching again as his fingers combed through her hair, lifting it, testing its weight, its softness. His blood, thick and heavy, pounded in his temples. He had the urge to do a whole lot more than kiss her, but a busload of Japanese tourists pulled up next to them.

He released her, saying, "That should convince those bums that we haven't even noticed them." He hoped he sounded more relaxed than he felt.

Dana responded by fumbling in her purse and coming up with a pair of sunglasses. She slammed them on her face and stared straight ahead. Okay, she wasn't quite comfortable with what happened, but it was getting a helluva lot easier to kiss her.

He backed out of the lot and floored the accelerator. The men in the Toyota zipped out of the gas station. "Amateurs. We'd never spot a pro."

"What are we going to do?"

"Nothing. We're going to the beach. Let those jerks sweat away the afternoon while we're swimming."

They drove down the Hana highway with the Toyota not far behind, going past several scenic turnouts until they reached Maliko Bay. The secluded beach had no tourist facilities, so Rob pulled onto the shoulder of the road and parked. The men were forced to drive on or make themselves completely obvious.

"We're going down there?" Dana eyed the narrow trail between the rocks to the ellipse of powdered-sugar sand with misgivings.

"Sure. I've done it lots of times."

Dana started down the trail, carrying the towels and umbrella. Rob hoisted the cooler to his side and grabbed the sandwiches. They had the beach to themselves, so they spread the towels out and opened the umbrella for shade. He stripped off his clothes and tossed them on his towel.

She eased out of her linen shorts to reveal a white one-piece suit that was cut high on the sides, which made her legs look even longer. Even sexier. That was the good news. The bad news was the top came up to her chin. A swimsuit? Hell, no. Another power suit.

"Last one in buys lunch tomorrow." Dana ran toward the surf.

"Watch the undertow," Rob cautioned her. He loved this beach, but it did have a stronger current than most beaches in the area.

He let her have a good head start, knowing he could beat her. Then he charged across the beach, the hot sand burning the skin between his toes. He caught Dana at the water's edge and sprinted past her. Turning, he grinned.

No question about it. She was miffed—big time. She was much more competitive than he'd originally thought. He liked that in a woman; it made her more challenging.

"You're buying lunch tomorrow. We'll go to Casanova's in Makawao. I hear it has the best Italian food on Maui."

Dana waded out to him. "It has the best Italian food in Hawaii—period."

The slow, undulating waves rolled in, tumbling like dice across the shimmering sand, luring them into deeper water. Chains of crimson seaweed drifted up from the ocean floor, a playground for schools of flat-bodied yellow butterfly fish with circles of brilliant turquoise around their eyes. The sun-dappled sea and the bracing scent of the breeze blowing across the nearby pineapple fields made Rob smile.

Now, this was what he loved about Maui. Pineapples on the wind and deserted beaches. Too many people lived in Honolulu; it was impossible to find a deserted beach. The pineapple fields there had become cookie-cutter condos. But this was paradise.

When Dana reached waist-high water, she jackknifed into a dive that cleanly split the incoming wave. Rob watched her flawlessly stroking, swimming out farther. He followed, leisurely paddling after her.

She stopped, treading water, waiting for him. Her hair was slicked back into a smooth cap of rich chestnut that gleamed in the brilliant sunlight, making her face seem more delicate, more feminine. She had the damnedest eyes. Impossibly green, a stark contrast to the azure sea. Those eyes beckoned him.

Close up, her long, curved lashes were wet spikes of dark brown, giving her an exotic look. There was something in them that reminded him of the way she looked at him just before he kissed her. Then she smiled at him, that slow, feminine smile that was heart-stoppingly sensual without intending to be.

"I just love swimming," she said, happier than he'd ever heard her. "In high school I was on the swim team."

"So was I." He wondered if she realized how much they had in common. He playfully splashed her.

"Stop it," she cried, then laughed. Along with the hypnotic lull of the surf, her laughter hung in the summer air sounding so right.

"Let's dive for shells," he suggested, though there were several other things he'd rather do with her. He wondered if she knew that her conservative suit, when wet, conformed to every curve, becoming semitransparent and revealing her taut nipples.

Her smile crumpled. "Don't look, but the blue Toyota is back. They're driving very slowly along the ridge."

"They're probably checking us out with binoculars. We should at least look like we're having fun." He grabbed her and hoisted her up to his hips before she could utter more than an astonished gasp. "Put your legs around my waist."

She did as she was told, her slim legs circling him as she faced him, but she frowned, wrinkling her brow and tightening her lips. He ignored those signals and gazed into her eyes. A glimmer of panic hardened her vivid green eyes. And knifed right through him.

Why, he asked himself. Her past, he decided. Dana had never fully recovered from that fateful night. Had that bastard raped her? She'd made it sound as if Vanessa had attacked Hank and rescued her. Had Dana told him the truth?

If Vanessa had been too late, that would account for the panic not quite hidden in the depths of Dana's eyes. Her description of the incident that traumatic night returned with startling clarity. A young, defenseless girl. A bull of a man. And a dark shed.

Rob's heart filled with emotions he didn't have time to analyze. He'd been going about this all wrong, he decided. He'd been aggressive, not compassionate, daring her to reject him. The old Rob, the man he barely remembered anymore, would never have behaved like that.

Oh, it worked. Partway. It wasn't what she'd needed though. She might open up and kiss him back, but she wasn't going to give herself to him— the way he wanted—unless she trusted him.

"Trust me," he whispered even though there wasn't anyone around to hear them except the seagulls drifting overhead.

"Only as far as I can throw you." She tried to joke, but her voice was as flat as week-old beer.

He cradled her against him, bringing her so close that her breasts pillowed against his chest. He tamped down the surge of heat that flared in his groin. "I swear, Dana. I'll never hurt you."

"The car's driving off," she responded, breaking the spell. She dropped her legs and slipped into the water. Before he could call to her she was swimming away.

Just as well, he said to himself, then paused to watch the rhythmic stroking of her arms as she swam. *Oh, who the hell are you kidding?*

He dove under the next wave and swam along the bottom with smooth, sure strokes. Why was he trying so hard? He'd emotionally cut his losses when Ellen had left him. From then on he dated women, yet he never gave a damn about them one way or the other. How had he gotten himself so involved with Dana Hamilton?

He shot to the surface and took a gulp of fresh air, his thoughts reeling. Son of a bitch. Had the past changed him, making him hate women? Well, maybe. Once upon a time—ten years ago to be exact —he'd been nicer, more sensitive.

Plunging below the surface once more, he followed a colorful clown fish into the filigreed branches of delicate coral that swayed, dancing with the surge of the sea. Okay, be honest, he told himself. With each day his loneliness and alienation grew and he became more sarcastic, more aggressive—daring any woman to love him.

Stupid as it was, he blamed all women for what had happened to him. That's why he was such a smart ass. What a mouth. What an attitude. He didn't even like himself, so how could he expect Dana to like him?

For the first time he realized that on that fateful night he'd lost a lot more than his career, his marriage. And the son he loved and missed more each day. He'd lost himself. *So what in hell are you going to do about it?*

His lungs were burning, but he kept following the clown fish. It darted into a huge chunk of coral where the reef fish mated, laid eggs, and fed. Usually hovering over these coral condos cheered him. Not today.

He surfaced, flipping his head backward and flinging rivulets of water over his shoulder. He blinked rapidly, the salt water stinging his eyes. A cry split the warm summer air.

"Rob, help!" Dana was splashing wildly in the water halfway down the beach.

Had she encountered a stingray or a school of poisonous jellyfish? Rob took advantage of his powerful chest muscles, using the butterfly stroke to get to her as quickly as possible. She was doubled over, clutching her leg. He could tell the way she was gasping for breath that she was nearly exhausted.

"Ch-Charlie horse," she sputtered, pointing to her calf.

Treading water madly, Rob lifted her over his shoulder and grabbed her leg. The usually smooth calf muscle was knotted. He rubbed it with quick, firm strokes that made Dana moan. He knew it hurt, but there wasn't any other way to unkink the muscle.

"Better?" he asked, letting her slide down into his arms.

"Y-Yes." Trembling all over, she curled against his chest like a small child, her arm still clinging to his neck, her eyes squeezed shut.

"You're all right," he murmured into her wet hair, nestling her against his torso as he turned on his side. In a few strokes they were in shallower water and Rob stood up. Dana hadn't moved, her face tucked against the curve of his neck. He held her in his arms and slowly walked through the waves toward shore.

He settled her on the towels and lay down beside her. Slipping his arm around her, he pulled her against him, determined to stop her shaking. How long had he been down there? How many times had she called out for him?

Dana opened her eyes, her face just an inch from his; if he moved he'd be kissing her. "I'm sorry. I panicked. I couldn't see you and I had the strangest—"

"The strangest what?"

"The strangest premonition." She rolled her eyes in self-derision. "You've heard of the night marchers —that old Hawaiian legend that says if you hear the

160

ghosts of the ancient warriors trooping their way to the sea, then someone is going to die."

"Sure, I've heard that legend."

"My neighbor Mrs. Hurley keeps saying she hears the night marchers." Dana frowned. "I know it's silly, but when my leg cramped and I couldn't find you, all I could think was the undertow was going to sweep me out to sea. I knew I was going to drown. I could literally hear the night marchers."

Well, I'll be damned, Rob thought. Beneath her professional exterior Dana Hamilton was as superstitious as the islanders who could trace their ancestry back to King Kamehameha.

"Dana, what you heard was probably the blood pounding in your ears."

"I know," she conceded, her expression still dead serious. "That's the logical explanation. But, I swear, I thought I was going to die."

Rob had no idea what to say. He didn't put much stock in premonitions. Maybe the blackmailer had frightened Dana more than he'd realized. Beneath that veneer of composure was a far different person, and he couldn't help wondering what other secrets she kept hidden.

Dana moved into his arms and lowered her head to his shoulder, closing her eyes. Rob waited a minute, certain she'd move away, but she didn't. He ran his hand over her wet hair, deliberately soothing her in the same way he had when his son had been young and needed comfort. She snuggled closer, her hand sliding across his chest.

His body surged in response to her, heat unfurling in the pit of his stomach, then centering in his groin. There wasn't anything deliberately provocative in her movements, he realized. Something snapped inside him like a violin string that had been strung too tight. Why hadn't he realized the truth before? What Dana wanted, what she needed, was to be cuddled.

He didn't believe much of the psychobabble about getting in touch with your inner child, but he stopped to recall Dana's past. Raised by a sex siren. She must have spent hours alone without the love and comfort of a mother. He'd been lucky, Rob realized, not for the first time. Every night his mother had kissed him good night and told him she loved him, even when he'd been a teenager and hated it.

His father, too, had been a warm man. Before every football game he'd hug Rob and wish him luck. That's why Rob found it so easy to express his affection. He'd always hugged and kissed Zach, even when Ellen reminded him other fathers didn't "baby" their sons.

But Dana's life had been nothing like his.

She shifted positions, pillowing her head against his chest and snuggling closer yet, her hand clutching the curve of his chest. She did need someone to comfort her. And he was the one.

With his free hand Rob adjusted the umbrella so they were shaded. He lay there quietly, thinking about Dana's life, until the cadence of her breathing told him that she'd fallen asleep. Once he would have yearned to touch her more intimately. Now he kept his arm around her, content and feeling truly close to her for the first time.

Almost an hour passed before Dana awoke. She raised her head, obviously surprised to find herself against his chest. He reassured her with a smile—or tried to.

"How about lunch?" he asked to fill the awkward silence as he reached for the cooler and sandwiches.

She was sitting up when he turned back, her knees drawn to her chest and her arms locked around her legs. A protective stance if he'd ever seen one. He refused to let it dampen what had just happened. They were close now in a way they never had been.

He handed her an ice-cold can of Diet Coke. She popped the tab and a cool spray misted his arm. As they ate their lunch he was acutely aware that she was studying him. What was she thinking?

"Rob." The word hung in the air like one of the gulls overhead, suspended by an updraft. Somehow he knew he wasn't going to like whatever was coming next. He managed to meet her serious green eyes and still appear relaxed. "Tell me why you left the police force."

13

Rob gazed out at the shoreline, barely recognizing that the tide was inching closer and closer, pushed inexorably onward by the full moon that would shine tonight. Should he tell Dana? If he wanted to build on their closeness, now was the time to do it. He hesitated, his eyes still on the breaking waves that left garlands of foam as they retreated. Aw, hell, if he was going to have a relationship with Dana, he was going to have to tell her.

"Bruce Kenae and I were homicide detectives," he began, explaining how he knew the policeman he'd just visited. "There aren't that many murders in paradise. So we spent most of our time on loan to narcotics. That night we were wearing those black windbreakers with HONOLULU PD on the back in Day-Glo orange letters."

Dana nodded. "Too often the police shoot each other by mistake, right? It must have been hot though."

"Hotter than hell. I was always sopping wet after

a bust." He gazed into her eyes, wondering if he could actually discuss this with her. It was like re-living the longest night of his life all over again. "We had a tip that Chang, the Chinese mob boss, had a stash of drugs hidden in the Green Dragon Club. It was supposed to be in the main building. Bruce and I were told to search the annex."

He paused and she said, "You know, in all the years I've lived here I've only been to Chinatown once."

"It's hardly the tourist's side of paradise. A crazy quilt of apartments built in the last century and gin-seng shops linked by pitch black alleys." Even now he could almost smell the unique scent of China-town, a foul odor of garbage that had baked in the tropical sun and opium coming from the hookers' rooms above the street. "We ventured up the back stairs of the building we had been assigned to search. It was supposed to be vacant, but we heard giggling. We went up to the room and looked through the peephole. Two girls were slip-sliding a Japanese man."

"Slip-sliding?" Dana asked.

"The Oriental equivalent of a Mazola party. Na-ked women cover themselves with soap lather. The guy gets on top and slides around," he said, and Dana's eyes widened slightly. "I told Bruce to leave them alone. No sense ruining the bust. We tiptoed down the hall until we reached the center of the building. By now we'd gone through a maze of cor-ridors and we were just about lost.

"There was no electricity in that part of the building, so we used our flashlights. We went past one room with boxes of ginseng piled to the ceiling. I don't know what made me stop." Even now, years later, he couldn't explain the hunch that ultimately cost him his career, his family. How many times had he wished that they'd just kept going? "We checked the boxes. They were filled with heroin. I sent Bruce back to get the rest of the men."

"You didn't use a walkie-talkie to call them in?"

Rob shook his head, squinting against the late-afternoon sunlight. "Not with Chang. His guys have sophisticated scanners. If they knew what we had found, Bruce and I would have been dead and the whole stash gone before help could get to us."

"Didn't that violate procedure? Leaving you alone?"

"We didn't have any choice. While Bruce went for the team I guarded the boxes. Obviously, the contents had already been packaged and were ready to hit the streets. I heard a noise behind me. Someone was running from the room. I went after him and landed him with a flying tackle."

Rob stopped and took a deep breath, half-wishing he hadn't started this story. Dana gazed at him expectantly and he went on. "I'd assumed one of Chang's flunkies had fallen asleep while he was on guard duty, but as we were rolling around on the floor I discovered it was a woman."

"Chang had a woman guarding the drugs?"

"She wasn't guarding the drugs," he answered.

167

"It was Chang's girlfriend. She was trying to rip him off. Who'd miss a few packets in a stash that big?"

Dana waited for him to continue, her expression concerned. Obviously she knew what was coming.

"Turned out her name was Angela Morton. Blonde, blue-eyed, centerfold figure, and boy, could she cuss a blue streak. I arrested her, read her the Miranda, cuffed her, and took her to the back of the room behind the boxes. 'Hey, copper,' she yelled as I walked away. 'Your career's over, you fuck-up.' Now, she said this with the sweetest, most innocent smile you've ever seen. It was eerie . . . real eerie."

"She sounds like quite an actress."

"You got that right." How well he remembered Angela's total metamorphosis. "Bruce had gotten lost, so it was some time before the unit returned. At first everyone was so excited because this was the biggest bust in the islands. Then we heard Angela crying. When we walked back to where I'd left her, we saw her panties were off. Somehow she got out of them and kicked them across the room even though she was cuffed.

"Her white dress was dirty from my tackling her." He looked straight into Dana's eyes. "She was almost hysterical and kept insisting I raped her."

There was a moment's silence broken only by the rush of the surf on the sand. "Oh, Rob. That's terrible. Surely they didn't believe her."

"Bruce didn't. He and I worked closely together

168

on homicide, but a lot of the other men were on loan to narcotics for the bust. They barely knew me, and Angela was a helluva actress. I told them she was stealing from Chang, but she claimed she was only in the building to go to the slip-slide party. Everyone believed that. Who would dare to cross Chang by stealing from him?''

"No one," Dana said softly. "He'd kill them."

"That shot my credibility and made them wonder if I really had raped Angela.'' Rob searched the depths of Dana's green eyes, wondering if she really believed him or if there was a shadow of a doubt in her mind. He couldn't tell; she wore that noncommittal expression that she usually had when she was on the bench.

"What happened next?" she asked.

"Internal Affairs was called in. Something as serious as this required a thorough IA investigation. I went through the entire exam: sperm sample, pubic hair samples, endless questions. It was the worst.''

"That's what women who are raped feel like. How they're treated afterward is almost as bad as the attack," Dana said. "Now you know what it feels like.''

Her tone was matter-of-fact, but she might as well have backhanded him. He thought that she'd believed him, but she wasn't any different than most of the women he'd known. Rape was a sensitive subject; once you were accused, a shadow of doubt hung over you. He reminded himself that she'd had a life-altering experience when her sister had been raped.

She didn't know him, didn't care about him. No doubt she had heard all the rumors and had her own preconceived ideas about what had happened that night. Like most women, she suspected he was guilty and had gotten away with it. Why in hell had he bothered telling her anyway?

Dana studied Rob's face. There was no mistaking the earnestness of his expression or the wounded look in his eyes. And it was her fault, she thought with disgust.

She realized she held back, not allowing herself to become involved with people and their problems. No one had ever told her anything this intimate, and she hadn't been certain how to respond. Did she have to say something so insensitive?

She realized it had been a few seconds since he'd spoken. During that time she'd been thinking. She should say something, but what? Oh, Lord, she wasn't any good in these situations.

"Rob, I believe you." Her voice could barely be heard above the surf.

He rolled onto his stomach, put his head down on the towel, and closed his eyes, shutting her out. Obviously, she hadn't been convincing. He'd told her about the most traumatic crisis in his life, and she hadn't responded properly. What was wrong with her?

Once a boyfriend had called her cold, incapable

of showing her emotions. At the time she'd denied it, claiming she had a temper, which tended to flare unexpectedly. But now she wondered if he hadn't been right. For the first time she was experiencing honest-to-God emotion—not just a twinge of feeling that vanished like a wisp of smoke, but a bone-deep appreciation of what it meant to love and be loved.

She found it hard to tell anyone she cared about them, even Vanessa. Her sister knew how she felt, didn't she? Maybe not. Perhaps she needed to be more verbal. Only with Jason was she able to cuddle and say how much she loved him. It was easy because he was a child.

She gazed down at Rob's dark head, his hair almost dry now and curled slightly at the temples. A short while ago he'd carried her out of the water. She could still feel the panic-stricken beating of her heart as she gasped for breath.

The night marchers.

She'd been so certain that she'd heard them. Even though she didn't believe in any of that pooky-pooky stuff, she'd taken it as a premonition that she was going to die. Rob changed her mind, calming her and persuading her that nothing was wrong. Her life wasn't in danger.

So why couldn't she help him? Clearly he'd taken a risk in telling her such a personal story. He had reached out to her. And she had rejected him with a thoughtless comment. She had to do something—anything—before it was too late.

She touched him, running her hand along the

solid contours of his back. "Rob, look at me . . . please."

He rolled onto his side and faced her. His eyes searched hers, seeking her soul. In his gaze she detected profound sadness. And something else. Something she intuitively recognized because she'd felt it so often. Loneliness.

"I never—not for one second—questioned your story. I know you're innocent." She let the air seep out of her lungs in a breath that verged on a sigh.

For a long moment he merely looked at her. What else could she say? Finally he spoke. "You must have heard the rumors. Don't tell me you didn't have your doubts."

"I heard lots of wild stories, but all I knew for certain was that Internal Affairs had investigated a rape charge against you. Since their findings are sealed I had no way of knowing anything else, but your leaving the force so unexpectedly didn't look good." She tried to buffer her words with a reassuring smile; his hard stare didn't waver. "Before I hired you I asked Garth Bradford. He said it was all gossip."

"Good old Garth. At least I have one friend. Make that two. Bruce Kenae stood by me the whole time."

"Make that three friends." She smiled, or tried to. The desire to touch him was swift and sharp. She stifled the soft gasp that rose in her throat and looked down at her hand. It was inches from his bare chest, but she couldn't move it.

A strange look crossed his face. "I'm not interested in being just your friend. Hell, you're smart enough to figure that out."

She honestly didn't know what to say. Some secret part of her, the side that seldom took risks, wanted to take one now. Still, the right words eluded her. How could she say she was attracted to him, yet afraid of him? She didn't have the time to analyze what frightened her exactly. He simply wasn't the type of man she usually dated.

"You're worried about your career."

"No, I'm not," she responded quite truthfully, shocked by the bitterness in his voice. "I just don't think it would work. We're too different."

"Why don't we give it a try and see what happens?"

Rob moved closer to her, his muscular thigh grazing her bare leg. Droplets of water clung to the skein of hair on his chest, and she had to force her eyes not to stray downward to the masculine ridge revealed by his swim trunks. His physical presence had its appeal, she realized, but his size and forceful personality made her wary.

"If I catch the blackmailer, know what my fee's going to be?"

Her pulse skittered alarmingly. Something was happening between them, and it frightened her because she couldn't predict—or control—the outcome. Changing the subject seemed to be the only safe course. "Aren't you going to finish your story? What happened? The sperm sample you gave cleared your name, didn't it?"

14

The question had the desired effect. Dana had never seen a man become serious quite so quickly. "No. The sperm sample I gave did not clear me. Apparently she'd had sex with several men in the previous twenty-four hours."

"That's terrible," she said, her voice barely above a whisper. "The test should have proved you innocent, but with more than one partner—"

"It was still Angela's word against mine." There was more than a trace of bitterness in his voice. "It was a slow news week. No hijackings, no sightings of aliens, no politicians caught between the sheets with some bimbo. The media played the story for all it was worth. The brass cowered, scared shitless of a lawsuit. I had to do something to help myself.

"I called the FBI training center at Quantico and spoke with the man who trains perp pros. I'd been his student, so he was glad to help me. We figured Angela Morton was a hardcase with a record— somewhere."

"That was good thinking," Dana said, imagining how desperate Rob had been.

"It worked. She'd pulled similar stunts in L.A. and Seattle, suing police departments and accusing officers of rape when they arrested her for prostitution. L.A. had settled out of court for half a mil when she sued them. That made the brass even more nervous."

And willing to sacrifice you, she added silently. "What became of the money? Angela must have needed more or she wouldn't have been trying to steal drugs from Chang."

Rob shrugged, his bronzed shoulders gleaming in the afternoon sunlight. "Who knows? She never admitted to touching the drugs."

"What happened to Angela?"

"What do you think?"

She'd been in law school at Stanford at the time, so she wasn't familiar with the case, but she could guess. "The DA dropped the charges."

"Exactly." There was no mistaking the anger in Rob's voice. "Angela took the next flight to the mainland—one step ahead of Chang—and vanished."

"You were cleared, weren't you?"

"Yeah, IA dropped the investigation." His tone told her something else was wrong. What? "I had my badge again, but things were never the same. It affected my wife, Ellen, and our son, Zach, too."

She wanted to ask more about them, but couldn't quite muster the courage.

"There was never a trial. IA investigations are confidential. Since Angela hadn't been charged with a crime, it looked mighty suspicious—for me."

"What about the papers? Didn't they run stories about Angela's past?"

"Sure." The word came out like a curse. "They ran a story about her on page thirty-seven. I'd hoped it would clear my name. Boy, was I wrong."

"What about your wife?" she couldn't help asking.

"We'd been having problems," he admitted. "Ellen accepted a guest-lecturer position at Cal Tech in Los Angeles. It was supposed to be temporary, a way to shield our son from negative publicity, but even after IA cleared me she didn't come home." Rob's tone was flat now, yet Dana sensed the hurt and anger he wasn't expressing. "Then she filed for divorce. She claimed her career would suffer if she returned."

How could she? Dana wondered. Women often put their careers first, but there was a child to consider in this situation. Then she remembered Rob accusing her of not wanting to date him because of her career. Obviously, he'd been thinking of his wife's betrayal.

She was uncomfortably aware of another awkward silence. She managed to ask, "What about Zach?"

Rob's brows drew together and he studied the pattern on the beach towel for a moment before saying, "I asked for custody. I even tried to persuade the judge to keep Ellen in Hawaii. She had a good job here. We could have shared custody. The judge saw it as a career opportunity though. He granted Ellen custody and allowed her to move to California.''

Once again Dana didn't know what to say. She could understand the judge's decision. Most often custody was given to the mother, but she felt Rob truly loved his son and Zach would have been better off with Rob.

"Do you see Zach often?" she asked.

"No. I hardly know my boy. I would have moved there to be with him, but Ellen kept promising to come back here. I had my new business already established when I realized that she never intended to return.''

"Don't you go there to visit him?"

"Yes, but even then Ellen does her best to keep us apart.'' The anger in his voice was barely disguised now.

Dana didn't want to ask anything more about his personal life, realizing it was a wound that had never really healed and there was nothing she could do about it. Again she wished she were the compassionate type of woman who would have soothing words for moments like this.

"After the IA investigation I went into a tailspin," Rob admitted. "I kept asking myself why in hell I was bustin' my butt for a job when everyone kept acting as if I had some contagious disease.''

"You mean the other officers believed Angela?"

"Yeah, some of them did. It was the classic fall from grace. One minute I was the department's golden boy, the next I was shit." He shrugged as if to suggest he didn't care, but she could tell it still bothered him.

She shuddered inwardly, ashamed of herself. Innocent until proven guilty. She was a judge, someone who was supposed to live by that rule. But she hadn't. She'd been guilty of letting rumors and innuendos play on her own fears. She *had* believed there was truth in the gossip.

What kind of person was she? All week Rob Tagett had forced her to look in the mirror, and the more she looked, the less she liked what she saw. Was she uptight and cold—a person who judged others on the basis of gossip not facts?

"Don't feel sorry for me," Rob broke into her thoughts. "I came out okay. I parlayed my experience on the force into a security company that's a cash cow. I have a home on the beach, which I'd never have been able to afford on a policeman's salary."

His voice drifted lower. "The only loss is my son. Being a father is a lot more than biology. It's having a relationship. I miss Zach more as time goes on, not less."

She studied Rob as he finished telling her about losing his son. Obviously he loved the boy and that touched the deepest reaches of her heart. And it ran counter to her preconceived notions about him. There was such a charge of emotion every time he said Zach's name that she wanted to reach out and hug him.

"Not that I want to change the subject from anything so fascinating as my life, but our friends in the blue Toyota are back."

Dana resisted the urge to look up at the top of the bluff. She moved closer to Rob, feeling inadequate but needing to reassure him. "I want you to know that I do believe you. I'm sorry about what happened. I don't know how your wife could desert you. Loving someone means believing in them, trusting them."

"Ellen thought a scandal would reflect on her and spoil her chances for a promotion. It was easier to hightail it to L.A. than to stand by me."

"I would never have left you, no matter what the consequences." Dana sat up straighter, amazed and very shaken. Where had those words come from? How could she have said anything so personal?

Suddenly Rob smiled, an arresting smile of approval, telling her that—for once—she'd said the right thing. She mustered a tentative smile. Their gazes locked and they kept looking at each other until she smiled in earnest.

"You like me, Dana. Admit it." She had no intention of admitting anything, but she couldn't look away from him. He leaned closer, bending toward her mouth. "Admit it," he repeated, his voice husky and low.

"All right," she responded, amazed at the breathless quality of her voice. "I like you better—now that I've gotten to know you—than I ever thought I would."

Rob chuckled, a rich, masculine sound that vibrated deep in his chest. A warm glow suddenly flared into something more. His mouth, so close to hers seemed very tempting. She had no intention of parting her lips, but she did.

He made no move to kiss her. Instead, he cupped her face with his large hand, cradling it in his palm and stroking her lower lip with the pad of his thumb. A languorous weakness flowed through her body like the lulling sound of the surf rushing softly across the sand.

She should have moved away, but she didn't. She should have reminded him of the blue car on the bluff, but she didn't. She should have done something—anything—to break the spell, but she didn't.

They were shadowed by the umbrella, she assured herself. The men up there couldn't see anything except their legs. Still, they were on a public beach. He wasn't doing anything—exactly—but the rough pad of his thumb stroking her lip seemed unbelievably intimate.

He slid his hand across her cheek and into her hair. His fingers threaded through the damp tresses, the fingertips stroking her scalp. It was just a massage, she told herself, yet it seemed to be so much more than that.

This had to be some kind of sophisticated foreplay. He was seducing her, plain and simple, with the slow, hypnotic movement of his fingers.

The small sound that escaped her parted lips wasn't a moan, was it?

"I'm the one, baby," he whispered. "The one for you—and don't forget it."

She should have argued, but she couldn't. It was all she could do not to demand that he stop teasing her with his talented hands and kiss her. Really kiss her.

He seemed to sense that the fight had gone out of her. He caught her hair in his fist and gently drew her head back as he lowered her to the towel. His lips brushed the rim of her ear as he spoke, sending a rush of warm air with each word. "I'm the one. The only one."

He could make a woman—even the sanest woman—do anything, she thought, slow heat unfurling in her belly. She waited, anticipation welling inside her, anxious to see what he'd do next.

He kissed her ear, his agile tongue flicking across the sensitive skin in a light caress that was as soft as a butterfly's wing. And more arousing than any X-rated movie could ever be. Push him away, her mind ordered, but her body couldn't resist temptation.

With his free hand he pulled her closer until she was flush against the hard, strong length of him. Then he moved his head lower, kissing the curve of her neck while he held her head back to expose her neck and shoulders.

His lips left a moist trail of kisses down her neck to the sensitive base of her throat. This time a real moan did escape her lips. Oh, Lordy, why couldn't she tell him to stop?

Even when he nudged her legs apart, gently inserting his powerful knee between her thighs, she didn't say anything. How could she? His lips on her neck had her mesmerized, and his strong thigh, slightly rough with hair, was so arousing against her bare skin that she didn't dare speak. If she did, she might beg him to take her right here on the beach.

Suddenly his lips were exploring her breast, his hand cupping its fullness. Her conservative suit covered her, of course, but she might as well have been naked. He coaxed the soft peak into rigid proof of the effect he had on her. Painful currents of arousal rushed through her, and the surf seemed to be pounding in her temples, beating an erotic tattoo.

She arched upward as he pulled her taut nipple into his mouth, teasing it mercilessly through the sheer fabric. Somehow her hands were in his hair now, holding his head in place, encouraging him shamelessly.

She couldn't tell how long they lay there, half-hidden by the umbrella. In the distance the waves breaking on the beach seemed to be accompanied by the shrill cry of squabbling gulls. Rob raised his head and gazed into her eyes, his own eyes shadowed by thick, black lashes.

"I'm the one," he said yet again, his voice raw, a reflection of his desire.

He kissed her, his tongue dancing with hers, a

wild, uninhibited tango that encouraged her to move against him to relieve the sweet ache in her breasts. He kissed her with all the passion he'd shown the other times he'd kissed her, and yet there was a tenderness in this kiss, a gentleness in the way he held her that hadn't been there before.

The shrill cry of the gulls became a crescendo. Rob lifted his lips from hers. It wasn't gulls that she'd been hearing. A gaggle of kids streamed down the trail, followed by their mothers toting sand toys and coolers.

"There goes the neighborhood," Rob said with a laugh.

He positioned the umbrella so they were concealed from view. Then he looked at her, scanning the length of her body and stopping at her breasts. Beneath the damp fabric her nipples were peaked and her chest rose and fell rapidly. His gaze traveled slowly upward, but got only as far as her lips.

Like liquid heat, his body spread over hers, his strong knee grazing the sensitive skin of her inner thighs as he moved it upward until it could go no farther. Passion smoldered in his eyes. "See? What did I tell you? I'm the one."

His lips covered hers before she could respond, and his tongue invaded her mouth with trusting pressure as if he couldn't get enough of her while his knee rubbed against her with shocking intimacy.

When he finally raised his head there was more than a hint of triumph in his eyes. "Sorry we can't continue this. We don't want to give the kiddies a show, do we?"

Dana finger-combed her tousled hair, a little self-conscious about what had happened. Why, there were people nearby and Big Daddy's spies on the bluff. No doubt they'd loved every second even if they couldn't see much.

"Let's get out of here." She rose to her feet, not daring to look directly at Rob. What had he been trying to prove? He'd confided in her as if she really meant something to him, but now he seemed totally nonchalant, gathering up their things without a word about what had happened.

What did he really want from her? He must have some reason. Men didn't bare their souls without a motive, did they? Of course not. A woman would be a fool to place too much faith in a man, particularly one who so skillfully manipulated women.

Keep your mind on the blackmailer, she reminded herself as she followed Rob up the serpentine trail toward the top of the bluff. Suddenly there was a thumping in her ears. It was the heat, wasn't it? Boy, was she ever becoming superstitious. If she didn't know better, she'd swear she was hearing the night marchers.

15

Garth Bradford wheeled himself into his office, stopping just inside the door to let the welcome blast of air conditioning cool him. He loosened his tie and shed his jacket, then unbuttoned the top three buttons of what had once been an immaculately starched and pressed white shirt.

"I guess I chose the wrong profession," he joked as his secretary watched. Willa had been with him for years; she knew better than to try to help him. "The only place in the islands where men wear suits is in court—or in a coffin."

Willa laughed dutifully, the way she always did when he came back from court, hot and irritable. Today he'd successfully argued a motion to dismiss a case; he should be happy, but he wasn't. What was wrong with him? He'd begun to suspect that winning wasn't enough. Yet it had to be. What else was there?

Cooler now, he wheeled into his spacious office and transferred to his custom-made chair. He gazed out the high rise's window at Waikiki's sun-splashed surf with its endless parade of tubular waves that tumbled across the bay. Yellow catamarans and orange outrigger canoes glided across the water, competing for waves with sun-bronzed surfers and sunburned tourists on paddle-wheelers. Windsurfers darted between them like colorful butterflies.

A happy sight, he thought, deliberately not looking at the other view his prestigious corner office offered. If he glanced in the other direction he'd see Pearl Harbor and in the distance the U.S. *Arizona*, which would depress him even more. A monument to men for whom history had ended as they were making it.

Willa walked in, a discouraging stack of affidavits in one hand and a fistful of messages in the other. "Do you know a Vanessa Coltrane? She isn't one of *the* Coltranes, is she? Probably not." As usual Willa chatted on, answering her own questions. "Anyone that rich wouldn't be using a pay phone."

Was Vanessa calling to tell him Dana was in trouble? Garth wondered. Considering what he was paying Rob for this investigation, he should at least have gotten more than one sketchy report, but he hadn't. He wasn't certain how long he stared at the turquoise water, which beckoned him even though he hadn't been able to go to the beach in years. Willa had to buzz twice to get his attention.

"It's that Coltrane woman again," Willa told him, and he picked up the phone.

"This is Garth Bradford." Suddenly he sounded uncharacteristically formal.

"Thanks for taking my call." The voice was low-pitched with that sultry quality he remembered from last night's conversation.

"Is everything all right with Dana? How'd she take the news?"

"I told Rob and he broke it to her. I guess she's fine. They went off to the beach this morning."

So why are you calling me, Garth wondered, once again imagining the Dana look-alike with long, dark hair as free-flowing as waves on the sea. And long, sexy nails. He didn't know where the image of nails came from, but in his mind's eye he saw Vanessa's soft hands with long, tapering nails polished a dusky pink.

"I'm calling from a phone booth in Makawao. Just a minute while I put some money in, so we won't be interrupted."

Garth waited, his interest piqued as he pictured the small town. As a kid he'd loved to go to their annual rodeo. Makawao had been built in the early part of the last century. It looked like a western town with its blacksmith shop, general store, and hitching posts for the *paniolos*. The cowboys often rode in from the neighboring ranches. He couldn't visit anymore because his wheelchair refused to navigate the rough-hewn plank sidewalks.

Makawao had lots of upscale boutiques, where artists who favored the secluded up-country sold their work. He tried to imagine Vanessa outside a trendy boutique housed in an old livery stable, plinking quarters into one of the wooden phone booths that looked as if Wyatt Earp had just used it.

Willa was right: Anyone as rich as Vanessa Coltrane shouldn't be using a pay phone. Obviously Vanessa didn't want her call to be overheard, or she might not want someone to see his number on the monthly statement.

"I talked to Rob about you last night," Vanessa announced when she came back on the line. "He said you were the best attorney in the islands."

"Really?" Garth didn't know what else to say. He'd never been comfortable with compliments, and when one came from a beautiful woman he was even less comfortable.

"I'd like you to take my case."

He hesitated, wondering if she and Dana were involved in the same problem. Why hadn't Rob told him more? "Tell me about it."

"I'm married to Eric Coltrane. I guess you know the Coltranes," she said, an edge of bitterness in her voice.

Who didn't know the Coltranes? They were famous for their money and their arrogance. Garth had met Thornton Coltrane at several political functions. He called himself Big Daddy and acted like a pompous jerk.

"I want to divorce Eric. Could you help me? I know that's not your field, but this . . . this"—her voice broke—"isn't going to be easy. Big Daddy will get the best lawyer money can buy. He's determined to take my son away from me."

Garth hesitated; the anguished way she'd said "my son" tugged at his heartstrings. He imagined her in a hot phone booth, tears in her eyes and light dancing over the shadows of her dark hair. Common sense said to refuse, but he couldn't.

"I'll take your case," he said, careful to keep his tone professional. *Never become emotionally involved*; it was the cardinal rule for any lawyer. "Have you already left your husband?"

"No. If the Coltranes knew I was leaving they'd never let me take Jason. In two days Big Daddy will have almost a hundred people at the ranch for his birthday *luau*. I'm leaving then with Dana. There'll be so much going on, no one will miss us. Jason and I will live with Dana."

"I don't think that's a good idea. That's exactly where they'll look for you."

"You're right," she admitted, a definite quaver in her voice. "I don't have anywhere else to go."

"Let me think about it. I'll come up with someplace for you two," he said, although he had absolutely no idea where that might be.

The smell of smoldering banana leaves that had been dried for months in the sun filled the warm evening air, which for once didn't have nature's blessing—cooling trade winds. The up-country was usually cooler than the touristy beach area, but not now. Tonight there was a hot, restless, seething feeling in the tropical air.

Or maybe it was just her imagination.

Dana stood at the edge of the party, gazing across the paddock area to the *imu*. The underground pit had been dug and lined with dried banana leaves. In the Hawaiian tradition a *kalua* pig was being slow-roasted, while the *paniolos* were tending a spit where a steer was being cooked. It would be another two days before the feast was ready and all the guests had arrived for the luau.

Dana couldn't imagine any more people at the ranch. Already the helipad was surrounded by helicopters, lined up like bees around a hive. Many wealthy Hawaiians owned jet helicopters. It was by far the easiest and fastest way to travel between islands and land in even the remotest of spots like the ranch. Big Daddy owned a sleek Bell Ranger that was as fast as many jets, but Dana wasn't impressed.

Nor was she awed by Coltrane's rich friends, who were gathered tonight outside the main barn for a western party. Dressed in their Saturday night best with polished cowboy boots and fresh leis on the crowns of their hats, *paniolos* sat on bales of hay playing traditional Hawaiian tunes on slack-key guitars and ukuleles.

Dana wandered toward the stables where Big Daddy kept his Arabian horses. Without the trades blowing to muffle the sound, she could hear the lowing of cattle. The nearest range was a great distance from the house and the barn area was concealed by tall trees. Unless you came down to the paddocks, Kau Ranch seemed more like a resort than a working cattle ranch.

"Hey, babe. Where ya goin'?"

Dana turned and managed to smile at Rob. The last time she'd seen him he'd been chatting with her sister. It was almost as if she'd imagined what had happened between them on the beach. Maybe that was for the best. She certainly didn't know what to say.

They walked into the stables, the scent of horses and fresh hay eclipsing the smell of smoke. Like everything else on the ranch, the stables were a showplace. Every bit of tack was in place, bits shined, leather gleaming. Even the horses were brushed to a glossy finish as if they might step into a show ring at any moment.

"Let's see what's out back," Rob said, and she knew he wanted to have a private conversation.

"Do you think the stable's bugged?" she asked when they were outside.

Rob leaned against the rail of the training ring. "Around here you never know." He flashed her his bad-boy grin; she told herself she was immune, but it wasn't true. "I've reconnoitered and come up with a plan."

She folded her arms and stared down at her new cowboy boots. He was going to do it; he really was going to break into Big Daddy's suite.

"After dinner there'll be Western dancing," Rob

said with a smile. "That should be a hoot for the mainlanders who think all Hawaiians do is the hula."

"Big Daddy isn't very creative. Every year he has a Western night à la Hawaii so they can see what the up-country is all about. Tomorrow night will be the hula show, complete with Fijian fire eaters. The next night at his luau he'll have a big-name band from the mainland."

"Well, tonight they're serving *okolehao* during the dancing. I figure everyone will be in the bag after one drink."

"You're right." The home-brew made from the potent roots of the ti plant was the same drink they served at Coconut Willie's as Sex on the Beach. Rob could handle it, but she wasn't touching the stuff.

Rob gazed thoughtfully across the empty ring. He was wearing a black polo shirt and Nikes because she'd forgotten to tell him that there would be a party with a Western theme. No matter what he stood out from the crowd, but tonight even more so because everyone else was in Western attire, wearing outfits that cost more than any *paniolo* made in a lifetime of riding the range.

"Have you noticed the security men?" he asked.

Dana shook her head. She'd been too busy brooding about Rob; she hadn't paid much attention to the guests.

"They're the guys that are standing around—drinks in their hands—but they aren't drinking. They're watching everyone."

"I could ask Vanessa about them. She might know."

"I asked her if she knew a couple of the guys, and she didn't. She hasn't a clue that they're security men."

Dana had barely spoken to her sister today. Vanessa had returned from Makawao with lots of shopping bags. She'd waved, but hadn't stopped to talk. Tonight she'd arrived late to the party and went right to Rob's side.

Don't be jealous, Dana chided herself. After listening to Rob's story this afternoon, her feelings about him had changed. She . . . well, she wasn't sure exactly how she felt, but she didn't want to compete with her sister. A man could never come between them. They'd been through too much together. And now they were being threatened again. This was not the time to allow herself to become jealous.

"Here's the plan," Rob said. "When the dancing starts we'll join in, but we'll stare into each other's eyes like teenagers with rampaging hormones. No one will be surprised when we leave together. They'll figure we're going to hop in the sack."

A scuffling noise distracted them; it was a *paniolo* coming out of the bunkhouse. Rob waited until the cowboy had passed before speaking.

"I'll sneak up to Big Daddy's and see what's there. You watch and see when he leaves the party. I'm betting he stays to the very end. Isn't that what a good host does?"

"I guess," she mumbled. Really, she couldn't

imagine herself doing this. "You're going to give me a walkie-talkie so I can warn you when he's coming?"

"Right. I've got the state-of-the-art devices. I just bought them for my security company. They're the size of a pack of cards. That way you can slip it in your pocket if anyone comes along."

"If someone sees me, how'll I explain not being with you?"

"Tell them we had a fight."

He had an answer for everything, Dana decided but somehow she knew it wasn't going to be so easy, not with all those security men snooping around.

"Keep Big Daddy in your sight all the time. I figure he'll leave with Minerva and spend a little time in her bungalow. He certainly can't take her up to his suite if he's got all that electronic equipment up there." Rob looked over his shoulder toward the dance area. "Just be certain you warn me when he's coming."

Dana swallowed hard, praying nothing went wrong. Big Daddy's suite occupied the entire second floor of the west wing of the house, but there was only one way in. She would have to warn Rob in plenty of time if he was going to get away without being seen.

Rob tried his damnedest to two-step, but he kept landing on Dana's toes. The caller was attempting to teach the greenhorns from the mainland Western dancing Hawaiian style. Rob had shuffled his way through the Boot-Scooting Boogie and Slapping Leather with about as much grace as a hog on ice.

"Okay, partners," yelled the caller. "Ready to try the Tush Push?"

Rob pulled Dana closer, his nose brushing her fragrant hair. He'd had his hands on her all evening. He hadn't been crude, but he'd certainly given everyone the message. They were lovers.

"That's it," he said with a laugh. "We're outta here. Forget the Tush Push. I'm not bumping butts with a bunch of people I don't know."

Dana barely smiled. What was wrong with her? he wondered. She'd been strange since they'd left the beach. Just when he thought he'd forged something meaningful, she froze up.

Women. Go figure. Obviously, he was a big zilch in the relationship department. His experience with Ellen proved that. Dana, though, liked him—no matter how she acted. He'd tried not to come on too strong, reminding himself that she needed a sensitive man, but it was damn hard. He was the kind of guy that went after what he wanted. And he wanted Dana.

Good thing he hadn't told her everything. He'd told her just enough about the events following that fateful night to begin a relationship. She didn't need to know all his secrets—until he could really trust her. Trust? It was as foreign to him as life on Mars. Yet he knew at some point he was going to have to take a chance. And pray that history didn't repeat itself.

He kept his arm draped around Dana's shoulders as they made their way off the dance floor. The entire party had been held outside under a canopy of black sky dominated by a silvery lovers' moon. The trades had finally kicked in, making it cooler than when the party had begun and blowing the haunting scent of tropical flowers into the night air.

"Everyone seems to be having fun," Dana observed. "Hardly anyone's left."

Except Vanessa. She'd left—alone—a half hour ago. Rob didn't mention this to Dana. He wasn't certain what was going on between the sisters, but he was going to have to do something about Vanessa. He didn't appreciate her smile. He'd seen it on too many women's faces. It said "yes" before he'd even asked the question.

They walked silently toward the grove of kiawe trees that screened the family compound from the working part of the ranch. He took her hand, lacing their fingers together and giving her a reassuring squeeze. She didn't squeeze back, but she didn't pull away either.

"This is where I hid the walkie-talkies." Rob brushed aside the fronds of the fiddlehead fern and pulled out the plastic bag. He handed Dana hers. "You're clear on how to use it?"

She nodded, her beautiful face solemn in the bright moonlight. "Press the button to talk. Release to listen."

"You're not worried, are you?" Stupid question.

He could see that she was. "This is a no-brainer. If anything unexpected happens, just use your head."

"I'm worried that Big Daddy will catch you."

"What can he do? Kill me?" He chuckled, but he could see that she'd lost her sense of humor. "If you stay in the shadow of that banyan tree over by the corral, you'll see Big Daddy when he leaves. Follow him—at a distance—and warn me. Give me enough time to get out of there."

"I will," she promised, and he turned to go. She caught his arm, then brushed a quick kiss across his cheek. "Good luck."

Rob grinned as he sprinted up the gentle slope to the main house. Damn all, she was coming 'round. Slowly, to be sure, but Dana did care about him. He couldn't remember when he last felt this good about life. About himself.

Having just one entrance to the upper-level suite that Big Daddy occupied made him nervous. He wanted another way out—in case. What he'd do if he were cornered was a crapshoot at best. The tree ferns that brushed the second floor weren't sturdy enough to climb down. A smart guy always had a backup plan.

Ten minutes later he was winded but he was in Big Daddy's suite. The plantation shutters were closed. After the brilliant moonlight the room seemed unusually dark, except for the strange pinpricks of light. Rob pulled the walkie-talkie from his hip pocket.

"Ribbit," he croaked, hoping he sounded like one

of the multitude of up-country bullfrogs that inhabited the koi ponds. The code word was supposed to let Dana know he was inside, without alerting Big Daddy through one of his bugs.

"Ribbit," came her soft reply.

Okay, she was in place and Big Daddy hadn't moved. Time to go to work. He jammed the walkie-talkie into his pocket and yanked out his high beam flashlight. He flicked it on.

"Holy shit. You've got to be kidding."

16

Dana answered Rob's "ribbit" with a sigh of relief. He was inside the suite and Big Daddy was still at the party, dancing with Minerva. Glancing down at the luminous dial of her watch, Dana prayed their luck would hold. It shouldn't take Rob more than a few minutes, should it?

A skein of clouds swept across the moon, and she took advantage of the dimmer light to move away from the tree trunk. Rob had been clever in selecting the banyan tree as a lookout point. The tree was hundreds of years old, with a trunk as big as a giant redwood and exposed roots that spread out like tentacles. An octopus on tiptoes, she'd once told Jason when describing the tree. Some of the roots came up to her knees, while garlands of moss hung from the branches. Anyone looking this way probably wouldn't notice her. Still, she was jumpy, on edge in a way that she'd never been until now.

The music stopped and the caller announced a short break. Couples began to drift away from the dance area, heading for the guest cottages. A rain-scented wind whistled through the tree, fluttering the trailers of moss, heralding a shower.

"Please don't let it rain," she prayed in a whisper. It would be nothing more than a tropical shower—over in minutes—but it would end the party. In answer to her prayer, a strobe of moonlight hit the ground and seconds later the moon broke free.

She checked her watch and saw that Rob had been in Big Daddy's suite for less than five minutes. It seemed like two lifetimes. She waited, the walkie-talkie pressed to her ear, so she wouldn't miss the double *ribbit* that would signal Rob was out. What was keeping him?

"Oh, my God," she said out loud. Big Daddy was walking away from the party, his arm around Minerva.

Dana stifled a gasp of alarm. Be calm. At the very least Big Daddy would walk Minerva to her bungalow at the far end of the complex. That should give Rob plenty of time to complete the search and escape.

Dana edged out of the sheltering shadows of the banyan and followed them. When she reached the kiawe trees that screened the bunkhouse and corrals from the house, she paused, again thankful for the concealing shadows and the moon playing tag with the clouds.

Looking over her shoulder, she checked to see if any of the security men that Rob had pointed out were following her. The only people behind her

were a couple who'd imbibed too much *okolehao*.
They were weaving and singing an off-key rendition
of "Home on the Range."

Why did she have to wear an outfit without a
pocket? She wedged the small walkie-talkie into her
bra as best she could, deciding she didn't want to
meet anyone and have them ask what she had in her
hand. The cowboy boots she'd thought looked so
cute with her denim skirt magnified every footstep
as she walked along the crushed-lava path. Ahead,
Big Daddy and Minerva turned right instead of left.

"Where are they going?" Dana muttered to herself. "That isn't the way to Minerva's bungalow."
Should she *ribbit* three times, the signal to Rob that
he had to get out immediately?

"Not yet," answered the logical side of her brain,
the one that remained calm even when she was on
the verge of trembling. It didn't appear that they
were going to Big Daddy's, and they weren't going
to Minerva's either.

She hung back, conscious of how much better lit
this area was. Now the moon was beaming, working
against her, as was the "nightscaping," installed to
showcase the fabulous yard. The low-voltage lighting illuminated craggy red lava rocks surrounded
by lacy ferns and clusters of vibrant orchids.

Spotlights washed the branches of the trees, creating artful pools of light and shadow. Small tulip
lights that were hardly noticeable during the day
craned their necks downward, lighting the serpen-

tine path through the gardens to the guest cottages. The lagoon and stream were well lit too.

Rob had planned so carefully, anticipated so much, but he hadn't thought about the light. Or he simply hadn't warned her. There wasn't anyplace for her to hide. How was she supposed to keep an eye on Big Daddy if he went in somewhere? He and Minerva were out of sight now. She had no choice but to follow or lose track of him and jeopardize Rob.

"What's taking you so long?" she whispered downward as if Rob could hear her through the transmitter barely stuffed into her bra. Of course, he couldn't. She'd have to depress the button to send a message, but somehow talking to herself made her feel better.

She rounded the corner and spotted Big Daddy's white hair. It suddenly dawned on her where they were going. She didn't know whether to laugh or cry. He was taking Minerva into the grotto. He *had* been monitoring their conversations and thought the grotto was the perfect spot for kinky sex.

"Rob will howl, simply howl, when he hears this," she told herself.

Coltrane disappeared into the jungle of ferns with the wealthy widow. Dana quickly scanned the area and decided she should sit on a chaise by the pool where she could still see the entrance to the grotto. If anyone approached she could pretend to have passed out from too much *okolehao.*

"That won't work." Now she was talking out

loud. Get a grip! Just because there were three nude women with one buck-naked man in the spa, didn't mean they knew what she was doing. Quite the opposite. They were swilling *Okolehao*, too inebriated to even notice her.

Dana changed directions and ambled along the lava rock path. Keep moving, but keep the grotto in sight. She wandered along—deliberately unsteady on her feet as if she, too, had imbibed too much—and checked her watch. Now Rob had been in there almost eight minutes. Had someone caught him and he hadn't been able to signal her?

She meandered down by the cabanas and slowly turned, hearing a volley of laughter and a series of cannonball splashes. It didn't take much imagination to know the spa had become too hot and the nude group had jumped in the pool.

Without warning, the ferns at the entrance to the grotto parted and Minerva Mallory's red head emerged. Dana halted, hoping the shadows concealed her. Big Daddy followed Minerva. They never looked in her direction. Instead, they walked down the path toward Minerva's bungalow.

"That was a quickie," Dana wanted to yell and insult Big Daddy. What kind of a lover was he? Well, maybe the noise from the pool discouraged them. With luck they'd try again and give Rob a little more time. Surely, he had to be finishing up by now.

Naturally her luck had run out. Big Daddy walked Minerva to her door, but didn't go in. He turned quickly and headed back up the trail toward Dana.

She ducked into the shadows off the path and took the shortcut to the koi lagoon, where she'd be far enough away from Big Daddy to pull out the walkie-talkie.

"Don't panic," she warned herself in a tight-lipped whisper. "You have plenty of time." Before the thought could calm her, she tripped on a piece of lava rock that was hidden by creeping vines. She pitched forward, arms flailing, and stumbled into the stream that fed the koi lagoon.

Squish! Something spongy gave beneath her boot. Oh, Lordy, had she stepped on a koi fish? Some of them were more than one hundred years old and were the most expensive fish on the planet.

She glanced down and saw the cold water rushing over the tops of the boots she couldn't afford, but had bought anyway. She pulled up her skirt, its hem soaked, and lifted her foot. "How stupid," she said reflexively, then cursed herself. What if one of the security men heard her?

Luckily, she hadn't killed a fish. She'd merely stepped on a clump of moss. Warn Rob, she thought as she reached for the walkie-talkie that was still hidden in her bra.

"What are you doing?"

She jumped, floundering in the stream, almost falling again and splashing more water—if possible —into her boots. The voice had to belong to one of the security men. She turned, beaming a megawatt smile at him and crossing her eyes. *Please, let him think I'm dead drunk.*

"I'm watching the koi sleep." She did her best to slur her words.

He eyed her suspiciously. Maybe he wasn't buying this. But why else would she be up to her knees in water at this ungodly hour?

"Look," she said, bending over, desperate to convince him. Time was running out. She had to alert Rob. "See that two-hundred-year-old koi napping?"

She leaned closer, her back to him, and the walkie-talkie popped out of her bra. Without so much as a splash, it slid into the water. "You blew it. You jerk."

Straightening, she let out a curse. If Rob hadn't already been caught, he'd be discovered now, and it was all her fault.

The security man's hand latched over her arm, and he pulled her out of the creek. "I think I'd better get you to your room, miss. I'll take you there."

"I'm fine," she said, choking back her panic.

Before he could argue, she sprinted down the path and ducked into the bushes. Knowing the terrain well was one advantage of visiting so often. Now, if she could skirt the lagoon, she had a fighting chance of beating Big Daddy back to his suite. What she'd do when she got there, she wasn't certain. Still running, the water sloshing over the tops of her boots, she rounded the corner, crossed the main terrace, and dashed toward the west end of the house. Too late. Ahead was Coltrane, and he was almost to the entrance.

"Big Daddy," she screamed, certain she could be

heard in Honolulu and praying she'd alerted Rob. "I need to talk to you."

He was halfway up the stairs to his suite. "Now?"

"It's about Vanessa," she said loudly.

His black eyes tracked her like a shark stalking a dolphin. Oh, God, could she pull this off? He motioned for her to follow him, and she flew up the stairs, water slogging in her boots, mustering her courage. He unlocked the door with a security-card key. How had Rob gotten in? she wondered.

More important, how was he going to get out? He had to have heard her scream at Big Daddy, but he certainly hadn't come out the front door. He could jump out a window, she supposed. From the second story? That wasn't an encouraging thought.

"Come in," he said.

"I can't." She pointed to the water oozing from her boots. "I'll ruin everything."

"What happened?"

"I was watching the koi sleep."

That got him. Now he was looking at her as if she'd lost every marble she ever possessed. And then some. She crossed her eyes again, thankful for her ruined boots and wet skirt. Surely he believed she was drunk.

"When I was watching the koi sleeping, I heard the frogs. Ribbit! Ribbit! Ribbit!" She was shouting their signal just in case Rob hadn't heard her before. "Did you know frogs go ribbit, ribbit, ribbit?"

"What does this have to do with Vanessa?" Even

with crossed eyes she could see he was angry. His stare could freeze lava.

"Ooooh. You got something on your jeans," she replied, stalling.

He brushed off a piece of moss that he'd picked up in the grotto. "We'll discuss this in the morning."

"It'll just take a sec. That ribbit, ribbit, ribbit gave me an idea." She was shooting from the hip, making it up as she went. "Vanessa loves kids, right? Right. She should open a children's boutique and call it Toad in the Hole."

"I thought my bullfrogs gave you the idea."

"They did." She uncrossed her eyes; the world was beginning to swim and her tummy along with it. "But Toad in the Hole is so much cuter. So what do you think?"

"You had too much *okolehao*. We'll talk tomorrow." Before she could fire another lame idea at him, he closed the door.

She stood there a moment, eyes squeezed shut, and expelled a long breath to quell the flutter of nerves in her chest. Had Rob escaped? She raced down the steps, water squeaking in her boots, and around to the back of the west wing. It was darker back here—no need to waste money on nightscaping—but Rob wasn't there.

At least Rob hadn't broken his leg jumping out the window from the second story, or he'd be on the ground. He must have gone back to the bungalow. She just hadn't heard the signal because she'd lost the radio.

She returned to Makai House and saw it was dark. Where was Rob? She stopped on the terrace and yanked off her boots. Water gushed out, a symbol of all that had gone wrong.

She quickly changed clothes, putting on shorts and a T-shirt. Reaching for her sandals, she changed her mind. She was much more surefooted in her Nikes. Rob was out there somewhere, and she had to find him.

It was almost two now, and the timer had turned off the nightscaping. It was eerily quiet; the nude bathers cavorting in the pool had left. No one was around, not even the security men.

She stood in the moonlight, fighting the tight knot of fear that had been in her chest all night and had now become a block of lead. *Stay calm. Think.* Where could Rob be? The security men must have nabbed him. That's why none of them were patrolling the grounds. Where would their command center be? Somewhere near the stables, she decided, where they wouldn't be obvious to the guests.

She blessed her tennis shoes and the lovers' moon as she wended her way through the glade of trees. There was only one light visible, in one of the buildings at the far side of the paddocks. Edging her way along, she stayed in the shadows.

A pool of light spilled from the window, and she could hear raucous voices as she drew near. She ventured a little closer, determined to peek in and see if they had Rob. A rivulet of cold sweat coursed down between her shoulder blades.

"Hold 'em," came a masculine voice from inside the building.

She eased closer, one step at a time, and peered into the room. Cards? Yes. They were playing poker.

Where was Rob? She ducked back before someone spotted her and mentally calculated what she'd seen. This was a one-room bunkhouse lined with bunks. The security men were gathered at a table in the center.

"Yessiree," gloated one of them so loudly that she could hear, "you've got to know when to hold 'em and when to fold 'em. I win again."

Rob wasn't here. They'd never caught him. She almost sighed with pure relief, but another—more devastating—thought hit her. Could it be that Big Daddy's suite was booby-trapped? Was Rob still up there?

She needed help. She had no alternative but to awaken Vanessa, get her outside beyond the range of the bugs, and tell her everything. Then together they'd go up to Big Daddy's suite and demand to see Rob.

"It's a good thing Eric spends the night in town with his mistress," Dana whispered to herself. "At least we won't have to contend with him."

Approaching the house along the side where she knew Vanessa's room was, Dana heard voices and saw shadowy forms on the terrace outside her sister's room. She hung back, concealed by a trailing bougainvillea, and looked more closely.

The moon revealed her sister—dressed in a night-

gown that was nothing more than a whisper of silk
—and Rob. They were standing close, Vanessa's
hand on his arm, her head inclined slightly toward
him in that provocative stance she'd mastered while
most girls were in training bras. A treacherous lump
formed in Dana's throat and with it came a wellspring of anger, an emotion so all-powerful that it
staggered her. And confused her. Who was she angry with? Rob, for making her worry more than
she'd ever worried about a man in her entire life, or
her own sister?

You can bet I'll never worry like that again about
a man, she decided, battling to control her fury.
While she'd been searching for him, Rob had been
with Vanessa. What they'd shared on the beach
slipped away like a half-remembered dream.

To hell with him.

But what about Vanessa? You expected men to betray you, but not your own sister.

17

Rob looked down at Vanessa. "We've got to hurry. There's not much time."

She tugged on his arm, trying to draw him back into the house. Okay, he'd asked for it by knocking on her window so late at night. Now he'd have to set her straight. And then get the hell out of here while they still had a chance to escape.

"Don't you realize I'm crazy about Dana?" He took her hand off his arm.

The moonlight played across Vanessa's face, highlighting her smug expression. "If you're so crazy about her why are you here?"

"I'm your friend and I—"

"Oh, really?" She cut him off before he could explain why he'd come.

Her assumption that she could have any man she wanted irritated him, but he held his temper, reminding himself that this was Dana's sister. And that they needed to get away from Kau Ranch quickly. "Let's be friends for Dana's sake."

"Friends?" she parroted as if it were some foreign word.

"Yes. I think—" The sheer hatred he saw blazing in her eyes cut him off. Then the truth blindsided him, leaving him speechless for a moment, making him forget why he'd come. "You despise men, don't you?"

"Men take advantage of you—if you let them." The bitterness in her voice stunned him. Her beauty concealed a deeply troubled, unhappy person. "I love my sister. I'm not letting you hurt her."

"Great! So you want to hurt her yourself by coming on to her boyfriend?"

Vanessa shrugged. "She'll get over it."

"Aw, come on. She's old enough to take care of herself."

"With most men, but not with a man like you."

"Like me?" Out of the corner of his eye he picked up a movement in the shadows. He kept his eyes on Vanessa, but remained aware of the shadow.

"I know your reputation. You were driven off the force for raping a woman. They let you get away with it." Vanessa shook her head, her expression one of complete revulsion.

He had never—ever—been quite this furious. Vanessa Coltrane represented all the people who'd judged him—on gossip—and found him guilty. At first it had hurt him, but as the years passed and rumors persisted he'd protected himself with a mask of indifference. Now anger flared inside him, all the more powerful for having been suppressed so long.

"Come join us, Dana," he said, seeing movement in the shadows.

Dana emerged from the darkness and stood by her sister.

"Look. I know what happened that night in the shed," he began and saw Vanessa throw an incredulous look at Dana.

"I told him," Dana admitted. "I had to. Someone's blackmailing me. I received another threat. This time they told me to get out of Hawaii."

"Why didn't you tell me?"

"I should have, but I didn't want to worry you."

"What happened that night has scarred you both." He put his hand on Dana's shoulder. "Don't you see it? If you can't control a man you're not interested because—deep down—you're afraid of men."

"I don't know," Dana hedged. "I hadn't thought about it that way."

"Well, think about it, and we'll talk later." There was a lot more he wanted to say to Dana. Now was not the time.

"What about me?" asked Vanessa, sarcasm etching every syllable.

"You hate men. You flirt with them, sure, but you're really laughing at them, thinking they're easy marks. You use your looks to manipulate men."

"Wonderful," Vanessa said. "An armchair psychologist."

"Neither of you trust men," Rob went on, directing his comments to Dana.

"You got me out of bed in the middle of the night to listen to a bunch of psychological mumbo jumbo?" Vanessa interrupted.

"Hell, no. I woke you to tell you that we have to get out of here tonight. Right this minute."

"What did you find in Big Daddy's suite?" Dana asked.

"You were in his suite?" Vanessa was clearly shocked.

"Yes. I was trying to find out if he's the one blackmailing Dana." There might have been a touch of respect in Vanessa's eyes now, but he was too angry with her to care. He turned to Dana. "Not only has Coltrane got this whole place bugged, he's put minicameras in the televisions."

"You mean he's watching as well as listening?" Dana cried.

"No wonder he knows so much," Vanessa said.

Rob noticed that she didn't sound particularly surprised. He suspected that she knew what else he'd found, but he didn't ask. They'd wasted enough time talking already. They had to get out of here while they still could.

"Big Daddy has a video of you packing," Rob told Vanessa. "You hid the suitcases in your closet. He knows you're going to leave."

"That's why he brought in the security men," Dana said.

"You're right. He's no fool. He's guessed that

we'll try to leave during the luau. The security men are supposed to stop us quietly without disrupting the party."

"He can't hold us here," Dana said.

"No, but he can keep Jason."

"And he will," Vanessa assured them, tears sparkling in her eyes.

Once Rob might have comforted her, but not after the way she'd lashed out at him. "I've arranged for us to get out of here, but we have to leave *now*."

"The airport closed at eleven," Dana said.

"After I left Big Daddy's suite I went over to the helipad. One of the pilots is waiting to fly us to Honolulu." Rob studied Vanessa for a moment. He wasn't certain how to interpret what he'd discovered in Big Daddy's suite. How much did Vanessa know? "Are you sure you want to leave with Jason? If you are, we have to go now."

"I'm positive," Vanessa insisted, and he believed her. Maybe she didn't know anything. This whole situation was so bizarre that he didn't know what to think. "I've already hired Garth Bradford to handle the divorce."

"Really?" Rob couldn't believe Garth would accept a divorce case; then again, Vanessa might hate men, but she certainly had a way of manipulating them.

Dana looked surprised, but added, "Garth's the best."

"When you get Jason, whisper into his ear so the bug won't pick up what you're saying," Rob said.

"Don't turn on the lights. Movement in the room activates the television camera inside the TV. It can't record anything without light."

"The helipad isn't close," Dana said. "We'll have to carry everything. We don't dare start up a car and attract attention."

"I'll just bring Jason and a few of his things. I'll leave all my clothes. I can share Dana's."

Rob silently gave her credit. He would have expected her to moan about leaving her glamorous wardrobe behind, but she put her son first. Okay, maybe she wasn't as bad as he thought. Time would tell.

"We'll get our stuff and be right back," Rob said.

"How'd you get out of Big Daddy's suite?" Dana cross-examined him as they rushed down the path.

Rob couldn't help chuckling. "I heard you ribbiting at the top of your lungs. What happened to your walkie-talkie?"

"It fell into the koi pond," she confessed, then told him how it happened.

"That was quick thinking, Dana. The minute I heard you ribbiting I knew something had gone wrong and got out of there the way I'd come in. I went out the window and up to the roof. I slid down the rain gutter."

"I looked behind the house. I didn't see you."

"I hightailed it for the helipad and found a pilot who was willing to make a little money on the side."

"I was worried," Dana admitted. "I searched everywhere for you. I was coming to get Vanessa to help when I found you."

He stopped, his hand on her arm, bringing her to a halt too. Running his knuckles up the soft curve of her cheek, he said, "Worried, were you?"

"I thought Big Daddy had you locked up somewhere—or something."

He lowered his head and touched his lips to hers. Not really much of a kiss; he couldn't afford to indulge himself right now. It was great to know she cared enough about him to worry.

"Come on," he said, guiding her down the crushed-lava path. "We don't have much time."

He waited outside Makai House, gazing into the distance where the full moon hung low over the water, splashing silvery light on the high-spirited waves. The trade winds were now a fickle breeze, lifting the palm fronds and bringing the fragrant scent of the tropics to the balmy air. There was nothing more he'd rather do than sit out on the terrace with Dana and gaze at the stars, but there wasn't a second to lose.

Dana emerged, her purse slung over one shoulder. "I'm ready." She opened her shoulder bag and brought out a small canister. "This is really what I came back to get."

"Hair spray?" he asked. At a time like this? Women.

She flashed him a sly grin. "The label says it's Stay Put Hair Spray, but it's really pepper spray."

"Jesus! One blast of that will drop a charging rhino."

"With the Panama Jack's rapist running around, you can't be too careful." She jammed the can back into her bag. "If anyone tries to stop us tonight I'll zap them."

Rob didn't want to take the time to discuss what he'd discovered in the suite, but he needed Dana on his side. Vanessa was so hostile toward men that she might not listen to him. She would listen to her sister. ·

"Big Daddy is going to go ballistic when he finds Vanessa and Jason gone," he said. "He's going to come right to your house looking for them. We need to hide them somewhere."

"Good idea, but where?"

"I'm going to call Garth. He's already agreed to take the case. I'm certain he'll let Vanessa and Jason stay at his place until after I meet with Coltrane."

"Why are you going to meet with him?"

"I helped myself to a few of his tapes. They're hidden out by the helipad. When he sees I can prove he's worse than a Peeping Tom, I think he'll be willing to listen to reason."

"You stole his tapes?" She let out a long, audible breath. "I suppose you had to do that to get proof."

"Damn right. Otherwise your sister can plan on joint custody or maybe even losing Jason if the Coltranes muster enough power."

"Big Daddy will make good on his blackmail

threat if we don't have leverage against him," Dana agreed.

"We have to pressure Coltrane, but I don't think he sent you the knife."

"If he didn't, who did?"

"This is a strange one. I'll be damned if I know who's out to get you."

The shrill ring of the telephone woke Garth; it was followed by the fluttering of Puni's wings as he woke too. Garth shook his head, trying to get his bearings. He was out on the lanai with Puni on his shoulder. Obviously he'd fallen asleep while gazing at the sea.

What time was it? Almost three-thirty. Anyone calling at this hour had to be in real trouble, Garth decided. They'd probably heard the Miranda and howled for a lawyer. He wheeled himself inside, a spurt of excitement sharpening his sleep-dulled brain. Maybe this would be an interesting case. He needed something to get himself out of this funk.

"Hello?" he said, answering the telephone and flipping on the light at the same time.

That was a mistake. The light hit Puni and he came to life. Stomping on Garth's shoulder, he chanted, "Sue the bastards! Sue the bastards! Sue their asses."

"Garth? Is that you?" It was Rob Tagett's unmistakable voice.

Garth cradled the receiver against his shoulder and put his hand over Puni's head to shut him up.

"It's me. Where are you? What's that noise? It sounds like you're in a wind tunnel."

"Close," Rob yelled. "I'm in a helicopter heading for Hickum Field. I need a huge favor—two of them actually."

"Shoot," Garth said, ignoring Puni nipping at his fingers.

"Can you pick us up? We land in about twenty minutes."

"I'll come get you, but you'll land before I can get there." Hickum Field was the military airport on the other side of the city, where the heliport was located. "What else do you need?"

"Would you mind letting Vanessa Coltrane and her son spend the night with you? We had to get out of there in a hell of a hurry. I'm expecting Big Daddy to come looking for them tomorrow. I don't want him to find them."

Garth hesitated. Vanessa Coltrane. The sensuous voice on the telephone. Dark, silky hair and long, tapered fingernails. He had no business getting anywhere near this woman.

"Sure. There's plenty of room here," Garth heard himself say.

He was still questioning his decision when he pulled up to the terminal in his customized van with Puni on his shoulder. The bird wasn't quite asleep or awake. When they were in a dark area he'd nod off, but if they pulled up under a streetlight Puni would threaten to sue. Garth stopped the van in front of the dark terminal and saw Rob waiting. He told himself that he didn't care what Vanessa Coltrane thought. He'd deliberately not changed his wrinkled clothes and had brought Puni along.

"Thanks for coming," Rob said after he'd opened the side door of the van.

"No problem," Garth said, watching as Rob helped Dana into the backseat and tossed in a few bags. Then he opened the door to the front seat beside Garth.

The most incredibly beautiful woman Garth had ever seen slid into his van. She wasn't a brunette like Dana. Vanessa Coltrane was a classy blonde with eyes as blue as the island sky. Cradled in her arms was a sleeping boy. One of her hands was on his bottom, supporting his weight, and the other was across the back of his neck.

He couldn't take his eyes off the hand on the boy's neck. A loving hand, gently stroking the child. A hand crowned by long oval nails painted a dusky mauve.

"Thank you so much for coming for us," Vanessa said. "I—"

"Sue the bastards," screeched Puni, who'd been awakened by the van's interior light. "Sue the bastards! Sue their asses."

Garth clamped his hand over Puni's head, but it was too late. The boy was already awake.

"Mommie, where are we?" He squinted at Garth.

Vanessa kissed the top of her son's head. "We're visiting Aunt Dana, remember?"

Jason's eyes were open wide now and he was staring at Puni, fascinated. "What's his name?"

"You ask him," Garth said gently. Jason had his mother's arresting blue eyes and blonde hair, but his jaw was the Coltranes', right down to the dimple on his chin that would become a deep cleft as he grew older.

"What's your name?" Jason asked.

"Puni." The bird stomped on Garth's shoulder. "Puni. Puni."

"That means *little*," Vanessa told her son, and Garth didn't bother to correct her.

"I'm Jason." He pointed to himself. "Say *Jason*."

"Jaa-son. Jaa-son."

Jason clapped his little hands and laughed. "Puni."

"Jaa-son. Jaa-son." Puni ruffled his feathers, flashing brilliant crimson.

"Will he sit on my shoulder?" Jason asked Garth.

Garth shook his head. Puni was a difficult parrot, who didn't like many people. He especially hated the cleaning lady and would spit birdseed over the freshly mopped floor just to annoy her. "He's shy."

Jason leaned closer. "Puni, don't be afraid. I'm your friend."

Garth stole a glance at Vanessa and found she was enthralled with her son, smiling as he tried to make friends with Puni. Despite her smile, her eyes looked sad, troubled.

"Thanks for coming out in the middle of the night," Dana said.

Garth glanced over his shoulder, momentarily having forgotten the other passengers, who were now settled in the backseat.

"Can I try to hold him?" Jason asked. "Puh-leeze?"

"Okay," Garth said, realizing no one could refuse this kid. "Put out your hand and see if he will walk up your arm to your shoulder."

Jason offered the parrot his hand, but Puni didn't budge. "Come on, Puni. I'm your friend. Come, Puni, come."

The parrot cocked his head, looked at Garth as if asking permission, then hopped onto Jason's hand and moonwalked up to his small shoulder. "Jaa-son. Jaa-son."

"Well, I'll be." Garth's eyes met Vanessa's, and he was greeted by a genuine smile of astonishing warmth. His heart backfired, but he kept his expression neutral, a trick he'd learned from years of court appearances.

"We're outta' here," Rob reminded him from the backseat as he slid the door shut and the interior became dark.

Garth used the hand controls that did the work his feet could no longer do and pulled away from the curb.

"Puni," said Jason. "What else can you say?"

"He doesn't talk when it's dark," Garth answered, still astonished the bird had gone to Jason. "He thinks that's time to sleep."

"Oh. We'll talk tomorrow." Jason ran his hand

over Puni's feathers, sounding more than a little sleepy himself.

They drove in silence through paradise's deserted streets. Garth braved a glance in Vanessa's direction as he came up to a corner and pretended to check for oncoming traffic. Jason had fallen asleep, his towhead pillowed against the fullness of his mother's bosom. Puni was asleep too, perched on the boy's shoulder, resting his head against Jason's cheek like the leaning tower of Pisa.

Garth lifted his eyes and saw that Vanessa was staring at him. He quickly looked away, paying careful attention to his driving. What did she see? A cripple with wrinkled clothes who smelled like a gym sock. Only a nut case would ride around with a parrot on his shoulder. Under the best conditions he was hardly the image of a powerhouse attorney, but now he felt especially foolish.

"Great parrot," Vanessa said, but she wasn't looking at Puni. She tilted her head slightly, sending a silky fall of blonde hair across her cheek, and treated him to another of her irresistible smiles.

He managed to smile back, and, incredibly, her smile widened.

18

"Rob," Dana said as they stood on the curb outside her house watching Garth drive away, "do you think we made a mistake calling Garth? He seems a little strange."

"Your sister affects men that way." He gave her a half smile and a wink. "Some of us are immune."

A hot flush raced up her neck to her cheeks, and Dana blessed the darkness. She was embarrassed at her overreacting, her jealousy. Her sister was only trying to protect her. And Rob . . . well, he did seem truly interested in her.

The neighborhood was dark except for the streetlight at the corner half-hidden by a coconut palm. Somewhere a dog barked; the sound carried through the tropical night along with the sweet scent of plumeria. They were alone now, really alone. It filled her with a strange inner excitement that almost frightened her.

"I've been thinking about what you said," she told him as he draped his arm around her shoulders and they began walking up the driveway to her house. "You think I choose men I can dominate, don't you?"

"Do you?"

"I'm not sure. It isn't a conscious decision."

He halted and drew her closer. "When you're traumatized the way you were, the mind calls on all its defense mechanisms. Subconsciously you've selected only men who make you feel safe—those you can control."

"Let me think about it a little more," she said.

The past was so ugly that Dana had deliberately blocked it from her thoughts. But you couldn't really escape anything that traumatic. It was there, a ghostlike presence, hovering in the shadows of her mind. If she was going to have a relationship with Rob, she'd have to deal with her own private demons. It could wait though; too much was at stake to indulge in self-analysis. She couldn't get on with her life until the blackmailer was caught.

"Do you think Big Daddy will show up here?" she asked. No matter what Rob's theory was, she still believed Coltrane was the blackmailer. Nothing else made sense.

They began walking toward the house again, and Rob held up the small duffel that contained the incriminating videos he'd taken from Big Daddy's suite. "As soon as it's light I'm hiding these. They're Vanessa's insurance. When Coltrane shows up—and believe me, he will—he'll want Vanessa and Jason back. That's when we hit him with the tapes."

"Why Vanessa? Won't he settle for Jason?"

Rob stopped again, his free arm still around her. "I found more than just a video camera monitoring station in his suite. Coltrane's sick. Obsessed."

She waited, fear coiling inside her stomach at his words and his concerned expression. They hadn't been able to talk during the flight over.

"There are cameras in the main house and in some of the cottages, but most of them are in Vanessa's house. He watches every move she makes."

"That's psychotic." Her heart shot up to her throat and lodged there. She couldn't imagine someone watching every move she made—day after day after day. An even more disgusting thought hit her. "There's a television in her bathroom—"

"Right. Big Daddy has an astonishing number of tapes of Vanessa; many of them would be considered pornographic."

"She'd die if she knew," Dana said.

"Too much was going on there for her not to have at least suspected."

"Maybe," Dana admitted. Once she'd been so close to her sister, but living with the Coltranes had put an invisible barrier between them. Perhaps the divorce would change things and they'd be close again.

She wasn't close to anyone, Dana realized, except Lillian Hurley. Her neighbor was so much older that it put a certain distance between them despite their fondness for each other. Distance. It was there in her relationship with Gwen Sihida too. Their relationship was defined—and confined—by their positions as judges.

With a growing sense of self-awareness, Dana realized that distance was the hallmark of all her relationships—even with women. What was she afraid of? What would it be like to really have a best friend?

She glanced sideways at Rob and wondered if she could ever be friends with a man like him. Friends and lovers. The old phrase echoed through the corridors of her mind. He would never settle for being just friends. Friends and lovers. It was a scary thought and one that would take some getting used to.

"What are you thinking?" Rob asked.

"*Kapu,*" Dana said, unwilling to discuss what she'd really been thinking. "That's the sign on the gate that lets you into Kau Ranch. In ancient Hawaii it meant *forbidden*. Incest, adultery, theft were *kapu*—punishable by death on the spot. I've always felt the old meaning suited Big Daddy. Now I know I was right."

"You surprise me, Dana." There was a low, husky pitch to his voice that sent a thrill of anticipation up her spine. "I'd never have guessed you were into Hawaiian lore. I can guarantee you won't be hearing the night marchers tonight."

Dana knew what he was implying and ignored it. "Speaking of the night marchers, that's Lillian Hurley's house over there." She pointed to the modest home that bordered her driveway. "I guess her daughter has arrived. That's a strange car in her driveway."

Rob didn't comment. Instead he gazed at her with a look so galvanizing that it sent a tremor of excitement rippling through her. They'd agreed he would spend the night with her so he'd be certain to be there when Big Daddy showed up, but they'd never discussed sleeping arrangements. After the way she'd behaved at the beach, she knew what Rob expected, and she wasn't sure she could say no.

Dana stopped at her front door and reached into the side pocket of her purse where she always kept her key. She unlocked the door; it swung open and they stepped inside. Her breath stalled in her throat. *Something was wrong.* She halted, her sixth sense telling her not to go any farther.

Rob bumped into her. "What's the matter?"

"The light in the hall is on a timer. It should be on."

"It burned out."

"Probably," she agreed, reaching for the light switch. The house was stuffy, the way it usually was after being left closed all day. The feeling that something was wrong persisted despite Rob's logical explanation. She flicked the light switch, once, twice. Nothing. "The power's out."

"Could be a blown fuse. Where's the fuse box?"

"In the kitch—" An explosion of light blinded her.

"Don't move, *brah*," boomed a man's voice from across the living room, "or we'll shoot."

In the backwash of the high-beam flashlight,

Dana could see two men built like brick walls. *Mokes*. The island tough guys, who spoke pidgin, using words like *brah* for brother. They were responsible for much of the crime in Honolulu. She'd seen enough of them in court to know how vicious they could be.

She couldn't make out their faces, but she did see the gleaming silver of a gun barrel. Rob's hand on the small of her back tensed. Her pulse thundered in her ears, making it impossible to think clearly, and droplets of sweat blossomed across the tops of her breasts.

"Hands in the air. *Hele on.*" *Get moving.*

"Do it." Rob dropped his camera bag and the duffel with the videos.

Her purse hit the floor, and she reached high. What did they want? This didn't have the earmarks of a simple robbery. They could have grabbed the TV and stereo and escaped out the back door when they heard them coming.

"Check the bags," said the *moke*, and Dana had her answer. They wanted the incriminating videos. How could Big Daddy have gotten these thugs to help him so soon? They'd left Kau Ranch only a little over two hours ago.

One of the men crossed the room, a high-beam flashlight in one hand, while the other man kept the gun trained on them. He ignored Rob's camera bag and grabbed the duffel with the videos.

Unzipping it, he said, *"Maika'i!"* *Beautiful.* He spoke a combination of pidgin and Hawaiian, his breath so strong you could walk to the mainland on it.

As he sauntered back to the *moke* holding the gun, Dana glanced up at Rob. She'd never seen him look this disheartened.

The man with the gun grunted with satisfaction as he inspected the contents of the duffel. "Be sure they don't have another one somewhere."

The other man lumbered over to them again and grabbed Dana's purse. He dumped the contents on the floor. "Nuthin'."

He emptied Rob's camera bag. The expensive Nikon hit the floor with a thump that sounded unusually loud in the stillness. "Nuthin' here either."

"Okay." The *moke* with the gun panned across the room with the flashlight. It settled on Dana, sweeping from her ankles to her eyebrows in slow motion. "Let's have some fun, *brah*."

Bile shot up Dana's throat as one man ambled toward them, his eyes on her. For a gut-wrenching second the world froze. Then she was thrown back in time. That night—so long ago—but never forgotten, returned with astonishing clarity.

She'd been helpless then too, she recalled, clenching her eyes shut, fighting an onslaught of terrifying memories. The young girl she'd been resurfaced, immobilized by fear. It was all she could do to force her eyes open.

Rob lunged forward. "Don't touch her!"

"Careful," she heard herself cry. The man had a

gun for God's sakes. But Rob didn't listen, stepping between her and the burly *moke*.

"Take care of him first," snarled the one with the gun.

Before his buddy could respond, Rob walloped him with a killer punch to the gut. The man's eyeballs shot upward and vanished into the back of his skull, leaving the whites glaring at her as he sank to his knees, clutching his middle.

Stark fear whipped the breath from Dana's lungs as Rob decked him. A brittle, splintering crack like a board breaking ripped through the room, and a geyser of blood shot from the man's nose. His buddy tracked Rob with the barrel of the gun like a hunter sighting a sure kill.

Please don't shoot Rob, Dana silently prayed.

"Hit him again and you're a dead man," warned the one with the gun.

Rob's arm was in motion to cold cock the man again, but he had the good sense to stop. Dana clamped her arms around herself and clenched her jaw to keep from screaming, terrified if she moved or made any sound, they'd kill Rob.

"You fuck-up." The man waved the gun and cursed his partner, who was still on his knees, one hand on his nose, blood trickling over his beefy fingers. "You hold the gun, *lolo*." *Dummy*.

Dana's pulse hammered in her ears, roaring with tremendous force. That's what people heard, she realized. Not the night marchers—just the sound of your own fear. As panicked as she was, Rob appeared unfazed, almost relaxed, but Dana knew better. There was a tenseness to his shoulders, a lethal calmness in his eyes.

His determined stance made her even more afraid. He'd do anything to save her—including getting himself killed. She couldn't just stand here like a cigar-store Indian. She couldn't let history repeat itself.

Do something. What? What could she do that wouldn't get them killed?

"Stand still or he'll shoot," screamed the *moke*.

"And let you beat the shit out of me?" Rob barked a laugh. "No way. Besides, he's a piss-poor shot. He's as likely to hit you as me."

Fists raised, he tracked Rob across the room. Rob lunged at the man, clobbering him with a full-bore punch to the gut. The man toppled forward, grabbing him. They tumbled to the floor and rolled over and over. Now Rob was on top, slamming his fist into the man's face, his free hand clutching the throat.

"Don't shoot," screamed Dana at the man with the gun. "You'll kill both of them."

The man aimed the gun, but didn't fire. Dana dropped to the floor, certain the fight had the men's undivided attention. On all fours she scrambled across the floor, searching for the pepper-spray canister from her purse.

A brush. Her wallet. A lipstick case. Her Filofax. No canister.

"Kokua!" Help! moaned the man pinned beneath

Rob. "Jump him if you cain't get a clear shot. He's gonna kill me."

The burly *moke*, blood still dribbling from his nose, shoved the gun into his waistband and dropped the flashlight. Its beam shot across the room, leaving Dana in darkness. He bellowed a primal curse, then, "Yaaahhh!!"

Panic was a breath away, held in check by the memory of how miserably she'd failed the last time —and the horrible consequences. She watched in terror as the man catapulted across the small space and onto Rob's back. He collapsed under the force of the heavier man's weight.

"Stop! Stop!" she screamed, but they ignored her.

Her stomach heaved, then took a terrifying plunge like a runaway roller coaster. *Dana, do something*. The canister of pepper spray had to be here somewhere. It had been in her purse earlier.

She scrambled across the wood floor, feeling in the darkness. Under the rim of the sofa she found the canister and yanked off the cap. Spinning around, she saw that the men had the best of Rob. One had pinned his arms behind his back while the other pummeled him with brutal punches.

She charged up, but they were so intent on the fight that they didn't know she was there. At the top of her lungs she screeched, "I'm going to shoot!"

They dropped Rob and rounded on her. She blasted them point-blank with a stream of pepper. The *mokes* sputtered, coughing and sneezing and cursing a blue streak. One of them sprang at her.

With watery eyes, she managed to shoot the charging man square in the face with another debilitating round of pepper. A direct hit to his eyes. "Aaaachou!" He sneezed like a rhino and collapsed to his knees, choking and gasping.

"Shit, *brah*," he cursed. "I cain't see. I cain't see shit."

"We got what we came for," his partner said, hauling him to his feet and pulling him out of Dana's range. She eyed the duffel, but it was slung over his shoulder and he still had the gun. "Let's get the fuck outta here."

With a volley of coughs and gut-wrenching sneezes, they staggered out the front door. The cloud of ultrafine pepper hung in the air like a poisonous gas. Dana knew that its effects, though disabling, were temporary. Her eyes were swollen almost shut from the pepper.

"Rob, darling." She cradled his jaw in her hand. Hot and sticky, blood seeped over her fingers from a cut on his lip.

His eyelids fluttered, then he sneezed. He squinted at her, his eyes as watery as hers. "Thanks, babe," he muttered. "Help me up."

It took all her strength to haul him to his feet. Hunkered over, coughing and obviously in pain, he leaned on her.

"Outside," he said, then sneezed.

A step at a time they trundled to the sliding glass doors that opened onto her lanai. The fresh air filled her lungs, a welcome relief from the pepper. She helped Rob to the chaise lounge that faced tranquil Maunalua Bay and Koko Head. He didn't complain, but she saw him wince as he lay down.

"I'm calling an ambulance and the police."

Rob's hand shot out and locked around her wrist. "No. I'll be fine."

"You could have internal injuries. A doctor needs—"

"No." There was no arguing with him, she thought. "I cut my lip, is all. Get some ice."

Cursing his stubbornness, she went inside and found the flashlight she kept in the drawer under the telephone. Seconds later she discovered the *mokes* had flipped the main breaker. She turned the lights on with trembling fingers.

Until that moment she'd been going on pure adrenaline. The digital lights on her stove and microwave came on, flashing to indicate a power failure. She sagged against the wall, weak with relief. *This time, you helped. You really helped.*

Well, don't stop now. Rob needs you. She mustered her strength and filled a plastic bag with ice. When she returned to the lanai Rob was lying there, eyes wide open, staring at Koko Head. He accepted the bag without a word and put it against his lip.

"I'm calling the police," she said.

"No, you're not. I'll take care of this."

"You can't take the law into your own hands."

"Watch me."

19

Garth parked the van in his garage and glanced over at Vanessa. She was awake, cradling Jason, who still had Puni on his shoulder. The little boy and the parrot looked so adorable, so blissfully asleep that he didn't want to open the door and break the spell. Before Garth dropped Rob and Dana off, Rob had told him about the videos he'd taken from Big Daddy's suite. Already Garth sensed just how ugly this case was going to get. Vanessa seemed stoic, resigned, but Jason was bound to get hurt if they weren't very careful.

The garage door closed with a muffled clank, reminding Garth that he had to get out. This was the part he hated, the reason he didn't like to take out women. Nothing, but nothing, was more humiliating than hauling his wheelchair from its space behind his seat, opening it, and hoisting his dead legs to the side so he could transfer from the car to the wheelchair.

"May I help?" Vanessa asked, reaching toward him.

"No." There was an edge to his voice that wasn't usually there. He didn't look around, not wanting to see Vanessa watching him, not wanting to feel less of a man.

The interior light awakened Puni, who became a welcome distraction. "Sue the bastards! Sue the bastards! Sue their asses."

"Puni," Jason said sleepily.

"Jaa-son. Jaa-son. Jaa-son."

Garth was in his chair and around to Vanessa's door in record time. He swung it open and reached out to take Jason from Vanessa. The little boy was light and so fascinated by the parrot moonwalking down his arm that he didn't notice that Garth was in a wheelchair. He punched his code onto the keypad and the door clicked open.

"Way co-o-ol," said Jason. "Jus' like the Power Rangers."

Garth hadn't seen the latest idols of the kindergarten set, but he knew they were fond of space age gadgets. And violence. "Would you like to put Puni to bed?"

"Yeah," Jason replied, and Garth could hear Vanessa walking behind them. What was she thinking? he wondered.

He wheeled into the kitchen to the alcove overlooking the ocean where Puni's huge cage stood surrounded by ferns. He opened the door. "Put him on that piece of wood. It's called a perch."

"Night-night, Puni," Jason said as Garth held him up.

"Now pull the cover over the cage," Garth said. "We'll take it off in the morning."

The cover in place, Jason hopped off Garth's lap and studied him for a moment. Here it comes, thought Garth.

"What's wrong with you?" Jason asked.

"I was hurt in an automobile accident and can't walk."

Jason nodded, but out of the corner of his eye Garth could see how uncomfortable Vanessa was. Children were often more accepting of his handicap than adults.

"It's time to go to bed." Vanessa picked up her son.

Garth led them down the hall into the guest wing. "Jason can stay in the room with twin beds. There's another room with a king-size bed for you."

"I'd better sleep in one of the twin beds. I don't want Jason to wake up in the night and not remember where he is."

Garth noticed Jason was already asleep, his blonde head nestled against the sensuous curve of his mother's neck. Her slim fingers crowned by those long, tapered nails were curved around Jason's back. Garth waited while Vanessa pulled down the covers and gently laid Jason across the bed. There was such love and heartfelt emotion in her eyes that Garth had to look away.

Remembering.

His mother used to look at him with the same unqualified love and devotion. The accident that crippled him had killed his parents. He missed them both, but to be honest he missed his mother more. He'd thought time would take care of things. It hadn't worked that way. He longed for his mother as much now as—maybe more than—he ever had.

Was there anything more precious than a mother's love? Just seeing Vanessa brushing her lips against her son's forehead had sent a pang of regret so sharp and deep that he had to inhale rapidly to make it go away.

Was anyone ever going to love him with half that much emotion? Was he ever going to love anyone that way? It seemed not. He had his career. That should be enough.

He whirled his chair around and was almost into the hall before he could trust his voice. "If you need anything let me know. I'm in the other wing."

He wheeled down the corridor and across the mammoth living room, clicking off lights as he went. Why was he so angry all of a sudden? The wellspring of hostility seemed to come from the deepest reaches of his soul, taking him by surprise. He was usually a happy person.

True, he'd felt a vague sense of ennui lately, a kind of boredom that he'd attributed to a career lull caused by a lack of interesting cases. Now he suspected it went deeper than that. He switched on the light in his room and sat there. Snap out of it, he told himself.

"Garth." Vanessa's voice was soft, but so unexpected that it startled him.

He flinched and turned around. She was standing in the doorway, her golden hair framed by the darkness in the hall and her long legs appearing even longer in those white shorts.

"Sorry to bother you," she said, "but I was wondering if I might borrow a T-shirt to sleep in. I only brought Jason's things."

"Sure." He started toward the huge armoire, but she dashed past him.

"Let me help."

He stopped. Jesus! Was he so pathetic that he seemed helpless, unable to open a simple armoire?

Vanessa reached the armoire and opened it, smiling a little too brightly over her shoulder at him. "Which drawer?"

"Third one down." He tried to keep the anger out of his voice, but failed miserably.

He wheeled over to the French doors that faced the pool and opened them. Outside he transferred from the wheelchair to the glider he often used when he couldn't sleep. He gazed at the sea, trying to let it comfort him. According to Hawaiian lore, on moonlit nights the *menehunes* danced on the waves, causing them to sparkle the way they were sparkling tonight. The ancient tale didn't comfort him the way it usually did. He heard Vanessa come out the door behind him, but didn't turn around.

"Have I done something wrong?" she asked.

He rarely lied, but this time he was tempted. Anything to get rid of her. Instead, he patted the space on the glider beside him. Vanessa hesitated, but she sat down, clutching his favorite T-shirt that read: Lawyers Do It in Their Briefs.

"Look!" His anger, a grenade in his gut, threatened to explode. He sucked in a deep breath and counted to three. "If we're going to work together, we need to get a few things straight. I was crippled when I was eighteen. I managed to put myself through college and law school without any help. Every day I go to work and function perfectly—on my own. I find it demeaning to have people rush to open doors as if I can't do it myself."

"I-I'm sorry," Vanessa stammered. "I just wanted to help."

The heartfelt emotion in her voice banished the anger he'd battled only moments ago. "I'll let you know when you can help me. Sometimes there are things I can't do."

"Tell me about the accident," she asked, her voice low.

He shrugged, unwilling to relive the unpleasant memory. "A drunk driver ran us off the road. My parents were killed on impact. I—" He stopped himself from saying he hadn't been so lucky.

Since when had he started feeling sorry for himself? What was wrong with him tonight? An image of a little boy and a parrot flashed through his mind. *Keisk*. Children. A home and a family. Now he knew what was wrong. A career just wasn't enough.

True, once that feeling of accomplishment had helped to overcome the loss of his parents and his debilitating injury. His career had given him pride and earned him the esteem of his peers. It also made him financially independent. Yet it wasn't enough.

"I can't believe it," Vanessa said. "Almost the same thing happened to us. I was sixteen when my father swerved to avoid a drunk driver. Dana and I were orphaned that night. We had no relatives, so we were sent to a foster home. It was terrible. We ran away and eventually made our way here."

Garth realized that he'd heard only part of the story. He'd represented enough people to know when information was being withheld.

"Nothing," Vanessa whispered, "nothing that happened to me can possibly compare with what you suffered."

"Don't feel sorry for me," he warned, his anger again surfacing. "I hate that as much as do-gooders who try to help. Not all wounds are physical. A lot of people are crippled psychologically and don't know how to get over it. At least I could see the way out."

The long silence made him anxious. What was she thinking? Was he wrong in believing she'd suffered as much as he had? Earlier, when Vanessa had seemed to be the perfect woman, he wouldn't have thought it possible, but now, hearing her speak of her youth made him believe that they had more in common than he ever would have suspected.

He bet those years following her parents' death

had been traumatic for Vanessa. He'd defended enough runaways who had been driven to a life of crime. Vanessa had escaped that, but she had suffered a psychological trauma. Of that he was dead certain.

He looked down and saw her hand inching across the small space between them, searching for his. Her fingers laced with his and she squeezed slightly. He looked down at her hand, fascinated by the long, tapered nails that were curled through his own slim fingers. The growing magnetism between them stunned him.

Vanessa said, "I've never met anyone like you."

Dana changed into a nightgown and went into the bathroom. She scrubbed her face, but didn't really see her reflection. Instead she saw Rob, the ice pack to his jaw, laying on the chaise outside. He'd refused to come inside.

She was so worried about him she couldn't possibly sleep. What if he had internal injuries and died before morning? Her stomach roiled spasmodically as she recalled how Rob had hurled himself at those men.

She'd been fighting it hard, but day by day, hour by hour, the more time that she spent with Rob, the more she cared about him. She felt protected—for the first time in her life. Rob would stay by her side and help her fend off the blackmailers the way he'd come to her defense tonight.

So why was she washing her face while he was

outside hurting? Because he'd insisted. He was accustomed to getting his way. Well, if they were going to have a relationship he'd have to learn to compromise.

She marched to the lanai and found Rob on the chaise, the ice bag held against his jaw.

"It takes two, you know."

Rob dropped the ice pack, revealing a vivid bruise that made her wince. "Two to what?"

"To have a relationship." She sat beside him, but didn't put her feet up. "I insist you tell me what you're thinking. You haven't said anything since those creeps left."

"What do you want me to say? I screwed up—big time—okay? I'm pissed as hell at myself." His voice was low, charged with emotion, and she could tell that he truly blamed himself for the loss of the tapes. "I should have known Big Daddy could pick up the phone and have some *mokes* waylay us."

"You couldn't have known that he'd discover the missing tapes so quickly."

"Wrong. I was in his suite, remember? I saw all the electronic gadgets he had. I must have tripped some hidden device. That's how he found out so fast."

"At least you got Vanessa and Jason out. I'm proud of you for that—for all you did."

"Hell, *you* saved *me*," he said, not sounding too happy about it, and she chalked it up to masculine pride. "I haven't been much help. I haven't found the blackmailer and I haven't helped your sister's custody case either."

"The fight's just beginning—on at least two fronts. But I can't tell you how glad I am to have you with me."

A sigh that seemed to well up from the bottom of his soul startled her. "I swear, I won't let you down again."

"You haven't let me down." She stared into his deep blue eyes, and for once the words came easily. "You've made me happy."

She swung her legs onto the chaise so she was reclining beside him. He grimaced, obviously in pain, but managed to put one arm around her. She gently rested her head on his shoulder.

The rhythmic *thump-thump* of his heart against her chest generated a longing deep within her. Her reaction wasn't just physical. It went far beyond that into a part of her psyche she'd never explored. What she wanted was intimacy. Someone special to share her life with.

She gazed at Rob and found him studying her. He had the most insightful eyes. They saw right through her. Then he smiled, his lips canted to one side because of his bruised jaw, and she was truly lost.

"You could have been shot—killed," she whispered.

"So what? I wasn't going to let you be raped again."

"Again?" The word came out much louder than

she intended, echoing in the darkness like the footsteps of the night marchers.

"The knife that man *'accidentally'* fell on. He got what he deserved. He raped you, didn't he?"

20

"How did you know?" she asked, hoping he'd believed the rest of her story about how Hank Rawlins had died.

Rob tried to shrug, but winced at the effort. "The FBI trained me to develop psychological profiles of criminals, remember? I didn't get a chance to use what the Feebies taught me while I was on the force, but it's helped me with my reporting. And I've been watching you."

The heartrending tenderness in his gaze astonished her. Tonight he'd proved that he cared enough to risk his life to protect her. Now he'd revealed that his interest in her wasn't new. It went back months or maybe even years.

"I've studied you closely these last few days. I rethought your story about the guy falling on the knife, then I put it all together."

She didn't bother to deny it. What good would it do to lie now? "I've never talked about being raped, not even to Vanessa."

"Sometimes talking helps."

"Sometimes," she admitted, "but sometimes it only brings back the pain. I've concentrated on the future, not the past, and that's been my salvation."

He gazed at her a moment, seemed set to argue, but said, "Okay. You'll tell me about it when you're ready."

He tenderly gathered her in his arms even though it must have hurt him. They cuddled, reclining on the chaise and watching the moonlight shimmering down on Koko Head. The trades had died down as they did most nights, leaving only a flicker of wind to rustle the palm trees.

"I wish you'd let me take you to a doctor."

"Know what would make me feel a lot better?" Slowly and seductively his gaze slid downward, taking in the filmy black nightgown, which had ridden up to reveal most of her thighs.

"You couldn't possibly. Not in your condition."

He chuckled, a masculine, sensuous sound that seemed to vibrate deep within her own chest. "You're right. I can barely move, but it would feel great to have you touch me the way you did the other night."

"What night?" Then she remembered. "I thought you were asleep. I—I—I—" How could she explain caressing him in such an intimate way?

"Couldn't resist me, could you?" His smile was so adorable that she couldn't help smiling back.

"I don't know what got into me," she said. "I honestly don't."

"I loved every second, but you left me with a stick of dynamite in my pants."

"Well, we certainly don't want to cause you any problems tonight."

"Why not? Everything else hurts."

She kissed his cheek, tenderly brushing her lips against the bristle of emerging whiskers. She meant to stop, she really did, but a few seconds later she found her lips on the curve of his neck. A trace of his after-shave mingled with his male scent and the smell of night-blooming jasmine that hung heavily in the soft night air. Beneath her lips, his pulse throbbed. She gently caressed his well-toned shoulders, savoring his strength and the slightly salty taste of his skin.

"I feel better already, darlin'." The slight inflection surprised her, once again reminding her that he'd grown up in Texas. His drawl seemed to appear most often when he was being amorous.

Suddenly it seemed ridiculous that they were joking, considering what they'd just been through. He'd saved her, and that couldn't be taken lightly. "How can I thank you for what you did tonight?"

"By remembering that we're a team. It took both of us."

She closed her eyes and nestled her head against the crook of his neck. Was he reading her mind? Earlier she'd thought much the same thing. Partners. She wasn't facing her problems alone anymore.

It was the most comforting thought she'd had in

years, and with it came a slow-dawning realization. She needed to love someone. All this time she'd thought in terms of someone to love her, not accepting that love was a two-way street. If she were honest she'd admit that she'd been afraid to love a man.

She let her hand drift down the solid plane of Rob's chest. He'd taken off his bloodied shirt, and the heat from his skin and the rasp of his hair reminded her that she was willingly, happily snuggling with a big, powerful man. A man who had just proven she could trust him with her life.

If you couldn't trust, you couldn't love. Take it easy, she reminded herself. *Don't make any commitments yet—even a mental one. Just ride with the tide and go with the flow; see where this takes you.*

She couldn't resist stroking him gently, being careful in case she was touching a bruised area. The muscular length of his torso intrigued her. He had a rugged, thoroughly masculine chest that she couldn't help kissing. She flicked her tongue over his skin. Once. Twice. How long had she wanted to taste him? Forever, it seemed.

In slow motion she ran her tongue over the surface until she found a nipple concealed by a whisk of hair. She blew a jet of cool air across it. Rob groaned, a low sound from deep in his throat that made her pulse skyrocket.

"Admit it," he demanded, his voice a shade shy of a whisper. "I'm the one—the only one for you. You want me. Don't be afraid of how you feel."

"I'm not." Now she had an entirely different fear. She was experiencing such an uncontrolled rush of longing that it frightened her more than she could ever have imagined. Yet it excited her too.

"Don't stop now." Rob stroked the back of her head, twining his fingers through her hair. "Touch every inch of my body."

With a sigh of anticipation, she lowered her head and kissed him again. She traced the solid contours of his torso with the liquid tip of her tongue. Tasting and kissing as she went.

"Ouch," groaned Rob, smiling.

Dana drew back. "Sorry. I have no business kissing you when you're in pain."

"You're better than any painkiller. Cuter too," he said, a teasing note in his voice, humor flirting in his eyes. "Besides, you don't want to stop, do you?"

She lowered her head and whispered, "No," against the warmth of his skin. She hadn't a clue why she was behaving so wantonly, but she craved him. From her flushed nipples to the sweet throbbing between her thighs—she wanted him. Only him.

The urge to touch him and kiss him bordered on the primitive. She didn't fight the feeling, didn't even try to. Instead, she explored him, lightly caressing him with her hands and kissing him. Occasionally she stopped to taste, or put her cheek to the wall of his chest and listen to the ever accelerating thump of his heart.

"Aw, hell," he muttered, his voice stripped to a husky growl by desire.

His breath was hot against the top of her head, and it sent a jolt of arousal through her. She sensuously stroked his hair-roughened chest, lightly teasing the skin by drawing the tips of her fingernails over it with tantalizing slowness.

His hands rested lightly on her hips, warm and solid. He flicked the sheer fabric aside and touched her bare skin with his hands. A depth charge of excitement exploded deep inside her. Slowly, ever so slowly, his hands coasted upward. Over the flare of her hips. To the curve of her waist. Up to the tender underside of her breasts.

There he stopped to cradle their fullness in the broad palms of his hands. His thumbs rested on her nipples, idly moving back and forth, coaxing the soft peaks into rigid proof of the effect he had on her.

"Take off the nightgown."

"Me?" she said, stalling.

"No, the man in the moon. Take it off. I want to see you."

She couldn't deny this man anything. Lifting her arms, she pulled the gown over the top of her head, then sent it swishing through the air. She remained on her knees and let the moonlight wash over her full breasts. Dusky pink areolas circled her pouting nipples, revealing how aroused she was, but she didn't care. She wet her lower lip with the tip of her tongue and tasted Rob's after-shave.

"God . . . you're beautiful." His heavy-lidded

eyes slowly drifted from her parted lips to the peaks of her breasts and lingered there.

She flinched under his intense gaze and her breasts swayed slightly, languidly moving like orchids in the island breeze. Rob's approving smile banished what little modesty remained, and she became keenly aware of an ache deep inside. The feeling increased, becoming a shudder of anticipation, as his gaze swept lower.

As surely as if he were actually touching her, she felt him scorching a path down the gentle swell of her hips and focusing on the juncture of her thighs, where pale blonde curls concealed her femininity. Heat shafted through her, arrowing to her most intimate place, her breath quickening. But she didn't look away.

Here she was, wearing nothing but a smile. "I can't believe I'm doing this."

"Stop kidding yourself, Dana. You have a wild streak. You've been dying to get into my pants."

She smiled, not bothering to deny it. Going back to the first night she'd met him years ago, she'd felt a certain thrill. Now she recognized that thrill was desire.

"Here I am"—Rob gave an overly dramatic sigh—"helpless. Have your way with me."

"I intend to."

She crouched over Rob, her legs straddling his hips. A soft moan caught in her throat. She'd never dreamed of taking charge like this, but then no one had ever told her that she'd want a man so much. It was a raw, primitive, physical pleasure, staggering in its intensity.

She longed to feel his mouth against hers, but his lower lip was split. She satisfied herself with the curve of his neck and the sensitive area behind his ear. Her bare breasts were so close to his chest that her nipples responded to the heat of his body by tightening even more. The hair on his chest tickled, adding to the excitement.

Driven by some forbidden impulse, she lowered her chest a fraction of an inch and let her breasts sink into the thatch of chest hair. *Oh, my.* She never dreamed a man could feel quite this good. Slowly, gently, she waltzed her taut nipples through the crinkly hair.

"See what you've done to me." He shoved her hand down to his crotch. Beneath his jeans he was rigid and throbbing slightly, his maleness a promise and a threat.

His hand slipped between her thighs, touching her intimately. Her breath stalled in her throat and for a second she indulged herself, closing her eyes and letting his talented fingers gently caress her with expert precision.

"Look at me, darlin'," he drawled, and she realized that he'd taken over.

She gripped his wrist and pulled his hand away. "You're in no condition to be giving orders."

"You wanna take charge? Great. You're just my type."

"Anything in a bra is your type."

"Right . . . Your Honor."

She ignored his teasing and reached for his belt buckle with trembling fingers. After fumbling with it for a second she managed to unhook it and yank down his zipper. The white fabric of his Joe Boxers and its familiar message, "Just Say Yo" stood out in the moonlight. She pressed her lips to his burgeoning erection, which was battling to be freed, and blew a hot current of breath through the fabric. "Yo." She smiled to herself. "Yo."

Rob moaned, but she ignored him, slipping her hand under the waistband of his shorts and homing in on his shaft. Thick and hot and amazingly hard, it still felt unexpectedly soft. She squeezed tight, moving her wrist up and down. Quickly glancing up at Rob, she saw that his face was contorted. He seemed to be in more pain than when the *mokes* hit him. She stopped, but didn't let go. It simply felt too good to hold him.

"For Christ's sake, don't stop now," Rob said, the words coming from deep in his chest.

That was all she needed to hear. She moved her lips over him, still amazed at the silkiness of the surface that belied the pulsing strength within. With her tongue she explored every inch. Somehow she peeled his clothes to his knees, driven by the insistent call of her own body. The moist heat between her thighs demanded release in a way that she'd never experienced before.

She held him in one hand, nuzzling the sensitive spot between her thighs with the rounded head of his erection. Slowly she eased over him, sheathing him a half inch at a time, opening herself to accept him.

Rob groaned loudly. "What is this? Cruel and unusual punishment?"

"You're too big," she said, teasing him.

"No way." His hands covered her hips, bringing her down on the iron heat of his sex.

He arched upward, thrusting deep inside her, then burrowed even farther. A shaft of exquisite pain shot right through her, and she paused for a moment to savor the bittersweet sensation. Instinctively she rocked slightly as she rode him, her head falling forward so she could watch him. Suddenly they were one, moving like dancers hearing a silent tango.

His eyes were squeezed shut and his teeth clamped down on his lower lip—despite the cut—while his powerful chest pumped up and down. That she could do this to him amazed her. And filled her with an overwhelming sense of power.

Within seconds her body contracted in a convulsion of pleasure so profound that she arched backward as an uncontrollable shudder racked her body. She gasped for air and flung her head from side to side. Above, the glittering stars in the swath of black sky seemed to be winking at her.

Rob tightened his grip on her hips and she felt him release. She gently lowered herself downward, careful not to collapse on top of him and hurt him.

She eased him onto his side, not letting their bodies part yet.

His intense eyes, now dilated until the blue was a mere shimmer around the ebony pupils, gazed at her with awe.

"You were absolutely right," she whispered. "I'm the one. The only woman for you."

21

The morning sunshine splashed through the windows, making the kitchen cheery. Usually this perked her up, but not today. Dana was so worried about Rob that nothing could make her feel better. After they'd made love she'd coaxed him into bed. They'd fallen asleep just as the first rays of sunshine backlit Koko Head. She'd awakened a short time later, but Rob was still in a deep sleep.

What if he had internal injuries? she asked herself. How selfishly she'd behaved, forcing herself on him. She should have channeled that energy into convincing him to see a doctor. "Great," she muttered. She barely had enough Kona beans for half a pot of coffee. Well, she'd have just half a cup and save the rest for Rob.

"Mornin'."

His unexpected appearance startled her, but not as much as the way he looked. His lip was swollen and a livid bruise covered his jaw. "How do you feel?"

He gingerly moved to the table and pulled out a chair. "Like I've been run over by a Mack truck. Twice."

"Coffee will make you feel better." Inane conversation, but she had no idea what else to say. She'd behaved so wantonly last night, so irresponsibly considering Rob's physical condition, that she was racked by spasms of guilt.

What had gotten into her?

She handed him the mug of coffee and tried to ignore the fact that he was wearing only Joe Boxers, which enhanced his masculinity and reminded her of last night. He was sitting now and grinning, totally relaxed, looking for all the world as if he'd spent countless nights with her.

"I'd better shower." Rob sipped his coffee, then added, "I want to be ready for Big Daddy. You don't happen to have a shirt around here that I could wear, do you? Mine's ruined."

"A friend left some clothes behind." She doubted if they would fit Rob, but it was worth a try. "Let's take a look."

They went into the guest room and opened the closet. She found the things an old boyfriend had left. Rob grabbed a shirt and waved it in front of her.

"Jesus H. Christ, I ask you, is it possible to wear too wild a shirt in Hawaii? I didn't think so. Well, I was wrong. This one needs a battery pack."

Dana didn't comment on the backhanded attack,

secretly pleased at his ill-concealed jealousy. Of course, the shirt didn't come close to fitting Rob.

"Try the T-shirt," she said.

In the frigid depths of his eyes she recognized anger. What could she say? There had been other men in her life. *Had.* That was the important word. After last night she couldn't imagine being with any other man.

Rob jerked the T-shirt out of her hand. The back was plastered with vibrant Day-Glo flowers and the front had hot-orange letters that read THE BIG KAHUNA. Grimacing in pain, Rob shrugged into it. The T-shirt stretched taut across his powerful torso, conforming to the muscular contours of his chest.

"It's better than nothing," Dana said.

"I look like fifty pounds of shit stuffed into a ten-pound sack," Rob said, arms belligerently crossed over his chest. "You and this guy are pretty cozy, huh?"

He fired the question at her with an attempt at a teasing tone, but she was getting to know him. When Rob was threatened, he resorted to sarcasm and became annoyingly domineering. Not knowing how to defuse the situation, she shrugged.

"Get rid of him."

"I was planning to date both of you," she tried to joke.

"No, you weren't. Sleeping with one man is hard enough for you. Two would be impossible. Besides, last night we made a commitment."

"Really?" There was a hint of arrogance to his

tone that sparked her temper. "Did I miss something?"

"I didn't see you pulling out a condom before you jumped on my bones."

"I don't know what got into me. I've never—"

He slipped his arm around her shoulders and gave her a gentle hug. "I'll bet you practice safe sex like a religion, but last night you got carried away."

Boy, had she! Why had she been so stupid? This was the nineties. Safe sex *should be* a religion. "I won't let it happen again."

"Yes, you will. I have no intention of using a condom. It's like taking a shower with your raincoat on. I love the way you feel—hot and wet." He grinned. "And real tight."

She squeezed her eyes shut, not believing they were talking about this. She'd never discussed sex with a man. She slowly opened her eyes and looked into his. "It's not safe."

"Don't worry. I've been careful. I don't intend to make love to anyone else but you, and I know you're not going to bed with another man." His look was so intense it sent a tremor through her. "We've made a commitment, haven't we?"

She nodded slowly, taken aback by his practical approach. Somehow she'd always associated commitments with roses and champagne, not frank discussions of safe sex in a brightly lit room. Perhaps this was better, a more direct, honest approach. Dealing with Rob Tagett would be a challenge. No doubt about it. He wasn't like any man that she knew.

I'm the one. The only one.

Somehow she'd known this even before she'd made love to him. Maybe she'd realized how she felt that afternoon on the beach. That's why she'd made love to him—and made a commitment.

He swung her into his arms and bent down to kiss her. He stopped as she brushed her finger across his swollen lip. They hugged, and she permitted herself to revel in the safety of being held, to savor the bone-deep warmth of his powerful body. And to realize she was no longer alone.

"Dana, I really care for you. I've been waiting for a chance to be with you since the night we met . . . years ago. The more time we spend together, the more sure I am that you were worth the wait."

She honestly didn't know what to say. She'd been hoping that he would tell her that he loved her, but maybe it was too soon. Could she say those words herself? No. Not yet. But she didn't doubt Rob cared about her. Last night he'd risked his life for her. Didn't actions speak louder than words?

They stood in the bedroom for a few minutes, cuddling each other, but not talking. She wished that they could spare the time to really get to know each other without all the problems she had. Why couldn't this have happened six months ago when her life had been simpler?

After a few minutes Rob said, "I'd better get in the shower."

"I'm going next door and tell Lillian that I'm back. I can see the street from her house. I'll run home if Big Daddy shows up."

Rob disappeared into the guest bath, and Dana checked her image in the hall mirror. She looked about the same, but she felt different. She'd suffered a severe psychological trauma and kept it hidden for so long that her suppressed emotions threatened to overwhelm her. Wrapping her arms around herself, she struggled to make sense of what had happened last night.

A crucial part of her, which she hadn't quite known was lost, had been found. Making love to Rob, taking charge, had given her a measure of self-control. But it went beyond that. Her response to him revealed a part of her psyche that she'd never explored: her willingness to trust a man enough to truly care about him. Until now she'd been able to go only so far before pulling back.

Last night she'd vaulted over that hurdle. Now she had an all-consuming need to discover everything about Rob. Everything. Oh, Lordy, she hadn't, had she? She hadn't fallen totally for Rob Tagett?

She tried to keep her mind on Lillian's problems, not on Rob, as she walked up to her friend's home. Would the daughter help her mother stay in the home she loved? Dana wondered. She pressed the bell and a woman in her mid-forties opened the door, greeting Dana with a challenging glare.

"Hi. I'm Dana Hamilton." She waved her hand

toward her house. "I live next door. You must be Lillian's daughter."

"Yeah, I'm Fran Martin." She spoke with a three-pack-a-day rasp. "So you're the hoity-toity judge who's filled Ma's head with crazy ideas about livin' alone."

Fran's hostility was so unexpected that for a moment it left Dana speechless. Didn't she care one iota about her mother? Maybe not. Fran never visited and rarely called. So why the sudden appearance?

"Ma's moving to the Twin Palms nursing home. They'll take care of her."

"Have you visited the facility?" Dana asked, keeping her tone light. Alienating this woman further wasn't going to help Lillian.

"Of course. It's very nice."

Dana doubted that Fran knew or cared about how the Twin Palms rated. Many facilities did nothing more than warehouse the elderly. Dana had never been inside the Twin Palms, but judging from the exterior—with paint so old the building appeared to be molting—it wasn't the best facility in Honolulu.

"Is Lillian home?" Dana asked, deciding to speak with her before confronting Fran.

"She's sleeping."

"At this hour? She's usually out in the garden by now."

"Ma's not feelin' so good."

"Have you called a doctor?"

"Nah. It's nuthin'."

"Maybe I'd better take a look at her." Dana barged in before Fran could object. "Lillian," she called.

"Dana?" The voice was weak. "That you?"

She walked into the bedroom and saw the drapes were drawn against the brilliant sun. Lillian was in bed, her face almost as pale as the pillow.

"You've been gone for weeks," Lillian said.

It had only been a few days. Lillian was losing it— a little—but did that mean she had to be yanked out of her home and sent to an institution?

"I'm back now." Dana sat at the edge of the bed. "Are you ill? Do you want me to call Dr. Winston?"

"No. I'm just tired." She looked at the door, seeming to check for her daughter, then lowered her voice to a whisper. "Fran's going to put me into a home. She took me to see it."

Lillian was silent for a moment, tears filling in her eyes. "It smelled awful. They had people strapped to their chairs to keep them from falling out. They were all lined up in the hall. I don't want to be sitting there with them."

Dana took Lillian's hand. It was thin, the blue veins raised. "Fran can't make you go there. Just tell her that you won't. I'll stand by you."

Lillian dabbed at her eyes with a lace-edged handkerchief. "You don't understand. If I don't sell the house and move to Twin Palms, Fran won't ever speak to me again."

"Does she call now, or come to see you?"

"No," Lillian admitted, tears now seeping over

her lashes. "But she says she's sorry and she's going to be better."

Dana thought this was about as likely as Mick Jaggar becoming the Pope, but she didn't voice her opinion. Lillian was a lonely old lady, and like many parents who were alienated from their children, she prayed that things would change. "If you sell the house, who's going to manage your money?"

"Fran will see that the nursing home gets money to keep me."

Exactly what Dana suspected. Fran didn't give a hoot about Lillian. She merely wanted the money. Lillian *would* end up strapped into a chair, broken-hearted. Alone.

"You don't have to go into a home. Let me talk to Fran," Dana said, although she had no idea how she could persuade such a hardcase to change her mind.

"I wish you were my daughter." Lillian squeezed Dana's hand, her fingers trembling. "I know you'd never toss me away like some worn-out old shoe."

Dana gazed at the older woman in despair. "We're calabash cousins, you know."

The Hawaiian term for friends who were as close as relatives garnered a suggestion of a smile from Lillian. She loved the island lore and often told Dana stories based on the ancient *menehune* legends like the night marchers.

"I'll help you all I can. You don't have to let Fran badger you into moving to Twin Palms."

"I know you will, sweetie, but . . ."

But what? Dana wanted to scream. Why wouldn't Lillian defy a daughter who didn't give a hoot about her anyway?

"I don't think it matters anymore," Lillian insisted. "I hear the night marchers all the time now. They're coming for me."

Dana sucked in a calming breath. First Lillian was convinced she'd spend her final days strapped to a chair at a decrepit nursing home; now she was certain she was going to die. She was confused and lonely, but she didn't need to be bullied by an ungrateful daughter. She needed tenderness and understanding.

"When I'm gone, promise me you'll take Molly. I don't want Fran to put her to sleep."

"Of course, I will," Dana said, picturing the marmalade-colored cat who'd wandered into the neighborhood and immediately found the softest touch on the block, Lillian Hurley. "But you and Molly are going to be together for a long time."

Lillian shook her head. "No. The night marchers keep getting closer and closer. I want to know those I love are in good hands."

A wild flash of grief ripped through Dana. What if Lillian died? She was such a sweet lady. Why hadn't Dana spent more time with her? Dana stroked her cheek, brushing Lillian's soft white hair off her face. "You know you can count on me. I'm positive you'll be fine and we'll work this out with Fran, but if something happens, I'll take care of Molly."

"I miss you already," Lillian whispered. "You're

the best thing that's ever happened to me. Since you moved in I've been happier. I tried to mother you a little, pretending you were my daughter."

A sob stalled in Dana's throat as she noticed the forlorn shadows beneath Lillian's eyes. In the older woman's expression she saw sadness and something deeper, something she intuitively recognized because she'd just discovered it. Love.

"I'd counted on being at your wedding," Lillian confessed. "You're going to be such a beautiful bride. But now I know I won't live that long. I won't see your children either. I wanted to hold them and cuddle them the way I did Fran."

Dana didn't trust her voice. If there was ever a perfect grandmother, it was Lillian. How could life be so unfair, cursing her with a daughter like Fran?

"Give me a hug and a kiss," Lillian said. "Tell me good-bye."

Dana gathered Lillian into her arms, surprised at Lillian's frailness. "I'm not telling you good-bye, because—"

"Don't worry, Dana. I'll be in a better place than the Twin Palms. I'll be with the *menehunes*, watching over you."

Tears welled up in Dana's eyes and she opened them wide to keep the tears at bay. Until now she hadn't realized how special Lillian was, how much she counted on seeing her each day. She couldn't face losing her.

"Hey, lady!" boomed Fran's voice from the other

room. "A limo just pulled up in front of your house."

Big Daddy! She'd forgotten all about him. She tried to let go of Lillian, promising herself she'd deal with Fran later, but Lillian refused to release her.

Frail arms locked around her, Lillian stared into Dana's eyes. "Promise me you won't forget me. I want somebody on this earth to remember that I lived and loved and did my best to be a good mother."

"Oh, Lillian. You *are* just like a mother to me. A wonderful, loving mother. I won't forget you, I swear."

"And promise me you'll be very careful after I'm gone." Her voice dropped until it was nothing more than a whisper on the wind. "The night marchers are coming for you next."

22

Night marchers? Dana thought as she sprinted across Lillian's backyard and into her own. Was Lillian really losing it? Or did she somehow sense danger? Well, Lillian did seem a bit off-kilter. But . . .

Dana had to admit that she'd felt a certain uneasiness, a chill of apprehension. It had certainly been with her that day at the beach. She wasn't prone to such thoughts, but that day when she'd been caught in the riptide, she'd believed that she had heard the night marchers.

Later that afternoon when she'd climbed the hill, she'd heard them again. Maybe it was a premonition. A warning.

She skirted the pygmy palm Lillian had planted for her earlier that summer and dodged the chaise where she'd made love to Rob. Breathless, she dashed through the back door into her kitchen.

Rob was waiting for her. "Let Coltrane do the talking. That way we'll know what he's up to. I've rigged your answering machine to record everything he says, but I doubt he'll be stupid enough to say anything incriminating."

"Good thinking," she replied.

Big Daddy was here. Now she would find out if he was the one blackmailing her. The bell rang, and the blood throbbed in Dana's temples as she followed Rob into the living room.

He sank onto the sofa and Dana quickly noticed he'd cleaned the room. There wasn't a trace of last night's brawl. Except for the cut on his lip, Rob didn't appear to have been in a fight. He'd shaved and must have found her makeup and used it to conceal the livid bruise that shadowed his jaw.

Dana raked her fingers through her hair, then opened the door. She longed to blast Coltrane with some cutting remark, but Rob's warning reminded her to keep a stranglehold on her temper.

"Where's Vanessa?" Big Daddy barged past her.

"She's in a safe place where you'll never find her." Rob's voice had the immutable ring of authority.

Coltrane halted, glaring at Rob, who was still seated, one arm casually draped over the back of the sofa. While his posture was relaxed, his expression was one Dana had never seen before. It clearly said: Don't screw with me.

Big Daddy's gaze swept the room as he seemed to consider his options. Finally he turned to Dana. "Let's talk this over."

Without waiting for an invitation he dropped into a chair, and Dana sat beside Rob. The older man looked at Dana, his black shark's eyes appearing even more threatening beneath the shock of arctic-white hair that glistened in the morning light. "Let's do a little horse trading. You've got what I want, and I've got what you want."

Here it comes, Dana thought. He *is* the black-mailer.

"You'll come up for election next year. I can help your campaign. I could deliver two ken clubs. Imagine all of them waving signs with your name on them."

This was the last thing she expected Big Daddy to say. True, she had been appointed to the bench and would have to run for election next year. She hadn't yet tackled how she would mount a campaign. Hawaiians disdained mainland media blitzes. During elections, supporters stood on street corners, waving posters with their candidate's name on them.

Mustering enough supporters to stand around in the broiling sun was an awesome challenge, but ken clubs, associations of Japanese-Americans who were very powerful in the islands, would be a godsend. To work her way up the judicial ladder Dana needed to hang on to her seat until she was appointed to a higher court. That meant running—and winning—in the next election. Big Daddy had to know how tempting his offer was.

"I'll get those ken clubs behind you," Big Daddy promised. He paused and grinned slyly. "I can convince them that you're the best judge around. All you have to do is persuade Vanessa and Jason to come home.''

Dana waited silently for him to mention Hank Rawlins's death, but he didn't. Finally she said, "This is Vanessa's decision, not mine. I won't trade my career for her happiness."

"Think twice," Big Daddy warned, rising to his feet. He crossed the room and yanked the plug out of the answering machine. "I can ruin you."

"Don't threaten her," Rob said, his voice low but forceful. "Think of what it would do to your reputation if people knew you were nothing more than a lowlife Peeping Tom who spies on his guests."

"You can't prove shit. It'll be my word against yours."

"True, but you know how devastating gossip can be. What if the story appeared in Mirah's column in the *Waikiki Tattler*?"

That got him. His wild brows furrowed into a deep vee above his eyes. The *Tattler*, the island tabloid devoted to muckraking, had a distinct fondness for reporting the real—or invented—sexual peccadilloes of well-known islanders. People claimed they never read it, yet its biweekly issues sold out.

"You're bluffing," Big Daddy said, but he didn't sound convinced. Again he turned to Dana. "I have witnesses who'll swear Vanessa is an unfit mother—a wacko. The court will give Eric full custody. You'll see."

Dana's temper flared and she almost lashed out at Big Daddy, but Rob's steadying hand on her arm reminded her to let Coltrane do the talking. As she stared at him, his expression like the devil's death mask, she realized this threat was his trump card.

An uneasy silence filled the room and she stole a quick glance at Rob. A flicker in his eyes confirmed her suspicions. A kaleidoscope of images whipped through her head. Big Daddy with bloody clothes from the pig sticking. The KAPU sign. Big Daddy "talking story" about the three sharks he'd killed.

The man was many things. A sneak. A pervert. A disgusting human being. But he wasn't the black-mailer. *He isn't the one blackmailing me.* The thought ricocheted through her brain. She almost gasped out loud, stopping herself just in time. Oh, my God, they'd been on the wrong track.

Big Daddy isn't the blackmailer.

This should have been a comforting thought, but it wasn't. There was someone else out there who hated her. An unknown enemy. Somehow that was even more chilling. Vanessa's divorce would make an enemy of Big Daddy. Now she would have two enemies. A double threat.

Concentrate on this situation, she told herself. She couldn't do anything about the blackmailer right now, but she could help Vanessa get away from the Coltranes. The thought of Big Daddy spying on her sister sickened her. What would become of Jason if this monster raised him?

Dana couldn't allow that to happen. She loved Jason, and she loved Vanessa too. She'd been there when Dana needed her. A mother, a sister, a best friend. Big Daddy could try to ruin her, but she wasn't giving up without the fight of her life.

Big Daddy rose, his eyes still on Dana. "Think it over carefully. Don't do anything you're going to regret."

"Speaking of regrets," Rob fired back, "the *mokes* you sent last night are going to get what they deserve—and so are you."

Garth awakened to the happy sounds of Puni and Jason chanting, "Sue the bastards! Sue the bastards! Sue their asses!"

He dressed and wheeled into the kitchen, cheered by the thoroughly domestic scene. Jason was sitting at the breakfast table with Puni moonwalking up his arm, while Vanessa made coffee.

"Morning," Garth muttered, uncertain of what to say. Last night they'd sat on the lanai, their hands linked, until the first etchings of a tropical dawn seeped up from the horizon in a misty mauve that soon became the sharp crimson halo of the sun. The cooing of dozens of awakening birds, harbingers of a new day, had reminded them that it was time to part.

They'd said good night, but he doubted either of them had slept much. He certainly hadn't; the few hours he'd spent in bed had done little to rest him. If anything, he was more keyed-up now—and less tired—than he had been in weeks. He couldn't help thinking about Vanessa. And wondering.

The telephone rang, and Vanessa hushed Jason

and Puni while Garth answered it. "Rob," he mouthed to Vanessa as he listened with mounting concern.

"What's wrong?" Vanessa asked after he hung up, and Garth rolled his eyes at Jason. Immediately she caught on. "Jason, why don't you take Puni outside?"

"Ooookay, Puni, here we go." Jason moonwalked backward to the door that opened onto the fern-filled lanai.

Vanessa joined him on the sofa in the alcove overlooking the lanai, her blue eyes troubled. "What happened?"

As gently as possible, Garth repeated what Big Daddy had said and the story of the *mokes* lying in wait for Dana and Rob. "They stole the tapes," he concluded, unable to keep the bitterness out of his voice. "Now there's no proof, no leverage against the Coltranes."

"Can't you do something?" she asked, her expression as beseeching as her voice.

He tenderly put his hand on Vanessa's shoulder and gazed into her eyes. "Let me be dead honest with you. The best you can hope for is joint custody with Eric, and that means Big Daddy will see Jason half the time. If the Coltranes carry out the threat to smear you as an unfit mother, you may very well lose custody of your son entirely."

"I'm a good mother," she insisted. "They can't—"

"The Coltranes have the money—and the influence—to get a number of the servants at the ranch, as well as his sons, to lie about you."

The pain in her eyes told him the words registered, but she didn't say anything. Her gaze drifted to the plate-glass window; through it they could see Jason frolicking with Puni.

"There might be a way." Vanessa's emotion-charged voice startled him.

"Like what?" he asked gently, unwilling to give her false hope.

She shrugged, then braced her hands against her tanned thighs. The long nails bit into the soft flesh, digging deeper as she kept her head averted.

"Is there something I should know?" Garth asked, dead certain she was withholding important information. He reached over and covered one hand with his, lacing his fingers through hers and gently lifting. Beneath her hand were half-moon indentations made by her nails. He took her hand and held it in both of his. "Tell me everything. I have to know the truth or I can't help you."

She studied him for a moment, seeming to judge whether or not she could trust him. "I think there's a way to fight the Coltranes and keep custody of Jason." She cast a swift glance at the lanai where Puni and Jason were playing. "Eric Coltrane wouldn't have any claim on Jason if he isn't his father, would he?"

Vanessa was grasping at straws, he thought. Jason had her beautiful blue eyes and platinum hair, but he had the Coltranes' square jaw and cleft chin.

"It won't work. The Coltranes' attorney will insist on a paternity test."

"Are those tests reliable?"

"If they're done properly in a good lab, paternity tests are accurate. I've had them done on occasion."

She smiled—grinned, actually—sending his heart into one long free-fall. What was going on here?

"That's what I was hoping, Garth. A paternity test will prove Eric isn't Jason's father."

23

Rob hung up the telephone, having just told Garth about the *mokes* and Big Daddy's visit. Across the room Dana was huddled on the sofa, her legs drawn up to her chest and her arms locked around her knees. Poor kid. With the tapes gone, she thought she'd let Vanessa down.

She hadn't been responsible. He'd gotten them into this mess. Shit! He should have anticipated the *mokes* coming after them. He'd been cocky, arrogant. Stupid. The shrill ringing of the telephone interrupted his thoughts and he watched Dana gracefully stride across the room to answer it.

"Hi, Gwen," she said, then paused to listen. "I came back early. . . . Ah, well, my sister is divorcing Eric Coltrane."

Rob wondered why she'd volunteered this information. How close was Dana to Gwen? He didn't really like Gwen.

Dana listened for a minute, twisting the telephone cord between her fingers. "Really? Where'd you hear that?" The anxious note in her voice alerted him. "Rob Tagett was there. . . . I did see a little of him."

He sank into a chair, his body still aching from the fight. So word had gotten back to Honolulu that he'd been with Dana at the Coltrane ranch. He wasn't surprised Gwen had gotten wind of it. The consummate politician, she would wonder what this meant for Dana's career.

"I suppose you're right," Dana said wearily, and Rob could just imagine the lecture she was getting from Gwen on how Dana's reputation would suffer if she spent time with him.

"You're kidding," Dana said, her eyes widening at whatever Gwen had just said. "Clements was only what? Forty-five?" She paused to listen. "Really? Just forty-one. That's too young to die of a heart attack, isn't it? . . . His poor wife and that darling little boy."

So Todd Clements was dead. Son of a bitch! Just went to prove you never knew. When your number was up, it was up. A damn shame, but this meant there'd be another opening on the superior court. Dana would get a second chance much sooner than anyone expected.

Rob wondered how Gwen really felt about Dana's name being on the list for superior court. Her father, Boss Sihida, was a force in political circles. He might try to get Gwen into Todd Clements' spot. Hell, Rob hoped not. The last thing Dana needed was to be pitted against a friend. In the islands it was hard enough to get women onto the bench. They didn't need to compete with each other.

Dana hung up, shaking her head. "Todd Clements died of a heart attack."

"That's too bad. He was a nice guy and a good judge."

"Gwen says I'm up for the vacancy. Big Daddy will do whatever he can to ruin it for me." She dropped onto the sofa beside him.

"Coltrane has power, but the governor's a tough cookie. He—"

"What if the blackmailer goes to the governor?"

"Without proof, it's just gossip." He studied her for a moment, the sunlight playing softly across her face. "How important is being a judge?"

She hesitated, then responded, "Careerwise, I want it more than anything. I always have—even when I was in law school. The day I was appointed to the municipal court was the happiest day of my life."

He nodded, remembering that was the night he'd met her. The DA had thrown a party to celebrate Dana's appointment. She'd been radiant. Her vitality, her energy had drawn him to her. Her intelligence had captivated him. From that night on, no other woman could compare.

He'd blown it with the tapes, but maybe he could make it up to Dana. "Your career's in jeopardy as long as the blackmailer is around. It can't be Big Daddy or he would have threatened you with it.

Let's talk about your other enemies again. I'm still suspicious of Judge Binkley."

"Davis Binkley hates me," she admitted. "You know he deliberately assigned me the Tenaka case the first week I was on the court."

Rob kept his mouth shut; the Tenaka case would always be a sore point between them. The superior court should have heard the child molester's case, but they dodged it, claiming their schedules were overloaded. It was too controversial for the muni court's presiding judge to handle, so Binkley passed it off to the rookie, Dana.

"He assigns me the worst cases, hoping I'll goof."

"So far, you've outsmarted him. Your decisions haven't been appealed. That's why you're up for the superior court."

"Judge Binkley has made no secret of how much he dislikes me. He even persuaded a friend's son to run for my seat on the municipal bench next year." She shook her head thoughtfully. "I keep remembering the blackmailer's message: *Get out of Hawaii*. There's nothing Binkley would like better. But how could he possibly know about my past?"

Rob didn't have an answer.

"There are several deputy DAs who can't stand me."

"Professional jealousy," Rob said. Dana's star had risen rapidly, eclipsing others who'd been around longer. He remembered the feeling from his days on the force when he'd shot ahead of many veteran officers. Meteoric rises made for spectacular crashes back to earth. Aw, hell, that wasn't going to happen to Dana, was it?

"This is a long shot, but I inherited my secretary, Anita, along with the office. She'd been Judge Gimble's secretary for years, and she adored him, probably because he put up with her sloppy work. I've written her up twice."

Rob knew the type. Protected by the civil-service system, they were just plain lazy. You could write them up a dozen times and still pay hell getting rid of them. "Has she done anything serious?"

"When she put my sentencing list into the computer, she somehow—after thirteen years on the job —'confused' the codes. So the jail received the information and released the wrong prisoners and kept those I'd wanted released."

"Petty things. Just what a secretary might do for revenge. Blackmail seems out of character. Anyway, how would she know about your past? It all comes back to that, you know."

"You're right. That's why I keep wondering if Vanessa's old boyfriend, Slade Carter, or one of his friends has come to Hawaii. Slade was right behind us that night. He probably found Hank's body and put two and two together."

"Makes sense," Rob admitted, "but why would he want you out of Hawaii?"

Dana threw up both hands. "I'm clueless."

"Well, I have an idea. Where did you say all this happened? Texas?"

He knew she'd deliberately not told him where

this had happened. With a desperation that came from a deep, secret corner of his soul, he wanted her to trust him. When had his feeling for her become an all-consuming passion? Startled by his own emotions, he looked away. He needed her to come to him, to want him so much that the past no longer mattered.

Last night he'd gotten his wish. She'd come to him and made love to him like no woman ever had. But with the light of day, Dana's fears had obviously returned.

The silence in the room thickened as she regarded him wordlessly, weighing her options. Finally she spoke. "Missouri. It happened in Gomper's Bend, Missouri. It's nothing more than a crook in the road near the Arkansas border."

Despite the pain from his split lip, he managed a smile. Knowing she trusted him triggered all his protective instincts. And something more. The divorce had sucked him dry emotionally, leaving him bitter and wary of relationships. Now he was ready to risk it all again.

"You know I'm crazy about you, don't you?" he asked and she nodded solemnly. "I'll do anything I can to help you. I want to go back there and nose around, but I need to know the whole truth about that night."

"Hank Rawlins was a no-good who was too lazy to work," Dana said. "He spent his time hunting and brewing rotgut whiskey, which they sold at the Road Kill Bar where Vanessa worked. We were trying to save money to go to California, so when Hank offered me five dollars to help him skin rabbits, I said yes." The pitch of her voice had gone up an octave, though her expression was calm. "He got me in the shed and . . . and . . ."

Rob gathered her in his arms and pressed his lips to the top of her head, cursing the bastard.

Dana drew back, staying in the circle of his arm. "Vanessa heard me crying hours after it was all over, and I was still crouched in that shed. She came to find me and Hank pounced on Vanessa."

The threat of tears was in her voice now. "I huddled in the corner like . . . like some beaten dog. I couldn't move. All I could do was watch."

She shrugged out of his protective embrace. He wasn't surprised. When emotionally threatened, Dana retreated, carefully maintaining the distance she kept between herself and the world.

"Do you know how that makes me feel?" The words, quite loud now, exploded out of her with such vehemence that Rob almost flinched. "I could have spared my sister the agony of that brute raping her—but I was a coward."

Coward. Coward. Coward. The word echoed through the room, triggering a suffocating memory that he'd rather forget. With it came empathy so powerful, he couldn't utter a word. Finally he managed to say, "You were young, and you'd been through a traumatic experience. It's understandable that fear paralyzed you."

"Well, I can't forgive myself. If I'd acted sooner . . ."

The psychological burden of this incident still weighed her down. Rob understood. Often forgiving your own weaknesses was more difficult than forgiving another person.

"Dana, let it go. Sometimes we have a second in which to act. If we don't the opportunity is gone—never to come again. Believe me, I know."

He put his arm around her, unsure of what to say. He recalled how he'd screwed up. And the devastating results.

"What do you mean?"

He didn't want to resurrect his past. He wanted her to see him as someone to lean on. Aw, hell, he wasn't perfect. Pretending he was had gotten him in trouble last time, but he wasn't going to make that mistake again. Dana meant too much to him.

"I resigned from the police force because I was a coward." He responded to her shocked expression with a curt nod. "That's right. I'd been touted as a hero, but I was a coward. Honey, you were just a little girl. No one would call you a coward."

"I don't believe you're a coward, not the way you went after those *mokes*."

"When that prostitute accused me of rape I should have brought it out into the open and fought it, but I didn't. I'd been the golden boy for so long that I thought things would work out. It's taken me a long time to admit the truth. You're the first person I've talked to about this. It hurts to have you know I was a coward, but it's done and nothing can change it."

"You were in a difficult position. You—"

"There are always excuses. I accept the truth and so should you."

Dana mulled over his words for a moment. "You want the truth . . . the whole truth?" Her tone reflected her pain and her tremendous strength of will. "Hank had raped Vanessa and was forcing her down again, when I summoned my courage and grabbed the rabbit-skinning knife off the hook."

She looked Rob directly in the eye. "Hank didn't fall on the knife. I stabbed him in the back."

24

Dana stared out her bedroom window at the palms etched in deep shadows against the moonlit sky. The curtains fluttered in the breeze. Fragrant plumeria scented the darkness, mingling with the loamy, earthy smell of the tropics. Usually she loved nights like this when the full moon—a lovers' moon—cast its magic on Koko Head, but not tonight.

She missed Rob already. After she'd explained what really happened to Hank Rawlins, Rob had consoled her, insisting she'd had no choice. Then he'd left for the airport, determined to get to Gomper's Bend and find Slade Carter, Vanessa's old boyfriend.

Rawlins got what he deserved. You had no other choice.

Rob's words had been reassuring—at the time. Now, though, alone in her bed, she had her doubts. How could she have killed another human being? She'd kept the memory of what she'd done locked away for years. She wondered how she had stepped up to the bench day after day and had the nerve to pass judgment on others.

How could she? No matter what her reasons, she had killed a man. She didn't deserve to be a judge.

The scene she'd blocked out for so many years still had the power to ruin her life. As the long-dead memories emerged, Dana relived that terror-filled night when she'd been fourteen.

Huddling in the corner of the filthy shed, immobilized by fear, she watched Hank assault Vanessa. *Why did you scream?* she asked herself. After Hank had attacked her he'd kept her locked in the shed for hours while he drank whiskey. If only she'd kept her mouth shut, Vanessa wouldn't have come to help her.

Vanessa's whimpering cries filled the shed. Though her young mind was barely functioning, Dana realized Hank intended to kill them. He'd told her that no one was ever going to find out what he'd done. She couldn't let him kill them.

"Mommie-e-e, help me!" cried Vanessa.

Her sister's plea echoed in Dana's brain—an incantation to the dead. Since their parents' deaths Vanessa had been so brave, being both mother and sister to Dana. But now Dana knew the truth. Vanessa had been afraid too. Her sister was just a girl in a woman's body.

For the first time Dana truly realized they had no one but themselves. She scanned the room, searching for something—anything—to use as a weapon. Then she'd spotted the rabbit knife.

Looking back over the span of twenty years, Dana realized she would have done the same thing all over again—only sooner. *Justice*. Sometimes it was a four-letter word. She truly believed Hank had gotten what he deserved. But she—and Vanessa—were still paying for his crime.

Rob had been right when he'd said they didn't trust men because they associated all men with Hank Rawlins. Dana closed her eyes, blocking out the moonlight, but not the wellspring of emotion she'd kept hidden for so many years. Yes, if it happened all over again she'd grab the knife—before Hank got to Vanessa, before her sister suffered his brutal assault the way she had.

The shrill sound of a siren startled Dana and she sat bolt upright in bed, memories of the past still swirling through her brain. Shouts came from the street, but she couldn't tell what they were saying. Dana charged to the window and yanked back the curtain. An ambulance was next door.

"Oh, my God! Something's happened to Lillian."

It took her a few seconds to throw on a robe and dash outside. By that time the paramedics were bringing out a gurney. Red then white, red then white, red then white flashed the strobe light of the ambulance as the body was brought out, draped in a white sheet. Two police cars were parked nearby, bursts of static and dispatch calls punctuating the stillness.

"No, no!" Dana cried. She pulled back the sheet. Lillian's face was an unnatural parchment color, yet peaceful, her lips curved into a suggestion of a smile.

"Oh, Lillian, no." Dana stared at the woman who'd loved her like a daughter. Something inside Dana broke, and a sob rose from her throat, a requiem of unparalleled sadness. She should have done more for Lillian, spent more time with her.

The EMT replaced the sheet and Dana said a silent farewell. A surge of guilt brought with it the weight of her loss, knowing she'd never see Lillian again. She'd never be able to share anything with her. How vividly she recalled the pride in the older woman's eyes when Dana spoke about one of her cases. A mother's pride. Yes, that's all Lillian ever had wanted to be—a loving mother.

From the shadows Dana saw Lillian's daughter, Fran, glaring at her. Normally she would have gone to console the woman, but Dana didn't trust her temper. She turned to Dr. Winston, who was standing nearby. "How did it happen?"

"Fran called to say her mother wasn't feeling well. I came right over. Just as I got here Lillian had a severe stroke," Dr. Winston replied. "No one could have saved Lillian. I found her pill case in the bathroom. It's been days since she'd taken her medication. Her blood pressure was in the stratosphere."

"Her daughter should have—"

"Lillian never told Fran that she needed those pills." Dr. Winston shrugged, his eyes on the ambulance as it pulled away. "I can't image why Lillian didn't mention it."

"She wanted to die," Dana whispered, more to herself than the doctor. "She wanted to pass away here, among the things she loved, in the home she and her husband had built—where she'd been happy. She was terrified of dying, lonely and forgotten, in some horrible nursing home."

And she didn't trust me to help her. Her sense of guilt went beyond words, beyond tears. She'd failed dear Lillian, failed her miserably.

Long after the ambulance had driven off, Dana stood at the curb, her eyes fastened on the curve in the road where the taillights had disappeared. She hardly heard the police cars pull away or Dr. Winston say good-bye. All she could think about was Lillian.

A dear friend. Almost her mother.

She trudged up the steps to her home, her heart unbearably heavy. As she passed through the living room the flashing light on her answering machine caught her eye. Rob, she thought, then realized it was just after midnight. He'd promised to call when he changed planes in Los Angeles, but he wouldn't be there until morning. She punched the buttons and heard Vanessa's voice.

"Garth has arranged a meeting with the Coltranes and their attorney for tomorrow at four." There was a strange upbeat quality to her sister's voice. "Garth wants to settle this before it gets to court. Can you be at his office about half an hour early? There's something I have to explain to you before Garth and I fight the Coltranes."

Garth and I? Well, well, it sounded as if they were becoming very friendly. At least Vanessa was prepared to fight Big Daddy. After the *mokes* had stolen the tapes Dana hadn't been certain Vanessa would risk it.

But what about me? Dana wondered. Where did she fit into her sister's life? She'd been conscious of a growing rift that she seemed powerless to overcome. She'd thought that Vanessa's leaving the Coltranes would bring them closer. Now she wasn't so sure. What had come between them?

"My career came between us," she said as she dropped into bed. A sigh that seemed to well up from the bottom of her soul filled the room. She'd made the same mistake with Lillian, she realized with growing alarm. She hadn't spent enough time with the people who counted.

Tears soaked the pillow as she mourned for Lillian until she finally fell asleep, carried into the unconscious world of her dreams by sheer exhaustion. For two nights now she'd had almost no sleep. She only dozed, awakened by images of the past and haunted by the present.

A noise brought her out of yet another disturbing dream. She sat up in bed and listened. There it was again. *Thump-thump-thump-thump.* It sounded like —but it couldn't be—the night marchers. Now in the darkest hours just before dawn Lillian's pro-

phetic warning echoed in her ears. *The night marchers are coming for you next.*

"You're going 'round the bend, Dana," she whispered to herself. "Next you'll be seeing ghosts."

She swung out of bed and silently padded down
the hall toward the noise. In the yard shadows
danced, made even deeper by the full moon. She
squinted into the darkness and the noise stopped.
Outside on her lanai a small shadow darted toward
the kitchen door. *Thump-thump-thump.*

Not the night marchers, but a cat. It wasn't just
any cat, she saw as a shaft of moonlight hit orange
fur. Lillian's cat, Molly. She opened the lanai door
and called, "Here, kitty, kitty, kitty."

Molly bounded over and rubbed her long fur
against Dana's legs. She meowed twice, a deep,
throaty sound that brought unexpected tears to
Dana's eyes. She picked up the cat, thinking that
Molly had never once come to her door until now.

The cat's collar with a small bell to warn birds
was missing. Lillian would never have taken it off.
Fran must have removed the collar and its identify-
ing tags. She wasn't even going to take her mother's
cat to the Humane Society, Dana thought, disgusted. She'd turned Molly loose to fend for herself.

"Would she do that to you?" she asked the kitty.
"Let's find out."

Guided by the moonlight, she left the house and
walked the short distance across the backyard to
Lillian's door, the cat tucked in her arms. The house
was dark except for the blue-white light of the televi-

sion in the den. Dana bent low and tested the lower half of the door. The pet door was bolted shut.

"Never mind," she whispered to Molly. "Lillian wanted me to have you."

She tiptoed down the path that she'd so often taken between their homes, knowing that this would be her last trip. Her beloved friend was gone.

I'll be with the menehunes, *watching over you.* Lillian's parting words were nothing more than a murmur in the rustling palms.

"Lillian told you where to come, didn't she?" Dana stroked Molly's soft fur. She smelled of jasmine from playing in the bushes. Deep in the cat's throat a low rumble of a purr began, accelerating with each stroke of Dana's hand. She knew she was being maudlin and even slightly irrational. Still, she couldn't seem to help herself.

The weight of the loss, knowing she'd never see Lillian again, swept through her. She'd never be able to share anything with her again. Pain reverberated through her, a keening cry from the depths of her soul. Death was terrifyingly final. There'd be no more star-filled tropic nights for Lillian, no more walks on the beach, no more working in the garden, no more petting Molly's silky fur. No more anything.

"I'm expecting a call from Rob Tagett," Dana told her secretary the next morning. "Put him through immediately. If I'm in court, have the clerk get me."

"Sure," Anita responded with all the enthusiasm of a person receiving the last rites.

Dana took a closer look at the woman and wondered if Anita hated her enough to blackmail her. Anita was arranging the intracourt documents. She was slower than a slug; the state would never have to worry about a stress claim.

Like many Hawaiian women, Anita had a penchant for gold bracelets. They covered her arm from wrist to elbow and tinkled as she moved, reminding Dana of Christmas bells. As usual, gold was the only color she wore. Her dress was as black as her eyes, which were now studying Dana suspiciously.

"Oh, I almost forgot. Judge Binkley wants to see you."

Dana walked into her office, her jaw clenched to keep from cursing, and tossed her briefcase on the desk. Anita conveniently "forgot" more than she remembered in a blatant attempt to sabotage Dana. As soon as she had a spare minute to fill out the myriad forms, she would report Anita again. This would be the third time that she'd written her up. With luck she could get rid of her this time.

Dana gazed at the Wyland print of dolphins playing with a whale, her eyes immediately going to the hidden world beneath the surface of the ocean. Just like people. There's so much concealed beneath the surface. It wasn't a comforting thought. Who was trying to ruin her life? It was obvious Anita despised her, but she couldn't possibly know about Dana's past.

She was still mulling over the situation as she walked down the hall for her meeting with Judge Binkley.

"Dana," called Gwen from her office.

Her friend wore an ivory Escada suit that was a perfect foil for her thick black hair and dark eyes. She smiled the warm smile she always had for Dana, and Dana smiled back.

"Have you heard anything?" Gwen asked.

She realized Gwen was talking about the superior court appointment. "Not a word. I'm on my way to the Black Lagoon. Binkley wants to see me."

"He's going to tell you that you're doing the arraignment calendar."

"The judicial pits. Yuck!" Dana said and Gwen laughed. All the judges hated working the arraignment calendar, which scheduled upcoming trials. "I've been on arraignments three times this year already. It can't be my turn again."

"Binkley's just trying to harass you. He knows you're up for that appointment." Gwen studied Dana for a moment, her dark eyes suddenly somber. "Don't blow it, Dana. Don't get mixed up with Rob Tagett."

Dana didn't know how to tell her friend that she was already involved—more than involved—with Rob. Gwen had dated him once and thought she knew him, but she didn't know the real Rob. No one did—no one but Dana. That thought brought an unexpected surge of affection.

"My brother's worried about your tooth." Gwen changed subjects, seemingly embarrassed by her own frankness. "He can fit you in this afternoon."

"I can't today. My sister needs me when she meets with the Coltranes and their lawyer." Dana didn't want to hurt Gwen's feelings, but she had no intention of letting her brother work on her again. "Maybe I'll call him later," Dana hedged, walking away with a wave of her hand. "Right now, I'm off to the Black Lagoon."

The urge to scream told her she had reached Judge Binkley's chambers. She entered and gave her name to his secretary. Photographs lined the walls, a rogues' gallery of Who's Who in Hawaii. Obviously, Judge Binkley aspired to a higher position, but he'd been stalled at this level for years.

Sixtyish, tanned, with a bald head sprouting tufts of gray hair, Davis Binkley was the presiding judge of the municipal court—in effect, her boss. A bigtime cage shaker and totally impressed with himself, his cronies were the men on the court. She and Gwen were the outsiders.

Dana walked into his chambers and Binkley looked up at her, but didn't smile or invite her to sit down. "You're on the arraignment calendar."

"Again?" she protested, even though experience had taught her that it wouldn't do any good.

"You scheduled several trials too close last time

and they had to be rescheduled. Attorneys protested. It caused a lot of problems.''

Dana battled to control her temper. There was no perfect schedule. Some trials went over, causing delays in other trials. She didn't make any more mistakes than any of the other judges when they worked the arraignment calendar.

He looked her in the eye and smiled. Actually he appeared to be gloating, and a knot of apprehension formed in her chest. "You know I don't listen to rumors, but I've been hearing things." He paused, obviously wanting to play the moment to the hilt, and she thought he'd heard about Rob. "What you do with your personal life is one thing, but this—this could be a problem.''

"What are you talking about?''

"Fran Martin's lawyer called. She's upset about her mother's will.''

"Lillian's will?'' Dana gasped. "The poor woman only died last night. What did Fran do? Wake the lawyer?''

"Maybe. She phoned him first thing this morning and claimed that you used undue influence on her late mother.''

"That's ridiculous. We were friends. That's all.'' She couldn't keep the anger out of her voice. Lillian deserved a better daughter than this.

"Fran Martin insists that you persuaded her mother to leave her out of the will.''

"We never discussed a will. Not once.''

"Good,'' he said, his tone clearly implying he

didn't believe her. "I have to investigate allegations of misconduct. You understand."

She understood, all right. Fran Martin's charges couldn't have come at a worse time. It would ruin her chances of getting that appointment—if the blackmailer didn't.

"You've got to admit, Dana, that it looks suspicious when a daughter is disinherited and a neighbor gets everything."

"Me?" She heard her own quick intake of breath. "Lillian left me everything?"

"Yes. It's suspicious. Mighty suspicious."

25

Dana was still shaken when she arrived at Garth's office hours later. What else could go wrong? It was bad enough that Lillian had died, but now her daughter wasn't going to let her rest in peace. She wished Rob was here with her and not on what was probably a wild-goose chase. He'd know what to do about Fran's threats.

What was she thinking? Rob had his own problems; he certainly didn't need hers. During his layover in L.A. he was meeting his son at the airport. From what Rob had told her, Zach was going through a difficult period. Rob hoped his wife would allow him to visit later that summer. Rob thought he could turn Zach around—if he had the chance.

Outside Garth's building, Vanessa was waiting for Dana. Dressed in a blue dress that emphasized her blonde hair and blue eyes, she dashed up and hugged Dana. "Thanks for coming," Vanessa said with a bright smile, and Dana realized her sister looked happier than she'd seen her in years. "Bad day in court?"

Dana glumly nodded, reluctant to trouble Vanessa with her problems. Her sister linked her arm with Dana's and led her over to the stone bench beneath the banyan tree. There they could have some privacy from the people coming and going from the high-rise tower.

"There's something I should have told you a long time ago," Vanessa began. "I just didn't have the courage."

"You shouldn't need courage to tell me anything." Dana took her sister's hand and held it in both of hers. "Vanessa, I love you. I know I haven't said it often enough, but I do."

Vanessa's expressive eyes misted with tears. She blinked them back and squeezed Dana's hand. "You know all I've ever wanted was a home and a family. I've never had your drive, your ambition. When Eric came along I thought he was perfect. I honestly did."

Vanessa's expression grew even more serious. "Things were fine—or so I thought—until we tried to have children. Nothing happened. We went to the doctor and discovered Eric had an extremely low sperm count. The only way for me to get pregnant was to collect his sperm and be artificially inseminated."

"I never realized you were having those problems."

"No one knew except Eric and his father."

LAST NIGHT

There was an edge of bitterness to Vanessa's voice that had become too familiar lately. No wonder. The Coltranes were even stranger than Dana had realized.

"I wanted to tell you, but Eric was terrified that someone would find out he couldn't father a child without medical assistance."

Dana nodded for her to continue.

"The insemination worked and I became pregnant. When Jason was born I thought my world was perfect. Then Eric stopped coming home at night. I confronted him and he said he'd married me to make his father happy. Now that the Coltranes had an heir, Eric was going back to his old girlfriend."

Dana's heart went out to her sister, imagining her trapped in a loveless marriage—with a child. "You must have been devastated. Why didn't you tell me?"

"Because you'd tried to warn me about the Coltranes and I hadn't listened. I decided that I owed it to Jason to make the best of it." For a moment Vanessa stared at her shoes. "I'm not as smart as you, Dana. I should have realized my father-in-law would try to raise Jason to be a macho jerk like his own sons. But I didn't, not at first anyway."

Vanessa stopped speaking as two men walked past. "When Jason was three I decided I wanted another child. I wasn't sleeping with Eric, of course, so I went back to the sperm bank, thinking they probably still had some of Eric's sperm." Vanessa's voice drifted into a hushed whisper.

"Did they?" Dana prompted after a few seconds' silence.

"There was a new doctor there." Vanessa attempted a smile. "You know how I affect some men. Well, he couldn't do enough for me. He got out all the old records and found there was plenty of sperm on hand, but it wasn't Eric's. It was Big Daddy's."

Dana heard her own quick intake of breath as she struggled to comprehend. "Oh, my God. You mean he's Jason's father?" The bile rose in her throat, and for a second she thought she might actually be ill. "That's beyond disgusting. That's . . . that's . . . sick!"

Vanessa silenced Dana, glaring at her with burning, reproachful eyes. "That's why I never told you. I knew how much you hated him. Now you'll hate Jason. I don't care who his father is. I love my son with all my heart."

"Oh, Vanessa, I didn't mean—"

"You'll be looking for Big Daddy in Jason, won't you?"

She had to confess that she'd never look at Jason in quite the same way. Then she remembered his small arms around her neck and him telling her about the wild pig that he'd confused with Wilbur from *Charlotte's Web*. Jason was still a sensitive child—nothing like his father. She did love him, and even this startling revelation could never change that.

"No, Vanessa, I won't be looking for Big Daddy in

Jason. Not at all. I'll be looking for you. He's your son. Never forget it."

Tears glistened on Vanessa's lashes, and she reached out with both arms to Dana. She drew Vanessa close, comforting her and praying that together they could get Jason away from the Coltranes.

"We'd better go upstairs," Dana said after a few minutes of silence. "We want to be ready for them."

"Garth is great with Jason," Vanessa commented as they rode the elevator to the top floor of the skyscraper. "You can't imagine how comforting that is after Eric ignoring him and Big Daddy trying to make him into 'a man.' Garth just lets Jason be himself—a little boy."

"How do you feel about Garth?"

"I've never met anyone like him. I know how hard it is to be alone in the world the way we were after Mom and Dad were killed. Imagine waking up and finding you're alone. Then you discover you'll never walk again. Garth was extraordinarily brave. He made a life for himself when so many would have given up."

"It's true," Dana said. "Everyone admires Garth."

"It's more than admiration, Dana. Knowing Garth makes me realize that all men aren't like the Coltranes or Hank. Lots of them have suffered as much as we have—or more."

The elevator door slid open and they walked down the hall toward Garth's office. Dana wanted to tell Vanessa about Rob, but there wasn't enough time. She also needed enough time to discuss that night when Hank had assaulted them. For years they'd avoided the topic—as if it had never happened. Rob was right; talking would help. You could never overcome an enemy until you faced him.

"I'm not returning to the ranch," Vanessa said emphatically.

"Even if it means losing Jason?"

"Garth will take care of Big Daddy, you'll see."

"It's not like you to put your faith in a man."

Vanessa opened the door to Garth's office. "It's nice to find a man you can put your faith in."

Garth sat in the conference room with Dana on one side and Vanessa on the other as Eric and Thornton Coltrane walked in with their attorney, Vince Adams, a legal thug who thrived on lucrative litigation. Garth let Adams strut his stuff, justifying his exorbitant fee by accusing Vanessa of everything but armed robbery.

Big Daddy sat silent as a tombstone, glaring at Garth. Evidently Adams had instructed him to be quiet, so he'd resorted to a stare that could freeze lava. It didn't fluster Garth. Coltrane was a pervert, plain and simple. Garth didn't take the moral high ground often, but this was one time he felt superior to another man.

Vince Adams finished explaining the very effective argument he'd present to the court. Garth glanced at Vanessa out of the corner of his eye and saw she was still composed, still trusting his judgment. *Oh, God, don't let me blow this.*

"We agree that you have an airtight case against Vanessa Coltrane, with all the witnesses who'll claim she's an unfit mother and everything," Garth said, not mentioning that Coltrane money paid for those witnesses.

For a moment Adams seemed taken aback, not expecting Garth to cave in so early and without a fee-bloating argument. Big Daddy grinned at Vanessa, an ugly, triumphant sneer. Vanessa stared back at him, her beautiful face a mask of composure.

Dana shifted in her seat and glared at the Coltranes. Big Daddy ignored her, concentrating on Vanessa and Garth instead. Eric Coltrane appeared so bored that nothing short of a bomb under his chair would get his attention.

"There's just one problem with your case," Garth said, his tone level.

"What's that?" Big Daddy blurted out.

"You can prove that Vanessa Coltrane is an unfit mother and custody should go to the father, but can you prove Eric is Jason's father?"

"Of course, we can—" Adams halted midsentence, reacting to his clients' stunned expressions.

Eric had appeared brain dead just moments ago, but now he was staring at Garth, slack-jawed. Big Daddy had turned the color of an eggplant, his unruly brows knit together, making him look like Rasputin.

Garth directed his next comment to Eric. "I have a laboratory ready to conduct a paternity test. Your blood will prove—"

Big Daddy vaulted to his feet. "Jason is a Coltrane. Just look at him."

"Eric is *not* Jason's father," Vanessa insisted. "A paternity test will prove it."

Big Daddy dropped into his chair, his face ashen.

"That's why I called everyone here today," Garth said, using the tone that convinced juries his clients were innocent. "I think we all want to avoid the spectacle of a public trial—for Jason's sake."

"She's an unfit mother." Adams pointed to Vanessa with an unflinching stare like a vulture. As tenacious as a used-car salesman, he was determined to prolong the case and up his billable hours. "The court will take Jason away."

Garth waited. This was the gamble: Was Big Daddy willing to risk exposing his perversion to get Jason? The silence from across the table was the answer he'd been praying for. Big Daddy had an ego the size of the Hindenburg, and he wasn't about to reveal his true nature. Not even for his son.

Garth was so relieved that tears formed behind his eyes, tears that he hadn't allowed himself since he watched both his parents being lowered into the ground and realized he'd spend the rest of his life in a wheelchair. Alone.

Without feeling a thing, he knew Vanessa's hand

was on his knee. Her fingers, crowned by those gorgeous nails, curved around his leg, silently communicating her relief.

Big Daddy lurched to his feet and yelled at Vanessa, "You'll be sorry. You'll beg me to forgive you. I swear it!"

Rob leaned against the open door of the phone booth and listened to Dana's phone ring. God damn, where was she? It was past midnight in Honolulu and early morning in Missouri. Already the temperature was nudging triple digits, sealing his shirt to his skin and giving him what promised to be the mother of all headaches.

Hell, it wasn't the weather that was getting to him. It was Zach. What was he going to do about his son? Or was it already too late? And how would Dana react to his news?

He was hanging up when he heard Dana's voice. "Hey, where've you been?" he asked.

"Rob." That's all she said, but the sound of her voice made him smile for the first time since he'd met Zach and Ellen at the airport in L.A.

"Sorry I didn't call when I changed planes, but I barely made my flight."

"Did something happen with Zach?"

"Yeah." He sucked in his breath and gazed at Joe Mama's, the two-bit diner where he'd had breakfast. "His mother caught him with pills in his pocket. She thinks he's experimenting with drugs. He denies it, but . . ."

"Oh, no. What are you going to do?"

"Ellen wants to send him away to school." Even now he could hear Ellen sobbing as they'd sat in the terminal's coffee shop and discussed Zach's future. This time he didn't give in to her tears. If he didn't take charge he'd lose his son to drugs. "I want him to come live with me."

"Is that what Zach wants?"

He slumped against the wall of the phone booth. "Who the hell knows? The kid barely said two words. He just sulked while we talked."

"You're doing the right thing. Zach needs your guidance. Bring him here and get counseling. You can turn him around."

She hadn't seen the petulant teenager his son had become. *Love you forever.* His son's voice echoed down through the years. Zach used to say that when Rob kissed him good night. That was then and this is now, Rob told himself. Inside the hostile teen he had to find that lost little boy.

"How does Ellen feel about Zach moving here?"

"She agreed. She knows she's in over her head." He didn't curse Ellen the way he wanted to. She'd done her best over the years to keep Zach away from him. Now she was willing to dump the problem in his lap, and blame him if it didn't work out.

What had he seen in her? He didn't know anymore, but he was dead certain of one thing. He loved his son. And he'd do anything to help him.

"I give a lot of counseling referrals for first-time drug offenders. I think Dr. Ho at Brigham Young

University in Laie has the most success. I'll make an appointment for you and Zach."

"Thanks." The word came out like a sigh. He didn't know what he expected. Didn't she understand this would change the course of their relationship? He couldn't spend his nights with her when Zach needed constant supervision.

She answered his unspoken question. "We'll work this out, Rob. You'll see."

"I know." She was being so great about this that he tried to sound upbeat for her sake. "Anything else happening?"

She told him all about Jason and the scene at Garth's with Big Daddy. Rob whistled softly. "I'm blown away. I've never heard of anything like that. Still, it's in character. The man's a voyeur, an eavesdropper, and worse. When he couldn't get what he wanted he did it the sneaky way."

"I'm afraid he's going to do something terrible. You should have seen him. He was so angry that I thought he'd have a coronary."

"No such luck."

Dana laughed. "I'm nervous. He's a powerful man."

Rob couldn't deny that. "He'll do something sneaky. Watch your blind side."

"Don't worry about me. It's Vanessa he's after. Anyway, I have plenty of problems of my own. I may be the subject of a judicial review."

"What? Why?"

He listened with growing concern as she explained about Lillian's death and the inheritance, but he didn't alarm her. "Look. It's just Davis Binkley being a total prick. He hasn't got anything worth calling for a review. He wants to keep you from getting that appointment."

"This will do it."

The infinite sadness in her voice tore at him, just as seeing his son had earlier. He loved them both, but he seemed powerless to help them. Dana wanted that appointment. He'd do anything to help her get it. That's why he'd come halfway across the country. Maybe he should have stayed home, maybe she needed him more there.

"Dana, I'm two hours from Gomper's Bend. I'll check out the situation there and fly right home."

"Call me as soon as you know anything."

Rob hung up with the nagging suspicion that he was a hound dog on a cold trail. He wasn't going to find a damn thing in Gomper's Bend. The answer wasn't in the past; it was in the present.

26

The following morning Dana was late for court. Molly had gone out and wouldn't come when she called her. No doubt Lillian's kitty was sulking because all Dana had to feed her the night before was cottage cheese. After searching for fifteen minutes she finally located Molly under the oleander bush and brought her into the house.

Last night Lillian's home had been dark. It didn't appear that her daughter was staying there, but Dana didn't want to take any chances. She kept worrying that Fran would return and steal Molly just to spite her.

"You're late," Anita said with a sly grin as Dana rushed into her office.

"Tell the clerk that I'm on my way."

Minutes later she was seated at her bench, trying to breathe normally and not look as flustered as she felt, when she discovered she had the wrong file folder. It was some old case, not the arraignment list that she was supposed to finish today. She ignored the disgruntled expressions of the half dozen attorneys who were waiting to schedule their cases. She wasn't usually late or disorganized, but wasn't everyone entitled to a bad day?

Motioning for her bailiff, Gus Mahala, to come to the bench, she cursed Anita. Dana knew she'd put the arraignment file on top of her desk. Anita must have switched files.

Dana resisted the urge to run back into her chambers and strangle Anita. Enough was enough! As soon as court was dismissed she was going to the personnel office and demand that Anita be replaced. Forget filling out a bunch of forms and waiting for a formal hearing. She wasn't putting up with this conniving woman another day.

"Is something wrong, Judge Hamilton?" Gus asked in a low tone.

Gus had the biggest smile and the gentlest disposition of anyone she knew. If he actually had to draw the gun holstered to his belt he'd probably scare himself to death. He claimed that he could trace his ancestors back to King Kamehameha, and Dana didn't doubt it. Gus didn't lie or gossip. That's why she'd called on him instead of the clerk, who was a magpie and Anita's close friend.

"Gus, my secretary goofed. Please go into my office and bring me the file marked 'Arraignment Schedule.' "

After this upsetting start, the rest of the morning wasn't much better. Defense attorneys couldn't coordinate their schedules with the prosecution; there was a shortage of public defenders and she had to appoint *pro bono* attorneys, which required telephone calls; worst of all, there was an acute shortage of courtrooms because of the overflow from the superior court. Finally she recessed for lunch and went to meet Gwen in the cafeteria.

She scanned the crowded room and saw Gwen seated at a table with her father. Gwen's back was to her, but judging from the angry expression on Boss Sihida's face, this wasn't a pleasant conversation. Not wanting to interrupt, Dana dallied in the food line, finally selecting a half-wilted spinach salad.

Out of the corner of her eye she watched Boss Sihida. Naturally he was dressed for a funeral. No one knew why he always wore black in such a hot climate, but he did. A small man with a surprisingly muscular build and a full head of black hair sprinkled with gray, Gwen's father had made a fortune with crack seed.

In ancient times Chinese warriors had been given bits of salted plum with a cracked pit to carry with them and eat over long periods of time. Shanghaied Chinese sailors brought the treat to the islands. Although Boss Sihida was the son of Japanese immigrants, he'd immediately seen how popular the Chinese snack food could be. He packaged the product, promoting it as the islands' answer to trail mix. Now every food store in the islands sold multiflavored packages of Sihida crack seed.

Even though Dana gave Boss Sihida credit for being a successful businessman, she didn't like him. She'd met him several times and he'd been polite and hospitable, but there was something about him that disturbed her. As she approached their table and Gwen looked up at her with a relieved smile, Dana realized why she didn't like Boss Sihida. He was too much like Big Daddy. He lived totally through his children, ruthlessly dominating them.

Boss rose as she came to the table, bowing slightly in the traditional Japanese way. "Good afternoon, Dana."

She smiled as sincerely as she could. It never hurt to have Boss Sihida in your camp—especially with the Coltranes gunning for you. "It's nice to see you again."

Boss studied her a second. "I wish I could stay, but I have an appointment." He left without another word to his daughter.

Dana sat down, embarrassed for her friend. How could her father treat her that way? It was worse at home, she thought, recalling the time she'd been invited to dinner. It was obvious Boss Sihida put his sons first, even the one who'd shunned politics for dentistry.

"I've got good news," Gwen said, her face flushed with excitement. "My name is on the list for that superior court spot that came up when Judge Clements died."

"It is?" Dana had intended to discuss the judicial review with Gwen, but considering that they were now competitors that didn't seem wise. How sad, she thought. The system made it hard for women to be close friends.

"Aren't you happy for me?" Gwen's almond eyes narrowed, making Dana ashamed of herself.

"Of course, I'm thrilled for you, Gwen. I just wish we didn't have to compete for the same position."

"That's life," Gwen responded, then she leaned closer. "By the way, what happened with your sister's divorce?"

"Vanessa will get sole custody of Jason."

"Really? They came to terms that fast? Unbelievable."

"Well, you know Garth Bradford."

"I certainly do," Gwen responded with genuine admiration. "If I had his brains I'd be on the Supreme Court by now."

The court was Gwen's life. She was close to her family, especially her brother, but didn't have any outside interests. That's not going to be me, Dana told herself, thinking about Rob. She was going to have a real life. And she wasn't going to be heartbroken if she didn't make superior court. Too many things were more important.

Gwen whispered, "I hear the police are about to arrest the Panama Jack's rapist."

"Really? That'll be a relief for women on the island."

Gwen looked around the room. "Rob Tagett isn't here. He's probably down at the station waiting for the story to break."

Dana wanted to tell Gwen about Rob but didn't.

She felt she owed it to Vanessa to discuss it with her first. Her sister's confession had changed things between them. They were well on their way to being close again.

"Don't look now, but here comes Binkley's secretary."

Dana didn't turn around, but a chill of apprehension waltzed up her spine.

"Judge Hamilton." Dana recognized the officious tone and turned to face Binkley's secretary. "His Honor would like to see you."

The secretary didn't wait for a response; she was gone in a second, lost among the lunchtime crowd, and Dana inhaled sharply, wondering what was wrong now. She stared down at her half-eaten spinach salad. "I'd better see what Hizzoner wants. I'm already behind with the arraignment schedule. I need to be in court right on time."

A few minutes later Dana was sitting in Binkley's office waiting for him to get off the telephone. The chill of apprehension she'd felt earlier was now a cold sweat.

Binkley hung up and gazed at her with a paternal expression, but she knew he was less than sympathetic. "We have a problem."

The royal "we," she thought. Like a king, Binkley took his position as presiding judge with regal authority. Her temper flared. "*We* don't have a problem. *I* have a problem. Isn't that what you really mean?"

He huffed, indignant. "It's come to my attention

that you were involved in a murder when you were younger."

She managed what she hoped was an outraged expression, her thoughts reeling. How could he know? "What on earth are you talking about?"

"There's no statute of limitations on child molestation . . . or murder. If you were involved in a crime you could be charged."

"So call the police. Charge me."

It was a bluff, but it worked. "Well, I haven't seen the file yet. I just heard about it. I was hoping you'd fill me in."

He tried his ingratiating smile on her, but she didn't capitulate. Binkley didn't have any evidence —yet. He wanted her to confess.

"There's nothing to tell you." She rose, striving to appear self-confident, and headed for the door, knowing Binkley hated anyone to get up before he'd dismissed them.

"I'll have the evidence tonight." His´ words caught her by surprise, and she was glad her back was to him. "I've called a judicial review for tomorrow at three."

She willed a smile onto her trembling lips and faced him. "I'll be there."

Somehow she made it back to her own chambers. She collapsed in her chair and put her head down on her desk. The blackmailer had gone to Binkley. Who was it? It didn't matter anymore. The truth would come out.

She had killed a man—no denying it. And no

more running from it. In some strange way that set her free. Once the truth was known she'd never have to hide from it again. Maybe she didn't deserve to be a judge. After all, she had killed a man. This might just be her punishment.

Considering the circumstances, Garth could probably save her from prison, but her career was over. She'd never be a judge again. So what? She would have worse problems. She'd be disbarred for concealing her crime. How would she support herself?

What would happen to her?

"Pun-iii." Jason's happy laughter rang out from the shower as Garth reached for a towel. Puni and Jason had spent the morning running through the sprinklers. The last thing they needed was a shower, but Jason insisted that Garth show him how to keep Puni clean.

There wasn't much to it, of course. It was simply a matter of running warm water over his feathers and taking care not to get the spray into his eyes. They'd been in there a half hour, singing and splashing each other. Who would have thought the ornery bird needed a little boy to make him happy?

He tapped on the shower door. "Okay, guys. Time to come out."

"Do we have to?" Jason asked and Puni backed him up with a few disgruntled chirps.

"Yes. I need you to help me with the barbecue. We're making hamburgers, remember?"

Dripping wet, Jason emerged. Garth, taking care

not to knock Puni off Jason's shoulder, draped him in an oversized towel that hung on him like a choir robe. The bird fluttered his wings. Droplets of water sprayed across Garth's face and dappled his polo shirt. He toweled off Jason, conscious of the child's questioning eyes on him.

"Am I going to live here now?" Jason asked.

Vanessa had already explained to Jason that they'd be living with Dana as soon as the beds were delivered. She'd told him that they wouldn't be returning to Kau Ranch, yet Jason kept asking questions. Obviously the child was upset.

"You'll be staying with Aunt Dana, remember? But you'll visit me . . . all the time," Garth said, hearing his own insecurity in his voice. He hoped he was going to be part of Vanessa and Jason's lives, but he wasn't sure.

Jason crawled into Garth's lap and snuggled against his chest. Yes, there were advantages to being in a wheelchair. You had a lap available at all times. Obviously Jason needed the security of being held. The boy had been ignored by the man he believed was his father and prodded into being "a man" by his real father. Naturally he responded to someone who held him and told him stories.

His thumb now in his mouth, Jason closed his eyes. Puni was nodding off too, his head bobbing. Garth thought he heard the bird say, "Sue!"

"So adorable," Garth muttered as he gazed down at Jason. He couldn't help himself. He kissed Jason's damp head, breathing in the fresh scent of soap and feeling the moist heat of the child's body.

For a moment he indulged himself, cuddling the boy closer and wishing Jason was his son. He lifted his head and caught their reflection in the mirror, a sleeping child with his parrot and a man holding him as if he was the most precious thing in the world.

A movement in the side mirror distracted him. Vanessa. How long had she been there? She silently walked across the marble floor and put her hand on his shoulder. "Let's put him down for his nap."

They put Jason to bed and Puni in his cage, then sat on the lanai overlooking the pool and the ocean. The trades were strong, as they often were in the late afternoon, blowing a cooling breeze in from the sea.

"I don't know how to thank you," Vanessa said.

"Forget it," he said. She'd thanked him dozens of times already. What was there left to say? *Stay here with me.*

Vanessa leaned toward him, her expression serious. "I've been thinking . . . Jason seems so happy here." She paused, her eyes dropping to her lap where her hands were clasped together. "You're very good with him."

His pulse kicked up a beat. What was she getting at? "He's a great kid."

Her eyes met his. "What about me?" she asked, her voice low, full of emotion.

She had to know how he felt about her, didn't

she? Maybe not. She'd told him about being raped and that Eric had married her only to make his father happy. Despite being drop-dead gorgeous, Vanessa was insecure. He could understand how she felt. His astonishing success at law didn't make him confident when he was outside the courtroom.

"You're fantastic." Now it was his turn to pause; he didn't know exactly what to say. "I'm hoping that we can see each other even after you've moved in with Dana."

Vanessa touched his arm. Her slim fingers, crowned by those sexy nails, curved around his biceps.

"I'd like to see you . . . without Jason," she said.

"Don't move out," he heard himself say.

"We barely know each other." She scooted closer, her hand still on his arm, squeezing slightly now.

Maybe asking her to stay wasn't such a good idea after all. She was grateful to him, sure, but she didn't feel the same way he did.

"I'd like to try," she said, her voice charged with emotion, "but I'm afraid that I'll let you down. You see, I was . . . I mean, I wasn't much of a wife. No wonder Eric went back to his girlfriend."

"Why not?" he asked, already suspecting what the answer might be.

"I kept thinking about Hank Rawlins," she said, confirming his suspicions. She'd told him about the rape. Not getting help hadn't made the problem go away. "I hate having sex."

"We'll take it a step at a time. Baby steps. First I

want you to see a counselor. You need to talk out your feelings with a professional."

"You're right," she agreed with a slight smile. "I should have done it long ago. Pretending it never happened didn't work."

He looked out at the sea, a shimmering mirror in the late-afternoon sun. A disturbing thought hit him like a punch to his gut. Did she find him attractive because he was in a wheelchair? Did she see him as less threatening with his disability? That was even worse than pitying him, trying to help him all the time.

"What's the matter?" she asked.

He faced her again, admitting to himself just how much he wanted this to work, yet accepting that the odds against their relationship were tremendous. "Just because I'm in a wheelchair doesn't mean I can't have sex."

"I know," she said. "That's why I'm afraid I'll disappoint you."

Relief swept through him so sharp and hard that he had to suck in his breath for a second to let the ache in his chest ease. "You won't disappoint me. We'll have to work together. Making love to someone with a handicap isn't the same as what you're—" The smile that lit her face stopped him. "What's wrong?"

"You've never even kissed me, and here we are discussing sex."

"I can fix that." He pulled her close and touched his lips to hers, holding himself in check. He longed to hug her tight and kiss her the way he'd wanted to kiss her for days now, but he needed to be gentle. Her eyes were closed, the lashes thick and silky. Her soft lips were parted against his.

Suddenly her arms were around his neck and her mouth was pressed against his. She kissed him with a hunger that matched his own. For the first time he let himself hope that their relationship might have a chance. For the first time he allowed himself to dream of a life beyond his career.

"Garth." The word came out like a sigh. She rested her head on his shoulder and breathed a kiss into the sensitive curve of his neck.

They sat on the lanai, cuddling and kissing until Garth heard a noise from inside the house. Vanessa sat up straight and listened.

"Sue the bastards! Sue the bastards! Sue their asses!"

She looked at him and smiled, her lips still moist from kissing. "They're ba-a-a-ack!"

27

Molly was waiting at the door for Dana, purring as loud as a lawn mower and swishing her tail. Dana reached down and gave her a loving pat.

"At least someone's glad to see me."

The afternoon had been utterly humiliating. She still felt the hot flush of embarrassment and the tightness in her chest that she'd experienced as she'd completed scheduling the arraignments. Every eye seemed to be on her. Accusing her. Condemning her.

News about the review had spread around the courthouse in a heartbeat. The attorneys cast suspicious looks at her, not bothering to disguise their contempt. She knew she had a reputation for being a tough judge, but she thought she had people's respect. She told herself that she didn't care, but that wasn't really true. Is this what Rob went through— every day? Knowing looks? Hushed whispers?

She'd dropped by Garth's house after work to see her sister and tell them about the judicial review.

Garth had insisted she was overreacting, claiming people did like and respect her. Well, he hadn't been there.

"Garth's too wrapped up in Vanessa and Jason to really know what's going on," she told Molly as the kitty trotted into the kitchen, leading the way to her bowl. "And Vanessa's crazy about him too."

Any fool could see those two were falling in love, Dana thought with a sigh. Vanessa had announced that she wouldn't be moving in with Dana. "It'll give Jason time to adjust," her sister had said, but Dana knew better. Vanessa was concerned about Jason, but that was just an excuse to stay with Garth and slowly test their relationship.

Dana put the sack of groceries she'd picked up at the all-night market on the counter. "Not a bad idea, really. It happened so fast."

Molly ignored Dana's chatter, circling her bowl impatiently.

Dana reached into the bag and brought out a can of Fancy Feast. "No more of the dreaded cottage cheese. I've got five different kinds of cat food. Let's try this one first."

She popped the lid, and the overpowering aroma of fish filled the air, making Dana gag, but Molly didn't care. As soon as Dana emptied the can, the cat did a face plant in her bowl. Dana leaned back against the counter, watching Molly gobble, recalling what Garth had told her at dinner.

"Stonewall it during the review," Garth had instructed. "See what they have to say. I'll bet it's nothing more than a lot of hot air."

"Stonewall it." She tossed the can in the recycling basket. "Easier said than done."

Too exhausted to work, Dana went into the bedroom. The phone rang as she was undressing. It was just after eleven, which was late for anyone to be calling. She grabbed the receiver, thinking it had to be Rob, but it wasn't.

"Sorry to call so late, but I was worried about you," Gwen said. "I hear Binkley has called for a judicial review. Why?"

"Garth Bradford says this is just an attempt to discredit me so I won't get that appointment."

"You consulted Garth? You can't bring a lawyer into the review. You have to go in alone."

How well she knew that. Dana dreaded facing the review by herself. If she could have anyone with her, she'd want Rob. "Garth invited me to dinner, and I asked him what he thought."

"Oh. That's smart," Gwen said. "I guess he told you about getting the inquiry letter that came this afternoon."

"What letter?" Dana sank down onto the bed. Now what?

"Whenever there's a review the presiding judge has to send letters to the legal community to see if there are additional complaints."

"Oh, yes. I remember," Dana responded. What would her peers say about her, she wondered with a growing sense of apprehension.

"Don't worry about the inquiry letter," Gwen said. "The review will be over before anyone sifts through their mail and finds the letter."

Dana didn't challenge her friend. No doubt Gwen was being supportive, but Dana remembered the condemning glares she'd received that afternoon. She had enemies—more than she'd imagined— who'd respond to the inquiry letter.

"Don't be upset."

"I'm not," Dana assured her with a lot more confidence than she actually felt. "I just want to get this farce over with."

"It'll be easy, you'll see." Gwen tried to be reassuring, but failed. "I heard that you have a new secretary."

"Yes," Dana said, recalling the scene she'd had with the stubborn personnel director that afternoon. "I put up with all I could. They can't fire Anita until she's had a hearing, so they've transferred her. I'm getting someone new tomorrow."

"Good for you," Gwen said. "Well, it's late. I'd better go. Good luck with the review. Stop by my chambers when it's over."

Dana hung up, flopped back on her bed, and closed her eyes, telling herself that she'd get up in a minute and change into a nightgown. An image of Lillian weeding her garden appeared in her mind, then one of Jason marching around Garth's house with Puni on his shoulder. Yes. There were more important things in her life than her career.

She heard a faint noise, a distant sound with a

hollow echo. Dana sat up and realized she'd fallen asleep and Molly had curled up beside her. The noise sounded a second time, seeming sharper now in the empty house. The doorbell, she realized, and quickly glanced at the alarm clock. Not yet midnight. Who would be at her door at this hour? Had the Panama Jack's rapist been arrested yet?

"Forget the rapist. It could be the blackmailer," she whispered to Molly, who was now awake. "They don't make house calls, do they?"

She tiptoed to the front door with Molly at her heels, wishing she'd bought another can of pepper spray. She'd left the lights on in the living room, but thankfully the curtains were drawn. Whoever was outside couldn't see in.

The *mokes*, she thought with a shudder. Rob insisted they'd gotten what they wanted and she was safe. She knew if he'd thought she was in any danger he would never have left.

Peering out the tiny peephole, she gasped and jumped back. "Oh, my God," she muttered half under her breath. No one in their right mind would open a door to this guy. A *moke* would be an improvement over this weirdo.

She almost dialed 911, but decided to take another peek. A boy about fifteen stood at her door. He was about six feet tall and had a series of small gold hoops in his ear, not in the lobe but halfway up like a punk rock star. It looked as if someone had put a bowl over his head and buzz-cut the hair below so you could see his white scalp. The longer hair on top had been dyed an iridescent maroon.

Heavens! Had someone put a curse on him? She drew back, realizing that there was something familiar about him. Cautiously she put her eye to the peephole just as he hit the doorbell again. The blast of noise in the empty house rang a bell in her mind. Rob. This boy was a younger, punked-out version of Rob Tagett. It had to be his son, but how did he know about her? How had he gotten her address?

"Who is it?" she called to confirm his identity.

"Zach Tagett. I want to talk to you."

She swung open the door and tried to keep her expression calm, as if weirdos rang her bell every day. Backpack slung over one shoulder, Zach walked in with the same athletic stride she associated with Rob. Molly took one look at the boy, crouched low, arched her back, and hissed.

Dana said, "I guess you know who I am or you wouldn't be here."

"Yeah," he said, and she instantly knew that he didn't like her. Great! Here she was counting on her personal life to pull her through this crisis, and Rob's son hated her on sight.

"Isn't it a little late to be out?" Oh, God. She sounded like an uptight parent, but she didn't know what else to say.

"I had to sneak out of the hotel while Mom was asleep," Zach admitted, and she realized he'd inherited his father's talent for being disarmingly honest. He shifted the backpack to the other shoulder, his deep blue eyes—his father's eyes—staring at her. "Leave Dad alone. He and Mom are getting together again. We're moving back here."

She wasn't certain how to respond. Just what had Rob told Zach about her? "I'm sure your father explained—"

"Yeah, all he does is talk and talk and talk." Zach dropped to his knees and held out his hand to Molly. The cat gingerly approached.

"How did you find me?"

"Dad told me about you. When I got here I called the courthouse. Your secretary gave me your address."

Anger welled up inside her with such astonishing swiftness that she had to struggle to hide it from Zach, not wanting him to think she was upset with him. She was furious with Anita. Her secretary knew better than to give anyone her address. What if Zach had been a dangerous felon with a grudge against her?

She smiled to herself. Now the haughty personnel director couldn't deny that Anita deserved to be fired. Civil-service employee or not, the woman was a menace.

"Look," she said as gently as possible, "I didn't come between your parents. Your father and I only became . . . involved recently."

"Mom and Dad are getting back together."

His tone was petulant like a child's, and Dana realized that was just what he was. A child in a man's body. But the question remained: Was this reconciliation real or Zach's wishful thinking? Rob hadn't mentioned anything about his wife coming to Hawaii with his son.

"My father doesn't care about you," he said as he patted Molly. "He doesn't care about anyone."

She was stunned by his impudent attitude, but refused to show it. "Your father called me after he saw you in L.A. He's terribly worried about you. He loves you very much."

"Yeah, right." He shrugged, making a show of not caring. He didn't fool Dana. "I didn't do nuthin'. Some guy gave me those pills, but I wasn't going to take them. Then Mom goes and makes a big deal out of it."

She'd seen more than her share of youthful offenders who'd begun with pills they claimed they never were going to take, but she resisted the urge to lecture him. "You'll have a fresh start here."

"Yeah." He wandered across the room, stopped in front of the bookcase, and pulled out a Stephen King book. "I read this. Way cool."

She walked over to him and took *The Stand* off the shelf. "I think this one's better. Why don't you take it with you?"

He accepted the book with a curt nod that again reminded her of Rob when he didn't know what to say.

"Call me when you finish it," she said, "and we'll discuss it."

His shocked expression almost made her smile. Evidently he wasn't accustomed to an adult wanting his opinion on a book. It made her wonder about his relationship with his mother, reinforcing her belief that he'd be better off with Rob.

"How did you get here?" she asked to fill the awkward silence.

"Hitched."

She almost gasped. The young were fearless. Terrible things happened to other people—not to them. A corner of her mind always warned her that bad things do happen to good people. She'd learned that the night her parents had been killed.

"I'll drive you back to your hotel," she said.

She drove him to the Waikiki Surf, chattering nonstop about things teenagers did in the islands. Zach listened intently, but said little.

He got out of the car, muttering, "Thanks."

Dana watched him disappear into the lobby. Would he ever accept her? Would she even get the chance, or would Rob go back to his ex-wife?

She drove away, quickly checking her rearview mirror to be certain she wasn't being followed. There were very few cars on the street at this hour. The only noise was the throbbing beat of the music coming from the popular night spot Panama Jack's. Her doors were already locked, but she double-checked them anyway, recalling that the rapist got his name for following women as they left the nightclub.

Back home she wearily opened the door and heard the phone ringing. She dashed across the room, tripping over Molly, who'd stationed herself on the throw rug, and grabbed the telephone.

"Dana?" came Rob's voice after her breathless hello.

She started to tell him about Zach, but the background noise sidetracked her. "Where are you?"

"In the airport in St. Louis. I'm coming home," he said, a smile in his voice.

"What happened?" She dropped to the floor beside Molly. "What did you find out?"

"I drove right to Gompers Bend and found Slade Carter. He's running the Whiz-In Mini Mart. Bald with a potbelly. He's a nice guy. He remembered you and Vanessa."

"What did he say about that night?"

"He drove into the parking lot and found Hank. He was dead, all right—dead drunk. You hadn't killed him. He'd passed out. The knife was stuck in his ribs. It didn't do much damage."

Relief so intense it felt like pain centered deep in her chest. She picked up Molly and held the kitty to her breast. "I didn't kill him?"

"No, angel, you didn't." The affection in his voice was unmistakable. If he'd been with her his arms would have been around her.

Now she knew what they meant when they said the weight of the world had been lifted from your shoulders. That's just how she felt. As a judge she'd stood for law and order. And justice. Yet she had felt like a fraud. Not anymore. She hadn't committed any crime. Thank heavens.

"Thank God. All these years I thought—" She stopped, a warning bell ringing in her brain. "Hank. He's here. He told the blackmailer—"

"No, babe. Hank Rawlins is in prison for raping a ten-year-old girl."

A suffocating sensation tightened her throat, and she clutched Molly so hard that the cat clawed at her. "I should have gone to the police, then that little girl would have been safe."

"Dana, you were a child yourself, and you were on the run."

"True, but I'm not keeping quiet any longer. When Hank comes up for parole Vanessa and I will testify against releasing him."

"Good idea."

"I can't thank you enough. I don't know what to say." She wanted to tell him she loved him, yet the words eluded her entirely. She needed to say how she felt about him in a nonthreatening way, not wanting him to feel trapped. But she'd never said those words to a man and they wouldn't come now.

"I've got some ideas on how you can thank me."

"Seriously, Rob. This has been hanging over my head for years. Now I feel . . . free."

"I'm glad I could help. I wanted to do this for you. Just don't make me out to be a hero. Hell, it was incredibly easy. I drove into town and in less than ten minutes found Slade."

"He must have told someone. That's how the blackmailer knows."

"No. Slade thought Hank had been in a fight."

"Really? That's exactly what we wanted the police to think when they found his body. I guess for two teenagers we were pretty smart."

"Slade isn't the brightest bulb in the chandelier. Of course, Hank never admitted raping anyone, so Slade just assumed Vanessa had gotten tired of him and left for California."

"Then how could anyone know? It doesn't make sense."

Rob was silent for a moment, and she heard a flight announcement. "Have you or Vanessa ever been hypnotized?"

She could see what he meant. Under hypnosis they might have revealed something they wouldn't have otherwise. "I never have been and Vanessa hasn't mentioned it, but I'll ask."

"It's a long shot. The blackmailer doesn't have any real evidence. He's just trying to scare you."

"He's doing more than just trying to scare me. Someone's using this to try to ruin my career." She took a minute to tell him about the review, finishing by saying, "It begins tomorrow at three."

"My plane won't land in time for me to see you before the hearing starts. I'll wait until it's over to see you. Don't worry. The bit with Hank is nothing, but I am concerned about the will. Is there anyone around who really knew Lillian, someone who could back you up?"

"Dr. Winston treated her for thirty-some years. She might have confided in him. She was always bringing him plants and things. I could ask him—"

346

"Dana, it's the last call for my plane. I'll see you tomorrow. Just hang tough. This is going to be all right. You'll see."

There wasn't enough time to tell him about Zach. She dropped the receiver into the cradle with the odd sensation she'd made a serious mistake.

28

By the time Rob walked through the metal detector and into the courthouse, he knew that Dana was in Judge Binkley's chambers for the review, so he stopped to call for his messages, hoping Zach had left word. The last time he'd checked his messages, Ellen had tersely informed him that she'd brought Zach to Honolulu.

"What in hell is she doing here?" he muttered to the walls of the phone booth. Zach wasn't supposed to arrive until next week. Had she decided to bring Zach for a visit but not allow him to stay? With Ellen you never knew. If she had changed her mind she was in for a fight.

There was only one message on his machine and it was from Garth, saying it was urgent that Rob call him right away. When he didn't get an answer at his son's hotel, he called Garth's office and was told he was in Judge Hamilton's chambers. Makes sense, Rob thought as he rode the elevator up to the third floor. Garth and Vanessa were probably here to give

Dana moral support. He wondered if Dana had remembered to ask her sister if she'd ever been hypnotized.

It was a shot in the dark, but he didn't have a better theory. Someone knew something, yet they hadn't bothered to check it out. Or maybe they didn't know where to look. They'd tried to capitalize on a kernel of information, which turned out to be misinformation. He walked into Dana's office, still pondering the question.

"I'm looking for Garth Bradford." The secretary inclined her head toward the closed door to Dana's office. He knocked and Garth called for him to come in. "What's—" He stopped, jarred by the sight of Jason sitting in Dana's chair with Puni on his shoulder.

"Sue the bastards! Sue the bastards! Sue their asses!" the twosome chanted, and Rob couldn't help chuckling.

Vanessa jumped up from her seat beside Garth and gave Rob a hug worthy of a sumo wrestler. "Dana told me the news. How can we thank you?"

She looked so damn happy that he felt guilty. He was getting more credit than he deserved—but loving it. "You and Garth could make me dinner," he said, looking at Garth and noticing the intense expression on his face.

Before Vanessa could answer Garth said to her, "Why don't you take Jason and Puni outside and see if Puni has a contribution to make?"

Vanessa held out her hand to her son, who shook

his head. "Puni doesn't have a conbution. He pooed with the pigeons when we came in."

"Now, sweetie," Vanessa began, and Jason's lower lip jutted out.

"What did we agree?" Garth asked Jason, his tone kind, yet forceful.

"I would mind 'cause there aren't any children here and this is special."

Garth beamed him the smile that won over countless juries. Jason hopped down from the chair and followed his mother outside without another word.

"Close the door," Garth said quietly, and the fine hairs across the back of Rob's neck prickled. Christ! What now?

Rob shut the door and took the seat beside Garth. "What's wrong?"

"I got a call from one of my sources." Garth hesitated, measuring him for a moment. "You're going to be arrested and charged with the Panama Jack's rapes."

Fear mushroomed inside him, an emotion so powerful that the force of it staggered him. "That's impossible. Why would the police think I did it?"

A flickering shadow in Garth's eyes sent Rob's stomach into a free-fall. "A victim picked you out of a six-pack, Rob."

He let out his breath, blowing upward, ruffling the hair on his forehead. Shit! A six-pack was a series of six photographs. Five of them were head shots of policemen, while the sixth was a suspect.

He vaulted to his feet. "What was I doing in a six-pack?"

"They're desperate, Rob. They're looking at repeat offenders."

"I was cleared. They don't have any right to show my photo."

"Were you at Panama Jack's last Monday night?"

Rob almost said no, then he remembered. "Yeah. Chuck Mahole at UH ran some tests for me on the blackmail note Dana received. He wouldn't take any money. He wanted to have a drink at Panama Jack's." He raked his hand through his hair. "Hell, I was only there half an hour."

Garth patted the seat beside him and Rob dropped into the chair. "I know you didn't do it, Rob. I suspect it's just Big Daddy making trouble."

"That son of a bitch. My son's here. He's going to live with me. If my wife gets wind of this she won't let him stay."

Garth's earnest eyes shifted, and Rob knew he didn't want to hear whatever else he was going to say. "I understand they have more evidence. What, I'm not sure, but I'm trying to find out. They plan to arrest you by the end of the week."

As if someone had coldcocked him with a knock-out punch, Rob gasped, every breath of air leaving his body at once. It was a few seconds before the magnitude of what Garth said finally registered. Numb with shock and anger, he said, "I learned my lesson last time. This time I'm fighting the charges —out in the open."

"I'm with you all the way," Garth assured him, "but this could get real ugly."

Rob rose and walked over to the Wyland print, feeling like the tiny rainbow fish about to be devoured by the shark. "My son's at a crossroads in his life. He doesn't need this."

"What about Dana?" Garth asked quietly.

"Dana," Rob echoed. "The last thing her career needs right now is to have her name linked with mine. Don't tell her anything about this. Let me handle her."

Dana stared at the three men across the table from her. Collis Hwang, head of the state commission on judicial performance, was older than she expected, but had a reputation as a fair man. Adam Pinsky, the young lawyer with him, kept eyeing her and shifting in his seat. Judge Binkley would present the charges. She would be given a chance to explain her actions, then the two men from the commission would decide her fate.

"Let's begin," Hwang said, checking his watch. It was almost three-thirty. Judge Binkley had kept them waiting almost a half hour.

"Sorry to have kept you waiting, but I was expecting more . . . uh . . . information about this . . . uh . . . problem," Binkley said, and Dana smothered a smile. It wouldn't do to appear too cocky yet, but she knew the "evidence" he'd been hoping to get about Hank Rawlins's murder hadn't appeared.

"What problem are we talking about?" Hwang's

impatience echoed through the teak-paneled chamber.

Davis Binkley cleared his throat. "Let's start with the first charge. If the evidence arrives, my secretary will bring it in." He cleared his throat again, obviously flustered by the missing evidence. "Fran Martin claims that Ms. Hamilton used undue influence to convince her mother to change her will."

Hwang scanned the documents that Binkley handed them, then gazed at the golf trophies mounted on the wall, waiting while Pinsky read every word. Dana struggled to remain calm. She knew this charge, although less serious than the other, had more potential to ruin her career. She could prove that Hank was alive; she couldn't prove she hadn't influenced Lillian Hurley.

"You can see how serious this charge is," prompted Binkley.

Hwang frowned slightly, and Dana had the impression that he'd seen far more serious charges. "What do you have to say, Judge Hamilton?"

"I never discussed Lillian's will with her. Never. She was my neighbor, and we became friends. I had no idea she'd left me anything. I—"

Binkley cut in. "Her daughter claims—"

"I read the statement," Hwang interrupted. "It's Judge Hamilton's turn."

Dana stifled a sigh of relief. Binkley was alienating Hwang. She couldn't tell what Pinsky was thinking, but he kept staring at her. "Lillian Hurley's doctor is waiting outside," Dana said, praying Dr.

Winston had arrived. "He can tell you more about Lillian's state of mind. He treated her for over thirty years."

"That's highly irregular," Binkley said. "Reviews use written statements. If you don't have a state—"

"I have Dr. Winston's statement." Dana reached for her briefcase, silently blessing Rob for prompting her to contact the doctor. "I just thought the seriousness of the charge warranted a personal appearance."

"Send him in," Hwang said, and Binkley reluctantly hit the intercom.

Dr. Winston was an impressive witness, Dana decided as the older gentleman entered the room. Tall, with an erect posture that suggested military training, he projected self-confidence and honesty.

"Dr. Winston, there's been some confusion about the changes in Lillian Hurley's will. Had she ever discussed it with you?" asked Judge Binkley.

"No, she never mentioned it," Dr. Winston admitted, and Binkley shot Hwang a look that clearly said, "I rest my case." But the doctor wasn't finished. "She did speak about her daughter. Quite often in fact. Fran was a bitter disappointment to Lillian. Her daughter never called, never visited."

He paused, and Dana realized he had a flair for drama. "And I mean *never*. Not on Christmas, not on Mother's Day, not on Lillian's birthday. I don't know how she could be so cruel to such a sweet old lady. Lillian was quite depressed about it, but she perked up when Dana moved next door."

Dr. Winston continued, explaining about Lillian's high blood pressure and the arrangements Dana had made so the older woman could live at home. She tried to gauge the effect of the doctor's words, knowing intuitively that Hwang, not Pinsky, would decide her fate, but it was impossible to read the older man's expression.

"Dana became a substitute daughter to Lillian," Dr. Winston concluded. "She loved Dana, truly loved her. I would have been stunned if she'd left anything to her own daughter. She appeared like a bolt out of the blue last week just to wheedle money out of Lillian."

"Thank you for coming," Binkley choked out the words, and the doctor left with a reassuring smile at Dana.

"There isn't any merit to this charge," Hwang concluded, and Pinsky rubber-stamped his colleague's assessment with an enthusiastic nod.

"We-l-l, the daughter says—" Binkley sputtered.

"I read the statement." Hwang raised his voice for the first time. "The daughter makes lots of accusations. What does the lawyer's statement say?"

Pinsky spoke up. "Lillian Hurley had never willed her home and small savings account to her daughter. Before she changed the will last year, all the money was to go to the Society to Preserve Hawaii's Native Plants and Flowers."

"True, but—"

"But nothing," Hwang said, cutting off Binkley. "What's the next charge?"

Dana was positive her sigh of relief could be heard all the way to Diamond Head, but no one in the room seemed to notice it. Relief quickly became anger, though, as she watched Binkley fumble with the second file folder. Undoubtedly Big Daddy was behind this, but he'd found a willing puppet.

"I . . . uh . . . didn't . . . uh . . . get the evidence I was expecting," Binkley said. "We may have to postpone this review until—"

"Why don't you tell us the charges?" Dana interjected. She didn't want this hanging over her head a minute longer than necessary. "Perhaps I can help."

"Good idea," Hwang added. "Let's see if we can clear this up now."

"I have information that Ms. Hamilton was involved in a murder."

"May we see the statements?" Hwang asked, and Binkley grudgingly handed them each a single sheet of paper that Hwang read in an instant. "An anonymous tip? You insisted on a review with nothing more than an anonymous tip? That's ridiculous. People are always angry with judges. They'll say anything to get them in trouble."

"I spoke with the caller myself. The information sounded reliable." A mottled flush crept up Binkley's neck. "I was supposed to get additional evidence, but it hasn't arrived yet."

"It'll never come, because I was never involved in a homicide," Dana informed the men. "The anonymous tip is about something that happened to me

357

when I was fourteen. Obviously, the person doesn't have all the facts."

Dana paused a moment, not quite comfortable discussing this with these men. She'd hardly been able to tell the story to Rob. She didn't have a choice; her future was at stake. "When I was fourteen a man lured me to a shack and raped me. My sister tried to rescue me, only to have him attack her. I stabbed him—so we could escape—but I didn't kill him."

She leaned forward, her eyes on Hwang's. "Hank Rawlins is a vicious criminal who's in prison in Missouri for raping a ten-year-old child. I would have done anything to spare her the pain, the suffering. It's a crime a victim lives with forever."

"My God," Pinsky muttered, shaking his head sadly. "I know just what you mean. My wife was raped several years ago. We're still going to counseling."

Hwang scalded Binkley with a disgusted look, then snapped his briefcase shut. "I don't know why you called for a review."

Dana couldn't resist. "I do. My sister is divorcing Thornton Coltrane's son. He's furious with us. He'll do anything to ruin my career."

Hwang glared at Binkley. "Did Coltrane contact you?"

"No," he responded a little too quickly.

"I have ways of checking, you know. If you're lying I'll have you reviewed—and be a witness."

Hwang's long fingers drummed his briefcase as he waited for an answer.

"He called when he heard about the will," Binkley conceded, "and encouraged me to go ahead with the review—now—when Dana was being considered for superior court. I wouldn't have done it, of course, had I not thought the charges against Ms. Hamilton—"

"Judge Hamilton," Hwang corrected, standing. "I'm reporting that these charges against Judge Hamilton were frivolous, entirely without merit."

Pinsky rose, telling Binkley, "I'll be reporting to the governor that you should be reprimanded. Not only have you used trumped-up charges against Judge Hamilton, you've failed to mention the petition."

"What petition?" Hwang asked, echoing Dana's thoughts.

Binkley shuffled through a stack of files. "Here, I was just about to show it to you." He handed a folder to Hwang. "I sent out an inquiry letter, asking about Ms.—Judge Hamilton's performance. This came to my office this morning."

Pinsky smiled at Dana. "Everyone that's anyone in the legal community signed a petition saying you were a fine judge—the best."

"Really?" Dana gasped. She *was* paranoid, certain that everyone looking at her was condemning her, when they'd actually been supporting her.

"Sure," Pinsky said with an encouraging smile. "The DA started it. He said you were the best prosecutor he ever had and that you were an even better judge.''

Hwang tucked the petition into his briefcase. ''Your name's on the list for superior court. I'm going to make certain that the governor sees this.''

''Thank you,'' she managed to say. She was overwhelmed by the rapid turn of events. Usually the wheels of justice moved as slowly as a postal worker on Valium, but not this time.

Even more surprising was the support of her colleagues. She'd been worried about nothing, imagining all sorts of things. She was liked and respected. Relief flooded her, making her feel weak and shaky. And incredibly happy. She could hardly wait to tell Rob.

''Come on.'' Pinsky guided her to the door, and Dana couldn't help thinking that Rob was right. There were plenty of good men around. Adam Pinsky's wife was fortunate to have married such a sensitive man.

Dana admitted that she was guilty of having a closed mind. People were people; some were good and others were bad. She hadn't looked for the good men like Garth Bradford, Adam Pinsky, Collis Hwang. And Rob Tagett.

Back in her office, Jason and Puni were asleep in her chair, but Dana was greeted enthusiastically by Vanessa and Garth.

''I was expecting Rob,'' she said, still hugging Vanessa.

''He had to leave,'' Garth said.

"Before he saw me?" she asked, and Garth solemnly nodded. "Is something wrong?"

Garth hesitated, then said in a troubled undertone, "I think he's worried about his son."

29

The sun, stalking the day's last clouds across the horizon, slowly disappeared into the sea as Dana drove toward Rob's home on the north shore. She rolled down her window, welcoming the stiff breeze. The air here was as warm as it was in Honolulu, but the stronger breeze swept farther inland, bringing a salt mist that she could taste on her lips and feel in her hair.

It had taken her longer than she'd expected to take the tidal wave of calls from colleagues congratulating her on the results of the review. Then she'd had to complete several probation reports and prepare the arraignment calendar so her new secretary could input it into the computer.

Should she have called Rob before coming? she wondered, pulling into his driveway. Garth said Rob had gone home, and Dana knew that Zach wasn't with him. His mother had taken him to Maui to visit her friends. This might be their only chance to be alone for some time.

Why had he left before the review was even over? Garth said he'd called Rob on his car phone the minute he knew the results—even before she'd come back to her office—but it still bothered her that Rob hadn't waited. Was there truth to what Zach had said? Was Rob considering getting back together with Ellen?

"There it is again," she muttered to herself. "Distrust rears its ugly head." She turned off the motor, then gripped the steering wheel. *Rob had faith in you. He went all the way to Gomper's Bend to prove it. He needs support now. He's terrified of losing his son to drugs.*

Those fortifying words in mind, she marched along the path toward the front of the house, which faced the beach. Rob was on the deck, stretched out on a chaise, a bottle of Primo beer in one hand. Surely he'd heard her footsteps, but he didn't turn to face her. Instead he kept his eyes on the horde of surfers riding the high-cresting waves, backlit by the setting sun. Then she noticed the fresh bruise on the rise of his cheek.

"Rob, you're hurt."

"Nah. I bumped into something." He turned and put down the bottle.

Instinctively she knew he'd found one or both of the *mokes* who'd attacked them and settled the score, but she didn't challenge him.

"Garth told me about the review . . . and the petition. Congratulations."

She detected distance in his tone, preoccupation.

A nervous flutter in her chest, she looked around. "I wanted to thank you in person for checking on Hank Rawlins. I don't know why it didn't occur to me to do that years ago. Now I won't have to spend the rest of my life looking over my shoulder."

He unenthusiastically patted the chair next to him, inviting her to sit. "Don't make it more than it is. I did some routine investigating. That's all."

She dropped into the chair beside him, suddenly feeling exhausted and at a loss for words. This was a side of Rob she hadn't seen before, and she realized she didn't know him as well as she'd thought. Tentatively she said, "Zach came to see me."

"Really?" Now she had his full attention. "When?"

"He dropped by late last night."

"To check you out." Rob chuckled. "A chip off the old block."

She tried to joke. "You had maroon hair too?"

Rob gazed at her, his blue eyes reflecting the dying embers of the sunset, seeming unusually intense. "No, but I went for good-looking women."

Dana could have told him Zach hated her on sight, but didn't. Rob, it seemed, had enough to worry about without this.

"Did he happen to say what he was doing today? I haven't been able to reach him."

"Last night he told me that his mother was taking him to Maui to visit her friends."

"Great! Naturally, she didn't bother to leave me a message."

His tone indicated nothing but contempt, almost prompting Dana to ask where she stood. But she didn't. A growing awareness that something was wrong kept her silent.

Rob watched the last flicker of light disappear into the sea, the sun setting on paradise. After Garth had told him that he would be arrested, Rob had made up his mind not to see Dana. He planned to throw everything he had into this fight, and he didn't want Dana caught in the crossfire.

More than anything, she wanted to move up the judicial ladder. The review had backfired—big time. Instead of disgracing her, it had rallied the legal community to her side. When the governor saw the petition he was certain to appoint Dana to that superior court vacancy.

It might be days or even weeks before the governor acted. If Dana's name became associated with the most notorious criminal in the islands, her chances would be ruined. No way would he let that happen.

He'd thought that leaving before she came out of the review would have discouraged Dana and made her question his interest in her. But this wasn't the old Dana. The woman sitting beside him was someone new.

A wild card.

That thought frightened him. He didn't want her involved in this mess. If Big Daddy was out to frame him, he wanted to fight him on his own terms. Only a fool would refuse to admit that Big Daddy wielded power in the islands. Dana had escaped this time, but she might not again.

Rob could see now that he wasn't going to be able to put her off by ignoring her. It was going to take a helluva lot more than that. He was going to have to get rid of her. That meant he would have to hurt her.

He ventured a glance at Dana and saw her hair fluttering in a cat's paw of wind. The sassy precision cut needed a trim, and close inspection revealed her blonde roots. She looked younger than usual. And nervous.

He couldn't blame her; he was behaving like an insensitive prick. What choice did he have? Like sharks spotting blood in the water, the media would eat him alive. And ruin Dana's career too, if he wasn't careful.

"I've made an appointment for you and Zach with Dr. Ho for counseling," she told him. "Monday at two."

"Great." Come Monday he would be in jail. He was going to have to talk to Zach, hope he'd listen, then send him home with Ellen. And pray his son could stay out of trouble.

"Zach will be fine, you'll see," Dana said gently.

Her look was so sympathetic, so concerned that he had to brace his hands against the chaise to keep himself from leaping up to hug her. And ask her to stick with him through this mess.

Dana rose. "I'd better go. I've got a cat waiting to be fed."

She sounded as uncomfortable as hell, and it was his fault. "You scored a big victory," he heard himself say. "I'm proud of you. Why don't you feed your cat, and I'll pick you up at eight-thirty and take you out to celebrate."

The grateful smile she beamed at him hurt worse than any of the *mokes'* punches. "I'll be ready."

Rob drove up to Dana's curb. *What in hell are you doing?* he asked himself for the hundredth time.

He turned off the ignition and silently acknowledged the truth. He had to let Dana go, but he wasn't ready quite yet. He wanted to take her to a restaurant where they could talk. Being alone was too tempting. If he touched her, kissed her, he'd never let her go. Tonight they'd enjoy the evening, then he'd tell her. What he was going to say exactly, Rob had no idea. But he'd think of something. He always did.

"You coward. You're just postponing the inevitable," he told his reflection in the rearview mirror. But he couldn't help himself. He couldn't stay away from her.

Dana answered his knock and he grinned quickly to hide his surprise. She wasn't dressed to go anywhere. Instead she wore white shorts and a blue blouse knotted at the waist. Her hair was damp around the edges from the shower.

"I picked up steaks," Dana said breathlessly. "I

thought it would be more fun to barbecue here . . . and talk."

Uh-oh. Just what he didn't want—to be alone with her. And temptation. She grabbed his hand and pulled him inside.

"Open the wine while I toss the salad."

He followed her to the kitchen, where a marmalade cat looked up suspiciously from her bowl for about a half second before deciding he was of no interest. Rob grabbed the bottle, thankful to have something to do.

"Tell me about the review. I want to hear every detail."

Dana launched into the story, also seeming grateful to have a safe topic of conversation. He listened intently, imagining her poise under such pressure and hearing the relief underscoring every word.

"Collis Hwang took the petition to the governor. Hwang thinks I still have a good chance of getting that superior court appointment," Dana concluded.

"I'm betting on it," Rob responded, and she blessed him with a melt-your-heart smile that left no doubt that this was her fondest dream, assuring him that leaving her was his only option.

"I'm not counting on being appointed," she told him. "It's enough just to get out of that blackmailer's clutches. Now I can get on with my life."

Rob poured the chardonnay into glasses. "Binkley admitted Big Daddy contacted him about the inquiry, but he denied that he was the one who told him about Hank's so-called murder, right?"

"Yes. Binkley claimed an anonymous caller tipped him." Dana waved the paring knife she was using on the carrots. "I'm certain it's someone Big Daddy had call."

"We still don't know who the blackmailer is."

"Does it matter? Thanks to you, I don't have anything to hide." Dana left the salad and walked toward him. "Vanessa is free, and Jason's safe. What more could we want?"

He tried to smile, wishing he could share her happiness. But rape charges hung over him, threatening to take Dana and his son. He'd called several contacts on the force, trying to see what evidence they had against him. No one knew—or would tell him—anything.

"I'm sorry." Dana stopped in front of him, her flawless green eyes filled with concern. "I wasn't thinking. What more do we want? We want Zach to weather this crisis. We want him to live with you and be happy."

"Yeah," was all he could say. Like a swimmer caught in one of the north shore's deadly undertows, he was being swept so far away from shore that nothing could save him.

"Do you want to talk about it?" Dana's eyes bored through his, seeking his soul.

Rob was tempted to spill his guts, but he held back. He could still hear the joyful echo in the kitchen when she'd said she might be named to that vacancy on the superior court. With luck she'd get that appointment before he was arrested. Sure as hell, he didn't want her defending him and ruining her chances.

Dana twined her arms around his neck, moving closer and gently pressing her body against his until the soft swells of her bosom molded against his chest. She looked him directly in the eyes. "I love you, Rob."

He couldn't help himself, he honestly couldn't, yet he tried. He gripped the counter with both hands for a second. The tender, expectant look in her eyes touched him in a way he never could have anticipated. He threw his arms around her, anchoring her to his chest.

The air left Dana's lungs in a soft gasp as Rob hugged her. Feeling the tears spring to her eyes, she closed them. Thank God, she said to herself. Rob had been acting so strangely that she hadn't known where she stood.

This at least was familiar territory; she wasn't adrift in some uncharted sea. Her lips trembling, she returned his kiss. A shiver of longing tripped up her spine, sending chills across her breasts. This was what she wanted and needed. Someone special, someone who cared about her, someone she could truly love. She sighed and rested her head against his sturdy chest, content.

His hands skimmed across her body and paused to caress her intimately while his tongue danced with hers. Roving fingers found their way under her blouse to the clasp of her bra. With a flick of his

371

wrist it was undone and her breast was cradled in the palm of his hand.

"You're beautiful, so beautiful," Rob whispered.

"Yes," she whispered, believing for the first time in her body's beauty instead of being afraid of it. She pressed her hips forward as her nipple tightened under the pressure of his thumb. Both breasts felt hot and achy now. She wanted his mouth on them the way it had been the other night.

Her pulse pounded in her temples, making her head spin, and she knew she was out of control. Images flashed through her mind so quickly she didn't have time to react: She was backed up against the refrigerator, her blouse dangling from one wrist; then she was sliding to the floor in slow motion; suddenly she was naked, yet she had no memory of undressing or being undressed.

Maybe she wasn't out of control. Perhaps it was Rob who'd gone over some invisible edge. He was everywhere at once, his touch tender but undeniably urgent—as if he couldn't get enough of her.

"Slow down," she whispered, wanting to make this last—forever.

He misunderstood and thought she wasn't aroused enough. His lips left hers and traced a moist trail down the sensitive curve of her neck. She buried her face against his neck and inhaled his sensuous earthy scent, clutching his hair, threading its soft fullness through her fingers, comparing it to the wiry hair on his chest as it abraded her sensitive nipples.

Rob! She thought. *Rob . . . oh, Rob!*

She'd waited so long—all her life—to be swept away like this. Once such domination, such unbridled passion would have frightened her. Not anymore.

His turgid erection pulsed against her naked thigh and she tried to remember when he'd taken off his clothes, but quickly decided it didn't matter. All that mattered was the subtle movement of his tongue as it glided down past her navel, tasting, circling, tasting again.

"Oh, my . . . more. Give me more," she cried.

"You got it, babe." His hands were under her now, digging into the softness of her buttocks and gently spreading her legs apart. The sensitive skin responded with a flare of heat that centered in her groin.

"Oh, yes," she cried out.

That spurred him on; he centered himself between her legs and blew across the cluster of curls. His hot breath felt cool against the moist skin—and unbelievably erotic. His head dipped and his tongue invaded her most intimate places with smooth, sure strokes.

She clutched at his powerful shoulders and held him there, mesmerized by the prospect of imminent release. Ripples of anticipation coursed through her with each tantalizing stroke of his tongue. Suddenly he was inside her, with a jolt that felt as if he'd shot right through her. She welcomed him with an instinctive upward thrust of her hips, wrapping her legs around him and matching his ever increasing rhythm with her own.

Her lungs were burning from lack of air and her eyes were watering—she wasn't sure why—when she realized she was seconds from climaxing. Too soon, she tried to shout, but the pounding of hips and the ramrod hardness between her thighs silenced her.

He stopped, still buried to the hilt inside her, and gazed into her eyes. "I'm the one. The only one— and don't you ever forget it."

"I know," she whispered. "You are the one."

She wanted this exquisite feeling to last forever, but it didn't. In a starburst of ecstasy that bordered on pain, she catapulted over the edge. Seconds later Rob followed, collapsing on top of her, utterly exhausted. She held him to her breast, not wanting the experience to end.

She honestly couldn't recall being this happy, this content. Yet here she was buck naked on the kitchen floor with her elbow in Molly's Meow Mix—euphorically happy. So this was love.

It was minutes before she found her voice. By then Rob had rolled off her and was staring at the kitchen ceiling. He seemed troubled.

"Maybe we should put the steaks on the barbecue," she suggested, thinking they should talk.

Rob levered himself up on one elbow and ran his hand over the supple curve of her hip and glided between her thighs with his talented fingers. "Screw the steaks."

In seconds they were in her bedroom on top of the new comforter she'd splurged on. This time he drew her to him more gently, his earlier intensity replaced by such tenderness it made her heart ache.

Too soon morning came, an apricot glow that backlit Koko Head in a wreath of light. Dana cracked one eye, realizing she must have fallen asleep. When had they stopped making love?

She turned to touch his cheek and make sure this was real, not some erotic dream, but he was gone. Nothing more than an indentation in the pillow said he'd ever been there. Suddenly a hollow feeling of being lost swept over her. It was the same helpless sensation she'd had at her parents' funeral when she'd stared at the twin caskets and realized they were never coming back.

The beckoning scent of coffee brewing brought her to her senses. Rob was in the kitchen. Was she ever going to stop being so insecure?

She hopped out of bed and dashed into the bathroom, where she found her robe. "Oh, Lordy," she moaned at her reflection.

Dark circles shadowed her eyes and her hair was a mass of tangles, but she looked as happy as Molly after a bowl of stinky fish. She quickly splashed cold water on her face and brushed her teeth. Rob appeared with a mug of coffee as she struggled to get the comb through her hair. "It'll be a week before you get a brush through the back of your hair." He gave her a triumphant smile. "After last night."

She giggled, accepting the mug with a heartfelt smile. "You rat."

The words wiped the grin off his face. "Come on. Let's talk."

She followed him to the kitchen with a growing sense of apprehension that she kept telling herself was unfounded. She'd been paranoid, thinking everyone was against her, and she'd been wrong.

I'm the one.

Yes. As wild as it seemed, Rob Tagett was the one for her. The only one. If she'd had any doubts about that last night changed her mind.

He faced her with the hard-edged reporter's expression that she remembered so well from the days when she'd first seen him around the courthouse. "I don't know any way to say this but to be completely honest."

A primitive warning sounded in her brain. Suddenly she felt as hollow as his voice sounded.

"I'm not going to be seeing you anymore."

The statement was so cold, so matter-of-fact, it caused her heart to lurch painfully as she stood transfixed, staring at him. Could this be Rob, the man who'd so tenderly made love to her all night? There had to be an explanation. Then it dawned on her.

"We can work around Zach. I realize that he'll take most of your time. I won't be able to stay overnight or have you here because you'll need to be with him, but—"

Rob raised his hand to cut her off. "It's not just Zach. It's . . ."

He seemed to be searching for words that wouldn't come, and she heard his harsh intake of breath. The transformation took but the flicker of her lashes. Suddenly, anything that had been between them was gone.

"It's Ellen, isn't it?" she asked, bitterness underscoring each word despite her valiant attempt to remain calm. "Zach said you were getting back together. Is it true?"

His gaze, so level before, shifted to Molly, who was at his feet, rubbing shamelessly against his legs. "Yeah. Ellen and I are going to give it another try. Zach needs both his parents right now."

"What about us?" she whispered, positive if her voice rose she'd be screaming at him. "What about last night?"

30

By the time Dana reached her office she'd stopped trembling. Hurt had flared into anger, making her so furious she could hardly think. How dare Rob spend the night with her—then blithely announce that he was going back to his wife? She should have known better than to trust him. Every fiber of her being had warned her again and again, but she hadn't listened. *Well, look at it as a valuable lesson. Lead with your head, not your heart.*

Still his parting words echoed through her soul. "What about last night?" he'd said, parroting back her own words with the emphasis on *what*.

The air suspended in her lungs, she had salvaged what little of her pride remained and shoved him out the door, slamming it so hard Molly ran and hid under the sofa.

"That jerk!" she said to the security camera scanning the entrance to the courthouse. The words didn't bring much comfort as she shouldered her way through the swinging doors into the building.

She smiled bravely at the attendant monitoring the metal detector, but her smile vanished long before she reached her office.

Betrayal whiplashed through her, bringing a sheen of tears to her eyes. The ache in her chest swelled to a sob. It took all her willpower not to break down as she passed people in the hall. Her tightly knit emotions unraveled like an old sweater, a host of conflicting emotions warring inside her.

She loved him. No. She hated him.

She *had* to hate him. It was the only way to survive. Anger and work, she decided. The emotional vise eased a bit as she thought about work. Grinding, hard work that would keep her busy until she was ready to drop was the solution.

Inside her chambers she gazed morosely at the mountain of papers on her desk. Thank God she wasn't due in juvenile court until afternoon, she thought, looking at the Wyland sea-life print. She wasn't certain how long she'd been staring at the picture when she heard a knock.

Vanessa entered and sat in one of the wing chairs opposite Dana's desk. "I tried to reach you last night, but your phone was out of order . . . or something."

Dana came around the desk to sit beside her sister, not wanting to tell her that Rob had taken the phone off the hook so they wouldn't be disturbed. She should be able to discuss this with Vanessa, she decided as she sat down. If there was distance between them, wasn't that due to her inability to talk about her feelings?

"Rob came over—" Dana began, then broke off, not knowing how to explain what happened.

"I knew it." Vanessa smiled. "He's crazy about you."

"He's crazy, all right, crazy enough to tell me we're 'committed,' then go back to his ex-wife." The wellspring of hurt that she'd been suppressing erupted with startling vehemence. "He's a real bastard."

"Why would he go back to her—after all this time?"

"His son's having problems. Rob thinks a solid family will help."

"But they've been divorced for years."

"It doesn't make sense, does it? But what do you expect? He's a man."

Vanessa studied her for a moment, her dazzling blue eyes solemn. "I thought we'd worked through all that when we talked. Don't tar all men with the same brush."

"You're right," Dana admitted with a sigh. "Garth's a treasure, and Pinsky and Hwang are wonderful too. I guess I just don't have luck with my personal relationships."

"I suspect something is troubling Rob," Vanessa said. "That's why I came to see you. Last night I overheard Garth talking on the phone about evidence. When I asked him about it he said it was confidential. I may be mistaken, but I thought he was talking about evidence against Rob."

"I don't give a damn about him."

Vanessa put her hand on Dana's shoulder and gazed into her eyes. "There's one thing Garth taught me that's priceless. Face the truth and it isn't nearly as frightening. Once I accepted what Big Daddy had done, I could deal with it. You need to accept the possibility that Rob has chosen his ex-wife over you. Don't deny it by saying you don't care—when you do."

It took Dana a minute to bring herself to say, "You're right. I care about him, that's why I'm so angry. That's why this hurts so much."

"Do you love him?"

"Yes," she admitted, experiencing an overwhelming sense of relief. Sharing this with her sister wouldn't take away the pain, but the ache eased a bit. "How could I be so wrong about him?"

"Trust your heart," Vanessa said quietly. "If you think he's the one, then I'll bet he is. Everything will work out, you'll see."

The one. The words brought a too familiar stab of regret. Of longing. Of loneliness too long denied. Of what might have been, but was never to be.

Vanessa rose. "Why don't you come by for dinner tonight?"

Dana wished her sister the best and truly believed she would find happiness with Garth, but tonight she couldn't bear to be with the lovebirds. "There's a sunset service for Lillian Hurley. I'm going there, then home to sleep."

Vanessa started to protest, but stopped. "Call me if you need me. And definitely let me know if Rob's in trouble. No matter what happened between you two, he's really helped us."

Vanessa left, and Dana called for Gus Mahala, certain her bailiff would know the latest courthouse gossip. Gus was the open, gregarious type, who inspired confidences even though he didn't gossip himself. No only that, Gus had numerous relatives sprinkled throughout the court system, giving him lots of contacts.

Gus came through the door, beaming. "You need me?"

She motioned for him to close the door, not wanting anyone to overhear them. "I don't usually listen to gossip, but I heard a disturbing rumor. I wonder if you would help me verify it?" She inhaled a calming breath as he nodded. "Is Rob Tagett in some kind of trouble?"

"My cousin Theo let it slip after a few brews," Gus confessed. "Don't mention his name. He'll lose his job in the police department."

"I won't say a word."

"I don't know much. Theo just said Tagett's going to be charged with the Panama Jack's rapes."

Totally astonished, Dana vaulted to her feet. A thousand possibilities had whirled through her mind, but not this. Never this. "That's impossible. They can't have any evidence."

"I dunno. They must have something. The police department sent the case to the DA."

Dana couldn't suppress a shudder. The police department sent only cases with enough evidence to prosecute to the district attorney. What could they possibly have on Rob?

Propping himself up on one elbow, Rob watched his son struggling with his windsurfer at Ho'okipa Beach on the north shore not far from his house. Rob had left Dana's early that morning, disgusted with himself and thoroughly disheartened. Christ, he was a real bastard.

I love you.

Dana's words echoed through his head, touching the secret reaches of his soul. The way she'd whispered the words, almost a plea, threatened to bring tears to his eyes. He longed to change things, but wishing and hoping wouldn't make any difference. If he was going to be arrested—for damn sure it looked that way—he wasn't going to drag her down with him.

"Okay, did you have to be such a schmuck about it?" he muttered to himself.

Letting her go was the hardest damn thing he'd ever done. He honestly hadn't had a clue what to say until she mentioned him getting back together with Ellen. That gave him the out he needed, all right. He'd been a real prick, but he didn't have a choice.

He gazed at the windsurfers, trying to forget what

a bastard he'd been, as Zach stumbled onshore, dragging his windsurfer, clearly discouraged. He collapsed beside Rob saying, "Nukin' winds, man. Never seen anything like it."

Rob almost chuckled. Nukin' winds—killer winds. What did Zach expect? Ho'okipa Beach was *the* windsurfing mecca. Just because Zach could ride the waves in California didn't mean he could cut it here—without a lot of work.

"Aren't you going back?" Rob asked as his son reached for his backpack.

"Nah. I'm reading."

"Really? What?"

Zach held up Stephen King's *The Stand*. "Dana gave it to me. Saved me from having to talk to Mom's nerdy friends in Maui."

Dana? Rob leaned back and studied the pure white strafers that clouded the north shore's sky, while his son buried his nose in the book. Rob closed his eyes, hearing the mournful sound of the door slamming when Dana threw him out. It echoed over and over and over, reminding him of all he'd lost.

"What did you think of Dana?" Rob ventured.

Zach didn't look up. "She's okay . . . I guess."

Okay didn't come close, but Rob refused to draw his son into a comparison of two distinctly different women—Ellen and Dana Hamilton. In his heart, though, he knew the difference.

"Zach, did you tell Dana that your mother and I are getting back together?"

His son studied the page for a time before looking up. Rob pushed his sunglasses to the top of his head so he could look directly into Zach's eyes.

"Yeah. I wanted to scare her off."

"Why? I barely mentioned her."

"I could tell that you're hot for her. I wanted to get rid of her." Zach began reading his book again.

Rob reached out and pulled it away. "Explain why you lied to Dana." He didn't mention that this lie had given him the out he wanted—when he desperately needed it.

Zach sat up, his spine rigid, his arms locking around his knees. "I knew what would happen. I've been down that trail, dude."

Dude? Rob seethed, imagining what would have happened to him had he called his father "dude." "Tell me."

Zach lifted his shoulders as if words escaped him. Of course, he didn't realize that this might be one of the last private conversations they'd have for—who knew?—weeks or months or, God forbid, years.

"Okay," Zach exploded. "I hate Mom's nerdy boyfriend and his two prissy daughters. Nuthin' I do around them is right. Nuthin'."

Rob knew Ellen had been dating a man who had two young daughters. He could imagine how different they'd be from a teenage boy. "I know what you mean. Girls that age are numbnuts. What does that have to do with Dana?"

Zach buried his fist in the sand, then glared at

386

Rob. "Mom's going to marry the nerd. Then you're going to marry Dana and have some dumb baby."

I'll be left alone. Rob read between the lines. He reached over and ruffled his son's hair. "I'm not marrying Dana, and I'm not having any more children."

It hurt to say it, but it was true. Somewhere in his deepest self he'd seen himself with another child— like a young Zach—Dana's child. That wasn't to be, and it hurt more than he ever could have imagined.

"You're not marrying Dana? Why? She's way cool."

Rob almost smiled at the contradictions in his son's adolescent logic, proof positive that teenagers were trapped in the Twilight Zone. Zach liked Dana, but he was afraid that she'd have a child who'd steal his father's affection. It was unbearably sad. How he remembered his own youth! He'd enjoyed a loving family. Even now, in his darkest hour, their upbringing gave him strength.

Rob decided he had to level with his son—even if he risked losing him. "Dana's a damn good judge. I don't want her to jeopardize her career by being involved with me."

Zach measured him with wary eyes. "I don't get it."

"Do you remember what made your mother leave me?" Rob wasn't entirely certain what Ellen had told Zach after they'd moved to L.A. He'd seen his son many times, yet they'd never discussed this. It reminded him of Dana and how she'd never discussed Hank Rawlins with her sister. When the hurt was deep enough, it was nearly impossible to talk about it.

"They said you raped somebody, but you didn't."

Rob silently applauded Ellen. Despite the energy she'd put into keeping him apart from Zach, at least she'd told him the truth. "Right. Well, it seems that I'm about to be charged with rape again."

"Unfuckingbelievable! You'd never do that."

Rob's throat closed up at the unqualified vote of confidence. God, he loved this boy with his oversize body and convoluted logic.

"Zach, let me tell you what's happening." His son listened intently as Rob described what he knew about the latest accusation.

"Just like Stephen King," Zach responded. "It's the stand between good and evil. That's what's happening to you."

"You're right. I have to take a stand, but it'll be difficult with you here. I may have to send you back to L.A."

Zach catapulted to his feet. "Fuck that shit. I'm stayin' right here with you. I'm going to help."

"I know you—" The cellular telephone in Rob's satchel rang and he grabbed it, hoping it was Garth. It was.

"Good news," Garth said. "You're not going to be arrested tomorrow. They're waiting until after the weekend. Monday's the day."

Rob slowly punched the END button, uncertain what this news meant. The DA went over cases recommended by the police with a fine-tooth comb. They rarely tried anything but slam-dunk cases. The rest they plea-bargained or dropped; it was simply too costly to proceed.

The Panama Jack's rapist was different. He'd terrorized the community and—more important—threatened tourists. That case could go to trial on a lot less evidence. Still, the DA would want to make certain they had enough to bring in a guilty verdict before risking his precious conviction record.

What evidence could they possibly have?

31

The memorial service for Lillian Hurley was held in the garden of the Society to Preserve Hawaii's Native Plants and Flowers. Dana couldn't imagine a more fitting site. For years Lillian had worked tirelessly for the organization. Dana moved through the mourners searching for Lillian's daughter, but Fran Martin wasn't among the small group gathered under the cooling shade of a hala tree. Just as well, Dana thought. Her temper had a hair trigger today; no telling what she might do to the woman.

Dr. Winston walked up to her. "We'd like you to say a few words about Lillian right after the director makes the presentation."

Inwardly Dana groaned. She wasn't prepared to speak; she was afraid she'd burst into tears if she tried. "What about her daughter—"

"She had Lillian cremated and left town. The director of the society made the funeral arrangements," he said, shaking his head. "You were closer to Lillian than anyone. Can't you say a few words?"

Dana fingered the lehua lei that was draped over one arm. "I'll do my best."

The director motioned for the group to join him in front of a statue of King Kamehameha, which was a smaller replica of the towering statue that stood in front of the government offices downtown near the courthouse.

"We're gathered to honor the memory of one of our dearest friends," the director began. "Lillian Hurley was a founding member of this society. Just after the war she recognized that Hawaii's unique plants and flowers might be wiped from the face of this earth unless we took action to preserve our heritage of plants and flowers that exist nowhere else on earth except in these blessed islands."

He draped a ten-foot-long lei of rare white epidendrum orchids with throats of deep scarlet over King Kamehameha's outstretched arm. Each June on the anniversary of the king's birthday, hundreds of tribute leis were placed on the majestic statue in the center of Honolulu. A lei here, on this statue, was a similar honor for someone who'd made a special contribution to Hawaiian culture.

"Before we pray for dear Lillian, her close friend Judge Dana Hamilton would like to say a few words."

No, I wouldn't, Dana thought as she moved to the front of the group, a droplet of perspiration trickling down between her breasts. She'd much rather keep her thoughts about Lillian to herself, but she didn't have any choice. She walked carefully, taking her time, not wanting to step on the lei that trailed down from her arm and brushed the diachondra, trying to gather her thoughts for a fitting tribute. As she looked up over the heads of the group, hoping for inspiration, she saw a man across the enormous garden standing in the shadows of the building's arcade.

Rob? It couldn't be. She squinted against the sun pitched low in the sky, but the silhouette remained concealed by the shadows. He wouldn't be here, she assured herself. Her imagination was working overtime.

Ever since Gus had told her about the rape charges, her mind had been in turmoil. Rob was a rat—the king of rats—but he was being falsely accused. She wanted to help him and settle the score, so she wouldn't feel she owed him anything for finding out about Hank Rawlins, but she didn't know how.

Concentrate, she told herself as she realized everyone was staring at her, waiting for her to begin. The words came, but from where she'd never be able to say. They merely flowed from her—right from the heart.

"Lillian, we're all gathered here to honor you. I know one of your fondest wishes was to have grandchildren. I'm sorry you didn't have that joy, but you must realize you've brought happiness to more children and grandchildren than you'll ever know. By saving from extinction so many plants and flowers, you've given Hawaii's children—and the children of the world—a precious treasure. You made a difference in so many lives. Few people can make that claim."

She lifted the long lehua lei and stood on tiptoe to drape it over King Kamehameha's extended arm. Native to Hawaii's up-country, the lehua was one of the first trees to reestablish itself on lava fields after a volcano-eruption. Its flower, a red pom-pom with spikelike petals, had always been one of Lillian's favorites.

Facing the group again, Dana noticed that the shadow in the arcade had moved, retreating farther into the shadows. She couldn't possibly identify the person. Her part of the memorial service was over once she'd placed the lei, but she needed to say more.

"Lillian Hurley not only loved plants, she was the type of person who welcomed stray animals—or people. I know. When I moved next door to her, she befriended me, and despite our ages that friendship grew."

Dana paused to gather her thoughts. "Shortly before she died, Lillian expressed to me her fear of dying without anyone remembering that she'd lived and loved and had been a good mother. I know that was a silly thought. Just look at how many of us are here."

Not nearly as many as there should be, she thought silently, but then, the society was quite small. "I'm donating enough money for a special Lillian Hurley plot, where visitors can see rare flowers without having to trek up the slopes of some volcano or through impenetrable rain forest."

A spontaneous round of applause startled her. She'd almost forgotten the group around her. For some reason she was talking to the person across the garden, cloaked in the shadows. She sensed a kindred spirit, she thought, then realized Lillian's death, the hearing, Rob's betrayal—everything had happened so fast that she was reacting emotionally.

"Lillian worked so hard and loved everyone so much that I want to make certain her memory never dies," Dana continued. "I'll put a special plaque on a marker. It'll be engraved with Lillian's favorite quote. It's a line from G. K. Chesterton: *The best way to love anything is as if it might be lost.*

"This plot will ensure that she's with us still. In the flowers she loved. In the breathtaking sunsets. In the sun's sparkle on Hawaii's azure sea." Dana heard the quaver in her own voice. "She'll be with us. Forever in our hearts."

She stepped back to let the director lead the group in prayer, tears dewing her lashes. In her blurred vision as she dropped her head to pray, she saw the man in the shadows turn and leave.

Exhausted, Dana entered her chambers the following morning. She'd been up all night, disturbed by Lillian's funeral and haunted by the image of a man standing at the back of the garden, silently giving her moral support. She kept telling herself that it was her imagination that made her believe it was Rob.

It's just guilt, she decided. Rob had helped her get Vanessa and Jason away from Big Daddy. Then he'd gone to Gomper's Bend and set her free. He was a heartless rat though. *What about last night?* Like a dying heartbeat his words echoed through her, bringing a sensation of unparalleled anguish and despair.

Still, she felt she owed him something. The only way to help Rob was risky. She'd just survived the judicial review, so what she was contemplating was pure insanity. If word got out she'd lose any chance she had of getting that appointment.

She waited until four-thirty, through the longest day of her life, before sneaking into the DA's office, praying no one would see her. Friday afternoons fell under the *ukupau* philosophy, which meant finish your job and take off the rest of the day. On Friday, people miraculously declared their work done in the early afternoon and left to get a head start on the weekend.

Even Al Homuku's secretary was gone when Dana slipped into the DA's office, but she could hear Al on the telephone. She wasn't surprised that he was still there. She'd spent several years as a prosecutor under him; Al didn't believe in *ukupau*.

She waited, her pulse pounding in her ears like the night marchers, until she heard Al hang up the telephone. She knocked lightly on his half-open door and he bellowed for her to come in.

LAST NIGHT

Tan and fit, Al Homuku had a wealth of jet black hair and dark eyes that attested to his Hawaiian ancestry, but he always dressed as if he'd just stepped onto the Via Venetto. He adored Italian suits and long-sleeved shirts with French cuffs, when most of the men in the islands wore short-sleeved shirts and took off their jackets the second they had a chance.

Today the fiftyish prosecutor was dressed in a dove gray suit and a tie of vibrant cranberry with a matching handkerchief flaring out of the pocket. He didn't have to pull his feet out from under the desk for Dana to know he was wearing the same scuffed black wing tips he'd had for years. As stylish as he was, as expensive as his suits were, Al had only two old pairs of shoes—black and brown.

No one had ever figured out why Al splurged on Italian suits and ties worth a week's wages yet never bought new shoes. He was an odd duck, but a fair man. Dana had enjoyed working for him. She was counting on their past relationship and Al's unbridled ambition to become attorney general.

"Dana." Al rose to his feet. "Hey, this is a surprise. Have a seat."

Dana dropped into the well-worn chair opposite his desk the way she had countless times when she'd been an assistant DA and had come to his office to discuss a case. Now, though, she was frightened.

Al took his seat again, grinning at her. "You don't have to thank me. As soon as I saw Binkley's letter of inquiry, I got the petition going. The rest was easy. People just passed it around."

"I really appreciate it," Dana managed to say. Knowing that Al had initiated the petition made this even harder. "Thank you so much."

"You're judge material. No question about it. And I found you right here in this office. I wasn't about to let that son of a bitch Binkley sabotage your career."

"If there's ever anything I can do for you—"

"I'm planning on running for attorney general. I'm counting on your vote."

"Of course." She hesitated, unsure of what to say next. After an embarrassingly long pause she said, "I need to ask you something."

Al's grin broadened. "Shoot."

"I understand your office is preparing to charge Rob Tagett with the Panama Jack's rapes. I want to know what evidence you have."

His smile collapsed and became a grim line that complemented his furrowed brow. He stared at her for a full second before rising, coming around the desk, and hitching one leg over the top so he was half-sitting, facing her.

"I'm going to pretend you never said that. You have a fantastic career ahead of you; don't ruin it with an obstruction of justice charge. You know it's unethical for a judge to interfere with the prosecution of any case. If anyone found out you'd come to me, you'd never get to superior court."

She stared at his scuffed shoe, which was swinging back and forth, a clear indication of how upset Al was. "I've weighed the consequences." She met his eyes. "Believe me, I wouldn't be here if I had any choice."

"Jesus! What has that bastard Tagett got? A secret love potion? Women fall all over him." Al shook his head. "He'll be the kiss of death for your career."

She couldn't blame him for being angry. This went against every judicial ethic she held so dear, but somehow rules didn't matter anymore. She could still hear Rob telling her how he lost his son the first time. She couldn't let it happen again.

She played her ace. "I'm here because I want to help you." Al's eyes widened in utter disbelief. Before he could say anything she rushed on. "I know you want to be attorney general. This case will do it —if you have the right man."

"We have proof," Al said, but he didn't sound completely certain.

"I know for a fact Rob is innocent and I can prove it." She let her words settle in, acknowledging that sometimes loving someone meant you had to bluff. Or even lie. "If you tell me what evidence you have, I can help you. But if you muff this case you won't be moving across the street to the state house."

32

"Love you." Ellen kissed Zach on the cheek and hugged him.

Zach stoically accepted her kiss like a typical teenage boy. "Bye, Mom."

Ellen's blue eyes drifted over Rob as she spoke to her son. "Take care. Call me if you need me."

"We won't need you, Mom. Dad's taking me to counseling on Monday. I'll be fine. You'll see."

If his situation hadn't been so pathetic, Rob might have smiled. Telling Zach his problems had brought them closer. They had two whole days to spend together. After that, who knew? The future shimmered like a mirage, out of focus, out of reach.

"I've got to go," Ellen said as they called her flight. She hurried away, then turned back, tears in her eyes.

"Aw, cripes," Zach mumbled. "She always cries."

"Umm-hmm." Rob didn't add that this was how Ellen manipulated men. He didn't have to; Zach was already learning.

Ellen disappeared down the Jetway, and Rob couldn't help comparing her to Dana. Had he ever really been in love with Ellen? Okay, sure, he'd married her and told himself he loved her. Now that he'd met Dana he couldn't imagine loving any other woman.

"So do we hit the beach, or what?" Zach asked.

He ruffled his son's hair, silently blessing Ellen for giving him Zach. She might not have stood by him, but Zach was remarkably loyal.

"Your choice," Rob said. "What do you want to do?"

"Is it too expensive to fly over to Kauai and see Grandma? I haven't seen her in years. She always writes and sends me stuff."

"Great idea. Let's give her a call. We don't want to get there and find she's out playing bridge or something."

Rob's mother was home, and they flew to the garden isle. Zach hadn't been there since he was a child, but he'd seen *Jurassic Park* and knew it had been filmed there. He insisted on renting a Jeep and dragging his father and grandmother through the rain forest looking for a T-Rex.

It was late Saturday night—early Sunday morning, actually—by the time they caught a return flight and drove home. The message light on his machine was flashing but Rob sent Zach to bed before picking up his messages. It had been such a wonderful day. He didn't want to spoil it with more bad news.

The first message was from the editor-in-chief at

the *Honolulu Sun*, wanting to know when he could expect Rob's next article. The next message was from Garth.

"Just thought you'd want to know. Dana's been appointed to the superior court. We're having a cocktail party tomorrow night to celebrate. Come over about six and bring Zach."

"I'm not going to know anyone," Zach said for the third time as they pulled up to Garth's home on Honolulu's Gold Coast.

"I want you to meet my friends." Rob tried to reassure him even though he was more than a little amazed at the number of cars lining the street.

They walked through the open gates that towered above their heads into a huge courtyard filled with majestic date palms and tropical plants. In the center was a work of modern art, a fountain that sent a sheet of water ten feet wide down a slab of polished marble, where it disappeared into a bed of orchids without letting a drop of water splash on the plants.

"Wow!" Zach said. "Get a load of this place."

"It belongs to the best lawyer in the islands. His parents were killed in an automobile crash and Garth was left penniless—at eighteen. Everything he has, he's earned himself."

Zach nodded, but Rob doubted he was impressed. He'd deliberately not mentioned Garth's handicap. He wanted his son to realize there were worse things in the world than your parents divorcing. And you could overcome them.

There wasn't any need to ring the bell; the unusually tall door, which seemed to reach the classic Japanese roof of sky blue ceramic tiles, was open. The chatter from inside was accompanied by the typically Hawaiian sound of a slack-key guitar playing an island ballad. Rob glanced around, recognizing most people.

He spotted Al Homuku standing in the corner of the vast, marble-floored living room sipping a drink. Their eyes met, and Rob shot him a look that could back down a pit bull, then turned to find Dana, but he didn't see her.

"Let's go out to the pool," Rob told Zach, and they maneuvered through the crowd to the wide terrace that faced the bay.

Floating candles studded the black-bottom pool, glowing in the dark water like stars in the night sky. At the far end of the pool, where the beach began, was a bar. Rob was half-tempted to order a Stoli straight up, except that he had his son with him and he was driving. Suddenly, something clasped his knees.

"Rob! Rob!" It was Jason Coltrane, his little arms outstretched to be picked up. With a pang of nostalgia he remembered Zach asking to be held in just the same way.

"Howdy, partner." Rob hoisted Jason to his hip. "This is my son, Zach."

Jason stared at Zach. "What's wrong with your hair? Why's it pink?"

"I like it like that." Zach's chin jutted out, proving he'd inherited more than his father's eyes.

Jason missed the sarcasm. "Oh, cool. Like a Power Ranger."

Rob wasn't aware of any Power Ranger with maroon hair, but then he wasn't up on kindergarten idols these days. Garth wheeled up just in time to save the conversation.

"Hey, Rob. Glad you could come." Garth spun his chair around to face Zach. "You must be Zach. I'm Garth Bradford."

Zach's jaw hit his shoelaces as they shook hands. "Hi."

"Garth's my calabash cousin," Jason proudly announced.

"Your what?" Zach asked.

"It's an old Hawaiian custom to call friends who are as close as family 'calabash cousins.' In olden days families used to eat from the same calabash gourd. That's where it started," Rob said.

"Hi." Vanessa Coltrane appeared and put her hand on Garth's shoulder, curling her fingers into the fabric of the shirt he wore in a way that said they were more than "cousins."

Rob almost laughed at Zach's astonished expression. He doubted Zach had met many women as beautiful as Vanessa. Most certainly he had never met anyone like Garth.

"Wanna see my parrot?" Jason asked Zach, clearly not put off by his pink hair or mesmerized expression. "He'll sue your ass."

"A-a-ah, sure," Zach answered, and Jason hopped down and led him away.

Rob opened his mouth to ask where Dana was, when a troop from the public defender's office descended on Garth. Obviously they were fresh out of law school and hadn't been disillusioned by defending drug addicts, child molesters, and repeat offenders who cycled through the system like bad pennies. The attorneys marked time in the PD's office until their talons were sharp enough to venture out on their own.

He wandered across the pool area to the beach. The sun was haloed by a warm mist as it floated on the horizon, casting its last light on the sea. He waited, silently watching until the sun disappeared and the mist rose, touching the emerging stars and screening them like a honeycomb veil. How often had he watched a sunset and taken it for granted?

No more. Facing prison was a sobering thought. The sunrises and sunsets he took for granted—along with much of his life—would be history if he didn't win this fight. Frustrated, he admitted there wasn't a damn thing he could do until he knew what evidence they had.

"Rob." He spun around and found Vanessa walking up to him. "I want to thank you again for all you did to help us. If I can ever—"

"It was nothing. Simple, really. I just found out the truth."

"It changed our lives—mine and Dana's." She put a soft hand on his shoulder, and he had yet another taste of Vanessa's charm, but this time it was a friendly gesture, not a seductive one. "Garth and I met with Big Daddy last night."

Rob tensed; he believed Coltrane was behind his troubles. He had tried to sabotage Dana and now he was after him.

"Big Daddy is really upset. He's terrified of losing Jason forever. He's willing to do whatever we ask. We've worked out an arrangement for supervised visitations so he can see Jason."

"Really? Why? Coltrane's a creep."

"Oh, Rob. He's so pathetic, so beaten." She inhaled sharply, holding raw emotion in check. "Still, he's Jason's father. Garth and I discussed it. I have no right to keep them apart. When Jason's old enough we're going to tell him the truth. Then he can decide for himself about seeing his father. Until then Big Daddy's on his best behavior. He doesn't want to chance losing Jason."

"You're doing the right thing," Rob conceded, but he thought Garth would make a better father. With luck, his relationship with Vanessa would work out.

One of the caterers needed Vanessa, and she disappeared, leaving Rob to wonder. If Coltrane wasn't behind his troubles, who was? He'd tracked down the *mokes* and beat the crap out of them. He had a couple of cuts and a lot of bruises, but the *mokes* had talked. They claimed Big Daddy had sent them after the tapes. Maybe their theft of the tapes had nothing to do with the blackmail scheme or his own problems. Rob stood, staring out to sea, pondering the situation, until he lost track of time.

He walked back toward the house, scanning the crowd for Dana. Nothing. Surely she wouldn't be this late for her own party. He surveyed the room again and his gaze came to rest on the sensuous back of a blonde.

Dana? Couldn't be. But the blonde slowly turned, giving him a view of her profile. *I'll be a son of a bitch. It is Dana.*

Her hair was a soft, natural blonde several shades darker than her sister's. She wore a slip dress in a soft shade of lavender that accented her slim figure. A touch more eye makeup than usual highlighted her long-lashed green eyes. The noose around his heart tightened. Without knowing he moved, he walked closer. A man stood beside Dana, his stance proprietary. Anger like invisible lightning arced through Rob.

"Hold it," he muttered half under his breath. She was much better off with some corporate wienie or another attorney than she was with him. She'd said she loved him and he'd given her the big kiss-off. What right did he have to be jealous?

Christ, she was gorgeous though. He'd hate to be a lawyer trying to concentrate in her court. There was something about Dana's striking green eyes and dark blonde hair that made her even more breathtaking than her sister.

Keep your distance, he cautioned himself, knowing he had a hard time staying away from her. He'd

A daughter who's run away from home.
A mother who's run away from herself.

RACHEL LEE

Snow in September

The tragedy of her husband's death has taken its toll on
both Meg Williams and her teenage daughter, Allie.
Now Allie has run away.

Sheriff Earl Sanders feels a responsibility to look after
Meg and Allie. Though he's determined not to let his love
and desire for his best friend's widow make her life even
harder, he's doing all he can to find her daughter. And as
days and nights pass, some startling secrets come to light.
Truths too painful to accept have stretched a family to
the breaking point, until a woman who nearly lost
everything discovers what matters most.

"A magnificent presence in romantic fiction.
Rachel Lee is an author to treasure forever."
—*Romantic Times Magazine*

On sale mid-April 2000 wherever paperbacks are sold!

MIRA

HELEN R. MYERS

Six years ago the town of Split Creek, Texas, was rocked to its core when a young woman was brutally murdered. Her killer was never found. Now another girl has disappeared....

When Faith Ramey's abandoned car is discovered, the town feels an unwelcome sense of déjà vu. Police Chief Jared Morgan doesn't want to believe there's a connection, but Faith's sister Michaele is beginning to suspect otherwise.

LST

As secrets and scandals are exposed, old fears— and new—spawn doubt and suspicion. Is a sinister stranger lurking behind the murder and Faith's disappearance—or does someone in Split Creek have blood on their hands? Only Michaele's fierce determination—and her trust in Jared—will help her see the truth hidden in plain sight.

"Ms. Myers gives readers an incredible depth of storytelling."
—*Romantic Times*

On sale mid-March 2000 wherever paperbacks are sold!

MIRA

Visit us at www.mirabooks.com

MHRM572

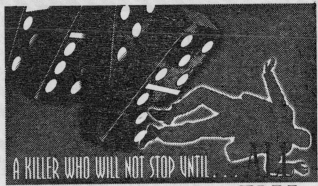

A KILLER WHO WILL NOT STOP UNTIL....

Men are dying unexpectedly in Charlotte, North Carolina—all victims of bizarre accidents. Only a small-town cop, Melanie May, sees the pattern: a serial killer targeting men who have slipped through the fingers of justice.

FALL DOWN

ERICA SPINDLER

Working with FBI profiler Connor Parks, Melanie is shocked to realize they've created a profile that fits someone in her *own* life...a cunning killer, without remorse and bent on vengence.

"Spindler's lastest moves fast and takes no prisoners."
—*Publishers Weekly* on *Cause for Alarm*

On sale mid-March 2000 wherever paperbacks are sold!

MIRA

If you enjoyed what you just read,
then we've got an offer you can't resist!

Take 2 bestselling love stories FREE!

Plus get a FREE surprise gift!

One small spark ignites the entire city of Chicago, but amid the chaos, a chance encounter leads to an unexpected new love....

THE HOSTAGE

As Deborah Sinclair confronts her powerful father, determined to refuse the society marriage he has arranged for her, a stranger with vengeance on his mind suddenly appears and takes the fragile, sheltered heiress hostage.

Swept off to Isle Royale, Deborah finds herself the pawn in Tom Silver's dangerous game of revenge. Soon she begins to understand the injustice that fuels his anger, an injustice wrought by her own family. And as winter imprisons the isolated land, she finds herself a hostage of her own heart....

SUSAN WIGGS

MIRA

"...draws readers in with delightful characters, engaging dialogue, humor, emotion and sizzling sensuality."
—*Costa Mesa Sunday Times* on *The Charm School*

On sale mid-April 2000 wherever paperbacks are sold!

Visit us at www.mirabooks.com

MSW592

Stella Cameron

| 66463 | MOONTIDE | ___ $5.50 U.S. | ___ $6.50 CAN. |
| 66495 | UNDERCURRENTS | ___ $5.99 U.S. | ___ $6.99 CAN. |

(limited quantities available)

TOTAL AMOUNT	$_____
POSTAGE & HANDLING	$_____
($1.00 for one book; 50¢ for each additional)	
APPLICABLE TAXES*	$_____
TOTAL PAYABLE	$_____
(check or money order—please do not send cash)	

To order, complete this form and send it, along with a check or money order for the total above, payable to MIRA Books®, to: **In the U.S.:** 3010 Walden Avenue, P.O. Box 9077, Buffalo, NY 14269-9077; **In Canada:** P.O. Box 636, Fort Erie, Ontario L2A 5X3.

Name:_____
Address:_____ City:_____
State/Prov.:_____ Zip/Postal Code:_____
Account Number (if applicable):_____
075 CSAS

*New York residents remit applicable sales taxes.
 Canadian residents remit applicable GST and provincial taxes.

MIRA®

gone to Lillian Hurley's memorial service just so he could see Dana. Her tribute had almost undone him. *The best way to love anything is as if it might be lost.*

He'd lost all right—big time.

"Rob, great to see you."

He found Gwen Sihida at his shoulder smiling that smile he remembered only too well from the time he'd taken her out. "Great day for Dana, isn't it?"

"Sure is." He tried to sound upbeat.

"So . . . what have you been up to?" Gwen asked, but he didn't want to talk.

He politely muttered something and went to find Zach. No way could he stand around the rest of the night and watch Dana with another man. Rob wandered through the crowd, smiling, but he would rather have walked barefoot through the Sahara. His chest tightened each time someone called his name, each time he paused and had to say a few words. Every second he wondered who was out to get him—and why.

He should have listened to his sixth sense. All along he'd felt that Big Daddy wasn't behind Dana's problems. Going to Kau Ranch had been a wild-goose chase. So had the trip to Gomper's Bend. Granted, it had helped Dana, but he wasn't one bit closer to finding the blackmailer.

He finally found Zach and Jason on the lanai, teaching the parrot some new four-letter words.

Typical boys. "Hey, guys, cut it out. Try teaching him 'Puni wants a cracker.' "

Zach howled and Jason collapsed in a fit of giggles. Even Puni ruffled his feathers in disgust. Obviously Rob wasn't cool.

"I'm ready to go," Rob said.

"We were just putting Puni to bed," Zach responded.

"Put him in his cage, then meet me out front by the fountain."

He returned to the living room, meaning to go straight to the fountain, but he stopped, half-hidden behind a fern that belonged on a Tarzan set, his eyes on Dana. The crowd had thinned; the party was drawing to a close. The nerd with Dana headed for the bar with two empty glasses. Zach emerged from the kitchen and walked right up to Dana. Uh-oh.

"*The Stand* was way cool," he heard Zach tell Dana as he walked over, set to stop Zach before he said something that might upset her.

"I'm glad you liked it," Dana said, her eyes now on Rob.

"Congrats . . . Your Honor," Rob joked.

Dana's dynamic green eyes met his, and beneath the surface he detected a depth charge of hurt and betrayal. How well he knew that feeling. But he'd done the right thing. Dana had the appointment she'd coveted. He hadn't drawn her into quicksand that would drag them both under.

For a moment they stood transfixed, unspoken feelings eddying between them. He wanted to say something—anything—to show her he wasn't a complete bastard, but he was hopelessly lost at expressing himself. He attempted a smile. "I like your hair. Why the change?"

"Everything in my life has changed." The serrated edge to her voice softened as she glanced at Zach. "It's the new me."

Rob got the message. "Well, congratulations on the appointment."

A bewildering surge of tenderness swept through him. He leaned down, meaning to quickly brush her cheek with a kiss, but he found his lips touching hers. His knees turned to putty.

This might be all he'd ever have of the woman he truly loved. He couldn't resist putting his arms around her and drawing her close. Passion flared inside him, hot and breathtakingly intense. She arched the small of her back, torturing him with the lush softness of her breasts as they molded against his torso.

The feel of her mouth beneath his sent the pit of his stomach into a wild swirl as his tongue found hers, his hardening body pressing against hers. He wanted to kiss her until . . . until the world went away. Hell, he really wanted to spirit her away to some secluded spot on the beach where he could peel off the wisp of a dress she was wearing and make slow, shattering love to her all night.

From some distant corner of his mind a warning bell sounded. You're out of control, it said. But he didn't want to listen. She belonged with him, cradled in his arms like this. Forever.

This was the last time he was going to be able to hold her and kiss her. He'd lost her, and knowing that made this moment, this kiss even more precious. He longed to tell her how much he loved her, truly loved her. *Love you forever.*

Dana tried to move away, but he wouldn't let her go. He kept kissing her, his eyes squeezed shut to keep the cold, stark world of reality at bay a few seconds longer.

Zach yanked on his arm, bringing him back to the present. Releasing her was almost impossible. He knew he'd spend the rest of his life missing her. Longing for her kiss, her soft laugh, her loving touch. There are no sadder words than *what might have been.*

Rob pulled away and saw that the nerd had returned and was glaring at him. He beamed his "fuck you" grin at the jerk and walked away.

"Jeez, Dad, did you have to cause a scene?"

33

It was more than an hour later when they walked out of McDonald's on Waikiki with three Big Macs, two jumbo fries, and a chocolate shake under Zach's belt. Rob hadn't eaten a thing. He couldn't remember the last time he'd been hungry.

Unlocking his Porsche, he heard the phone ringing.

"You left before I could talk to you," Garth told him.

"Yeah, well . . ." What could he say? After making an ass out of himself with Dana, he'd gladly let Zach drag him out for fast food. He slid behind the wheel, then reached over and unlocked the door for his son.

"I have some news," Garth said, a smile in his voice. "The DA dropped the case. You're not going to be arrested."

Rob gasped, the air leaving his chest in a painful rush. *Thank you, God.* His breath seeped back into his lungs and he prayed he wasn't dreaming this. *Please let this be true.*

"You have Dana to thank," Garth continued. "She went to the DA and convinced him to show her the evidence against you."

"How did she know that I was being charged? I never told her a thing."

"Well . . . ah, I suspect I might have a leak around here."

Vanessa had told Dana, Rob decided. "She did this before her appointment came through, didn't she?"

"Right. She risked getting hit with an obstruction of justice charge."

She loved him, she truly loved him. A suffocating sensation tightened his throat. He hadn't cried in years and he wasn't going to break down now, but he felt like it. Instead, he leaned his head against the side window and closed his eyes for a second. He didn't deserve to have her risk everything for him. How had he gotten so damn lucky?

"Rob, are you there?"

"Yeah." He lifted his head, aware that Zach was watching him. "I guess they didn't have any real evidence since they folded so easily."

"They had a damn good case. That tourist IDed your picture; you were seen at Panama Jack's. And here's the kicker. Your pubic hairs came up on a comb-through with one of the victims'."

"That's impossible," Rob said flatly.

"No. They were yours. Remember the sample you

gave for the Internal Affairs investigation? The lab analysis was on file. A perfect match."

"How the hell did that happen?"

"Dana figured it out. Somebody bribed one of the clerks in the evidence unit. The sample you gave was still in the evidence locker. Under pressure the clerk admitted he was bribed to switch your sample with the hairs found on the victim."

"Son of a bitch!" He could have been convicted—easily. He glanced at Zach, who was staring at him with questioning eyes. Dana had put her career on the line for him. Knowing what she risked made him unbearably grateful—and madder than hell. When he caught the person behind this, swear to God, he'd kill him. "Who bribed the clerk? Big Daddy?"

"No. Vanessa and I met with him. I'm positive he won't do anything to jeopardize his relationship with Jason. The bribe was handled over the phone and the clerk was paid in cash, so it's hard to trace, but the DA's investigating."

"Let me know the minute you find out."

He hung up, then bear-hugged Zach even though he knew his son was at the age where he hated displays of affection. Rob couldn't help himself, any more than he could have kept himself from kissing Dana earlier.

"Jeez, Dad, what happened?"

Rob slowly told Zach about the evidence against him, then explained what Dana had done.

"She believed in you, Dad. Why didn't you tell her to begin with?"

"I didn't want to hurt her chances of being appointed to superior court."

Zach shook his head, his thick hair shifting across his forehead so the maroon tint caught the light. "You didn't trust Dana. You thought she'd bail out on you the way Mom did."

"No—" Rob started to protest. But Zach was right. Rob had told himself that he was protecting Dana. In reality he'd been shielding himself from another devastating betrayal. He honestly couldn't have faced an ordeal like this, expecting Dana to stand by his side only to have her desert him. He'd been through that once, and he hadn't been willing to risk it again. So he'd taken the easy way out.

"Go to her," Zach said. "Tell her you love her. Don't blow this."

"I thought you didn't like her. This was the woman you tried to scare off, remember?"

Zach drummed his fingers on his thigh. "I was dead wrong. What did you used to tell me? *Love you forever.* She loves you, Dad. Can't you see it? This is her way of saying she'll love you forever."

Rob was too astonished to say anything. Sometimes his son seemed incredibly immature for his age—searching for a T-Rex and playing with a parrot—but at other times he had the insight of a world-weary old man. Dana did love him. She wasn't the cooey, kissy-face type like Ellen, who

416

tossed the word *love* around like a two-bit coin. Dana had said it only once. But she meant it.

Love you forever.

"Have I told you lately that I love you?" he asked Zach.

"Aw, Dad, don't start." He leaned over and turned the key in the ignition. "Drive over to Dana's and tell it to her."

"She's probably with—"

"The nerd. That's why you better get there quick."

Rob stepped on the accelerator and bullied his way into the stream of traffic, thinking he had a helluva lot of explaining to do. Dana would want to know why he hadn't confided in her. He'd pushed, insisting she trust him—then he hadn't trusted her. Damn it. He loved her. That meant he should have trusted her.

Would she even consider taking him back? After the cruel way he'd said "*What* about last night," he wouldn't blame her if she told him to fuck off and die. He was mulling over what he'd say to Dana when the phone rang. It was Garth again.

"Vanessa just found something quite disturbing. Lots of guests brought flowers or cards to the party. She found a Li-See among them."

"Really?" The red envelopes were given on special occasions. They contained money and were supposed to bring luck. The Chinese tradition had been adopted by Hawaiians. Naturally people would have brought Li-Sees to Dana.

"The Li-See didn't have money in it," Garth said.

"It had a note that said: *The night marchers are on the way.*"

"Meaning Dana's going to die."

"That's exactly what Vanessa thought. Maybe she's overreacting, but Vanessa thinks the blackmailer plans to kill Dana. We tried to reach her, but no one answered. She was going out to dinner with the guy who brought her to the party."

"We'll go over there and wait for her." Rob hung up, the fine hairs across the back of his neck prickling. He yanked the steering wheel to the right and gunned the engine, swerving around the slow-moving car in front of them.

"What's wrong, Dad?"

He explained to Zach about the blackmailer, glossing over the part about the rape and the stabbing as best he could without lying. Zach's eyes were wide with surprise when he finished.

"Do you think someone is trying to kill Dana?"

Rob spun onto the side street that led to Dana's house. "I hope not, but all along we've misjudged the blackmailer. We've got to warn her," he said, praying it wasn't already too late.

"Party-time!" Zach said as they neared Dana's home and found cars lining both sides of the street.

Rob spotted a sleek black Lexus in Dana's driveway. "She's home."

"The nerd's with her."

"Looks like it." Rob drove farther down the street and shoehorned the Porsche into a spot. "I'm getting rid of the jerk."

"Way to go, Dad."

Rob swung open the door. "Stay here. I'll be right back."

"Uh-huh." Zach seemed more interested in the kids streaming into the party than anything Rob was saying.

The soft breeze carried the sweet scent of plumeria and the raucous sounds of heavy-metal music. Rob crossed the street, alarmed because Dana's porch light was off and only a dim light, probably the night-light, seemed to be on in the living room. He rushed up the drive, dodging the Lexus. A loud noise from the party across the street stopped him, and he glanced over his shoulder.

The moonlight gleamed off the car's windshield, and he spotted the blue and gold security sticker. The sticker admitted cars to the courthouse's security garage. Okay, so maybe she'd come home with another judge or someone from the DA's office. They all worked in the same building.

His sixth sense kicked in. Son of a bitch! Why hadn't he figured it out before now? It had been totally, completely obvious. But he'd been too distracted by everything else going on to realize who was after Dana.

Was it too late? Now the house was as dark as a crypt. Someone had turned off the night-light. His pulse thrummed in his temples, making it hard to think. He had to get in there; he didn't have time to go for help. *Just don't let it be too late.*

Guided by the bright light of the full moon, he

went around to the back of the house and peered in the windows. Not a light in the whole place. He tried the back door and discovered it was unlocked. He eased it open and stepped inside, squinting into the blackness.

"Watch out!" He instantly recognized Dana's voice.

Pain exploded along the side of his head in a thousand pinpricks of light. He staggered forward, his pulse kicking into overdrive. *Dana is in trouble. Don't let her down now.*

He lurched sideways, figuring the kitchen counter had to be nearby. If only he could get to it he could get his bearings. His fingers found the cool tile. *Whack.* The second, more vicious blow buckled his knees. A whirling vortex of darkness sucked him under.

"No-o-o," he heard himself moan.

Someone said something, but despite his best efforts he couldn't open his eyes to identify the person talking. The pain in his head, like a shard of jagged glass slowly being twisted, kept him from thinking clearly. He'd blacked out—but for how long? Minutes? Hours?

A tugging sensation, then he felt himself sliding. Someone was slowly dragging him across the floor, he realized. Where was he? Through a miasma of pain and confusion, his scrambled thoughts jelled. He was in Dana's house. Sounds were sharper now, clearer. A voice. If he could just concentrate a little more, he could understand what being said.

Again he tried to open his eyes, but failed. He was more lucid though, and he decided not to struggle. If they thought he was helpless he might surprise them.

"Put him on the bed," he heard a voice say.

"I can't. He's too heavy."

Dana! He bit the inside of his lip to keep from calling her name. It was her hands he felt under his arms. She tried to hoist him onto a bed, but all she did was move him into an upright position. His head hung forward, his chin on his chest, and he eased his eyes open just a slit. His belt buckle swam in his clouded vision. A white-hot lance of pain speared through his head.

"Come on, Dana. You can get him onto that bed."

Rob recognized the voice. Gwen Sihida. Just as he suspected. With a jolt of self-loathing he cursed himself for getting sidetracked by Big Daddy and Vanessa's problems. He'd overlooked the obvious.

The night marchers are coming for you.

Was Gwen capable of murder? Well, hell, she hadn't clobbered him to be friendly. Often the craziest people appeared sane, he reminded himself.

He heard Dana gasp for breath as she tried to lift his shoulders enough to get his torso on the bed. He aided her efforts by slumping in the right direction. She managed to move him by shoving his hips. Again he helped by rolling onto the bed, making sure to tangle his arms and legs to appear unconscious.

He knew Dana realized he was conscious. He had

to assume Gwen was armed, or Dana wouldn't be taking orders from her.

Gentle hands straightened his arms and pulled the awkwardly bent leg into position. Her palm touched his brow and smoothed back his hair. "He needs a doctor."

"Haven't you figured it out yet? You're dead. You're both dead," Gwen said. "Domestic violence. You know how popular it is these days."

Rob decided there wasn't any advantage to be gained by playing possum any longer. He levered himself up on his elbows and opened his eyes, ignoring the nauseating explosion of pain that sent a starburst of color across his field of vision.

Someone had turned on a lamp, and its dim light cast shadows across the small room. A blurry Gwen, holding a revolver, stood not far from the bed. Nearby was Dana, concern for him etching her beautiful face.

"It'll never work," Rob said, surprised at how calm and forceful his voice sounded despite the debilitating blows to his head that still had him off-kilter.

"Prince Charming awakens. How sweet."

Dana tried to move to his side. Gwen waved her back with the gun.

"You can kill us, but the police will never chalk it up to domestic violence." He managed to scoot into a sitting position and lock his arms around his knees so he wouldn't topple over. "There won't be powder burns on my hands. The position of the bodies and dozens of other details will be out of sync."

"That's right," Dana chimed in. "You'll never get away with this."

"You both think I'm stupid, don't you? Neither of you *ever* gave me any credit for being brilliant. You're just like my father."

The look of pure hatred in Gwen's eyes almost made Rob panic. It wasn't going to be easy to reason with her, and he was so woozy that he didn't think he could overpower her without getting killed —or worse, getting Dana killed.

"Now my father—the almighty Boss Sihida— thinks I'm worthless because some bimbo was appointed to superior court instead of me."

"That's why she was blackmailing me," Dana told Rob. "Gwen lost the election to superior court last year. She claims she'll never be able to muster the political backing to run again."

Rob tried to placate her. "I'm sure your father—"

"I had to beg my father for help last time. He said that I'd never win unless I was the incumbent judge. Islanders don't vote for pushy women. But if I'm appointed to fill a vacancy and do well, I'll have no trouble being elected."

Rob couldn't argue with her logic. "Is a seat on the court worth killing for?"

"I tried to get rid of Dana, to make this easy, but she refused to leave."

Rob couldn't help saying, "She doesn't scare easily."

Gwen huffed her disgust. "Dana could fall in a cesspool and come out smelling like a rose. Binkley calls for a judicial review. What happens? She beats the charges. And everyone rallies around the golden girl. Well, I'm sure it's going to be a touching funeral. I can hardly wait."

"Gwen," Rob said, "we can work this out. Let's—"

"Don't patronize me! I've gone this far. There's no turning back."

"Okay, just how do you plan on getting away with murder?" Rob asked just to keep her going. With each passing second he was feeling stronger. He was going to have to rush her and risk being killed —or die anyway.

"During the fight a lamp will tip over. The fire will destroy enough evidence so that the police won't look for powder burns."

Rob opened his mouth to say the angles of the wounds might tip them off, but the doorbell rang. It had to be Zach looking for him. Gwen aimed the gun at Dana.

"I'm not expecting—"

"It's probably one of those drunk kids from that brawl across the street," Rob said, cutting Dana off. "They'll go away in a minute."

Please God, he prayed silently, get Zach out of here. He was certain Gwen hadn't seen Zach at the party. He'd spent most of the time on the lanai off the kitchen with that mouthy parrot. If Gwen discovered it was his son at the door, she'd kill Zach too.

The bell rang again, then there was a long silence during which Gwen never lowered the gun. Now Zach was punching the bell, the chimes echoing through the house like a death knell.

34

The doorbell stopped ringing as suddenly as it had begun. The silence was as unsettling as the noise, and Dana sensed that Gwen was on the brink. Any second she could squeeze the trigger. Dana had been shaky since she'd accepted Gwen's offer to drive her home from the party and Gwen had pulled a gun. But now, having Rob with her and seeing he wasn't too badly hurt, she felt calmer. They couldn't die like this. They had too much to live for. Together they could outsmart Gwen.

Those thoughts uppermost in her mind, Dana began to talk, hoping to distract Gwen. "Why don't you tell Rob how you knew he'd come over, how you watched as his car drove up the street."

"Who could miss a silver Porsche?" Gwen asked.

Dana noted the way Rob's eyes narrowed slightly at this information. What was wrong, she wondered. Then it hit her. Zach. He'd been at the party with Rob. There hadn't been enough time to take him home and return.

Gwen must not have seen Zach. That wasn't surprising. Dana had watched Rob prowling around Garth's place, but she hadn't seen Zach until he walked up to her. Zach had to have been the person ringing the doorbell. Would he think to call the police? Or would he go back to the car and turn on the radio full blast? With teenagers you never knew.

"What made you think I'd come over?" Rob asked Gwen.

"Because you're crazy about *her*."

There was such fury in Gwen's voice that Dana decided there was an element of jealousy behind Gwen's actions. Granted, Boss Sihida's expectations were at the root of Gwen's problems, but she'd gone out with Rob and must have been upset when he hadn't called her again.

"Now the two of you can be together through eternity." She raised the gun, pointing at Dana's heart.

"Wait a second!" Rob yelled, and Dana felt the blood surge to her temples as she anticipated the shot. "I understand how you bribed an evidence clerk to frame me. Clever. Very clever." Gwen beamed despite the sarcastic tone in his voice. "How did you know about the man who raped Dana and Vanessa?"

"I should let you go to your graves wondering," Gwen said, but Dana realized she wanted to brag. She was relishing every moment, letting them suffer with the knowledge she was going to kill them.

"I'm sure it's a very simple explanation—"

"It wasn't simple." Gwen raised her voice an octave. "This was brilliant, and it would have worked until you snooped around."

"Okay, what was so brilliant?" Rob asked. "You didn't know the whole story. You thought Hank died."

Gwen shrugged off this oversight. "When Dana was medicated, having her wisdom teeth removed, she blabbed. My brother said that she'd killed what's-his-name."

Dana couldn't help gasping. Never—ever—had she thought that she'd been the source of the information. But now that she looked back to the ordeal at the dentist's, she remembered how oddly Gwen's brother had acted. Well, no wonder. He thought he'd just treated a cold-blooded killer.

"Gwen's extremely resourceful," Dana said, praying Zach had called the police. "She made certain Binkley found out about the so-called murder, but she managed to shift the blame to Big Daddy."

"It was easy. Once I found out about the divorce I made an anonymous call to Thornton Coltrane. He took it from there."

"You made lots of anonymous calls," Rob said.

"I just played on people's fear and greed."

Rob's brow furrowed and he shook his head derisively. "I really did underestimate you, Gwen. I never even suspected—"

"Meeeee-ooow!" Molly screeched from the hall as if her tail had been caught in a door. The cat bolted into the room, shot across Gwen's feet, and vaulted onto the bed, landing on Rob. Right behind her bar-reled Zach at a dead run.

"Christ!" Gwen screamed, seeing the maroon-haired kid with the weird earrings appearing out of the darkness like a swamp monster.

If Dana hadn't been so terrified she would have laughed. Until she saw the tire iron in Zach's hand. Gwen cocked the gun.

"Dana! Zach! Hit the floor!" yelled Rob, jumping off the bed.

Dana didn't have a second to think—she just acted, hurling herself at Gwen. She pivoted, leveling the gun at Dana's chest. Dana ducked, trying to fling herself at Gwen's waist and take her down before she fired. Suddenly, Dana heard a pop like a twig snapping, a deceptively soft sound.

Searing pain ripped through her torso. She careened to the right, bumping into the bed, then reeled backward, clutching her chest. Dimly, she heard a *thwack* and saw out of the corner of her eye that Rob was tackling Gwen just as Zach hit her with the tire iron.

Gwen was out cold; they were safe. Dana stared at the blood dripping from her fingers, the pain spiking suddenly, stealing the air from her lungs, keeping her from crying out. Her blood? Couldn't be, she thought, as the room cycloned around her, then mercifully cloaked her in darkness.

"Dana! Dana!" Rob yelled as he saw her slump to the floor. "Oh, God, no!" He huddled over her limp form, saying her name over and over and over as he ripped off her blouse to check the wound.

"I'm calling nine-one-one!" Zach cried.

Rob tore part of the sheet off the bed and tried to stanch the blood flowing from her chest. "You're going to be fine, darling. I promise."

Her lids fluttered, slowly opening. She gazed at him with eyes so dilated and unfocused that he wasn't certain she could actually see him.

"Cold," she whispered, her voice weak. "So cold."

She was going into shock. He grabbed the comforter and tucked it around her. "Better?"

"You . . . you didn't give me a chance. I loved you, but you didn't give me a chance." Her lids slammed shut and her head lolled back against his shoulder.

He cradled her in his arms. *Don't let her die without letting me tell her I love her.* "I love you, Dana," he whispered, even though he knew she couldn't hear him.

He didn't know how long he'd sat there, holding her, whispering his innermost feelings until the piercing wail of an ambulance broke into his thoughts. He looked up and found Zach hovering over Gwen, the tire iron raised in his hand even though she was out cold. Seconds later police and med techs rushed into the room.

"We'll take her now," one of the med techs said, and Rob surrendered Dana's lifeless form.

* * *

"It's my fault," Rob explained to Vanessa and Garth as they waited at the hospital. Dana had been in surgery for over an hour. "I should have been with Dana, then Gwen wouldn't have taken her by surprise."

"Gwen would have found another way," Garth assured him.

"She's a psychopath," Vanessa added.

Rob paced the hall, trying to pass the time. Then he sat in stoic silence and watched the second hand on the waiting-room clock. Nothing helped. The next hour crawled by even slower than the first. When the doctor finally came in to speak with them, Zach was sleeping on a sofa with Jason curled up beside him, his head in Zach's lap.

"She's lost a lot of blood, but she's going to be fine," Dr. Scott said.

"Thank God," Rob cried.

"May we see her?" Vanessa asked.

"She won't know you're there. She's sedated."

It didn't matter; the three of them wanted to see Dana, to see for themselves that she'd survived. There wasn't much to see. A small form lying helpless, linked to a bank of monitors by a jungle of wires and tubes. Her face was leached of color, appearing even paler with her blonde hair. Her lips—how many times had he kissed them?—were slightly blue. She didn't look as if she had the strength to make it another minute, let alone through the long night.

"I'm staying with her," Rob announced. He had to be by her side—this time.

Vanessa started to protest, but Garth touched her arm. "Let's take Zach home with us," he said. "We'll be back first thing in the morning."

Rob awakened his son while Vanessa lifted Jason onto Garth's lap. He wheeled the sleeping boy down the hall. Like a family, Rob realized vaguely.

"Is Dana okay?" Zach asked, his eyes heavy with sleep.

"She's going to be fine." Rob gazed into his son's eyes, a mirror image of his own. "You were very brave, you know. You saved us."

A dull flush shot up Zach's neck to his cheeks. "Nah. Dana saved us."

An image of Dana hurling herself at Gwen flashed across his mind. "You're right, son. She put her career at risk to clear my name, then charged Gwen to keep her from killing you. I owe her . . . more than I can ever repay."

Zach heaved a sigh, blowing air upward and lifting his maroon bangs. "I feel like a real ass for lying to her."

"She'll understand. I promise."

"You better marry her. She's way cool. Way cool."

"I hope she'll have me. After the way I've acted, I don't know."

"Get real. She'll marry you." Zach offered him a sudden, arresting smile. "I won't mind if you have a kid like Jason."

"Could be a little girl. But knowing Dana, she

won't be the prissy kind." Rob cleared his throat, not knowing what to say exactly, but realizing there would never be a better time to reassure his son. "No matter what, I'll always love you. They took you away from me when you weren't much older than Jason. I've missed you every day since."

He hugged Zach, and surprisingly his son hugged him back even harder. "If Dana will have us, we'll be a family again. That's what I want. I love you both. Love you forever."

"Aw, Dad, come on," Zach said, but there were tears in his eyes.

She awakened slowly, floating upward in a dreamlike trance. She was on Maui, high in the up-country, stretched out in a meadow of white ginger, staring up at the ribbons of clouds that were waltzing across the sky. Above her, like a reigning monarch, towered Haleakala. The volcano's peak looked black against the deep blue sky.

"Dana . . . Dana," she heard someone calling from a hillock far away. She tried to say something, but words wouldn't come. Instead, a fretful moan escaped her lips. Through slitted eyes she saw a silhouette of a man. She mustered the strength to whisper, "Rob?"

"It's me, angel." He squeezed her hand. "You're going to be all right."

The floating sensation evaporated, replaced by a pain so sharp that it hurt to breathe. "Where am I?"

She listened as he explained about her surgery.

Most of it barely registered. "Don't leave me," she whispered, her voice dropping with each word, her strength ebbing quickly. "Promise me."

It was noon before she awakened again, but Rob never left her side. Daylight made Dana appear stronger, healthier despite the armada of frightening-looking machines. Her color was better, her lips no longer blue.

"How are you doing?" Rob asked, stroking her forehead.

"Better," she said. "What's wrong with me?"

"The bullet lodged in your shoulder. You'll be sore for a while, but you'll be as good as new in no time."

"Gwen?"

"She's in the jail's hospital with a mild concussion."

Dana didn't say another word; she merely gazed at him with those fantastic green eyes.

"I really like you as a blonde, you know. What made you to do it?"

"I decided to be the real me. I've been hiding for too many years."

"I like it. I like it," he said, but he knew that wasn't what she wanted to hear. "I don't know how to thank you for clearing me. If you hadn't I might very well have been convicted. I'd have lost Zach. And you."

He cradled her cheek in his hand, knowing he was inadequately expressing what was in his heart.

"You were willing to sacrifice everything—for me. You have no idea how that makes me feel, do you?"

She shrugged—or tried to—but the effort brought tears to her eyes. Her entire shoulder was encased in bandages. It would take weeks of physical therapy before she could move her arm.

"Dana, I love you. Don't you know that?"

She looked at him blankly as if he were discussing some new life form or some damn mathematical equation. She wasn't going to make this easy for him—not that he blamed her.

"I should have told you that I was about to be arrested, but I wanted to protect you. I didn't want—"

"No, you didn't. That may have been part of it, but fess up, Rob. You didn't trust me. You thought I'd desert you."

What could he say? It was the truth. Even Zach had seen it. "You're right. I wanted to tell you, but I couldn't. I made a mistake. I can't change the past. All I can do is ask you to forgive me."

"I forgave you the minute I walked into the DA's office to try to help you."

There ought to be words to express the heartfelt emotion he was experiencing, but all he could say was "I love you."

"I knew that when you kissed me at the party." She managed a sly smile. "No man kisses a woman like that just to say congratulations."

Rob chuckled. "You got that right. Zach said I made a scene."

"You did, and you were really good at it."

"Well, I wasn't so good at discovering Gwen was out to get you." He shook his head. "I never suspected her."

"Who would think she'd kill anyone over a place on the bench?"

"I guess Boss Sihida is just as intimidating as Big Daddy. Gwen wanted to please him at all costs."

"That's true," Dana agreed. "But you have to realize that Gwen doesn't have a life beyond her career. That's why it was so important to her." Dana reached for his hand, able to move only so far without disturbing the IV. Her fingers were icy; he cradled them in his warm palm. "I learned something when Lillian died. People are more important than careers. That's why I had no trouble walking into the DA's office and asking about the evidence."

"I love you more than I can say. I'm sorry I didn't trust you. I was wrong. Dead wrong."

"Don't let it happen again," Dana warned him with a smile. Then she stared at the small bandage on his temple. "How's your head? She really conked you with that frying pan."

"I've got two killer lumps and the grandmother of all headaches. Wanna kiss it and make it better?"

"You bet," she said.

"Seriously, Dana." He turned her hand over and kissed the palm. "I want you to marry me."

"Have you discussed this with Zach? I don't think he likes me."

"He changed his mind. Actually, *he* insisted I

drive over to your house. Despite how smart Gwen thinks she is, I would have waited until later except that Zach wanted me to tell you how much I love you."

"Really? How sweet. I'm prepared to love him—maroon hair and all." She blessed him with her sassiest smile.

He bent over and gently kissed her. "Love you forever."